Praise for Boyd Morrison's thrillers

'Boyd Morrison's novel, *The Noah's Ark Quest*, is a stunning thriller with a premise as ingenious as it is flawlessly executed. Lightning-paced, chillingly real, here is a novel that will have you holding your breath until the last page is turned. One of the best debuts I've read this year' **James Rollins**

'When it comes to thrillers, Boyd Morrison has the Midas touch' **Chris Kuzneski**

'A bang-a-minute blockbuster' **The Times**

'A roller coaster ride of gun-blazing action, fascinating historical references, and a nail-biting battle of wits ... Move over Dan Brown, and give Boyd Morrison a try' **Lisa Gardner**

'A rip-roaring thriller which has the reader entranced from first page to last ... Hold on tight as the pace is akin to that of a white water raft ride – furious bouts of life-threatening action then a spell of calm before the next onslaught on your senses!' *CrimeSquad.com*

'Heart-stopping action, biblical history, mysticism, a stunning archeological find and mind-boggling evil results in a breathcatching adventure ... a pitch-perfect combination of plot, action and dialogue' *RT Book Reviews*

'Full of action, villainy, and close calls. Fans of James Rollins, Matthew Reilly, and Douglas Preston take note' *Booklist*

'The perfect blend of historical mysticism and clever, classical thriller plotting. Imagine the famed Ark rediscovered and reinvented to form the seeds of a modern day conspiracy. Boyd Morrison manages that flawlessly in this blisteringly paced tale' **Jon Land**

'A perfect thriller' Crimespree Magazine

ALSO BY BOYD MORRISON

THE
CATALYST

BOYD MORRISON

SPHERE

First published in the United States in 2011 by Pocket Books,
an imprint of Simon & Schuster (US)
First published in Great Britain in 2014 by Sphere

A CIP catalogue record for this book
is available from the British Library.

ISBN 978-0-7515-4720-7

Printed and bound in Great Britain by
Clays Ltd, St Ives plc

Papers used by Sphere are from well-managed forests
and other responsible sources.

MIX
Paper from
responsible sources
FSC® C104740

Sphere
An imprint of
Little, Brown Book Group
100 Victoria Embankment
London EC4Y 0DY

An Hachette UK Company
www.hachette.co.uk

www.littlebrown.co.uk

For my brother and sisters:
Marty, Beth, Barby, and Nancy.

ACKNOWLEDGEMENTS

As always I'm indebted to the people who helped me polish this story into the novel you're holding.

When you have an agent as wonderful as Irene Goodman, you thank your lucky stars, and I'm grateful to a constellation of them.

My foreign rights agents, Danny Baror and Heather Baror-Shapiro, continue to be the gold standard of the business.

I'm amazed at how my editor, Abby Zidle, could focus on exactly where the story needed improvement. She's a joy to work with.

Although I consulted with several people on this book, any errors in fact or detail, whether intentional or not, are mine alone.

Thanks to my good friend and trauma surgeon, Dr Erik Van Eaton, for assisting me with the medical minutiae.

I sincerely appreciate the long hours and hard work my sister, Elizabeth Morrison, and my father-in-law, Frank Moretti, put into giving me their valued feedback.

And to my wife, Randi, all I can say is thanks for never letting me give up. Your confidence inspires me.

We are not here to sell a parcel of boilers and vats, but the potentiality of growing rich beyond the dreams of avarice.

Samuel Johnson

K *evin, the same men who killed Stein are after me.* Michael Ward's fingers trembled as he lifted his hands from the keyboard. Because he didn't have Kevin's cell phone number, Ward had tried his home a dozen times, but he kept getting the damned answering machine. Leaving a message was out of the question. Even email could be intercepted, so he'd have to choose his words carefully.

He needed a cigarette badly. His hand fumbled through his shirt pocket and removed the pack of Marlboros. Only one left. He'd have to get another pack on the way to the airport.

He lit the cigarette despite the shaking and took a deep drag, trying to pull every milligram of precious nicotine into his system. He felt the smoke fill his lungs, and the trembling subsided. His attention returned to the words on the screen. He wanted to laugh at their absurdity, but he was afraid if he started he wouldn't be able to stop.

A wave of nausea hit him. Ward shook off the feeling. There wasn't much left in his stomach anyway, just half a bottle of Pepto-Bismol he'd drained when he got home. He'd been spending the Friday in his South Texas University office, working and listening to the radio, when he'd heard the news of Herbert Stein's death. The story had been short, but it was enough. An execution-style shooting, the body thrown in a Dumpster. He got sick twice, once in his office trash can and again before climbing into his Mercedes. He didn't feel like a man who was about retire to the Bahamas with ten million dollars.

He checked the progress of his download. The backup of his hard disk to the USB drive had another three minutes to go. With the cigarette stuck in his mouth, he continued typing.

> Caroline and I are leaving Houston. I think we'll be
> safe where we're going, but I need your help to be sure.
> NV117 wasn't a failure. You know the equipment. The
> key to everything else you need is in your thesis. I made
> a deal with Clay

'May we come in, Dr Ward?'

Ward jerked at the sound of the voice. He recognized too well the distinct enunciation of each syllable and his heart started pounding. He turned his head to see two men standing in the doorway to his study. David Lobec and, behind him, Richard Bern, Clayton Tarnwell's men here to finalize the deal. They were early. The meeting wasn't supposed to be for another two hours.

He silently cursed himself for not grabbing the passports and running as soon as he got home. He'd been careful not to call ahead in case the phones were tapped, but they'd found him anyway.

Five minutes, he'd told Caroline when he burst through the front door. *Pack whatever you can in five minutes, then we head straight to Intercontinental and get the first flight out.* She'd begun to protest, asking if he'd lost his mind. *I'll explain everything in the car, but we need to get the hell out of here.* When he'd practically shoved her up the stairs, she'd gotten the message. He was dead serious. Now they were out of time, and Ward's mind raced for options.

Out of the corner of his eye, he saw the blinking cursor on the screen and realized that the words on the computer might be seen from in front of his desk. Without glancing back at the monitor, he pressed the F4 key as he turned the chair to face his visitors. The message disappeared from the screen.

'I'm sorry, Mr Lobec,' Ward said, rising from his seat. 'I didn't hear the doorbell.' The waver in his voice betrayed his attempt to remain calm. He took another puff from the cigarette.

Lobec smiled and strode in without waiting for the invitation he had asked for.

'Disgusting habit,' he said, plucking the cigarette from Ward's lips. He stubbed it out in a heavily stained brass ashtray. 'Much better. Now we can all breathe while we talk.'

He sat in one of the leather chairs. Bern remained standing behind him.

'Please sit down,' Lobec said.

'You're early,' said Ward, lowering himself into his chair. 'I wasn't expecting you until six thirty.' The clock on the study's mantel said 4:23.

'Of course you weren't. You expected to be far away by the time we arrived. I'm happy to surprise you.'

He wasn't tall, no more than five foot ten, but Lobec carried a quiet confidence that made him more imposing than a man six inches taller. His thick ebony hair, a marked contrast to his fair complexion and slate-gray eyes, was combed straight back. His gray suit was tailored, perfectly fitting his athletic frame. Lobec was not a handsome man: his nose angled downward and crooked, his chin was weak but his eyes were always alert and focused. Despite being intimidated by Lobec, Ward couldn't help but admire the man's presence.

Lobec's younger associate was the same height as Lobec but about fifty pounds heavier, most of it muscle. Bern lacked Lobec's sense of style, wearing an ill-fitting blue suit that looked a size too large. His brown hair was cut in a Marine-style crew, and boredom radiated from his perpetual frown and sleepy eyes. Beyond the visual, Ward knew hardly anything about the man. He'd never uttered more than a few unintelligible greetings.

Ward forced a smile, knowing he'd never be able to overpower either one of them, let alone both. Despite his four-inch height advantage over the two men, his large paunch and fleshy jowls clearly marked him as a professor whose sole exercise was swinging a golf club. Since the fall semester didn't begin until next week, he was dressed in the three-hundred-dollar sweatsuit he normally wore on weekends. Otherwise, Ward was the archetype of a distinguished professor, down to the thin, graying hair and wire-rimmed glasses. Judging by Lobec's attitude, he didn't appear to pose much of a threat.

'I don't know what you mean,' Ward said. 'I was just finishing up some—'

'You *do* know what I mean.' Lobec seemed more amused than annoyed. 'We've been searching for you for the last hour. You didn't take your normal route from the office today. Maybe you can tell us why.'

He had suspected they were watching him, and now Lobec's statement confirmed it. After hearing the news about Herbert Stein's murder, Ward had taken the precaution of leaving through the subbasement to another building, hoping to elude his observers for just the ten minutes he needed to hide his insurance. Apparently, he had been successful.

'How do you know what route I take?' Ward was stalling, trying to think.

'The same way we know how you've been able to afford a half-million-dollar home and a Mercedes on a professor's salary.' Lobec scanned the tastefully decorated study, with its mahogany desk, black leather sofa, golf awards, and memorabilia, then looked out the window at the gated community's eighteen-hole championship golf course in the final stages of construction before his eyes returned to Ward. 'Although lately your situation has taken a turn for the worse, hasn't it? Mr Tarnwell mentioned your reputation for successful ventures in the stock market. It's a pity your appraisal of Chromosotics wasn't as shrewd.'

Ward's jaw dropped. He had received a hot tip about a local company called Chromosotics that was about to go to market with a new drug. FDA approval was a sure thing, his source had told him. After the initial press release, the stock soared to four times its original price, and Ward leveraged himself to the hilt to buy more shares. But within a month, a report leaked test results detailing serious side effects of the new drug. With the probability of FDA approval virtually nil, the stock plummeted. Ward couldn't have given shares away. Before the deal with Tarnwell came along, he was on the verge of bankruptcy. Not even Caroline knew.

As Ward sat dumbfounded, Lobec continued. 'I mention these facts merely to impress upon you that our resources for gathering information are quite formidable. Should you and your wife think of leaving Houston, we *would* find you.'

Suddenly, Ward remembered Caroline packing upstairs. She should have come down by now. He saw a nasty gleam in Lobec's eyes.

Ward jumped from his seat. 'Caroline!' There was no response. He moved toward Lobec. 'Where is she, dammit?'

Bern tensed and took a step forward. Lobec, the smile never leaving his face, calmly reached into his jacket and pulled out an automatic pistol.

'Mrs Ward is safe for the moment, but I wouldn't want any rash behavior on your part to jeopardize that safety.'

'You won't shoot me. Somebody will hear.'

'I know as well as you do that you and your wife are the first, and currently only, occupants on this block,' Lobec said with a tone that could have frozen lava. 'I have a silencer, but there really is no need for it. Now, please sit down or I'll ask Mr Bern to assist you.'

Seeing that he had no choice, Ward reluctantly sat. The fear that had gripped him moments before was now competing with the anger seething just below it. Despite their problems, Ward loved his wife, and the thought of these bastards manhandling her was repulsive to him.

'What does Clay want?' he asked, his voice barely above a whisper.

'First of all, he would like the ten million dollars you've stolen from him.'

'I didn't steal it! He paid me that ten million. And he's supposed to pay me another twenty million when he gets Adamas.'

'Second,' Lobec continued, 'we want the names of every person you've told about Adamas.'

Ward's eyes narrowed. 'If you don't let us go, you'll never see Adamas, and Clay will get nothing for his ten million.'

'Spare us, Dr Ward. We already have the details of your process in our possession.'

Ward sat back as if slapped in the face. That was impossible. There was only one copy of his notebook, and it was stored in a safe place. The meeting tonight was to go over the specifics of the final transaction. On Monday he was planning to retrieve the notebook, copy it, and give the copy to a lawyer before handing the original over to Tarnwell in return for the additional twenty million. The lawyer would turn the copy in to the authorities only if something happened to Ward. But something had happened to the lawyer first. The lawyer was Herbert Stein, and he had been murdered.

Ward sputtered, 'But you couldn't—'

'You've been observed for the past two weeks, Dr Ward. We've also had a chance to thoroughly itemize the contents of your office. We have everything we need.'

Something was wrong. He had safely hidden his notebook a month ago and hadn't returned to its secure location since then. He certainly didn't keep it in his office, and he doubted even someone as powerful as Tarnwell could retrieve the notebook from its hiding place.

Ward needed to know if Lobec was lying. 'Then you have the videotape as well, I suppose.'

Lobec's irritating smile finally dissolved. 'You're bluffing. There *is* no videotape.'

It was Ward smiling now. They had the false duplicate notebook he'd written and stashed in his office as a safeguard.

'So Clay *doesn't* have Adamas,' he said. 'That's too bad. When my friends find the videotape and the notebook, Clay is going to see a billion dollars evaporate. That is, if you don't let us go.' This time he *was* bluffing. No one else knew of Adamas or the notebook's location.

Lobec's smile returned. 'Surely you learned what happened to your new attorney, Mr Stein, or you wouldn't have led us on this merry chase. I must say, Mr Stein was quite forceful about his need to protect his clients' interests. But when I removed his index finger, he told us about your attempt to retain his services – in great detail, in fact. No doubt your friends will be as obliging, with the proper incentive.'

Despite his horror, Ward tried to feign confidence. 'You can't possibly know who they are.'

'That's correct,' Lobec said, nodding. 'But I think you'll be willing to tell us. Especially if you don't want to see your beautiful wife damaged by Mr Bern.' Lobec glanced toward Bern and nodded in Ward's direction.

Ward's stomach sank. He now realized they would never let him go. They'd torture the information about the notebook's location out of him. Once they had that, there would be no reason to keep either of them alive. In fact, with him out of the way, there would be no one to dispute Tarnwell's claim that he was the inventor of Adamas. With that realization, Ward knew he had to take whatever chance he saw.

Bern, his bored expression unwavering, walked around

the desk and bent over to grab Ward's arm. As he did so, his jacket fell open and Ward saw a semiautomatic pistol holstered under his left armpit. When Bern wrapped his meaty hand around Ward's arm, Ward sagged as if overcome with despair, his 250 pounds throwing Bern off balance in the process. He plunged his free hand into Bern's jacket, found the pistol, and yanked it from the holster.

Bern snapped back and grabbed Ward's wrist, pointing the gun toward the ceiling. To the side, he could see Lobec aiming his pistol at them but not firing, probably not wanting to kill Ward until he got the information he needed. Bern's other hand grabbed at the gun. He pried at Ward's hand, but Ward gripped the gun with tenacity born of desperation.

Ward tried forcing the gun into Bern's face. Bern deflected it as Ward pulled the trigger, and a deafening blast rent the air. A chunk of the ceiling hit Ward as Bern whirled them around and into the wall. He pulled Ward's arm down, trying to use leverage to wrest the gun away. With one hand still on Ward's wrist, Bern slid the other up the gun's barrel and jerked downward. Another shot rang out, and the gun dropped to the floor.

Bern stepped back to retrieve the weapon. Ward ignored him, his face contorted with agony. A red stain grew on his right shoulder, but it was his left shoulder that throbbed. The excruciating pain spread to his chest. His eyes searched for the source of the agony, but the only obvious wound was from the gunshot. Then he understood. The heart attack Caroline had always predicted. The smoking, the greasy foods, the lack of exercise. She'd nagged him for years. Now it was going to keep Tarnwell from getting what he wanted. He tried to laugh, but the sound came out as only a weak gargle. He staggered forward a step and fell to his knees. Bern stood aside as Ward pitched over.

Ward looked up, his vision tunneling. Through the tunnel, he could see Lobec's eyes hovering only a foot from his face. Lobec shook Ward and spoke. Although his voice was only a muddy jumble, Ward felt himself responding, not really understanding what he was saying. He saw Lobec's face turn and start searching, stopping when he came to the computer screen. He followed Lobec's gaze there. The last thing Ward ever saw was the phrase *Message sent to: N. Kevin Hamilton.*

TWO

Slamming the apartment door behind him, Kevin Hamilton sprinted to his car. As he ran, he pulled a Rockets cap over his wet, tangled hair and shoved his wallet into the front pocket of his shorts. One of his shoes was still untied, and the laces slapped against his bare ankles. He didn't dare stop to tie it. If he didn't get to the South Texas University campus in twenty minutes, his life would be over.

Kevin had just finished toweling off from a late-afternoon shower when he'd thought to check the emails in his South Texas University in-box. The first one had stopped him cold. He'd read the email twice to make sure he'd understood it correctly, then frantically called the number under the signature. Getting only voicemail, he had printed out the email message and scrambled into the first clothes he could find. The long-sleeved button-down shirt he'd ripped from a closet hanger was wildly incongruous with the workout shorts and tennis shoes, but he didn't care. Besides, he'd seen a lot worse on other graduate students.

He jumped into his Mustang and tossed the printout

onto the front seat. As he inserted the ignition key, Kevin rested his other hand on the steering wheel, then immediately pulled it back with a gasp. Even this late in the day, the September sun was still strong enough to heat the leather to scorching temperatures. Gripping the cooler lower part of the wheel, he turned the key.

The Mustang wheezed for a few seconds, then nothing. Kevin swore under his breath. He'd had the car for nine years – won it in a radio contest when he was still in high school. For the first two years he lived the teenage male's dream of owning a flaming red V-8 hot rod. But since then, it had started to slowly fall apart. The rear hatch release, the gas gauge, the car alarm, and the right window switch were all broken. The latest frustration was its difficulty starting. He'd been meaning to get it fixed, but money had been tight.

He tried again, mouthing a silent prayer. The car rumbled to life.

'Yes!' Kevin shouted. He tore out of the parking space and headed for the exit.

The Mustang roared through the lot of the Sycamore apartment complex until Kevin had to brake for the closed security gate. The ten-foot-high gate slid sideways on a track and always seemed to move slower when he was in a hurry, but it actually took no more than eight seconds to open fully.

He pounded on the steering wheel and glanced at the dashboard clock. 4:43. It was going to be close.

As soon as the opening was wide enough, Kevin accelerated onto the street. The traffic didn't leave much room for maneuvering, so he was stuck with its plodding pace, changing lanes over and over, looking for any opening he could exploit.

When he finally reached the STU campus, the dashboard clock read 4:59.

Kevin found an empty spot marked 'RESERVED' right in front of Braden Hall. He took the printout from the front seat and bounded up the steps into the granite administration building to the second floor, where he reached a glass door with 'Office of Financial Aid and Student Affairs' etched on the front. He had the door halfway open when a woman on the other side of the door reached out to stop him.

'The office is closed,' she said. He recognized the woman immediately. Her name was Teri Linley. She was an undergraduate with curly brown hair and makeup so thick it looked like it had been applied with crayons. Kevin knew her because he had graded a first-year chemistry course over a year ago, and she had been the biggest pain in the class, complaining about every little point he took off her exams.

She didn't give Kevin a second glance and tried closing the door. He held the handle firmly.

'Teri, I have to see Dean Baker,' he said.

Teri examined her watch dramatically. 'It's after five. We're closed.' Her expression was annoyance mixed with impatience. She wanted to be out of there.

'I know it's late, but I have to talk to her.'

She shook her head. 'You'll have to come back Monday.'

'I can't.' Kevin waved the email at her. 'This says I have to see her before the end of today.'

'As far as this office is concerned,' she said, 'the day has ended.'

Kevin pointed toward the office hallway. 'I know Dean Baker's still here. Her light's on.'

'I didn't say she wasn't here. I said we were closed.' Teri pulled on the door again. Kevin wouldn't let it budge.

'What are you doing?' she said. 'Let go.'

'I'm not letting go of this door until I get to see her.'

Teri hesitated, turning her head to look down the hallway.

'I promise you'll get out of here a lot faster if you let me in.'

She turned back and held his gaze for a couple of seconds with a look of disgusted resignation. She let go of the door and threw up her hands. 'Fine. Come on.'

Teri went back to the front desk, and Kevin walked down to the professor's office.

He rapped lightly on the open door. 'Dr Baker?'

Julia Baker, dean of STU Financial Aid and Student Affairs, looked up, her eyes peering over reading glasses with the unmistakable gaze of authority. Her straight red hair and angular face dusted with freckles complemented an expensive-looking gray dress accented by a turquoise scarf. He suddenly felt self-conscious about his own appearance but didn't take off his cap, knowing his hair would look even worse.

'Sorry to bother you so late—' he began.

'Not at all,' Dean Baker said with a smile. 'Please have a seat.' She gestured to one of the chairs in front of the desk and Kevin sat. 'I've been expecting you, Kevin.'

'You know who I am?' he said. She had been hired away from the University of Oklahoma during the summer. Kevin had never met her before.

'Of course. I recognize you from your application photo.' She turned to her computer, tapped a few keys, and then peered at the screen. 'Your GPA is stellar. I want to make sure our best students get every chance to succeed, no matter what problems they've had.'

'I came over as soon as I read your email.'

'I sent the email out August twenty-second. That was almost three weeks ago.'

'I don't use my STU account very often. I didn't take any classes this summer and I work off campus.'

'I see.' She tapped a few more keys. 'It says here that last year you were offered a research assistantship by Michael Ward and that you accepted.'

'I did have one with Dr Ward until eight months ago. He fired me.'

'I know, but your file doesn't say why.'

'There was an accident in the lab. Some equipment got destroyed. Some expensive equipment. He thought it was my fault.'

'Was it? You didn't appeal the decision.'

'I can't say for sure. Both of us were in the lab at the time, but I was the one who set up the equipment, so I got the blame. He fired me right after the accident. I didn't get a chance to inspect the equipment closely.'

'Would you like me to speak to Dr Ward for you?'

Kevin shook his head. Even if she could do it, he wouldn't go back to work for the arrogant asshole. 'No, thanks. After I was fired, none of the other chemistry professors had any open positions. I found a temporary job at Memorial Hermann in the diagnostic lab while waiting to hear about my application for research assistantships this coming school year.'

'You like the job?'

Kevin shrugged. 'It pays the rent.'

'But not your tuition.'

'Without a research assistantship, STU won't waive my tuition for the coming year. I can't afford the cost, even with the school loans.'

'And that's why I was offering you a chance at this opportunity.'

The reason for her email. The reason Kevin had raced over. He shifted uncomfortably in the chair.

'I know. And I really appreciate it.'

'I sent that email – and two follow-ups, I might add – to see if you were interested in an open position as a teaching assistant, which would also guarantee you a tuition waiver. I was very clear that I needed to hear from you so that we could set up an interview before the end of today, and that if you didn't respond, I would let the chemistry department offer it to another student.'

Kevin began to speak, but Dean Baker held up her hand. 'Unfortunately, I have to finish preparing for a speech I'm to give at five thirty. We'll have to discuss your options further on Monday.'

'But without the waiver—'

'Kevin, you're an outstanding student. You have strong potential, but you could have been more proactive in pursuing assistantships. However, if you come in early on Monday, I think we can work out an arrangement. The office opens at eight. Now, please close my door on your way out.' She went back to reading the papers on her desk.

Kevin tried not to let her see him sigh with relief. 'Thank you,' he said, gently closing the door behind him.

Teri was waiting by the door as he entered the main office. She was talking to a huge bodybuilder type, no doubt her boyfriend. When she saw Kevin, the disgusted look returned to her face, accompanied by a scowl from the bodybuilder. She nodded in his direction and whispered, 'Finally.'

Kevin pretended to ignore them. He smiled, pushed the door open, and strolled down the hall, feeling much better than when he had run through it ten minutes before.

His life wasn't over after all.

THREE

David Lobec closed the bedroom curtains in case someone happened to drive by on the otherwise deserted suburban street outside. Their car was on the opposite side of the house where it couldn't be seen from the street.

Richard Bern spoke from behind him. 'So, did Ward say anything important?'

He turned to see Bern carefully place Michael Ward on the bed next to his wife. Ward had already been stripped and put into his pajamas. Caroline Ward, dressed in a negligee, looked as if she were sleeping peacefully next to him, belying the fact that Lobec had smothered her with a pillow.

'What do you mean?' Lobec said.

'When he was whispering right before he died, it looked like he was telling you something.'

Lobec's expression didn't change. 'No, he was babbling.' He took an unopened switchblade out of his pocket and threw it to Bern, who caught it with ease.

'I thought you were kidding about this,' Bern said, his eyes wide.

'It's your bullet,' Lobec said. 'Therefore, you take it out. Would you like to explain to Mr Tarnwell why Ward's death wasn't ruled an accident?'

Bern slowly shook his head, pondering the thought. Tarnwell was a bear of a man, a stout six foot six, and still every inch the football player he used to be. Everyone in his employ feared him. Everyone except Lobec. He had other reasons for obeying Tarnwell.

Lobec handed Bern a pair of latex gloves and put a pair on himself.

'I didn't think so,' he said. 'When you're through, wipe down everything in the room that we might have touched. Then come down and remove the slug from the office ceiling.'

Lobec left the bedroom and stopped at the upstairs smoke detector. He took the battery out and slipped it into his pocket. He would do the same to the others. It wasn't uncommon for firemen to find brand-new houses burned to the ground with the occupants still inside because they had forgotten to install batteries in their smoke detectors. The Wards, both smokers, would be another sad story the firemen would use to warn second graders and their parents.

Once Lobec and Bern were through searching the house and Ward's computer for anything associated with Adamas or the missing ten million dollars, flames would consume the building long before the fire department could arrive on the scene.

Lobec smiled at his own ingenuity. With the gas fueling

a raging inferno, it would be difficult to verify a definitive cause of death from the charred remains. Unless, of course, the coroner found a bullet in one of the corpses. And Bern was taking care of that.

Several issues still troubled Lobec, and he stopped smiling at the thought. Who was N. Kevin Hamilton? And what did it mean that the key to Adamas was in his thesis? He'd noticed Ward finish typing on his keyboard just as they walked into his office, but Lobec had thought little of it at the time. Now it could be a significant problem.

Lobec needed to know more. After emptying the other two smoke detectors, he headed for Ward's office. The next item on the agenda was to look for anything regarding N. Kevin Hamilton. Unless they found him quickly, the message might find its way to the police. He couldn't let that happen. In more ways than one, the authorities' involvement would be disastrous for Lobec.

Reggae blasted from the stereo of the stifling, overcrowded house as Kevin threaded his way to Nigel Hudson's kitchen. Although it was only nine o'clock, Nigel's traditional beginning-of-the-semester party was well under way. After returning to his apartment and changing into shorts and a T-shirt, Kevin had made a run to McDonald's and watched TV until he got the text from Erica Jensen that she was heading to the party. As he walked through the bodies gyrating to the music, he scanned the crowd but couldn't see her.

In the kitchen Kevin spotted Nigel at the keg and tapped

him on the shoulder. His friend turned and grasped his hand while giving him a quick man-hug.

'You made it!' Nigel said as he thrust a beer into Kevin's hand.

'Thanks. Wouldn't miss it.' Kevin glanced around again.

'She's in the bathroom.'

'Who?'

'You know who. Are you going to ask her out?'

'I can tell you've been drinking,' Kevin said, taking a fortifying drink. 'Your accent's back.'

Nigel, an immigrant from Jamaica who'd been a U.S. resident for fifteen years, was meticulously fashionable and the most gregarious person at South Texas. He was also one of the few friends from his undergraduate years at Texas A&M that Kevin kept in touch with.

Nigel shot him a bemused look. 'Don't change the subject. You've been waiting for this ever since she broke up with that surgical resident.'

Kevin shrugged and looked around at Nigel's business school friends, most of whom he didn't know. 'It's only been a month since she booted Luke's ass out for cheating on her, and she's still got two weeks left on her ER rotation. You know how busy med students are. It might not be the right time.'

'"Might not be the right time"? You're kidding, right? If you don't ask her out, *I* will.'

Kevin's head snapped back to Nigel, who put up his hands.

'Joking!' Nigel's eyes shifted to something over Kevin's shoulder. 'Well, look who we have here.'

Kevin fought the impulse to whirl around. Though they both worked at the hospital, he had seen Erica only sporadically since her breakup, catching just a few lunches with her and her friends. He'd invited her to the party in the hopes that they'd have some time to chat one-on-one. They'd gotten to know each other through their jobs and then at parties and other get-togethers, but Luke or her friends had always been hovering around. This was finally his chance to see what more could happen.

He turned slowly, but his heart sank when he saw that it wasn't Erica.

A voluptuous blonde, maybe five feet tall and shoehorned into a low-cut black dress, walked over to Nigel, hugged him tightly, and gave him a peck on the cheek.

'How are you, Nigel?' she said with exaggerated flair. 'I haven't seen you in hours.' She turned to Kevin and smiled up at him. 'And who is your friend here?'

'Kevin,' Nigel said, 'this is Heather. She's a classmate of mine.'

They shook hands. She had a surprisingly firm grip for someone her size, but then Kevin realized that a limp handshake wouldn't get a business school graduate very far.

Nigel said he'd mix her a cocktail and walked away, leaving Kevin and Heather alone.

Heather said something that Kevin couldn't hear over the music. He said, 'Excuse me?' and bent down to put his ear closer to her mouth. Her spicy perfume and the tequila on her breath engulfed his nose. The cut of her dress wasn't sleazy, but it left little to the imagination. He turned his head so he wouldn't give the impression that he was staring into her cleavage.

'I said you're cute,' she repeated, raising her voice. 'You're not in the business school, are you? I would have noticed you before.'

Normally, Kevin's stomach would be doing flips by now from the compliment, but tonight it was oddly silent.

'I'm getting my Ph.D. in chemistry. Nigel was my roommate last year.'

'Nigel's great, isn't he? I'm taking a class with him. He helps me a lot with my homework.'

I'll bet he does, thought Kevin.

'Did you go to South Texas for your undergrad too?' she asked, putting her hand on Kevin's arm to balance herself.

'A&M.' He held up his class ring, the words Texas A&M encircling the border. South Texas and A&M were huge rivals. 'Some people don't speak to me when they find out.'

She tilted her head and one end of her mouth turned up. 'I won't hold it against you.'

'So, how long have you been here?' he said.

'I started last year. There's no way to advance at the bank I work for unless you have an MBA, so I thought night school—'

'Heather!' A brunette ran up to Heather and began talking to her, looking at Kevin several times, but he couldn't hear them over the stereo. He breathed a sigh of relief and was about to excuse himself when Heather spoke.

'This is Darcy. We were going to a club and wondered if you wanted to join us. Do you like jazz?'

Kevin loved jazz. 'It's not really my thing,' he said, and looked down at his shorts. 'Besides, I'm not dressed for it.'

'Sure you are. I think you look great.'

'Maybe some other time.'

'Well, if you ever want to go, you can reach me at this number.' She produced a card from her purse. 'It was nice to meet you. Hope to see you again.' She put the card in his hand. Her finger trailed down his arm as she moved away.

Kevin slid the card into his pocket without reading it. He'd toss it in the trash later.

He slowly turned and caught his breath when he saw Erica smiling at him from across the room. Her naturally curly hair was cut in a low-maintenance bob, and a few brown locks dangled over her left eye in a saucy way. She raised her eyebrows, and Kevin immediately realized she'd been watching his exchange with Heather.

Dressed in a tank top, miniskirt, and heels, Erica made her way over and threw her arms wide, pulling him into a quick hug.

'Glad you came,' Kevin said. 'You look really ...' He was trying to figure out how far to go with the compliment – pretty? beautiful? good? – but Erica interrupted him.

'Different?' she said, drawing out the vowels with her Texas twang. 'Yeah, it's nice to be out of scrubs for a change.'

Now his compliment would seem lame, so Kevin just said, 'I bet.'

'Nice job, by the way,' she said. 'That girl looked like she was into you.'

'Nah. I don't think I was her type.'

'Wasn't her type? She was hanging all over you like drapes on a curtain rod. At least you got her number.'

'Yeah, well, we'll see.'

'Don't worry,' she said. 'If it doesn't work out, we can always find you someone else. There are a ton of girls at this party.'

'You don't have to do that.' This was not the way Kevin had seen the conversation going.

'Hey, what are friends for?'

Kevin took another gulp of beer. 'What about you?'

Erica shook her head. 'I've decided I don't have time for relationships right now. Too exhausting. I need to focus on med school. Besides, now I'll have more time to hang out with you.' She patted him on the shoulder like he was her big brother.

Kevin gave her a smile that he hoped was convincing enough, but inside he was dying. The dreaded 'Let's just be friends' speech wasn't even needed. He had skipped directly to it with no intervening steps. *Brilliant, Hamilton. Really suave.*

He decided to move off the topic. 'How come I didn't see you at lunch today?'

She wrinkled her nose as if she got a whiff of something

disgusting. 'Sorry about that. I was on the phone. Money problems. Family problems. It's a long story.'

'If it makes you feel any better, I'm right there with you on both. I had to meet with the dean of student affairs today. And you don't even want to hear about my dad.'

'Sure I do.'

Before he could go on, he was shocked into silence when he saw a tall black-haired guy who wouldn't have looked out of place on a Times Square billboard. He was the type who always had the perfect amount of stubble on his chiseled cheekbones. Hanging on to his arm was a curvaceous Asian beauty.

Kevin couldn't understand why Luke was at the party, but he couldn't let Erica see her ex. He tried to usher her into another room, but she caught him staring and turned in time to see Luke plant a sloppy kiss on the girl before she left his side.

Luke saw them, and instead of heading the other direction, he came straight toward them.

'Well, this is awkward,' Luke said casually as he poured himself a beer.

'What are you doing here?' Erica said.

'Sun was invited. Apparently, she knows the guy who rents the house.' He straightened up and took a drink without the slightest trace of remorse on his face. 'You are looking beautiful tonight, I must say.' He simply nodded at Kevin.

She and Luke saw each other at the hospital occasionally

out of necessity, but Kevin was sure this was the first time they'd been together in a social setting since they broke up. Kevin wasn't surprised to see Luke with another girl already.

Kevin leaned over to him and said, 'Dude, why don't you just find another party?'

'Don't worry, Kev. We'll leave in a few.' Kevin hated when someone called him Kev.

'Can't you see this isn't cool?'

Luke took another drink and shrugged. 'It's gonna happen. Might as well get over it now.'

'It's okay, Kevin,' Erica said. 'I was just going anyway.'

'See you, babe,' Luke said as he smiled at them and walked out of the kitchen.

'Sorry about that,' Kevin said. 'I didn't know he was going to be here.'

'Not your fault,' she said. 'But I'm not going to stay. It's too ... I just don't want to deal with it right now.'

'You sure? He'll be gone soon.'

Erica cast a quick glance toward the direction Luke had exited, then back to Kevin. 'I'll give you a call tomorrow. Maybe we can get some lunch.'

He nodded to show he understood. 'You want me to walk you out?'

Erica shook her head. 'You're sweet,' she said as she gave him a hug. 'Thanks for sticking up for me.' She left through the door Luke hadn't used.

Nigel returned to the keg.

'Where's Erica?' he said.

'She called it a night.'

Nigel frowned. 'Already? Did everything go the way you planned?'

'Just about the exact opposite,' Kevin said, then gulped his beer. He handed the empty cup to Nigel. 'Now, shut up and pour me another one.'

'**T**hat son of a bitch!' Clayton Tarnwell's finger stabbed the limousine's intercom button. 'Get Senders on the phone now.' His deep voice boomed, revealing just a hint of Texas drawl. David Lobec, who was sitting across from Tarnwell, didn't flinch.

Tarnwell's personal secretary was in the front seat, hidden by the opaque glass partition. 'Sir, Senders is still in Yosemite camping with his family. He'll be out of pocket until tomorrow night.'

Tarnwell looked outside in time to see a sign saying 'Welcome to Houston' whiz by. It was seven o'clock on a Saturday morning and traffic out of the airport was light. 'Didn't he take his satellite phone with him?'

'It's in his office.'

Christ, he thought, *I've got some morons working for me. First, the problem with Stein, now this.* 'When does ZurBank open?'

'Two thirty Monday morning, Houston time.'

'Then call that idiot's house and leave a message that if he isn't in my office by two thirty A.M. on Monday, he can kiss his ass good-bye.'

'Yes, sir. Will you be needing the Gulfstream again on Tuesday as planned?'

'No. Cancel the trip to Wyoming. Murphy can take care of that. But I've got to go back to D.C. on Thursday for the meeting with the National Mining Association. Tell them we fly out Wednesday night, eight o'clock. And get another pilot. I almost lost a filling on that landing.'

As the CEO of Tarnwell Mining and Chemical, Clayton Tarnwell spent a substantial amount of his time in Washington. He had made most of his money taking advantage of loopholes in U.S. mining laws, buying land from the government at ridiculously low prices and then stripping every last precious mineral from it, leaving the residue to be disposed of at taxpayer expense.

Lately he had diversified into the chemical industry, relying on his mining interests to provide the raw material. And the only way to make the most of his investments was to ensure that his presence was felt on Capitol Hill. Usually, he took Lobec with him to Washington for special operations with which he didn't want to be directly associated, but this time Lobec had stayed behind to take care of Ward.

Ward was a special case. Probably once in a lifetime.

Tarnwell took a bottle of water from the limo's fridge and looked back at Lobec. 'That's all Ward said? Nothing about the money?'

Lobec shook his head. 'He died before I could get anything further from him. It must have been a heart attack. The wound was in the shoulder, not nearly severe enough to cause immediate death.'

'And you're sure he didn't have the account number hidden somewhere in the house?'

'We took several hours to search it. There was a safe, but nothing was in it besides some insurance documents and jewelry. The computer also looked fruitless, but I copied all of the files and gave them to Mitch Hornung to see if anything is there.'

Tarnwell nodded and took a swig of water. Hornung was his resident hacker. If anything was on the computer, Mitch would find it.

'We were quite thorough,' Lobec continued, 'but it's very possible that something as small as a piece of paper with a number on it could have been overlooked.'

'What about his university office? On the computer there, maybe?'

'I checked the campus office, the lab, and the office computer after we were finished with his house. I could see nothing about Adamas or the Swiss account. Of course, Hornung has those files as well, so we won't be certain until later today. I believe, however, that Ward must have memorized the account information.'

'Damn! I told Senders this was going to happen. That dumbshit is going to work twenty-four hours a day until he gets my money back.'

'I was under the impression that the money could not be transferred without our knowledge.'

Tarnwell threw his hands up. 'That's what *I* thought! That moron!'

Milton Senders, Tarnwell's chief financial officer, had been responsible for transferring the ten million dollars to an account he set up for Ward in Switzerland. Tarnwell had no intention of letting Ward keep the money, but Ward was no dummy, so Tarnwell needed to make the transaction look legitimate to get Ward to give him the notebook. Senders assured Tarnwell that the risk of losing the money was minimal. He had created an escrow account in which Ward could withdraw small amounts to maintain the illusion that he had control of the money, giving up maybe a few thousand for the sake of appearances. Large transactions had to be approved by Tarnwell, and Ward hadn't made any. But last night they found that the account was virtually empty. Ward somehow slipped ten million dollars past the security measures.

'We don't even know how Ward did it,' Tarnwell said. 'It's almost as if he had help.' Then his huge frame suddenly went rigid and he narrowed his eyes at Lobec. 'David, you *have* told me everything, haven't you? I mean, I can trust you. I know I can. But I just want to hear it from you.'

Lobec looked him in the eye. 'Mr Tarnwell, I owe you my life. What more can I say?'

'You're damn right you owe me. If it weren't for me, you'd still be rotting in La Mesa.' Tarnwell smiled to himself when he saw Lobec's mouth twitch at the mention of the Mexican prison that had been Lobec's home for two years. The only reason Tarnwell had gotten him out was because he'd needed a good security man, one who wasn't afraid to get his hands dirty. Through some contacts he'd heard Lobec was one of the best mercenaries money could buy, imprisoned only because his previous employer had ratted him out to avoid a sentence.

'You are very generous, Mr Tarnwell. I would never betray that generosity.'

'That's what I like to hear. You're the best man I've got, David. You know how to get things done, and I appreciate that.' Tarnwell leaned forward and lowered his voice. 'But if I ever so much as have an inkling that you're not being straight with me, you'll be on the next truck to Tijuana.'

Lobec narrowed his eyes. 'I understand.'

'Good,' Tarnwell said. 'Now, tell me about how you took care of the house. Everything went as planned, I assume?'

'It should look like the fire started with a smoldering cigarette. I extinguished the stove's pilot light and left the gas on. As I understand from the initial police reports, the entire house was consumed. The bodies were nearly cremated. The police haven't even positively identified them yet.'

'Do you think it'll be enough to cover Ward's gunshot wound?'

'Definitely for the next week. Fortunately, the county coroner's office is swamped with bodies from the Baytown refinery explosion. Ward's autopsy won't even begin until that's finished. With the bodies burned so badly, they may never know what really happened.'

'It doesn't matter anyway. They have no way to link me to him. And at least we have the notebook.'

'Right before his scuffle with Bern, Ward did mention something about a videotape,' Lobec said. 'He also said that you don't really have the notebook.'

Tarnwell waved his hand. 'He was bluffing. I would in his situation. Don't worry about it. The lab should have Adamas up and running any time now. And the lawyers started the patent ball rolling yesterday.' A smile spread across Tarnwell's face, and a set of perfect teeth showed through. He leaned his head back and closed his eyes, stretching his long legs onto the seat next to Lobec.

Lobec cleared his throat. 'There is one detail that remains.'

Except for his mouth, Tarnwell didn't move. 'Then take care of it.'

'I will. But I thought you should know. It seems that Ward sent an email before we arrived.'

Tarnwell's head jerked up. 'Do you know who it went to?'

'It was sent to an N. Kevin Hamilton.'

'Who is he?'

'We found a number of references to him in Ward's files.

He's in his third year of graduate school at South Texas University. He worked with Ward until January. Of course, Bern and I searched his apartment as soon as we were finished with Ward.' Lobec passed a picture to Tarnwell. 'This was the most prominently displayed photo in his apartment. I took my own snapshot of it, of course.'

It showed a smiling man in his twenties with thick brown hair. He was wearing a Texas A&M T-shirt and jeans and was standing next to a lanky brunette with long tan legs extending from a pair of white shorts.

'Who's the girl?' Tarnwell said, handing the photo back.

'We don't know yet, but we're looking into it. Her first name is Erica. He had several photos like it in his desk, and one of them had their names written on the back.'

'What was in the message?'

Lobec handed a sheet of paper to Tarnwell with the email on it. Tarnwell cursed under his breath as he read it.

'This tells him everything!'

'Not everything. At least we stopped Ward before he wrote your full name.'

'What's this about the key being in his thesis?'

'Hornung downloaded Hamilton's master's thesis from his computer and is going through it, but we'll need Hamilton to tell us what it has to do with Adamas.'

'It doesn't sound like you've brought him in yet.'

'He wasn't there when we arrived last night, which is why we're trying to find this girl. He could be at her place. Bern is watching his apartment and we have a tap under way on his home phone. I'll join Bern after we reach your office. Do you have any specific instructions?'

'Find out what Hamilton knows. I mean anything. And videotape the interrogation for me. I can't be there, but I want to see it. Then get rid of him.'

'It is possible that Hamilton knows nothing,' Lobec said.

Tarnwell took a sip of coffee and leaned his head back again. 'Nobody ever said life was fair.'

Kevin's eyes fluttered, and the pounding in his head convinced him that he was conscious. The sun was up; no other source of light could be as excruciatingly painful. He made a halfhearted attempt to turn over, but his stomach argued and won. Besides, it didn't feel like his muscles would respond.

He lay in the same position for an hour, awake the entire time, his brain seemingly three sizes too big for his skull. Suddenly a chain saw started in the next room and he sat bolt upright. He pried his eyes open enough to see Nigel in the kitchen, standing over a coffee grinder.

Looking around, he realized that he had slept on Nigel's couch. He wondered how he'd squeezed his six-foot-two length into the tiny area between the armrests. He was bare from the waist up and a blanket was balled up at the end of the couch. Various cups and bottles littered the floor around him. He also noticed the stale smell of beer for the first time. The pounding in his head returned to full strength and nausea gripped him. He ran to the bathroom.

After emptying the contents of his stomach and then his bladder into the toilet, Kevin turned to the mirror and found just about what he was expecting. His face was unusually pale and his hair looked rather comical. On one side it stood straight out in all directions, on the other it was matted from sleep. He hadn't bothered to remove his contacts, so his eyes were dry and bloodshot.

Feeling slightly better after vomiting, he rifled through the medicine cabinet and found a bottle of Extra Strength Tylenol. He carried it into the kitchen, where he'd get a Diet Coke to soothe his stomach.

The television came on in the living room as he grabbed a can from the fridge. He put a caplet into his hand, thought about it, added another, then popped both into his mouth and took a small sip of the soda. He held the cool can to his forehead as he walked back to the living room.

Nigel was sitting on the couch with a cup of coffee, surfing the channels with the remote. Kevin had never known him to look anything but impeccable, even early in the morning, and today was no exception. He was already showered and fully dressed, as if he hadn't had a sip of alcohol the previous night.

With a slight grunt, Kevin sank into the La-Z-Boy.

'Good morning, beautiful,' Nigel said with a smile.

Kevin turned toward him and gave him a dirty look. 'I hate you.'

'I told you the Jell-O shots were strong, but you didn't want to listen.'

'You had just as many as I did.'

'I also drink more often than every six months.'

'So do I. But now I'm thinking about quitting altogether.'

Kevin watched TV and brooded quietly. Conversation was not generally part of his morning routine. As Kevin nursed his drink, Nigel flipped past a face on the screen that Kevin immediately recognized.

He almost spit out the soda. After swallowing, he sputtered, 'Wait! Turn it back!'

'What?' Nigel said, as he reversed directions on the remote.

Four channels down, Kevin saw it. 'There! Stop!'

Nigel stopped on what was apparently a local TV news broadcast and looked over at him with a puzzled expression. 'What—'

'Shh! Turn it up.' Kevin stared incredulously at the screen. To the right of the anchorwoman's head was a photo of Michael Ward. The picture had been taken when Ward still had a beard, but it was definitely him.

Nigel thumbed the remote, and the program became audible.

'... where we take you live to Lisa Hernandez. Lisa, what can you tell us?'

The image shifted to a woman standing in front of the blackened ruins of what used to be a house. Wisps of smoke could still be seen rising in the calm air. The only things left standing were a crumbling chimney and the scorched remains of a large tree. Police and firefighters mingled in the background.

'Joan, at two o'clock this morning, residents of this usually quiet north Houston suburb were awakened by an enormous explosion. When firefighters arrived on the scene, they found the home of Michael Ward, a South Texas University chemistry professor, burning out of control. As you can see, the fire is now contained, but not before two firefighters succumbed to heat exhaustion in this morning's sweltering conditions. When the heat of the fire had subsided enough for a search, the charred remains of two people were found in the rubble.'

The TV cut to a clip of two black plastic bags lying behind a van marked 'Harris County Coroner.' Kevin's grip on the soda can tightened.

'The police haven't issued a statement as yet, but sources close to the investigation believe they could only be the bodies of Dr Ward and his wife, Caroline.'

Kevin continued silently watching, shaking his head in disbelief.

Joan asked, 'Has the cause of the fire been determined, Lisa?'

'The cause of the fire has not yet been determined, Joan, but arson investigators are on the premises and foul play has not been ruled out. Speculation now is that the fire was started by a cigarette and spread to the gas lines, which then caused the explosion. The house is in a relatively new development and is the first on the block to be occupied, which may explain why the fire was not reported soon enough to prevent this horrible tragedy. This is Lisa Hernandez reporting live from Spring. Joan.'

'Thank you, Lisa. We understand the police are expected to make a statement within the next hour, and when they do, H-News, Houston's only twenty-four-hour news source, will bring it to you live. Turning to other news, police say drugs may be involved in the execution-style shooting of an attorney whose body was found yesterday morning ...' Nigel pressed the mute button on the remote.

'You knew that professor, didn't you?' he said.

'He was the one who fired me eight months ago.'

'Wow, that's wild.'

Kevin stared out the window. When the accident had happened and he'd been fired, Kevin had wished a lot of bad things on Dr Ward, but never death. Yet, he didn't feel grief about the loss, either. He really didn't know how he felt.

'Kevin,' Nigel said, 'are you all right?'

'Yeah, I'm fine. It's just weird.'

'Did you know him well?'

'Well enough. That's why it's so strange. Ward was a jerk, but he was also a careful guy, almost anal. I guess I'm just surprised that that kind of accident would happen to him.'

'I hear about these things happening to smokers all the time.'

'So do I. I'm just surprised he'd be that careless.'

They sat in silence for a few minutes. Kevin decided he

needed to get back to his apartment and started to search for the rest of his clothes. He found his shirt and shoes under a pizza box and put them on. The hangover was still there, but it was down to a dull throbbing.

'If you need anything, give me a call,' Nigel said.

'Really, I'm okay. Don't worry about it.'

Kevin walked out into the bright September morning. The newscast was right about the temperature. The heat was already shimmering off the driveway's pavement.

He had to crank the Mustang several times before the engine turned over. He automatically switched on the radio, which was usually tuned to the local rock station, and then figured that he needed a little silence this morning and shut the radio off. As he released the parking brake and shifted into first, he looked at the trip odometer, which was how he gauged his gas level. Just enough to make it back to his apartment and a nice, cool shower.

SIX

The Sycamore apartment complex was nowhere near the South Texas University campus. It was located on the west side of Houston, just outside the Loop, far from the high-crime area around the university where the cheapest apartments were, but not quite into the more expensive suburbs. It was relatively safe, with a security gate and fence encircling the complex, and the rent for a one-bedroom apartment was affordable. The only drawback was the commute, which could take over thirty minutes during the morning rush-hour drive.

Like most complexes in the city, sprawling parking lots surrounded long rows of nondescript three-level buildings, which in turn overlooked courtyards with the de rigueur swimming pools that were used practically year-round. Hedges and small strips of grass separated the buildings from the sidewalks. The only thing that made the Sycamore stand out from other complexes, and in defiance of the complex's name, was the abundance of large oaks shading cars from the relentless heat. In the far corner of the lot, inside a Chevy sedan parked under one of these oaks, sat David Lobec and Richard Bern.

Bern was dozing, taking a break while Lobec read the short dossier they had compiled on Kevin Hamilton in the last few hours, cobbled together from the internet, his school files, a quick search of his apartment, and Texas Department of Public Safety records. Every thirty seconds, as if he had a built-in chronometer, Lobec would look up to observe Kevin's first-floor apartment, whose front door faced the parking lot.

A truck with the words 'Four Seasons Landscaping' emblazoned across its side in large green letters rumbled to a stop twenty yards in front of them. A man with no shirt and a huge gut hanging over a pair of greasy shorts climbed out and proceeded to unload a riding lawn mower from the trailer hitched to the truck. Lobec, who hadn't seen snow in the five years he'd been in Houston, wanted to ask the man when the other three seasons would arrive.

The mower belched a plume of smoke and the engine rose to an unmuffled crescendo, drowning out the distant sound of the street traffic and waking Bern. He looked around for the source of noise and through the car's heavily tinted windows saw the fat man ride onto the grass.

'Damn! And I was having a great dream.' He turned to Lobec, who cringed at what he knew was coming. He'd heard this kind of thing a nauseating number of times from Bern.

'Oh, man, what a dream!' Bern continued. 'In this one I

was like Frankenstein, right? You know, making my own person? Except, I wasn't making a monster. I was making my dream girl from parts of all the girls who've ever been in the *Sports Illustrated* swimsuit issue, cutting out one girl's leg from this picture and another girl's jugs from that picture. She was just hit by lightning, right? She was alive, buck naked, right on the table in front of me! So she got up and she was just about to—'

'You may save the details for your memoirs, Mr Bern.'

Bern gave him a quizzical look. 'Sometimes I don't know if you're really human, Lobec. You got any hormones at all?'

'I prefer to separate my sexual urges from my professional functions, and I suggest you attempt the same, if at all possible. It may help you better concentrate on your work.'

'What's there to concentrate on? This guy ain't even home.' He put a pair of headphones up to his ears and punched a button on a machine sitting on the seat next to him. 'The bug and the tap are working fine. What else am I supposed to do?'

Lobec looked around the parking lot. Every few minutes a person or two would emerge from the building complex and get into one of the cars. 'Perhaps we should discuss the new plan we'll follow when Kevin Hamilton returns.'

'New plan? Too many people around for you?'

'Yes. Instead of approaching him at his apartment, we'll monitor his telephone calls and wait. If no particular urgency arises, we'll let him leave the apartment and stop his car in a more secluded area. I assume you have your identification with you?'

'Yeah, I got it.' Bern took out his wallet and flipped it open, revealing a Houston Police Department badge and identification. Lobec nodded and Bern returned it to his pocket. 'But I'm sick of the name Kaplan. I think I'll get Sheryl to make me a new ID after this op is over. What do you think of Braddock?'

'No. This is the third identification you've had this year. Changing aliases too often can compromise an operation. It may be difficult to remember in times of stress.'

'Afraid you'll forget it?' Bern smirked.

'I wasn't speaking about myself. Do I have to I bring up the incident last year with the OGP?'

Bern's smirk dissolved. The Old Growth Protectorate was a fringe environmental group bent on radical, sometimes militant defense of primeval forests. Clayton Tarnwell had never even heard of them until his company announced plans to open a copper strip mine on virgin forest land in Montana. When the OGP threatened to destroy his mining equipment, Tarnwell sent Lobec to persuade the group's leader to share his knowledge of their plans. Bern and Lobec had been wearing ski masks, but during the interrogation, Bern slipped and used Lobec's name, requiring a more permanent method of dealing with OGP's founder.

'What's all this stuff about Adamas, anyway?' Bern said, clumsily changing the subject. 'Is that some new chemical Tarnwell's trying to make?'

'You know as much as I do about Dr Ward's process. I am not well versed in the chemical sciences, and Mr Tarnwell has not seen fit to brief me on the details. I think for both our sakes it's better not to talk about it.'

'Was he pissed about Stein?'

'You could say that.'

'Well, it's not like it was our fault those kids found the body when they were playing in that Dumpster.' Bern pulled a cigarette from the pack of Marlboros in his front pocket and stuck it in his mouth, then pulled a Bic lighter from the same pocket. 'That lot looked so deserted, I thought it would be months before anyone would look in—'

'Mr Bern,' Lobec said, his voice a dagger's edge, 'what have I asked you not to do in my presence?'

The Bic's flame flickered two inches in front of the unlit cigarette. Bern's eyes widened when he realized what he'd done and he sat up straight, releasing the Bic's lever. 'I'm s-sorry, Lobec,' he said in a rush. 'I didn't mean to, it's just habit—'

'You know that smoking offends me, but you don't respect my wishes. That offends me even more. I sincerely hope further correction won't be necessary.'

Bern shook his head vigorously, and Lobec was satisfied that his point had been made. Bern had objected to his demands only twice, and he'd learned the second time that Lobec didn't take his smoking policy lightly. The burn scar on Bern's forearm proved that.

Now that Bern was awake, Lobec returned his full

attention to the folder in front of him and read from the beginning. He always liked to know as much as he could about the people he dealt with, even if it would be for only a short time.

Nicholas Kevin Hamilton. Age twenty-six. Only child. Valedictorian of Sam Houston High School in Dallas, Texas. According to old letters of acceptance he had stored in a file box, he applied to and was accepted by eight universities, including Stanford and MIT, but he attended Texas A&M on a National Merit Scholarship and ten thousand dollars a year in student loans. Graduated summa cum laude with a B.A. in chemistry. Mother: Frances May – died of cancer while he was at A&M. Father: Murray Hamilton – foreman for a construction firm in Dallas. Began graduate school at South Texas University in chemistry immediately after leaving A&M and was about to begin his third year of studies. He drove a nine-year-old red Ford Mustang GT, with three moving violations for speeding in the past three years.

'Is this all we have?' Lobec asked.

'Uh, no. I almost forgot,' Bern said. He pulled a notepad out of his pocket and flipped it open. 'Mitch called while you were with Tarnwell. After he was done with the DPS records, he accessed Hamilton's credit rating. It seems our student has had a little trouble paying his bills lately. He's been late with his rent three times this year, and he has a Visa and a MasterCard maxed out. Total limit nine thousand dollars.'

'What about the car?'

'Funny thing. There's no record of a loan on it. Must have been paid for with cash.'

'Life insurance?'

'No payout that Mitch could find. He has one checking account with the university's credit union, current balance $85.86. Hamilton's father probably bought the car for him.'

'Possibly.'

'Why do we have to get all this stuff this time, anyway? I thought we were just gonna find out what he knows and take him out.'

'Bern, in my experience I have noticed one unchanging characteristic among all of the ops I've conducted: No matter how simple an operation seems, there will always be complications. And when they arise, the more information you have, the more likely you'll be to succeed.'

Bern looked past Lobec's shoulder and nodded as he put the microphone in his ear. 'At least we don't have to wait too long to find out.'

Lobec turned to see a car pull into the parking lot. It was a red Mustang.

SEVEN

Kevin threaded the Mustang into his usual slot beside one of the parking lot's islands, pulled through one space, and lurched to a stop in the second with the car facing away from the apartment building and shaded by an oak. He sat there for a minute, turning his face back and forth through the refreshing blast of the air conditioner, trying to soothe his still-throbbing head. Ready to face the heat, he killed the engine and reluctantly opened the door to the humid air that sucked the coolness from the car. He was sweating by the time he reached his apartment.

He dropped his keys on the kitchen counter and walked through the tiny living room to his bedroom. After punching the thermostat to its lowest temperature, he glanced at the answering machine. The light shined steadily. No messages. Not that he used it much. He would have gotten rid of it and just used his cell phone if the landline weren't free with his internet service.

The battery on Kevin's cell phone was drained after he'd spent the night at Nigel's. He plugged in the charger and left it on the counter with his wallet.

Kevin ran his fingers through his oily hair and realized just how nasty he felt. He peeled off his sticky clothes and removed the contacts from his dry, itchy eyes. He spent the next ten minutes in the cold shower, letting the pulsating water massage his aches.

When he stepped out of the bathroom into the cooled air of the apartment, he felt refreshed. Wearing just a towel, he put on his glasses and went into the kitchen to open another can of Diet Coke. As he passed through the living room, he hit the space bar to wake his Mac and leaned over to turn on the TV, which he normally had on while he worked.

He stopped when he didn't see the remote on the coffee table. He searched for a minute and finally found it under the couch. How did it get there? He tried to remember the last time he watched TV. After a second, he shrugged, picked up the remote, and flipped on the alternative rock music channel.

After taking a gulp from the cold soda, he felt even better. He set the can on his desk and returned to the bedroom, where he put on workout shorts and a South Texas University T-shirt. The pair of beat-up flip-flops he slipped into completed his typical Saturday outfit.

As Kevin sat down at his desk, an anchorman was telling viewers what they'd be seeing when the news resumed at the top of the hour. He adjusted the keyboard and mouse to their correct positions and clicked the email icon.

He needed to get ready for the interview with Dean Baker on Monday. Maybe she was right that he should be more proactive in pursuing research opportunities. When he was fired earlier in the year, Kevin remembered printing a forum discussion on National Science Foundation grants. He started thumbing through his file drawer to find it, then abruptly stopped.

The files were all there, but something was wrong. What was it? And then it struck him.

He filed his folders alphabetically by the first author of the reference, with the stapled end up so he could grab and replace the references easily when he was working on his dissertation or writing a paper. It was a habit he had developed from years of research. Today the articles were in the exact order they always were, and the four file folders were in the correct order. But in every one of the folders, the stapled end of the article was at the *bottom* of the folder.

As he put the articles back in their correct orientation, Kevin didn't know what to make of it. Just another strange thing in an already odd morning, he thought.

Two new messages were in his Gmail in-box. The first message was from the American Chemical Society student chapter, probably asking for dues. He skipped it.

He smiled when he saw who the second message was from: Ted Huang, his best friend since coming to grad school. Ted had joined the program two years before him and had just accepted a teaching position at Virginia Tech. When Kevin last saw him, Ted and his wife, Janice, were moving to Blacksburg. Kevin had heard from him only once since he left and opened the message, eager to read the news.

> Kevin, I'm sorry I've haven't called in a while, but as you might guess it's been a madhouse getting ready for the semester. I've got three classes to teach, not to mention the conference coming up next Wednesday. Five days in Minneapolis. Janice is going with me because she has some family there, so it shouldn't be too bad.
>
> By the way, the lab is looking great, and the equipment they're giving me is incredible. That's about all. I've got to go. My presentation isn't done yet, and I only have the weekend to do it. Talk to you later.
>
> T

Kevin exited the message. He'd send a reply later. He logged into his STU account just in case Dean Baker had sent him something else.

As he raised the Diet Coke to take a sip, he noticed the bold line that indicated he had one new message. When he saw who the message was from, he froze, the can hovering in front of his face.

It was from Michael Ward. Sent at 4:23 P.M. yesterday.

Kevin placed the can precariously on the edge of the desk, feeling strangely repulsed that one of the last messages Ward had ever sent was waiting for him. Nevertheless, he had to read it. He opened the file.

Kevin was totally unprepared for the message he found. His heartbeat tripled as he read and reread the short message.

> Kevin, the same men who killed Stein are after me. Caroline and I are leaving Houston. I think we'll be safe where we're going, but I need your help to be sure. NV117 wasn't a failure. You know the equipment. The key to everything else you need is in your thesis. I made a deal with Clay

Questions filled Kevin's mind. Who was Stein? Where were Ward and his wife going? Who were these men he was talking about? They must be connected to Clay, whoever that was. And what did he mean NV117 wasn't a failure? Of course it was a failure – a huge failure, from Kevin's standpoint.

NV117 was a routine investigation into high-temperature superconductivity. They'd been conducting experiments like it for months with little success. Then the routine was shattered when it almost blew up in their faces. The damage to the equipment had been extensive, or so Kevin had been told. Ward hadn't let him back into the lab after the accident. Even if the experiment had turned out to be a success, the results they were expecting would have been interesting but certainly nothing revolutionary. Nothing worth killing for. It didn't make sense.

Maybe the message was a joke, Kevin thought, but he immediately dismissed the idea. No one he knew would have done something this bizarre, not when Ward's house had gone up in flames hours before. The only other possibility was that Ward had actually sent the message. If that was true, why write a message to Kevin? Why didn't Ward just call the police?

He looked at the last sentence, which made it seem as if Ward had been interrupted. Or maybe he'd been drunk and didn't realize he hadn't finished. He'd heard about smokers getting drunk and falling asleep with a lit cigarette. Maybe that's how the fire started. He cringed at the thought and studied the message again.

What did he mean that everything else he needed was in his thesis? Kevin's master's thesis on the design of metal nanoparticle catalysts had little to do with Ward's superconductor research. The only reason Kevin was working on the project was because Ward had needed someone who was familiar with the equipment and could help him use the catalysts in his experiment. How could anything in his thesis be the key?

The cordless phone rang in the bedroom. Kevin let it ring. He turned on the laser printer and selected the print option. The page fed in as the answering machine clicked on and played the announcement.

'This is the home of Kevin Hamilton. If you would like to hang up, please press one now. If you are selling something or asking for money, please press one now. Otherwise, leave a message and I'll get back to you.' The beep sounded, and he heard Erica's drawl.

'Kevin, it's me. Give me a call when you get back.'

Kevin ran into the bedroom and snatched up the phone. 'Erica. I'm here.' He stopped the recorder as he spoke. 'How are you doing?'

'I'm sorry I ducked out so quickly last night. I guess I should get used to seeing Luke show up with another girl.'

Kevin wanted to ask what she ever saw in a jerk like that, but he didn't know how to say it without making her feel worse. 'Are you all right?'

'I'm fine,' she said, but she didn't sound fine. She sounded as if she had been up all night, and Kevin knew that she was supposed to go on her ER rotation later this afternoon. He wasn't going to press the issue. 'I just got back from the pool. Why is your cell phone off?'

'Battery died,' Kevin said. 'It's charging now. Do you want to get lunch?'

'Sure. I was just calling because ... Have you seen the news today?'

'You mean about Dr Ward?'

'So it's the same Ward you've told me about?'

'The one who fired me, yes.' Kevin went over to the printer and picked up the copy of the email. 'Funny you should ask. I just got a message from him.'

'What do you mean?' Erica said. 'Today?'

'Just a few minutes ago. It was sent yesterday afternoon.' Kevin read the message to her.

'That's really weird,' Erica said. 'Have you called the police yet?'

'I hadn't gotten that far.'

'I heard something about arson on the radio.'

'They said they aren't ruling out arson, but they always say that.'

'Do you know who Stein or Clay are?'

'I had a high school math teacher named Joshua Clay, but I don't think that's him.'

'Do you know what any of it means?' Erica asked. 'What about your thesis?'

'I have no idea. But I do know what NV117 means. It was an experiment we were doing for the Department of Energy on superconductivity using a new kind of chemical structure.'

'Superconductivity? Would somebody kill him for it?'

'I can't imagine why. The experiment was a total failure. In fact, it was the one that got me fired. As far as I know, he stopped all work on it after the accident. Even if it wasn't a failure like the message said, it wouldn't have been groundbreaking. Certainly nothing worth killing for. We're probably getting worked up over nothing. Some people in the department said he was a drinker. He was probably wasted when he wrote it.' He told her his theory about the cigarette.

'That's certainly possible. I've seen three alcoholics in the ER who accidentally set fire to themselves with cigarettes. Still, the police should probably know about the message.'

'Yeah, I know. I'm just trying to avoid it because I know it's going to be a hassle. They might want me to go down to the station.'

'I'm going to shower off,' Erica said. 'Call me back after you talk to them.'

'Okay. Talk to you later.'

Kevin hung up, looked up the HPD Web site, and dialed the number for police headquarters. There wasn't really any reason to call 911.

He was put on hold three times as staff at the police station shuffled his call around to various departments. Each time someone new answered, he had to explain the situation all over again. As he waited for someone in Homicide to pick up, Kevin thought that at least his day couldn't get any stranger.

Lobec and Bern listened as a female voice on the line said, 'Homicide. Detective Chambers speaking.'

'Detective Chambers,' Kevin Hamilton said, 'I hope I've finally got the right person. I have a message from Dr Michael Ward. You know, the guy who died in the house fire last night?'

'What is your name, sir?' The voice was curt.

There was a pause. 'Uh, my name's Kevin Hamilton, one of Dr Ward's students. He sent me an email telling me that the same men who had killed Stein were after him. It seemed suspicious, so I thought I'd better let you know.'

'Herbert Stein is Guy Robley's case.'

There was another pause from Hamilton, this time longer. 'You mean, there really is someone named Stein?'

'He was found Saturday morning in a vacant lot near the

Astrodome. Shot twice and loaded into a Dumpster. Look, Detective Robley isn't here right now, but he should be back in about twenty minutes. Can he call you back then?'

'Wow. Okay. I'll stay here.' He gave her the number. 'Please have him call me as soon as he gets in.'

'All right.' Two clicks could be heard. Bern began to speak, but Lobec lifted his hand as another number was dialed. The LCD panel in front of him displayed the number of the girl named Erica Jensen, whom they had already identified with their caller ID unit. The line went straight to voice mail. Hamilton left her a message to call him and hung up the phone.

Finally, Lobec lowered his hand, and Bern spoke.

'What if he gets the cops involved?'

'We can't allow that. It's unfortunate that we didn't know of Hamilton's involvement in NV117 previously.' Lobec pulled out his .40 caliber SIG Sauer P230, a compact weapon easily concealed and modified to accommodate a silencer. He replaced it in his shoulder holster.

'We going in now?' Bern checked his badge and identification and grimaced again when he saw his alias.

'No, that would be unrealistic. The police would never arrive so quickly. Even so, we don't have much time. We'll wait ten minutes. If anyone calls in that time, we'll need to surprise him. Otherwise, we can introduce ourselves to him in the usual fashion.'

After shaving and changing into more presentable clothes, Kevin walked back to the living room, plopping himself at his desk. He searched Google for more info about the fire at Ward's house, but there wasn't anything new. Next he searched for Herbert Stein and found an article about the discovery of the lawyer's body. The police hadn't identified any suspects or motive in the murder.

Kevin played over the events of the last day again. One, his professor and the professor's wife were dead, supposedly from a house fire. Two, he had received email from Dr Ward – wait, change that: from Dr Ward's email *address* – claiming that someone was trying to kill him, possibly for a failed experiment that had actually worked. Three, Ward had made a some kind of deal with a person named Clay. Four, Herbert Stein, a person Kevin had never heard of until today, had been murdered.

Which left him with what? He looked at the printout again. He wished he could believe that this was all an elaborate hoax, that somebody owed him for a joke he had pulled at one time, but even the nerds in his chemistry department wouldn't stoop to something like this.

That left a high probability that the message really was from Dr Ward. Three dead people. Maybe all of them murdered. He was glad he had called the police.

A sharp knock on the door startled him. Kevin folded the printout and stuffed it into his pocket as he rose and walked over to the front door.

Normally during the day he would just open the door, although at night he always checked who it was first. Today was not normal. He looked through the foggy peephole and could make out two men in suits. He recognized neither of them.

'Who is it?' he said loudly.

'Detectives Barnett and Kaplan,' a well-spoken voice said. 'Guy Robley radioed us and asked us to stop by since we were in the neighborhood. He said he couldn't get to the phone right now to call you. If you'll crack the door, you can see our identification.'

At the mention of Detective Robley's name, Kevin calmed. Even so, he kept the chain on and inspected the IDs. They seemed all right to him, not that he'd know what fake badges looked like. Satisfied, he removed the chain and invited the officers to come in.

'Man, am I glad you're here.' The officer named Barnett looked to be in his late thirties and was neatly dressed in a gray suit and paisley tie. He looked more like a businessman than a cop. He scrutinized Kevin thoroughly but gave him a friendly smile. The other officer, Kaplan, was younger and more rumpled in his navy suit. Both were shorter than Kevin by about four inches. 'You guys must be hot. Can I get you something to drink?'

Barnett glanced at Kaplan and then shook his head. 'No, thank you. We just had a late breakfast, and I think we drank a pot of coffee between us.' As they sat down in the living room, his smile changed to a concerned frown. 'We are working on the Stein case with Guy. He said you called with some information concerning Mr Stein?'

'Actually, I was calling about a professor, Dr Michael Ward.'

'The professor from STU who died in the fire last night?' Barnett said.

'Yes, I go to STU. I worked with him for a year and a half until last January.'

Barnett's concerned expression deepened. 'This must be difficult for you. I'm sorry. Please, go on.'

'I wasn't very close to Dr Ward. I just worked for him.' Kevin told them everything that had happened to him since he woke up. During the story, Barnett asked a few questions for clarification, but Kaplan just scribbled on a notepad and said nothing. When Kevin got to the part about the message from Ward, Barnett stopped him.

'Do you know what the message means? This could be very important in our investigation into Mr Stein's death.'

'No, I don't. Maybe if Dr Ward had been able to finish it, I would have understood. The last sentence was cut off, as if he'd stopped typing abruptly.'

'Could I see this email message?' said Barnett.

'Sure,' Kevin said, 'I can even give you a copy.' He went to the Mac and printed them a fresh copy instead of giving them the crumpled one in his pocket. 'Do you really think it's from Dr Ward?'

Both officers read it intently. 'As you said yourself,' Barnett answered, 'this could have been typed by anyone and merely sent from his account. But I don't think we can rule out the possibility that it's real.'

For the first time, Kaplan spoke. His voice was surprisingly high for his size. 'What is NV117?'

'An experiment we were working on right before I stopped working with Dr Ward. It was research we were conducting for the Department of Energy.'

Kaplan glanced down at his notebook. 'So why would someone be after this superconducting experiment?' Kaplan said.

Kevin gave him a puzzled look. 'I have no idea. It's fairly harmless stuff. How did you—'

Barnett interrupted. 'Do you know what the key in your thesis is?'

Kevin shrugged. 'Nothing comes to mind. Like I said, the message wasn't finished.' He turned back toward Barnett and, for a split second, caught Barnett glaring at Kaplan. The look vanished quickly and smoothly, as if Kevin hadn't been meant to see it.

'Did you know Herbert Stein?' asked Barnett.

'Never heard of him before. Who was he? Some drug

dealer's lawyer?' The drug wave had hit Houston as hard as any other big city.

'Well,' Barnett said, 'of course, you understand that I can't reveal everything we know about the case, but I can tell you that he was a respectable attorney with a small practice in the Village. We can't say yet whether drugs were involved.'

'Was Dr Ward a client of his?'

'I don't recall that name from his records,' Kaplan said.

'I don't, either,' Barnett said. 'We'll check that out later. Have you seen a photo of Mr Stein?'

'No. The story on the Web didn't have one. I didn't even know he was a real person until I talked to Detective Chambers.'

'Mr Hamilton,' Barnett said, 'I wonder if we could ask you to come down to the station and look at a picture of Mr Stein.'

'Why?'

'If he and Dr Ward had some clandestine meetings – say, at the university? – a student such as yourself may have seen him. We also have some photos of other suspects. They may have been intermediaries between Mr Stein and Dr Ward, and we'd like you to take a look at them.'

Kevin nodded. 'Sure. No problem.' He looked down at his battered flip-flops. 'I have to put my shoes on.'

'That's all right, Mr Hamilton,' Barnett said. 'Go right ahead. We'll wait out here.'

Kevin ducked into the bedroom, closing the door behind him. His eyes felt better, so he took his glasses off and put his contact lenses back in. Just then the phone rang. He picked it up and started putting on his tennis shoes.

'Hello.'

'It's me,' Erica said. 'Somebody called right after you hung up, and I couldn't get him off the phone.'

'Never mind that. You are not going to believe what's going on. There really is a Stein. Herbert Stein. Actually, I should say there was. He was murdered two days ago.' Erica gasped. 'Now the cops are here, and they want me to go down to the station with them.'

'To look at a lineup?'

'No, just some pictures. It shouldn't take too long.'

The sound of a gas motor steadily grew as the landscaper's riding mower neared Kevin's apartment. He raised his voice.

'You still interested in lunch?'

There was a pause on the other end. 'All right, but no McDonald's.'

A click in the phone interrupted Erica's voice. He could barely make out the telltale beeping of the call-waiting signal over the din of the lawn mower. 'That's another call. Can you hang on?'

'Yes.'

Kevin depressed the switch.

'Hello?' He was practically yelling over the sound of the mower. He moved to the bathroom where it was quieter.

'Mr Hamilton, this is Detective Guy Robley of the HPD Homicide Division. Detective Chambers said you called about Herbert Stein.'

'Yes. Barnett and Kaplan are here. They explained about you not being able to get back to me.'

'Who?'

Kevin frowned. 'Detectives Barnett and Kaplan. They said you asked them to stop by my apartment. I was just about to leave with them to come down to the station.'

'What do you mean, Mr Hamilton? I didn't send anyone to your apartment.'

Kevin looked at the closed bedroom door. 'There must be some misunderstanding. Their names are Detectives Barnett and Kaplan.'

'Look, Mr Hamilton,' Robley said, 'I have no idea what you're talking about, but I don't know anyone by the name of Barnett or Kaplan.'

Lobec leaned against the wall by the bedroom door. He had moved over there to hear the phone conversation, but the noise of the lawn mower was drowning out Kevin's voice. No matter. He had heard most of the conversation with the girl-friend, and it didn't sound as if he had told her anything of importance. Besides, her home was going to be their next stop. So much easier to make their deaths appear as one accident.

He couldn't hear Kevin hang up the phone, but his voice called from the bedroom.

'I just have to go to the bathroom and then I'll be ready to go.'

Lobec heard the push-button lock click and the door shut. After waiting a minute, he peered into the bedroom.

Seeing that it was clear, he walked in. The obese man with the lawn mower turned his machine off. Lobec listened at the door of the bathroom. The fan was on. He heard nothing more.

He waited a few seconds. Still nothing.

He knocked on the door and asked if everything was all right. No response. He drew his pistol and tried the knob. Locked. He hit the flimsy door with his shoulder and rushed into the bathroom.

It took him only a second to scan the tiny room. Before his eyes reached it, he could feel the heat flowing through an open window, large enough for a man to fit through easily. He looked out. Hamilton's car was still in the lot, but the student was nowhere to be seen.

'Something must have tipped him off,' Bern said. 'He didn't take the car?'

Lobec turned toward Bern, who had joined him at the window, his pistol already drawn. He slapped Bern's right cheek hard, leaving an angry red mark.

'You idiot. Of course he was tipped off. You did it by mentioning superconductivity.'

'I heard *him* say superconductivity!'

'He said he was conducting an experiment. He didn't say "superconducting."'

'But I—'

'This is not a debate. His keys, wallet, and cell phone are in the kitchen. Get them in case he decides to come back. He must be in the apartment complex.'

Lobec heard talking coming from the bedroom. He and Bern rushed out of the bathroom to find Hamilton's greeting playing on the answering machine. When the machine beeped and started recording, Lobec recognized the voice.

'Kevin? Kevin, are you there? It's Erica. We got cut off. Kevin? If you've left for the police station, let me know when you get back.' After a few more seconds calling his name, she hung up.

Bern looked at Lobec. 'What do we do now? Same plan? Interrogation?'

Lobec gave Bern a cold stare, twisting the silencer onto his pistol. 'No. Hamilton obviously didn't know what the key in his thesis meant. Therefore, he's of no further use to us. When you find him, kill him.'

As he heard Barnett and Kaplan, or whoever they were, leave the bedroom, Kevin felt the air rush from his lungs. He hadn't even realized he had been holding his breath. Now he was breathing in huge gulps. His hiding place under the pile of laundry in the bedroom closet was tenuous at best. They would be back as soon as they realized he wasn't anywhere in the apartment complex. He needed to move.

His hands were shaking as he eased open the closet door. Once the lawn mower had stopped, he'd been able to hear everything they said in the bathroom. These guys were impersonating police officers and talking about killing him as if it were nothing more than an inconvenience.

When Detective Robley said that he had never heard of Barnett and Kaplan, Kevin had put the phone down without another word, knowing he'd never be able to convince Robley of his situation before the two impostors got suspicious. He also turned off the ringer so the other line with Erica wouldn't suddenly start ringing the phone.

The conversation with Robley made everything suddenly

click. The misplaced remote control and the incorrectly filed folders – the conclusion was obvious. Someone had been in his apartment last night. They had been very careful, but not perfect.

But the real clincher had been Kaplan's offhand question about superconductivity. Kevin had never mentioned it in their conversation, but he remembered talking to Erica about it, which meant his phone must have been tapped, which was also how they knew about his phone call to Robley. They were afraid he'd tell the police about the message from Ward. And they would probably also figure out who Erica was and where she lived.

Kevin crept out of the closet. The apartment was quiet. He kept his steps soft as he moved into the living room.

Per Barnett's order, Kaplan had taken Kevin's wallet, keys, and phone. Kevin opened the right desk drawer and flipped through the files he kept in there. Even though he was meticulous with his research files, his personal files were a mess. He didn't even label all of them. His stomach dropped when he didn't find what he was looking for on the first pass. As he went through the files a second time more carefully, his hands shook, and several times he glanced at the door. Finally, he found it in the tenth file and breathed a sigh of relief: the valet key he had gotten with the car but never used.

He poked his head out the door. No one was in sight. No choice – he had to go for it.

Kevin sprinted to the Mustang, all the while expecting a

bullet in the back. Thankful for once that the alarm was broken, he jammed the key into the door, his head swiveling as he quietly opened it. Still no sign of them. He got in and kept his head down as he eased the door shut.

He stuck the key in the ignition and turned it. The Mustang coughed, struggling to turn over. It cranked and cranked, but the engine wouldn't catch. Dammit! He let go and tried again. Same result.

'Not now,' he muttered to himself, glancing in the rearview mirror. He opened the window to let out some of the stifling heat. 'Come on. Come on.'

He turned the key again.

At the apartment complex's pedestrian entrance, Lobec saw no sign of Hamilton. It was unlikely their target had scaled one of the ten-foot-high fences encircling the apartment property. That left the driveway as the only route out of the complex.

Lobec returned to the gate, where Bern was waiting.

'I assume there was no sign of him,' Lobec said.

'No. But there's no way we wouldn't have seen him. The street's clear, and there's nowhere to hide.'

'It's the same on my side. He must still be in the complex.'

'You want me to wait here in case he tries to get out?' Bern said.

'We can't just wait for him to show up. We need to find him immediately, before he tries to call someone. We'll make one pass through the complex. If we can't find him, we have to assume that he found refuge with a neighbor.'

While Bern took the other side, Lobec skirted the western edge of the complex, looking under bushes, behind cars, and inside shadowed alcoves. Both of the pool areas were crowded with sun worshippers. Lobec kept his distance, not wanting to present a face that residents might remember should he have to shoot Hamilton, but there was no trace of their target. As he finished at the last courtyard, the one directly outside Hamilton's apartment, Bern came toward him.

'No luck. I've searched every inch of this place between here and the entrance. If he's here, I don't—'

Lobec raised his hand, cutting off Bern. Somewhere nearby an engine was turning over. It sounded like the rumble of a V-8 engine, which seemed to start but then abruptly died. He motioned for Bern to get the car and pulled the SIG Sauer from his jacket as he raced to the back of the building.

As he rounded the corner, he saw the Mustang at the far end of the lot. Someone was inside. Lobec ran toward it.

Kevin nervously searched the parking lot as he let the engine pause before trying again. He was just about to reach for the key when he caught motion out of the corner of his eye. To his right he saw a man sprinting from the opposite side of the parking lot. His hand fumbled for the ignition. The engine had almost started the last time, and it looked like he'd get only one more chance. He frantically turned the key.

The engine caught on the first crank. Kevin mashed his foot on the accelerator, but he was now surging with adrenaline and was almost unaware of how fast he released the clutch, nearly stalling. The car lurched forward, coughed, and then roared back to life, the needle on the tachometer leaping toward the redline. The rear wheels emitted an ear-piercing screech, and Kevin could smell the tires burning on the hot cement.

He twirled the steering wheel to the left, the Mustang gyrating wildly. Kevin tried to get it headed in the direction of the apartment complex exit. As he completed the 180-degree turn, he glanced out the window.

The man, whom he now recognized as the fake officer calling himself Barnett, stopped only fifty yards away and raised his arm, pointing it at Kevin. Kevin realized what was happening almost too late and ducked down as the passenger window disintegrated. He raised his arm to shield himself from the bits of glass ricocheting around the car's interior. Another bullet smashed the side mirror and others peppered the door. The tires finally gripped the pavement, and the Mustang shot past the end of the building and out of Barnett's sight.

Kevin saw the front gate approaching quickly and only then remembered he would need to wait for its sensor to detect the car's weight before opening. As the Mustang skidded to a halt, he looked in the mirror. A Chevy sedan rounded the corner a hundred yards back, stopping barely long enough for Barnett to yank the door open and jump in. The car leapt toward him and would close the distance in seconds.

Kevin gunned the engine as the gate crawled along its track, still only three-quarters open. It had always seemed slow, but this was agonizing. He looked in the mirror again. His pursuers were nearly on top of him. He couldn't wait.

The engine howled as the Mustang sprang forward, and Kevin winced when he heard metal tearing from the passenger side, the mirror ripped from its mounting. He turned right and floored it.

As he rocketed past a puttering Honda, he suddenly realized that he had no idea where he was going. He knew he had to get to the police, but until this moment it had never crossed his mind that he didn't actually know the location of a police station. The only contact he'd had with the police was a few tickets, but he'd always paid them through the mail. His only hope was to get caught in a speed trap. He'd cheerfully accept another citation if they would stop him.

He was coming up on the Loop, the beltway that encircled the city. The Chevy was lagging behind, but not as much as Kevin had hoped. Apparently, it had almost as much power as the Mustang's V-8, and the driver was putting it to good use.

Kevin was about to randomly pick a direction when a sign caught his eye. It advertised the wholesome atmosphere at Houston Baptist University. Kevin realized that he did know the location of a police station: the campus police station at South Texas University. At the rate he was going, he could be there in ten minutes. And the quickest way was to get on the freeway, which meant turning left.

After shooting through the highway underpass, he slowed only long enough to time the gap in the heavy opposing traffic. He saw an opening and punched the accelerator. The Mustang blasted through the intersection and swerved sickeningly, missing the front of a pickup by inches.

The Chevy tried the same maneuver, but it sideswiped a UPS truck, which knocked the battered car aside. Kevin was elated until he saw the Chevy rebound off another car and continue in his direction. He weaved past cars on the frontage road paralleling the freeway, honking the horn whenever someone blocked the way.

Kevin saw the freeway entrance ahead just past Beechnut Street. Once he was on the Loop, he'd be able to open it up and maybe even lose them altogether.

His fear ratcheted up a notch when he saw the traffic backed up at the stoplight. He'd be stopped for thirty seconds, easily long enough for the thugs following him to run up and drag him from the car, probably flashing badges all the way.

Kevin glanced at the stores lining the frontage road and noticed an entrance to a Lowe's hardware store on his right. He wrenched the wheel in that direction and flew into and over the steeply inclined parking lot entrance, mashing the nose of the Mustang in the process.

Rounding the corner of the Lowe's, he almost ran down an employee wheeling an empty shopping cart toward the storefront. The startled employee jumped back, pushing the cart directly into the Mustang's path. The car's nose hit it low, tossing the cart into the right half of the Mustang's windshield, creating a maze of cracks in the safety glass.

Kevin turned left and bypassed the crowded store entrance, racing across the empty fringes of the lot and struggling to see through the crazed windshield. He wiped sweat from his forehead, wishing he could use the air conditioner but not wanting to sap any power from the engine. Not that the air conditioner would do much good with the shattered passenger-side window.

He flew out of the lot onto Beechnut, but now he was heading away from the freeway. He took another look in his one remaining mirror. The Chevy was still there, a mere fifty yards behind.

The Mustang coughed. Kevin ignored the old car's wheeze as he tried to think of the best alternative route.

Up ahead Kevin saw the flashing signal of a railroad crossing. The gates were lowering. To his right he could see a train rumbling in his direction, its engine only a few hundred yards from the crossing. Turning around would be a bad move, because it'd give his pursuers a clean shot at him. There was some kind of business coming up on the right with a sign that said, CLEAN WATER TEXAS. He considered cutting through the lot, taking the chance that it had an outlet onto another road.

The Mustang coughed again. Kevin looked at the hood. No steam or smoke. It coughed again. In seconds the Mustang was sputtering, as if trying to catch its breath, the power falling off. Kevin glanced at the instrument cluster to see if the engine had overheated in the hot summer air. He gasped when he saw the gauges.

The trip odometer read 327 miles. The sputtering made sense now. The fuel tank was empty.

In his desperation to escape, he had forgotten that he'd driven home without filling up. Now he'd be lucky to make it another half mile before he was a sitting duck.

The train blew its air horn twice as it approached the crossing. Kevin suddenly realized what he had to do.

The barrier stretched across both two lanes, and a guardrail along the passing lane made it impossible to go around on the left. The only way around was to bypass the gate on the right.

The Mustang continued to sputter. With no other cars behind him, he could see the Chevy closing the gap. The train was only fifty yards from the crossing. He couldn't be sure, but it looked like he could make it. It didn't really matter. He had no other options. Kevin floored it, praying that there was enough gas left to get him across the tracks.

The sputtering got more violent, but the car responded, squirting around the clanging signal and shuddering as it bounced across the exposed rails. The looming train filled the passenger window, and the blast of the air horn deafened him.

It was only when he heard the clack of the train cars on the track behind him that Kevin realized he'd gotten across alive. The mountainous diesel had missed him by not more than five feet.

The other bit of good news was that the Chevy was stuck on the other side, but he didn't spend time celebrating. The Mustang limped forward, scraping the curb. Kevin coaxed it a hundred more feet before the engine died. He turned the key, hoping there were a few drops of fuel left. It was no use.

Kevin scrambled out of the car and quickly surveyed his surroundings, pausing for only a second to appraise the damage to his car. It was pitiful: the broken mirrors, the fractured windshield, the bullet holes, the wheel skewed from the impact with the train tracks. He didn't want to know what the passenger side looked like. *Better it than me,* he thought, and then searched the street for a hiding place.

Kevin wasn't heartened by what he saw. It was at least a hundred yards to the nearest neighborhood. On the left, a wide space for a series of high-voltage towers. On the right, a chain-link fence protecting construction equipment that lay dormant.

The last train car was visible in the distance. It would be there in thirty seconds. They'd catch him before he could get to any cover.

Kevin looked at the low-slung train cars piled high with lumber. Through the gaps he could see his pursuers trying to follow his movements. Then on his side of the signal he saw a waiting pickup that caught his attention. It looked like his best chance. He ran away from the crossing and angled across the street, using the idling traffic as cover to stay out of sight of the other side. When he was sure Barnett and Kaplan could no longer see him, he headed back toward the tracks.

In front of the crossing, near the back of the line of cars, was a black Dodge pickup with tinted windows. Its back window and bumper were festooned with stickers with the familiar maroon and white colors of Kevin's undergraduate alma mater. Many of them said 'Texas A&M' or 'Gig 'em, Aggies!'

He ran up to the passenger door, hoping that it might be less threatening in this era of carjackings, and knocked on the window. The electric window lowered to reveal a man around his age in a tank top and jeans. A gun rack was mounted on the back window, but it held only an umbrella.

'You got a problem, bud?' the man said.

'My damn car broke down,' Kevin said between gulps of air, 'and I was wondering if you could give a fellow Aggie some help.' He wiggled his class ring toward the man.

The man looked at the ring and a smile broke across his face. 'I'll always help another Ag in trouble. And today's your lucky day. My dad owns a garage. Maybe I can take a look at it and see if we can't get it fixed. Name's Bob Tinan.' Bob leaned over to extend his hand through the window, and Kevin took it.

'Kevin Hamilton.' Through the windshield, he could see the last train car approaching. 'Thanks, Bob, but I know what's wrong with it. It's the fuel injector.' Kevin jerked his thumb toward the Mustang. 'It was bound to happen sometime. The only way it's going to move now is behind a tow truck.'

Bob twisted around to look at the heavily damaged car behind them and turned back to Kevin. 'Hell, you're probably right. No sense messin' it up more than it already is. Come on in. There's a gas station with a tow truck a couple blocks from here.'

As Kevin climbed in and closed the door, the end of the train passed, and he could see the Chevy shoot under the opening gates.

'He's in a hell of a hurry,' Bob said with a chuckle as the Chevy raced by them. Kevin bent over, pretending to tie his shoes.

'What year did you graduate, Bob?'

Bob told him and drove toward the intersection. Kevin looked back at his car. Barnett and Kaplan were already out of the Chevy and slowly approaching the immobile vehicle, their guns discreetly held at their sides. By the time the pickup rounded the next curve out of sight, Barnett and Kaplan were back in their car and continuing their pursuit in the opposite direction.

TEN

From the Williams Tower, the eight-hundred-foot-tall suburban skyscraper on the West Loop, the railroad crossing on Beechnut was easily visible, as was most of the rest of Houston. It was one of the reasons that Clayton Tarnwell had chosen it for his vast office head-quarters. On clear days the Houston ship channel, more than ten miles to the east, could also be seen through the spaces between the silvery towers of downtown Houston. From this vantage point, Tarnwell could survey the vast metropolis as if he owned the entire expanse. He loved to watch the expressions of visitors as they walked into the enormous office toward the floor-to-ceiling picture window. It was an awe-inspiring view.

At the moment Clayton Tarnwell was paying no atten-tion to it whatsoever.

'What?' he screamed into the phone. 'Are you telling me that two experienced operatives couldn't handle the simple task of bringing in a college student?'

'I think you may want to hear the entire report,' David Lobec said from his car phone. 'And I recommend not discussing it any further over an open line. We can be there in less than ten minutes.'

He thought about using some choice words, but trusted Lobec's professional advice. Someone might be eavesdropping. 'You damn well better be!' He slammed the phone into the cradle, then stabbed the intercom button.

'Coffee. Now. And when Lobec gets here, send him right in.'

A female voice replied, 'Yes, sir.'

Tarnwell picked up the loan contracts he had been studying, then slapped them down on the desk without seeing any of the words. Damn! He was so close. After years of building his small but extremely profitable empire, he was now on the verge of leapfrogging into the ranks of the Forbes 400. Ward's Adamas process – no, *Tarnwell's* Adamas process, he corrected himself – was the key. Once he had the process patented, he would own the most lucrative invention of the last fifty years. He could truly be one of the richest men in the world. And now some pissant little college kid was getting in his way. He would not let that happen.

Tarnwell's office had all the trappings of a successful businessman: the teak coffee table, the leather sofa and antique Chippendale chairs he had bought at auction, the state-of-the-art media center on the far wall, the handmade oriental rug. A vast array of photographs adorned the office, most of them pictures of him posing with tennis pals from the club, local sports celebrities, a couple of congressmen, and a senator. They showed a tall, tan, rugged all-American boy living the American Dream.

But it wasn't enough. He was a nobody outside of Houston. He could get his share of attention in Washington in the mining and chemical circles, but he wasn't a big player, not like the chairmen of the mega-conglomerates. He was a barracuda in an ocean of killer whales.

He wanted to be more. *He* wanted to be one of the killer whales, maybe even the biggest. And thanks to Adamas, Tarnwell's name was on the brink of becoming a household word. He would be one of the most powerful men in the world. And this Hamilton snot was endangering everything.

The door to his office opened, and a shapely blonde emerged with a steaming mug of coffee. She handed it to Tarnwell and gave him a playful smile. Even though they were occasional lovers – one of the reasons she'd been hired in the first place – Tarnwell ignored her and went back to staring at the wall. She left the room without saying a word.

Moments later, Lobec walked in.

'Let's hear it,' Tarnwell said.

'These are Hamilton's,' Lobec said, throwing a wallet, a phone, and a set of keys onto the desk.

Without asking, he sat in one of the high-backed leather chairs and gave his report. He took Tarnwell through every detail of the morning's events, starting with their stakeout and finishing with the high-speed chase that ended at the rail crossing.

'He apparently received a ride from one of the vehicles

traveling in the other direction,' Lobec concluded. 'Otherwise, we would have seen him running. There were few places to hide within the immediate area.'

Tarnwell knew Lobec was capable, so he didn't waste time trying to assign blame. The most important thing was to find Hamilton. 'So he's got no car.'

'Correct. He'll have to get help from someone.'

'The police?'

'That's a distinct possibility. Since he contacted them before, we have to assume that he might try again.'

'What can we do about it?'

'There really isn't anything we need to do about it. I have several associates at the Houston Police Department. If Hamilton files a report at any station, I will know about it within fifteen minutes.'

'Did anyone at the apartment complex see you?'

'It's possible, but no one was in the parking lot. If they did see us, it was from a distance.'

'But Hamilton saw you. He can identify both of you.'

'He can describe us, but I assure you, the police have no photographs of either me or Bern.'

'Can we get to him while he's in there?'

'No, not unless he were put into a holding area where I have some contacts. In that case the police would find him in the morning quietly smothered to death. However, there is no reason to believe he'll be jailed. The police will take his statement, show him a few pictures, and then let him go. Once we know where he is, it is a simple matter to wait until he leaves the building. Actually, the best thing he could do for us is go to the police.'

'What if they provide him with protection?' Tarnwell said. 'You *did* try to kill him.' A flicker of amusement and disdain crossed Lobec's face, and Tarnwell knew he had made a suggestion which Lobec thought amateurish.

'Protection is offered only in special cases, such as to witnesses who have been threatened before testimony is to be given. The resources the police have are limited. It is highly unlikely they would provide protection to a student with a poor driving record who makes such an outrageous claim. There's no other evidence, and he has no idea why we were there.'

'Yes there is. The email message. And what about the car?'

'All traces of the message will be erased from the school's computer system by this afternoon. We still haven't determined what the thesis reference means, but Hamilton hasn't, either. As for the car, it was towed to a more suitable location: the Fourth Ward. The car will be stripped clean by thieves before the police find it.'

'Good thinking.' Tarnwell took a sip of his coffee, going through Hamilton's wallet while he thought. Nothing but a few credit cards, a driver's license, and a student ID. 'Then what are our options?' he finally asked. 'I don't like waiting for him to make a move.'

'There is not much more *we* can do, but *he* has several alternatives,' Lobec said.

'Such as?'

'Do you remember the picture I showed you this morning?'

'You mean the girl? What was her name?'

'Erica Jensen.'

'Have you given her name to Mitch?' Tarnwell knew Mitch Hornung could get any information they needed from the state records.

'Mr Hornung is working on it as we speak. We know he was confiding in her. If Hamilton doesn't go to the police, she is the next reasonable alternative. I've texted her photograph to our other operatives, who have been instructed to apprehend her on sight. When we have her full records, we'll relay her profile as well. I'll go to her residence as soon as we're done here.'

'What about friends or relatives?'

'We have operatives stationed at all of the most likely places Hamilton might go, but we have little information on his other friends. We should be able to get that in a few hours. Perhaps a day at most. I've also hired an operative in Dallas to keep an eye on Hamilton's father in case he makes contact with him.'

Tarnwell turned his chair and looked at the skyline. 'He'll go to the police as soon as he can. But he has no car and no wallet, and he's not going to get very far in Houston without either of those. That means he'll have to call a friend, maybe this Erica Jensen, to come get him.' He swiveled the chair back in Lobec's direction. 'We can't afford any more problems. You don't have to tell me when he gets to the police. And I don't care who picks him up. As soon as he leaves the station, take him out.'

Lobec cocked his head and raised an eyebrow. 'Is that a wise move, considering he will have just told his story to—'

'It won't matter. You said he had no evidence, but if he was involved with NV117, he may know about Adamas, and I can't chance that. Just make him disappear. And this time I don't want the body found. *Ever.* Think you can handle that?'

Erica looked at the phone, wondering if she should try Kevin's number again. For nearly thirty minutes she'd been calling and all she'd gotten was the answering machine.

Something bad had happened, she knew it – even if she didn't know why she was so sure. He could easily be so involved in something else that he didn't hear the phone. She remembered a few of their conversations while working at the hospital. He had focused so intently on her that he didn't hear someone call his name until she told him. But this was different. Before leaving with the police, he should have at least called to tell her that he would get back to her later. If he just forgot, she would be really pissed.

Erica picked up the phone and hit 'REDIAL.' She let it ring three times before hanging up, not knowing whether to be angry or worried.

Kevin's apartment was just a five-minute drive away. She grabbed her cell phone and purse and headed to the door.

As she pulled it open and felt the blast of heat invade her town house, her phone rang. The number was Kevin's. She hit the button to answer it.

'Kevin?' she asked, closing the door. 'What's going on?'

'Thank God I got you,' Kevin said, the relief in his voice palpable. 'Are you still at your condo?'

'Yes, but I was just leaving to come over to your apartment.'

'Don't come over!'

'So you're coming here?'

'No. I want you to get out of there.'

'What? Kevin, what's going on? I've been calling for half an—'

'I can't tell you right now, so don't ask.'

'Tell me what? You're not making sense. Just calm down.'

'I'm about as calm as I'll be until you come get me.'

'Come get you? Where's your car? Where *are* you?'

'I'm at . . .' He paused. 'Do you remember where I said I wanted to go for lunch on my birthday?'

'You wanted—'

'Don't say the name! Just answer yes or no.'

'Kevin, what is going on?'

'There's no time! They might have your place bugged.'

'Bugged? That's crazy!'

'Just answer me, *please*.'

'All right! Yes, I remember.'

'Good. I'm at the gas station across the street from there. I want you to leave the town house right now and come pick me up. Get your car keys and go.'

'Will you at least tell me—'

'No. I'll explain everything when you get here. Just get out of there.' With that, the phone clicked off. He had hung up.

She stared at the receiver, but for only a second. In the six months Erica had known Kevin, he had never once been irrational. A little absentminded maybe, but never irrational. And she didn't think he was starting now. She didn't know what was going on, but he was clearly terrified about her staying in the condo. That was enough for her.

She dropped the handset into the cradle and ran out of the town house, pausing only to lock the door. In ten seconds she was driving to a gas station across the street from Fuddruckers.

ELEVEN

The air-conditioning was on the fritz again, and Detective Guy Robley was sweating his ass off. The HPD headquarters was already at eighty-five degrees, and it was only going to get worse. Why did it always quit on the hottest day of the year?

Robley filled out the report as fast as he could type. As soon as he was done, he could hit the field again in his nice cool car. There was no way he was going to spend a minute longer in this hellhole than he had to. The phone rang and he stopped typing, looking at the black receiver with annoyance. He snatched it from the cradle.

'Robley.'

It was Joe Johnson, who was sitting on the other side of the homicide division office. 'Hey, Robe, some guy on the line says he has to talk to you. Says it's an emergency.'

'Who is it?'

'Name's Hamilton. Says he talked to you earlier about the Stein case.'

'That crank again? Dammit, what is it with the heat that brings out these nuts?'

'You want me to get rid of him?'

'No, I'll take care of it. Put him on.' Under his breath he muttered, 'Goddamned heat.'

As soon as the transfer was made, Robley could hear the noise of traffic in the background and the ding of a service station's bell.

'Detective Robley here.'

'Detective Robley, this is Kevin Hamilton. We spoke about thirty minutes ago.' The voice was slightly higher in pitch than the last time, but it was definitely the same guy.

'Yes, Mr Hamilton, I remember. We got disconnected.'

'I'm sorry, but I had to hang up.' He paused, as if struggling for words. 'Some men tried to kill me.'

Robley rolled his eyes. 'Someone tried to kill you, Mr Hamilton?' Johnson, who was watching him from across the room, shook his head and chuckled. 'You mean, while we were on the phone, or afterwards?'

'I know this sounds crazy, Detective, but these two guys who came to my door said they were cops, shot at me, and then chased me in a blue Chevy sedan.'

'Uh-huh. And did you get their license plate number?'

'Uh, no, I couldn't see it. They were behind me, and we were going too fast.'

'I see. Look, Mr Hamilton, why don't you come down to the station and make a statement? You know, give us a detailed description of the assailants and an account of the events.'

'Then what?'

'Then we'll see what we can do about it.'

'That's it? You'll see what you can do about it? Those guys tried to kill me! They know where I live!'

'Why would they want to kill you, Mr Hamilton?'

Another pause. 'I don't know. I think it has to do with this email I got from Dr Ward. You know, Michael Ward? The South Texas professor who died this morning? I used to work for him.'

'The professor and his wife who died in the house fire?'

'Yes, in the note he said the same people who killed Stein were after him. Then he said it has to do with an experiment we did together.'

'What's so special about this experiment?'

'I don't know.'

'You don't know.' Of course he didn't.

'Look, I do know that a guy in a business suit and his muscle-bound buddy came to my apartment this morning pretending to be cops and tried to shoot me.'

Robley wiped his forehead with a handkerchief. 'Where do you live?'

'The Sycamore apartments.'

The Sycamore was on the southwest side. No reports of shots fired came from that area this morning. 'Did anyone else at the Sycamore hear the shots?'

'I doubt it. They were using silencers.'

This was too much. 'Silencers? Mr Hamilton, you've seen too many movies.'

'If you don't believe me, my car is on Beechnut just east of the tracks. It has two bullet holes in the driver's door.'

Robley sighed. 'Okay, I'll check it out. But false reporting of a crime is a serious offense, Mr Hamilton. Do you want to stick with your story?'

'It's the truth! I swear!'

'Fine. Give me the license number on your car.' As Robley jotted the information on a notepad, he shook his head. Maybe it wasn't the heat that brought out the nuts. Maybe it was the humidity.

Kevin let out his breath in relief as he saw the familiar gray Honda pull into the Exxon station. He emerged from the shadows of the food mart and dashed to the car as she slowed. Even before she had stopped, he flung the door open and leapt in.

'Go. Romanelli's. It's dark and it shouldn't be too crowded yet.'

As Erica headed in the direction of the Italian restaurant, Kevin looked behind her to see if he could spot anybody following her, particularly a Chevy sedan.

'What's going on?' She glanced at him. Her dark eyebrows were furrowed in a mixture of concern, curiosity, and skepticism.

'In a minute. Turn here.'

'What?'

'I want to make sure you weren't followed.'

'Are you kidding?'

'No. Then take the first left. Go!'

'All right,' Erica said in a voice normally reserved for small children telling you about their imaginary friends.

After another three turns, Kevin was satisfied that they were alone. 'I know I must have sounded like a nut—'

'You still do.'

'Okay, I'm sounding like a nut. But I didn't want to be stranded at that gas station.' He leaned back and closed his eyes, welcoming the rest, and then told her about his encounter with Barnett and Kaplan. During the entire story, Erica didn't say a word. Kevin was relieved. The act of explaining what had happened helped to clarify the events in his mind. By the time he was finished, they were pulling into Romanelli's parking lot.

'Park in the back, out of sight,' Kevin said.

Erica pulled into a space in the almost empty lot. Turning off the engine, she said, 'Why aren't we at a police station? You said these guys tried to kill you.'

Kevin let out another sigh. 'The police don't believe me.'

'What? When did you talk to them?'

'After I called you, I called Detective Robley.'

'What did he say?'

'That he had never heard of the two men at my apartment who claimed to be Detectives Barnett and Kaplan. I probably sounded like a nut to Robley when I called him back from the gas station. He said I could make a statement, but that's about all. Maybe when they have the

Mustang, they'll believe me.' He looked at his watch. 'I'm supposed to call him back in about ten minutes to see if they found it. One thing's for sure, I'm not going down there until I know what's going on.'

'Why not? What else can you do?'

'I don't know. I can't go home. And for all I know, the police could be in on this. If those guys *were* cops, they'll know where I am the minute I set foot in the station. It's also possible that they know who *you* are.'

'Is that why you wanted me to leave the town house?'

Kevin nodded. 'Something bothered me about the conversation with the detectives, something Kaplan said. I told them about the message and the experiment, and then he asked me if this was all about superconductivity.'

'So?'

'I hadn't told them what kind of experiment it was. I had just told them we had conducted one. But Kaplan asked me specifically about my "superconducting" experiment. He couldn't have known that unless he'd heard you and me talking about it. The phone was bugged.'

'Come on, Kevin! Do you know how crazy this sounds?'

'Yes. And don't say I've been watching too many movies. Besides, they heard your voice on the answering machine when I was hiding in the closet.'

Erica tapped her fingers on the steering wheel. 'And you think they might have traced the phone call to my condo?'

'I think it's possible. For all we know, they could be over there right now.'

'This is crazy.'

'Tell me about it.'

'How about we continue this inside?' she said as she grabbed her purse. 'It's getting hot out here.'

Romanelli's was a new hot spot with so little light that identification of the food was difficult. The effect was supposed to be elegant privacy, but Kevin hated it. However, it was dark, which would help them stay out of sight. As they entered, he saw that the lunch rush hadn't started yet and most of the tables were empty. He asked the hostess for a dim booth in the far corner so he could keep an eye on the door from afar.

They both ordered Diet Cokes and told the waiter they needed some time to examine the menu.

After the waiter left, Erica said in a lowered voice, 'Are you sure these weren't policemen that Robley just didn't know? Maybe they thought you were some kind of fugitive trying to flee.'

'I heard every word they said. It was muffled in the closet, but I heard Barnett clearly. He said Kaplan should kill me if . . .' He looked at Erica's concerned expression, and now he didn't know if it was his safety she was really worried about. 'You don't believe me.' The thought that she wouldn't hadn't occurred to him until this point.

'Of course I believe you,' she said without a trace of condescension. 'I'm just trying to figure out what's going on. You said you didn't hear any shots.'

'He must have been using a silencer. It's actually called a suppressor, because it's not very silent, but the car's engine would have been loud enough to cover the sound.'

'How do you know that?'

Kevin shrugged. 'My dad was really into guns and took me out to the range all the time. Besides, I saw the bullet holes in the car door.'

'You could see them even with all the damage to the car?' she said.

'Yes.'

'Then why didn't they just kill you in the apartment?'

She had a point. 'I don't know. I don't even know why they would want to kill me in the first place. All I can figure is that it has something to do with the message from Dr Ward and experiment NV117.'

'Okay, let's assume somebody was trying to kill you because of the email he sent you. Then the answer has to be there. What exactly did it say? Something about—'

'Damn!' Kevin said. 'I totally forgot!' The printout. He still had it in his pocket. He dug out the paper and flattened it on the table between them.

Erica frowned as she read the message. Kevin focused on the line about the key being in his thesis. He still didn't know what it had to do with anything.

'What does it mean?' Erica said. 'What does your thesis have to do with Ward's experiment?'

'I don't know. But Ward wanted me to know that NV117 is what these guys are after.'

'Maybe they already have it and they didn't want you to find out about it.'

'Then why would they ask me what the reference to the thesis means?' he asked, receiving only a shrug in reply.

Kevin looked at his watch. It was time to call Robley back. 'I'll ask the bartender to use his phone.'

'Use mine.'

'No. He'll see your caller ID, and I don't want him to know I'm with you. Just in case.'

Leaving the printout with Erica, he went to the bar. After he convinced the bartender it would just be a local call, he dialed the number Robley had given him.

'Detective Robley.'

'It's Kevin Hamilton.'

'What are you trying to pull, Hamilton?'

This wasn't the response Kevin was expecting. 'What do you mean?'

'I checked with dispatch. Seems your Mustang was reported stolen at nine thirty this morning.'

'What?'

'Luckily, we've already found it. In the Fourth Ward.'

'The Fourth Ward? But it was out of gas. How did it ...' Kevin ran his fingers through his hair, searching for an explanation. 'They must have moved it. Did the officers who found it tell you about the bullet holes?'

'Yes, they did. They found exactly zero bullet holes.'

Kevin's mouth dropped open. 'That's impossible. I know I saw two bullet holes in the door.'

'They also found zero doors on the vehicle. It was totally stripped. Dispatch said it looked like it had the hell beat out of it too.'

'Detective, believe me. I know this sounds weird, even crazy. But this has something to do with Stein's—'

'Hamilton, I don't know what your angle is, and I don't care. I just want to get the hell out of this hothouse. If you want a copy of the report for your insurance company, fine. Call Traffic. I'm through.'

Kevin heard the phone slam down. He slammed his own receiver in return. Damn! Robley was probably bitching about Kevin to the other detectives at this very moment. And since he was the one handling the Stein case, Kevin wouldn't get help from anyone else trying to connect Ward's and Stein's deaths. If he went to the police again, they'd laugh him out of the station.

He plodded back to the table and slumped into the bench across from Erica.

She leaned forward. 'What's wrong?'

'They found the Mustang in the Fourth Ward, stripped. No evidence of any wrongdoing, other than my car being stolen and vandalized. The theft was reported at nine thirty this morning.'

'Nine thirty? But that's almost two hours ago.'

'These guys sure have some connections if they can make the police believe something like that. I'm screwed. No, I'm dead. Maybe when Robley finds my body, he'll believe me.'

'Kevin, you're not dead. And while you were on the

phone with Robley, I called the Houston police and asked
for Detectives Barnett and Kaplan. The only Barnett they
had was Emily Barnett in the vice squad, and there was no
Kaplan. They were obviously impersonating police officers,
so I'm sure if you go down to the police station and
explain—'

'Without evidence, I can't go down there. They'll just
think I'm making it up. And now I can't go back to my
apartment. I can't even go to *your* apartment. Neither of us
can go home.'

Erica put her hand on his. 'Kevin, there has to be a
rational explanation for all this.'

'Well, I can't figure out what it is. Those guys were
smooth. Man, were they smooth. They had to be professionals. Professionals sent to find me and bring me in. If
they couldn't do that, they were definitely going to kill me.
I could hear it in their voices. When Barnett talked about
killing me, he was cold. No emotion.'

The skepticism was still in Erica's voice. 'Then what are
we going to do?'

'Unless we can find out how my thesis is the key to
NV117, I have no idea.'

'So reread your thesis. Maybe you can figure it out.'

'How? It's on my computer. It might as well be on
Jupiter.'

'Doesn't the library have a copy?'

Kevin nearly slapped himself for being so stupid. *Of
course* the campus library held a copy, a requirement for all

theses and dissertations. There was also a digital version accessible from the STU on-campus system. A printout would take too long for the 150-page document. It would be easier just to check out the manuscript.

'Let me have your keys,' he said, grabbing for her purse. 'I'll be back in forty-five minutes.'

'Wait a minute, bud,' Erica said, sliding the purse off the table and into her lap. 'Don't you think the STU campus might be one place they're looking for you?'

'Erica, I have to go. If we can figure out how my thesis is involved, we might be able to take the evidence to the police. I'll buy a cap for a disguise.'

'With your height, they could spot you from across the quad.'

'We don't have a choice. I need to get it to have any shot at figuring this mess out.'

'You're overlooking the obvious. I can go.'

Kevin shook his head. 'No way. You're involved in this too much already.'

'Now, don't get chauvinistic on me. It's simple. They know what you look like. They don't know what *I* look like.'

'How do you know? What if they traced the call?'

'They haven't seen me in person. And I don't have time to be on Facebook or Twitter. Googling my name gets you nothing.'

Kevin didn't like it, but she was right. He would be identified too easily. And they *didn't* have a choice.

'All right,' he said grudgingly. 'Do you have your Mace with you?'

She pulled a cylinder out of her purse. 'Armed and ready,' she said with a smile. 'Maybe I'll even get to use what I learned in self-defense class.'

'Will you stop joking? This is serious.'

'I *am* serious. I took a class two years ago.'

'Why are you doing this?' Kevin asked.

'Because you're in trouble, and I help friends in trouble.'

'Thanks. Be careful.'

Erica gave his hand a squeeze. 'I'll be fine. If I'm not back in an hour, send the cavalry.'

The closest spot Erica could find to STU's Campbell Library was a quarter of a mile away, and the temperature was inching toward one hundred. She took a barrette from the glove box and clipped her hair into a ponytail before getting out of the car.

She tried to make some sense of Kevin's story as she hiked through the university's main entrance. It wasn't that she didn't believe him. In the six months she'd gotten to know Kevin, he'd become a good friend. Unlike Luke, a charming player who used his good looks to get what he wanted, Kevin was a steady, dependable guy. He wouldn't make up something like this. His fear was real.

Kevin was in trouble, and that was enough for her. When he got the thesis, maybe he could figure out why someone would take a shot at him.

Several other people dotted the campus, mostly students enjoying the slow day during the beginning of the term. A few older men and women strode purposefully across the quad, no doubt professors returning to their offices.

Erica reached the shadowed portico leading to the

library's main entrance and took off her sunglasses as she entered the lobby. All she had to do was find one of the catalog terminals and make sure the manuscript hadn't been checked out.

Across the main quad, a suntanned blond in his mid-twenties, wearing a gray suit and sunglasses and saddled with the name Vernon Francowiak, watched the woman entering the main library. His gait never slowed as he saw her disappear into the library's foyer, then he abruptly changed directions when he was sure he wouldn't be noticed.

Franco and two other men had been posted at the university to look for any signs of the student or his girlfriend, a picture of whom they had been texted only half an hour before from Bern. Franco's boss, Stan Wilson, was watching the building where Hamilton did the research with Ward while another man kept an eye on the campus police department. At the briefing this morning, Franco had been told to wander the main quad in the hope of seeing one or both of them, in case they tried seeking aid from a friend at the university.

The woman he'd seen enter the library fit the description, but he'd been too far away to make a positive ID from her photograph. He wasn't going to pass up any chance he might have of making a few points with Lobec, who Franco knew had Tarnwell's ear. He retreated to the cover of the physics building's shadows before opening his cell phone.

After one ring he heard, 'This is Wilson. Go ahead.'

'This is Franco. I have a possible on the woman.'

'Where?'

'She just entered the main library.'

'When?'

'Ten seconds ago. Should I follow?'

'No, the library's too big. She's got too much of a head start. She might come out before you find her.'

'But it hasn't been that long—'

'I said no.'

Franco swore under his breath, eager to get a chance to prove himself.

'How sure are you about her identity?' Wilson said.

'I was about a hundred yards away. Just a possible.'

Another short pause. 'The library has only one entrance. Wait outside to make a positive. If it's her, text me.'

'Then what?'

'Follow her until I join you. We'll make contact together.' Franco knew better. Wilson wanted to take the glory for himself.

'She's just a student. I can take her.'

Wilson's voice hardened. 'You have your orders. Understood?'

Franco clenched his teeth. 'Yes, sir.'

He hung up and shifted the fake HPD badge to his front pocket. As he walked toward the library's entrance, he unsnapped the restraining clip on his shoulder holster. No way was he going to let Wilson take the credit for this one.

*

Muted colors and warm lights bathed the library's information center. The lone staffer at the island reference desk looked up as Erica entered the room and then went back to reading his paperback when she didn't approach him. Computer terminals lined the room's walls, and Erica took the nearest one.

She stood as she typed Kevin's name into the library's database search. In a second she saw his thesis title: *On the dynamic and catalytic properties of composite metallic and carbon nanoparticles*, call number LD5655.V856. She'd have to head down to the basement to get it.

Rather than instilling a sense of wonder as edifices of learning and freedom, libraries always gave Erica the creeps, and this one only reinforced those feelings. The tall bookshelves interfered with the fluorescent lighting, which wasn't especially effective to begin with. Some bulbs flickered, others were burned out, and only the whisper of her sneakers along the linoleum broke the silence, making it seem as if she'd entered a dank catacomb. She could almost imagine that she was the first to set eyes on this place in a thousand years.

I bet at most two people have been in this stack in the past three months, Erica thought as she rounded the corner of the shelves where she would find the thesis. *Including me*.

She ran her fingers across the bindings as she walked down the stack, looking at the first two letters of the call numbers. KS. KT. L. LD. She stopped and examined each shelf until she found it on the bottom row. With theses available on the campus intranet, she guessed that the hardbound copy had never been checked out. She reached down and took it from the shelf.

As she stood, something fell out of the book, clinking as it hit the linoleum. She knelt and saw that it was a key wrapped in a Post-it note. She picked it up and opened the piece of paper. Erica recognized it as a key to a safe-deposit box. Stenciled on it was the number '645.' On the note, only three words were written: 'First Texas Bank.'

Erica's heart hammered in her chest as she realized Michael Ward's email was real. When he wrote that the key was in Kevin's thesis, he was being literal.

No one would hide a key to a safe-deposit box in the library. It was absurd. Yet, here it was. She trembled as she walked back toward the stairway.

'Miss!' said a voice from behind her.

With a gasp, she whirled to see a tall, gaunt man in jeans standing at the end of the stack.

'Do you know where the fiction section is?' he said, peering at a paper scrap in his hand. 'I'm completely lost.'

Franco felt his cell vibrate. He retreated farther behind the pillar from which he had been watching the front entrance of the library and pulled the phone from his pocket.

While keeping an eye on the entrance, he said, 'This is Franco. Go ahead.'

'It's Wilson. I just got an update from Hornung. Lobec and Bern used their Barnett and Kaplan identities to capture

Kevin Hamilton, but he escaped. Now his girlfriend is a top priority.'

'What's her name?'

'Erica Jensen,' Wilson said. 'She's a fourth-year med student at South Texas and is probably dating Hamilton.'

'So it's possible she's here to study in the library?'

'Did she have any books with her?'

'No. Just a purse.'

'Then probably not. Just wait outside, and don't let her get out of your sight once you make a positive ID. We already lost our boy once today. She's the best way to find him.'

'Acknowledged.'

Franco hung up. Just as he did so, the front door of the library opened and a woman burst through, out of breath. She was dark-haired, approximately five foot eight, with bright-green almond-shaped eyes that darted from side to side but did not see him behind the pillar. The T-shirt and shorts she wore conformed well to her slim frame, and her high cheekbones enhanced an already pretty face. The overall effect was a girl-next-door attractiveness that made her easily identifiable from this distance.

Franco looked at the photo in his hand and smiled. He now had a positive.

Erica scanned the people around her as she hurried back toward her car. The man who had scared her minutes before had been harmless, but she was still worried about the prospects of meeting one of Kevin's policemen. Her right hand clutched her purse with the thesis and the safe-deposit box key inside it, and her left was wrapped tightly around the Mace canister.

Footsteps rushed at her from behind. She turned, hoping it was only a student late for an appointment. Her breathing stopped when she saw a handsome young man wearing a suit. He had his hand raised. She couldn't see what he was holding, but he started to call to her.

'Miss Jensen! I need to speak with you!'

She didn't recognize him and had no idea how he knew who she was. She almost turned to run when she realized that he was flashing a badge.

He came to a stop in front of her. A fine sheen of sweat glistened on his face.

'Miss Jensen, my name is Detective Patrick with the HPD. It's urgent that I speak with you regarding Kevin Hamilton.'

After Kevin's story about the police detectives, she didn't know what to think. The badge looked authentic, but then, she had never seen a real badge before. If he wasn't a policeman, he was very convincing.

Nervously, she looked around again. She could see only two other people. Both were far away and moving out of the quad.

'What do you want?' she said. She could hear the nervousness in her voice, but she couldn't do much about it.

'Actually, this concerns both of you. I think it would be

better if we discussed it at the station.' He motioned in a direction away from her car. She didn't move.

'First, I want to know what this is about.'

'It's in connection with the death of a Dr Michael Ward last night. We have reason to believe Mr Hamilton might have some information that would be helpful in the case.'

'Why?' Erica asked.

'I'm afraid I can't discuss the specifics of the case. Have you seen Mr Hamilton this morning?'

She wasn't going to commit herself just yet. 'No, I just talked to him a little over the phone around nine thirty. He said a Detective Robley was going to call him. Do you know him?'

'Robley? The name doesn't sound familiar. But I'm with the arson squad, investigating Dr Ward's death as a possible homicide. Detective Robley is probably in another division. Do you know why Mr Hamilton would call him?'

The fact that he didn't know Robley might not mean anything, but she was still wary. 'He said it had something to do with Dr Ward, but I don't know what.'

'Then I'm sure you can understand why I have to speak with him. I'm going to have to ask you to come with me. I'd like you to help me locate Mr Hamilton. As I said, it's very urgent.' Again he motioned toward the west end of the campus.

She slowly walked in that direction with Detective Patrick beside her. He seemed all right, but she decided to try one more angle to confirm that he was legit.

'Detective Patrick, there was one other thing that might help. Kevin said he was talking to two police officers. I can't quite remember their names. I think one was Barnett. You might try one of them. He might even be with them.'

Patrick seemed to think for a second. Then he said, 'You must be talking about Detectives Barnett and Kaplan. We could try contacting them when—'

Erica whipped her hand up and blasted him in the face with the Mace. His hands went to his face, and he began screaming. As she ran, she could hear him yelling after her.

'You bitch!'

No one was in the quad anymore. She bolted for the nearest building, passing a sign that said 'Cooper Physics Building.' She pulled furiously on the door, but it wouldn't budge. Locked. She ran down to the next door. This one was wedged open with a piece of wood. She yanked it open, pausing only to look back at the police impersonator, who was now on his feet just forty yards behind her.

The literature that came with the Mace said a full-grown man would be incapacitated for twenty minutes. Either the claims were exaggerated or her aim had been off.

She kicked the wedge out and ran down the hallway. Turning, she was horrified to see that, instead of slamming shut, the door had hydraulic hinges. It was closing, but excruciatingly slowly.

Ahead, she saw a stairway and decided to take it. Over her footsteps echoing on the stone floor, she could hear Patrick slam the door open, sputtering as he did so. It sounded like he tripped and fell as he crossed the door's threshold, but she didn't dare turn to look. She took the steps two at a time.

The second-floor hallway was dark, but sunlight filtered through the office transoms. The stairway was about midway between the ends of the hall and topped out on this floor. She randomly chose left and started twisting knobs in an effort to find an unlocked door.

After trying three doors unsuccessfully, she came to the last room in the hall. She pushed down on the lever of the massive metal door and the latch clicked open. She pushed and slammed the door behind her. She scrabbled for the deadbolt and then realized it needed a key to lock from this side as well. Two wooden doorstops lay on the floor. She jammed them under the door. They'd hold for a minute, but not against sustained pounding.

Looking around the room, she now knew why it had a door different from the others on the floor. Surrounding her was thousands of dollars' worth of complex machinery and gadgets, the purpose of which she couldn't even guess. Somebody must have gone for coffee and had forgotten to lock the lab. He might be back any second or he might be gone for fifteen minutes. Not that some grad student would be able to protect her; Patrick's badge would make his story sound convincing.

Along one wall, storage cabinets stretched from floor to ceiling, and a huge metal box took up a quarter of the twenty-by-thirty-foot room. Jumbles of cable connected many of the devices together, and she almost tripped on one as she dialed 911 on her cell.

A series of rude beeps came back. No signal. The heavy steel door was blocking it, and the lab had no landline. Venturing back out would allow Patrick to catch her long before help could arrive.

As she desperately hunted for a hiding place, she noticed that a door on the metal box was slightly ajar. On a table next to it sat a heavy-duty padlock with the key still in it. The box's door had three steps leading up to it, putting the bottom of the door at mid-thigh level. She quickly examined the door handle mechanism, trying to ignore the fact that Patrick was going to be bashing against the laboratory door at any moment.

The thick steel handle had an eyelet that lined up with a similar eyelet in the door when the handle was closed. The padlock was big enough to go through both eyelets and lock the door. Erica opened the door wider and climbed the steps to look inside.

She'd seen a room like this once before while she was taking introductory physics. It was an anechoic chamber, used to study sound in an environment that was almost completely free of any echo. Large foam wedges covered the floor three feet below. A heavy wire mesh was suspended above the wedges to support experimenters and their mounted equipment. In the far corner, construction materials and a sheet of plywood leaned against the wall. The sound-absorbing foam covered only part of the wall and none of ceiling. Apparently, the chamber wasn't finished.

Erica frantically checked the inside of the door, hoping she could lock herself in until whoever was using the room returned, but there was nowhere to attach the padlock.

At that moment she heard a muffled pounding outside the chamber.

When Franco reached the top of the stairs, he saw the door slam on the room at the end of the hall and sprinted toward it, drawing his Glock pistol. With the automatic raised, he gently pushed down on the lever. He heard the click of the latch disengaging. No deadbolt.

He took out his phone while wiping his eyes with the sleeve of his jacket and called Wilson.

'Wilson.'

'It's Franco. I found her. The bitch Maced me!'

'What? You idiot! I told you not to contact her without me.'

'I had to when she came out of the library,' Franco lied. 'She ran as soon as she saw me.'

'Did she get away?'

'No, I'm in the physics building. I've got her trapped in one of the rooms on the second floor, but it's going to be tougher getting her to the car now. Get over here and help me out.'

'We're on our way.'

Franco threw the full weight of his body against the steel

door, ready to crouch and duck another Mace attack. He'd shoot her, but not to kill, much as he'd like to. Expecting the door to swing wide, he wasn't ready for the sudden stop after the door began to open. His head smacked against the steel with a resounding thud, and he almost fell to his knees.

Holding his head, he shook out the stars. Maybe his aim would be off just this once, and there would be a fatal accident. Lobec wouldn't like it, but tough shit. Franco had had just about enough of Erica Jensen.

He slammed his shoulder against the door, this time anticipating the shock. On the third try the door flew open.

He crouched as he'd originally intended, but no Mace came. A quick look around the room didn't reveal where she'd hidden.

Then he heard a faint series of tones coming from the direction of the open door of a large metal chamber in the opposite corner of the room. The sound of a cell phone ring tone. Tough luck for her. It didn't matter, though. He would have found her eventually.

He eased over to the door and opened it wider. He peeked around the corner. He couldn't see her inside the faintly lit chamber. He crept up the stairs, the Glock held at arm's length.

As he stepped onto the wire mesh, he knew where she was because of the deadened ringing coming from the direction of a four-by-eight sheet of plywood leaning against the far corner. The space behind it would leave plenty of room for someone to hide.

'Miss Jensen, I can hear your phone. I don't want to hurt you, but I will if I have to. And if you spray me again, I *will* hurt you.'

No response. This bitch was tougher than he thought. Not too bright, though. He slowly walked over to the plywood, then hooked his foot under it and kicked it aside.

The woman wasn't there. Only one thing sat on the wire mesh: a cell phone whose display read 'Timer Done.'

No!

He whipped around to see the door swinging shut.

Erica pushed on the chamber's outer door as hard as she could, but the enormous metal frame was as heavy as it looked and only with effort started to shut. She didn't dare look into the chamber, but she heard the police impersonator curse as he realized that she had merely set the timer on her phone and crammed herself into an empty equipment locker. If he had done even a cursory search of the room, he would have found her easily.

The lock in her hand poked her skin, but she pushed harder. The door was almost closed when fingers shot through the opening. The man's weight fell against the other side of the door, but it wasn't enough to halt the inertia of the door's massive bulk. His hand was crushed against the jamb. He let out a scream, and the weight momentarily lifted. The hand disappeared into the chamber.

Erica used the opportunity to latch the door. As she threaded the lock through the handle mechanism, gunshots rang out, and she nearly fell from the stairs in surprise. She looked down and saw with relief that the bullets, unable to penetrate the thick door, only made small protrusions on her side. Her fumbling hands finally got the lock in place just as the man began pounding on the other side, and she closed it with a satisfying click.

Suspecting that she didn't have much time before more police impostors arrived, she collected her purse and headed for the exit. The sound of hammering fists faded quickly as she ran down the hall.

THIRTEEN

Clay Tarnwell leaned into the drive, never taking his eyes off the ball, following through with the form he'd learned at Pinehurst. As soon as the ball left the tee, he knew he'd sliced it. The ball curved gracefully away from the center of the fairway and toward the stand of oaks lining the right side of the rough. It bounced once and then came to rest a good two hundred yards from the green. He'd be lucky to make a bogey on this hole, let alone par. It was a perfect shot, exactly where he'd wanted it.

A white-haired man sporting a straw hat, lime green pants, and a well-rounded paunch started laughing as soon as the ball hit the ground.

'If I didn't know you any better, Clay,' said the sweating man as he took his driver from the bag in the back of the golf cart, 'I'd say you shanked that one on purpose.'

'You're right, Vic,' said Tarnwell, trying to sound disgusted. 'And the next one is going in the left sand trap if I can make it. What do you think? Would a three iron do it?'

Vic Hanson laughed again and then lined up at the tee. After taking sufficient time to level his swing, he drove a beautiful shot at least fifty yards past Tarnwell's directly down the fairway.

Tarnwell shook his head as if to curse his luck, but the truth was he could have easily beaten his companion, probably by at least eight strokes. He played a four handicap but he had intentionally been missing the harder shots on the previous twelve holes. Now he saw a good chance to stay behind for a while, so he took it.

Not that Tarnwell wasn't competitive. He was, but only at one thing. Making money. All the he-man stuff was bullshit. Sure, he was good at it. A natural athlete all his life, Tarnwell had been gifted enough to play linebacker at the University of Michigan until a knee injury ended his career. He'd gotten a lot of sympathy at the time, but nobody seemed to realize that he didn't care.

Football was a means to an end, the method of putting himself through school, with majors in both business and chemistry. That was the ticket out of his father's shadow, the way to make even more than the vaunted Bernard Tarnwell ever dreamed of having. All his life, Clayton Tarnwell had seen the pot of gold at the end of the rainbow, and he couldn't care less how beautiful that rainbow was. If it could lead him to the pot, fine. Otherwise, it was just in the way.

And losing to this ass was just another means to that end. If he had to lose a few rounds of golf, so be it. As long as it got Vic Hanson in the mood to close a deal, he'd gladly piss into the wind.

They climbed into the cart, Tarnwell driving. Another of Hanson's little attempts to show who was in control. He never drove his own cars, preferring to leave that menial chore to his underlings. Tarnwell was glad to drive. He knew it would make Hanson happy.

'So, Clay,' said Hanson as they drove, 'you really think you can pull off this merger? If you can't, there's no way I could help save you or your company. Your credit would be ruined. You wouldn't be able to get a five-dollar loan with ten dollars collateral.'

Tarnwell suspected he would get this kind of response, which is exactly why he was trying to butter the old man up by losing.

'Vic, I know what I'm doing. I've given this a lot of thought, and there's just no way I can lose. Not with my ace. When the banks realize what this new invention means, they'll be throwing money at me.'

'Clay, the only reason I'm here, letting you pretend you're losing to me, is that your father was a good friend of mine. You're a suck-up and a cheat. But you were also loyal to your father and extremely good at making money. I never understood why Bernie didn't leave you his company. I suppose it was his attempt to teach you some values, late as it was, but I was as surprised as you were. Now you've built up your own company, almost as successful as your father's. I just don't want to see you blow it, son.'

The line about being *almost* as successful as his father grated on Tarnwell, but he managed to hold back a sneer.

His father had built up a mining company from scratch and then sold it for two hundred million dollars. When his father died during Clayton Tarnwell's senior year of college, the will left him with a pittance, less than a million, with the rest going to charity. Tarnwell was furious, betrayed by his own father, to whom he had shown unwavering devotion. He used his inheritance to start his own company, Tarnwell Mining and Chemical, just to show the world he was even better at making money than Bernard Tarnwell. Now he was one week away from proving that point.

'This buyout is important,' Tarnwell said. 'If it doesn't come through, it'll take me two years to get up to full production on Adamas. Forrestal Chemical has the facilities I need *now*. I've been trying to buy those facilities, but they won't sell. If I had them, I could be producing in two months. The only other choice is to buy the whole company. And without your support, I'll never get the loans I need for the leveraged buyout.'

'You're sure this Adamas process works? How has testing gone?'

Tarnwell pulled to a stop near his ball. 'Final validation is taking place as we speak. We should know the results by Tuesday. But I've seen the process myself. It works. Tarnwell Mining and Chemical already has an invention disclosure out, and the patent process will be well under way this week.'

'I certainly trust your business sense if nothing else. I

know you wouldn't do anything to con me.' Hanson looked at Tarnwell as if posing a question.

'Of course not. This is the wisest investment you'll ever make.'

Hanson paused and then nodded. 'I leave on a business trip Monday afternoon. Come to my office first thing Monday morning. We'll talk to Wayne Haddam over at First Texas. I'm sure we'll be able to work out a favorable agreement.'

'Thanks, Vic,' Tarnwell said as he climbed out of the cart. 'You won't be disappointed.'

'I'd better not be.'

Kevin looked around nervously as Erica punched her code into the ATM. The vestibule was partially enclosed, but he could see Kirby Drive easily from his position – as easily as the passing motorists could see him. He didn't like being exposed like this, especially when using an electronic device that could be traced.

Erica removed the maximum five hundred dollars from the receptacle and retrieved her debit card.

After she had picked Kevin up and told him what had happened at the university, they'd agreed that the people they were dealing with were probably resourceful enough to trace their credit cards. They hadn't discussed what to do next, but it seemed like a good idea to have as much cash on hand as possible, so they headed to an ATM that Erica didn't normally use. Since Barnett and Kaplan had taken Kevin's wallet, there was no way to get the eighty-six dollars in his checking account.

'It'll be another twenty-four hours before I can take out any more,' Erica said. Since her ordeal, Kevin noticed her

drawl had gotten thicker, but it was her only outward man-
ifestation of stress.

'Thanks for doing this,' he said as they walked toward
the Honda.

'I've got some extra saved up. We'll be okay.' Despite her
nonchalance, he could tell that she was still unnerved by her
close call at the library.

When they were back in the car, Erica sat staring at the
steering wheel as if in a trance.

'What now?' she said. She had already called the hospital and told them she couldn't come in for her ER shift
afternoon, making up a death in the family. Which had
almost come true.

'Start driving,' Kevin said. 'If they've hacked into your
account, they may know we just made a withdrawal from
this location.'

Erica started the car and turned south onto Kirby. 'What
do you think the chances are that they'll find this car? They
probably know my license plate number by now.'

'As long as we stay away from anywhere we usually
go,' Kevin said, 'it'll be pure coincidence if they see us. And
if they find us on some random street, then either our luck
is incredibly bad or they have so much intelligence and
manpower that we'll never get away from them. The
question is, how do we get into that safe-deposit box on
Monday?'

Erica seemed to come back to her senses and looked at
him. 'Ever since I found the key I've been thinking about

that. And I came up with only two possibilities. I don't like the first, which is that we give it to the police.'

'No way. As soon as we say it's from Ward, it'll get back to Robley. They'll just think it's another prank.'

'We could drop it off anonymously,' Erica said.

'What if the police just mail it to the bank? Who knows what'll happen? It's too risky.'

'Then the only other option is for you to use the key and open the safe-deposit box.'

'Me?'

'Well, they're not going to think *I'm* Michael Ward.'

'And you think I'll do better?'

'One time you told me that you filled out so many forms for Dr Ward that you probably signed his name better than he did.'

'That's true, but so what? You think I'm going to walk in there and just sign my name and they'll let me in?'

'Why not? Banks are so big nowadays that the odds of the bank officer knowing any one customer are a hundred to one. I've had a safe-deposit box before. All they make you do is show them your ID and sign your name.'

'I don't even have my own driver's license, let alone one that says Michael Ward.'

'Why don't we get you one?'

'You make it sound easy,' Kevin said. 'How can you stay so calm with all this?'

'The ER teaches you something about dealing with tense situations. Like facing armed gang members who insist you treat their knifed friend before you try to stop the guy who stabbed him from bleeding to death from a gunshot wound. Now, let's go get you a driver's license, Dr Ward.'

'And I guess you know how to do that,' Kevin said.

Erica just nodded and turned left, pointing the Honda toward the Astrodome.

As they passed the retracting gate of the Beechwood Manor apartment complex and entered its parking lot, Kevin's thoughts returned to the flight from his own complex. So much had happened already that it seemed as if days had passed since he'd heard of Dr Ward's death. He glanced at his watch. It had only been seven hours.

Kevin noticed a superficial similarity between his complex and this one. Perhaps they had been built by the same developer. But that's where the resemblance ended. The buildings here looked as if they hadn't been painted in ten years, and the pool they walked past was dirty and full of leaves. He was amazed that the electric gate still worked.

He wasn't sure that coming to this seedy area east of the Astrodome was a good idea. The person they were meeting was named Daryl Grotman, a University of Houston student Erica had treated a month ago for burns. Apparently, he had been concocting a contact explosive out of iodine and ammonia. Kevin was familiar with the compound. Ammonium triiodide, powerful stuff.

Daryl said he had heard about it from another student and wanted to see if he could make the pressure-sensitive explosive. During the mixing, which he'd conducted in his bedroom, he had the doors to his apartment open for ventilation and a breeze slammed the bedroom door shut. The change in air pressure was enough to detonate the explosive. Luckily, he'd been across the room at the time and only suffered shrapnel wounds to his arm. Still, the firefighters insisted that he go to the emergency room.

The guy didn't get out much, going on and on about every detail of his life as Erica bandaged him. He bragged to Erica about his side business and told her that if she ever needed any help, she should email him. Erica hadn't taken it seriously. Patients often professed that kind of gratitude and made up all kinds of stories. But she couldn't forget the email address Daryl had given her: FakeThemOut@hotmail.com.

After leaving the ATM, they had stopped at a public library to use a computer. Erica created a new account on a Web-based service in case her private email was being monitored and sent the email to Daryl. He must have remembered her because he responded within five minutes with his phone number. When she called from the library's pay phone and told him what she needed, he said that there would be no problem helping them out. All they needed to do was stop and get a passport photo taken of Kevin. A short trip to the nearest FedEx store did the job.

As they walked up to 215G, they heard heavy metal blasting from the apartment. Kevin didn't recognize the band, but it was hard-core. He wondered if the neighbors ever complained. Probably not.

After banging on the door three times, Erica tried the knob. It turned easily. She pushed it open.

Suddenly, as a chain stopped the door after only a few inches, the music turned off, and a shrill alarm wailed. Erica jumped back in surprise, colliding with Kevin.

Just as suddenly, the alarm shut off, and they heard someone inside yelling, 'Sorry! Sorry!'

The door shut again, the chain clinked, and then they were greeted by Daryl Grotman.

He was about the same height as Kevin but at least twenty pounds thinner. To Kevin, he looked starved. Although he was a junior in college, Daryl looked almost ten years older because of a thinning crown and wild, wiry beard. The only clue to his age was excessive acne visible above his heavy, black-framed glasses and on the scarred cheeks above his beard. He wore Birkenstock sandals, cutoff jeans shorts, and a black T-shirt festooned with the logo of a band called Raging Sperm.

'There's my doc! Look,' Daryl said, holding up his arm. 'All healed, thanks to you.'

'Hi again. This is the friend I was telling you about. Daryl Grotman, this is Kevin Hamilton.'

Daryl shook Kevin's hand vigorously. 'I hope you guys weren't blown away by the alarm. I rigged the system myself. Been a lot of break-ins in this rat trap. I meant to turn it off 'cause I knew you guys were coming over, but I got caught up with something. Come on in.'

Kevin followed Erica in but stopped in his tracks in

shock. He'd expected to see pizza boxes littering the floor, trash everywhere, dishes piled in the sink – typical computer nerd living.

What met them was the cleanest, neatest apartment Kevin had ever seen. It wasn't decorated to his taste, what with the posters of bands like Butthole Surfers and Blood Junkies covering the walls and row upon alphabetically organized row of comic books. But otherwise, it could have been a *Better Homes and Gardens* spread, albeit one featuring rooms with twenty thousand dollars' worth of computer equipment. Looking back at Daryl, Kevin noticed how spotless his clothes looked. There was zero trace of damage from the explosion.

'Yeah, I know,' said Daryl. 'Not what you pictured. I guess I'm just anal. Helps in my line of work, though.'

'What *is* your line of work?' asked Kevin.

'I thought Erica told you. I fake licenses. Sometimes other documents, passports, state IDs, but mostly licenses. I can do visas for six countries, but they take longer.'

'She did tell me. That's why we're here. But I didn't think it was a business.'

'Well, it's not something I'm going to do for the rest of my life. It sure helps pay the tuition, though. Computer science major, if you didn't guess, although I'm getting a minor in criminal science.'

'Looks like you're acing it,' Kevin muttered.

'How do you get so much business?' Erica asked, glaring at Kevin. 'Aren't you afraid of getting caught?'

'Not really. My orders come through anonymously online. Anyone looking for me would find a totally different name.'

'Which is?' Kevin asked.

'Dave Zugot. You know, I don't do too many of these in person.' He pointed at Kevin. 'You've *got* to be older than twenty-one.'

'Actually, I need a different name.'

Daryl nodded as if familiar with the request. 'Ah. Anyone in particular?'

'Yeah. A guy I'm trying to play a joke on.'

'Sure. Can I see the photos?'

Kevin handed them to him. After a quick inspection, Daryl slapped them onto a scanner and began to tap on the keyboard. A minute later, Kevin's picture was on the computer monitor. A minute after that, Kevin's face was superimposed over a Texas Department of Public Safety background curtain.

'Behold,' said Daryl, 'the wonders of photo manipulation software in all its glory.'

'I have to admit, that's pretty amazing,' said Kevin. 'You'd never know it wasn't taken at the DPS.'

Daryl smiled. '"It slices, dices, juliennes – but wait, there's more!"'

Erica pulled out her license and compared it to the picture on the screen. 'That's incredible. But how do you put the hologram on the plastic covering?'

'Not a problem. I've got a thousand just like that.' He showed them a box filled with plastic sheaths, all carrying the holographic imprint of the state of Texas.

'Where did you—'

'That's a little touchy. Let's just say that there was a mix-up at the manufacturer and a few thousand too many were made. Now! How do you want the license to read?'

Kevin spoke. 'Michael Jason Ward. Just make up the address. I don't have his new one yet.'

'You obviously haven't gotten the picture, Kevin. It's not a problem. If you have a couple of minutes, we can make your license look like the real thing. It'll take a little longer if you want his actual license number. The state computers are a little tougher than the credit bureaus. You want to be an organ donor?'

Kevin shook his head. 'The address is good enough.'

Two minutes later, Kevin was looking at the credit record of his professor on-screen, complete with card numbers, outstanding loans, and personal information.

'My God!' said Kevin. 'Erica—'

'I see it.'

Kevin couldn't believe it. On top of payments on a Mercedes and a Lexus, Ward was three months into a home loan worth $750,000. He was already a month behind.

'Man, you guys must be in some serious trouble.'

Kevin recoiled. 'What do you mean?'

'Well, it's none of my business, but you must either be desperate, greedy, or weird to be impersonating a guy who died yesterday. And the last two don't fit Erica. Besides, a college professor doesn't make that kind of money.'

Kevin and Erica exchanged worried looks.

'You'll still help us, won't you?' she asked.

'Hey, I'm not throwing any stones. Look around. I was just making an observation.'

'We don't want to get you involved,' said Kevin, his tension easing. 'What I mean is, we *are* in a lot of trouble, so you'll understand if we don't share much with you.'

'No problem. I'm not sure I'd want to know anyway.'

'Can you print that out for me?' Kevin said, pointing at the credit report on the monitor.

'It's already on the printer. So is your ID. All we need to do is have you sign it and then laminate it.' Daryl handed him the fake license.

'I'd like to ask another favor from you, Daryl,' said Kevin as he signed.

'Shoot.' A homemade lamination heater gobbled up the paper license inserted into the holographic plastic sleeve.

'We were thinking earlier that we shouldn't be using our credit cards because the records might be available to the people that are after us.'

Erica tilted her head in puzzlement but said nothing. She could see that Kevin had an idea.

'Smart move,' Daryl said. 'If they have a halfway decent hacker, they can get into your credit card company's database as easily as I accessed the credit bureau. Tracking you that way would be a cinch if you weren't careful.'

'Then maybe you can help us get a little breathing room.'

After they finished their business with Daryl, Kevin and Erica prepared to hole up for the night. They found a Wal-Mart and bought toiletries and a change of clothes for the two of them. Then they stopped at Antone's for some takeout.

They'd decided not to call their friends, not only because they didn't want to endanger them, but also because they didn't want to go anywhere they might logically be found. That meant they had to lie low for the next day and a half until the bank opened on Monday morning.

Erica wheeled the Honda into the back parking lot of the seedy-looking Tidal Moon motel, the first one they'd found that didn't require identification. The grimy man at the registration desk made them pay cash up front.

While Erica dumped their meager belongings on the bed, Kevin locked the door behind them, then peeked through the torn and spotted drapes. From their first-floor vantage point, he could see that it would be difficult to spot their car from the road. Satisfied, he pulled the drapes closed. Although it was safe for now, he didn't want to get complacent.

Erica announced that she wanted to take a shower before she ate and turned on the water in the bathroom. Ravenous, Kevin opened the bag from Antone's and began munching on a shrimp po' boy.

As he ate, he scanned the local channels for more news on Dr Ward or Herbert Stein. He saw stories about each of them, but nothing more than they had learned earlier. Apparently the police were still treating the fire as an accident without ruling out the possibility of arson.

Kevin sat dejected, listening to the water run in the bathroom. The more he thought about what was going on, the more confused he got. He could now reasonably assume that Dr Ward and his wife had been murdered. But why? What was in the safe-deposit box that somebody would kill for? How did Dr Ward get the money to buy that house and car? And why did he write that email to Kevin?

The worst part was that he had dragged Erica into this with him. He thought about leaving, doing the rest of it himself, but how would that help? Erica was already involved up to the hilt. She wouldn't be any safer without him than with him. Besides, once they had more proof – whatever that was – together their story would be much more convincing than from either of them alone.

Kevin heard the water shut off in the bathroom.

'Any news?' she called.

'No, nothing new.'

Erica came out with a towel wrapped tightly around

her. It barely reached her legs. Despite being exhausted by the day's events, Kevin couldn't help feeling both turned on and embarrassed at the same time. She grabbed the extra-long T-shirt she had bought and retreated to the bathroom.

'I'm starving,' she said. 'I hope the sandwiches are good.'

'Of course they are. Haven't you ever had a po' boy?'

Erica came out of the bathroom, her hair still wet. The T-shirt was almost as revealing as the towel had been. 'No. Abilene was known more for its good barbecue.' Using the wrapper as a placemat on the stained table, she sat and nibbled at her sandwich. 'Hey, this *is* good.'

'See? You should trust me.'

'I'll take that under advisement.'

'Good. Now it's my turn.' Kevin took his shower while Erica finished her sandwich. After he was done, he put on his new T-shirt and boxers.

When he came out of the bathroom, Erica was lying in bed, holding the remote.

'Now I remember why I stopped watching TV,' she said, turning it off and putting the remote on the nightstand.

'I thought it was because of med school.' Kevin pulled a pillow off the bed and walked over to the chair.

'That too. What are you doing?'

'Getting ready to go to sleep.'

'Over there?'

'Yeah. Well, you know, one bed ...' He shrugged. 'I thought ...'

'Don't be an idiot. I'm not going to make you sleep in that chair.'

'You sure?'

'I just took a shower, so I can't smell too bad. Are you afraid I'm going to bite you?'

'No, just trying to be chivalrous.'

'Well, stop it. We're both adults. Now, come on.'

Kevin climbed into bed as Erica switched off the lamp. The bed seemed even smaller now that he was in it. Erica was only a foot away.

'Isn't that more comfortable?' she asked.

'Mm-hm,' Kevin responded, although he felt extremely uncomfortable. She was turned toward him, her light breathing raising the hairs on his neck, the warmth of her body flowing to his.

'You're an interesting guy, Kevin,' she said, her voice groggy with fatigue.

'What do you mean?'

'I always thought you were just a nice guy.'

That surprised him. 'I'm not a nice guy?'

'Nice guys are boring. Reliable, but boring. Today wasn't boring.' Within a minute she was asleep. She had the med student gift for being able to sleep anywhere at any time.

Kevin turned over and gazed at her face, lit by the weak light coming through a crack in the curtain. He stayed awake a long time.

*

'This is it,' Lobec said, pointing at the Best Western. The last of the twilight was dwindling. The clock on the bank across the street flashed 9:03.

'You sure?' Bern replied, turning the rental car into the motel's parking lot. 'Mitch said there were two along this strip.'

'He also said it was the one closest to the interstate. The next one is almost in downtown New Orleans. Go in and see if they're here.'

Bern climbed out and lumbered into the lobby. Lobec saw him flash his police ID. That seemed to get the clerk's attention, and he tapped at the computer's keyboard. After a few minutes Bern trotted back out to the car.

'This is it, all right. But they haven't checked in yet. Probably just getting some dinner first. I'll bet we have them in less than two hours. What do you think?'

'I will be surprised if it's that easy.'

'God, you're hard to please. Mitch said they made the reservation at this motel three hours ago, guaranteed it with the girl's credit card. Then they stopped in Baton Rouge for gas two hours ago, also paid with the girl's credit card.'

'Doesn't it strike you as odd that they would reserve the room ahead of time?'

'Maybe they wanted to make sure they had a place to stay. What more do you want?'

'I want them in this car with us. When that happens, I'll be satisfied. Not a moment earlier.'

Lobec had been right to be cautious. An hour and a half

passed with no sign of the couple. He was thinking that he'd wait another half hour and no more when his cellular phone beeped.

'Yes.'

'It's Mitch. Thought you might like to know Erica Jensen just canceled the reservation at the Best Western. She also charged $11.58 at a convenience store in Biloxi, Mississippi, five minutes ago.'

'Has she made any other reservations?'

'No. But if they stay at another motel without making a guaranteed reservation, all they'll do is preauthorize it tonight. It won't be run through until tomorrow morning.'

'That's no good. They'll be gone before we can get there. They must be heading east for a reason. Check to see if they have any family or friends in the area.'

'I'm already searching the Biloxi area for matches.'

'No. Search Mississippi, then Alabama, Georgia, and Florida.' Lobec heard muffled curses at the end of the line. 'Anything else?'

'Yeah. Jensen called the hospital to tell them she wouldn't be in today or tomorrow. No way to know where the call was made from. One voice mail was left on each cell phone. The one to Hamilton's was a guy named Nigel asking if he wanted to grab some dinner. The one to Jensen's was the hospital returning her call. Neither cell phone was checked for messages.'

'Fine. Advise me when you have anything new.'

Lobec terminated the signal and dialed another number.

'Who're you calling?' Bern asked.

'The Gulfstream.'

'We going back to Houston?'

'No. Biloxi.'

Kevin and Erica bided their time until the bank opened on Monday morning. They drove around or ate in quiet out-of-the-way restaurants – any place where they wouldn't see familiar faces – then spent another awkward night in a different motel.

Using one of the prepaid cell phones they'd bought, Kevin had found that there were seven First Texas branches within five miles of campus. Luckily, Daryl was as skillful as he claimed and helped them find the correct branch. Ward had one deposit box with First Texas, but no accounts or loans. The bank was located in the Village, close to Rice University, and the safe-deposit box had been leased only two months before. No one would know he had the box unless they knew where to look. At ten after nine on Monday, Erica stopped the Honda next to the bank's front entrance.

'This shouldn't take long,' Kevin said, glancing at his watch. 'Damn!' He was supposed to be at the student affairs office an hour ago to meet with Dean Baker.

'What?'

He took a breath and then sighed. 'Nothing. I'm just ready for this whole business to be over with. I hope your idea works. The last thing we need is for them to call the police.'

'I guess it's possible the bank officer knows Ward, but I doubt it. They get people opening and closing boxes all the time. This branch is so big, you probably won't even get the same person that helped him lease the box.'

'Probably? Thanks.' Kevin pulled in a deep breath. 'Cross your fingers.'

Kevin stepped out of the Honda and walked into the immense lobby. Even at this early hour, the bank was bustling with activity. A line was already forming at the teller window, and well-dressed men and women moved about with determined authority. Kevin was dressed in a polo shirt, khaki pants, and loafers in the hope that they would make him look more like someone who would have a safe-deposit box.

Standing next to the central pillar, a security guard surveyed the lobby in measured glances. Kevin avoided his eyes and walked past. He clasped the fake ID in his pocket tightly.

He approached one of the dozen desks situated near the vault. Seated behind it was a young brunette with a name tag that said 'Martha Warsett' and then below it 'Management Trainee.' She looked up at Kevin and smiled broadly.

'Can I help you, sir?'

'Yes,' Kevin said as he sat. 'I would like to get into my safe-deposit box.'

She turned toward the terminal on her desk. 'Your name?'

This was it. 'Michael Ward.' He bounced his foot, praying that she didn't recognize the name.

He stood in front of the desk as she typed the name into the computer. After a second she turned back to him. 'Yes, Mr Ward. Box 645.'

Kevin stifled a sigh of relief.

As she opened a drawer to her left to retrieve some papers, she said, 'I'll just need to see two forms of ID and we'll get you signed in.'

Kevin felt as if he'd been jabbed in the kidneys.

'Two forms of ID? I only brought my driver's license.' He pulled the license out of his pocket and showed her.

'I'm sorry, Mr Ward. We require two IDs. Several incidents of fraud have forced us to make that change. It's for our customers' safety. I hope you understand.'

Kevin would have to chance going back to Daryl Grotman and getting another ID made, then risk returning and getting the person who had opened the account for Ward. 'I really need to get into my box. My tuition is due today, and I have a bond in my box that I need to cash. Is there any way you can make an exception?'

'I'm sorry, sir. Any form of ID will be acceptable. Credit card, student ID, or—'

'I'll have to go all the way back to my apartment, and by that time it'll be too late—'

Kevin felt a hand grab his left elbow. 'What are you doing here?' a female voice said.

He spun and was stunned to see a short blonde with her hair pinned up, wearing glasses and a dark gray business jacket and skirt. He was speechless, primarily because he didn't recall ever seeing her before.

'Don't tell me you forgot me already. We met at Nigel's party Friday. The jazz band was great, by the way. Sorry you missed it.'

The recollection of the tight black dress hit Kevin. He never would have recognized her if she hadn't spoken to him. Then he remembered her mentioning that she worked in a local bank.

He nodded. 'I'm glad.' he said, trying to regain his composure. He glanced at her name tag, which said 'Heather Whitcomb' and underneath 'Loan Officer.' He hadn't remembered her name from the party. He hoped her memory was just as bad.

'I mean, I'm sorry too. Of course I remember you, Heather.'

'Is it Kenneth?' she said.

'No,' Kevin said, smiling. 'Mike. Michael Ward.'

'I did have a little to drink that night.'

'That's okay. I cheated.' He pointed to the name tag.

Heather looked down and laughed. 'I didn't know this was your bank. I've never seen you here before.'

'I, uh, just have a safe-deposit box here. I opened it a couple of months ago and haven't been here since.'

Martha spoke. 'Mr Ward was trying to get into it, but he only had his driver's license. I was explaining our policy—'

'I think one ID will be enough for Mike. You don't have to be a stickler for the rules if you know the customer.' Heather winked at Kevin.

'Thanks,' he said. 'You just saved my life.'

'Can you remember my name now?' Heather said.

'I don't think that'll be a problem.'

'Then maybe I'll see you around.'

She started across the lobby, glancing back as she did.

Kevin's knees stopped shaking now that he had passed inspection. Martha led him to the vault, where she looked through a box of cards, removed one, and handed it to Kevin. On line one, it had Michael Ward's signature and the date the box was leased. Line two was blank, meaning Ward had never reopened the box.

Kevin tried to nonchalantly sign and date the card. He had practiced the signature for two hours yesterday. As he returned the card to Martha, he thought the resemblance to the original was close enough. Martha replaced the card after a thorough inspection.

Ward's safe-deposit box was one of the larger ones, about ten inches across and four inches high. Kevin gave Martha the key, and she used it to remove the long container from its sheath. By the way she handled it, it looked fairly light, which he confirmed when she gave it to him. It rattled a little as he took it along with the key.

'Would you like a private booth?'

'Please.'

Once inside the booth, Kevin took a deep breath and lifted the lid.

At the front of the box lay a digital camcorder videotape, the kind they used in the lab to record experiments. He took it out. It had been rewound to the beginning. The label on the tape said 'NV117.' He slipped the tape into his pocket.

Kevin tilted the box toward him, and a laboratory notebook slid to the front. He reached into the covered area at the back of the box, but nothing else was in it.

He carefully lifted the notebook out and turned it over. One word was handwritten on the front cover. In all capital letters it said, 'ADAMAS.' Kevin thought it was an odd title for a lab book.

He opened it. The front page looked as if it had been torn out. A date in February was printed at the top of the second page. Most of the notebook was filled with numbers, formulas, and chemical equations. Only a chemist would understand it.

Kevin quickly read the first page, stopping to reread every equation to make sure he had understood it correctly, not wanting to believe it. He skipped to the pages detailing the technical schematics of the equipment. He read them in disbelief. Then he saw the data. After five minutes he was convinced. Adamas worked.

Now he fully understood the danger he and Erica were in. The people who were after them would stop at nothing to get this notebook and kill them both for even knowing of its existence.

He shut the notebook, tucked it under his arm, and left the booth.

He passed Martha, who said, 'Is that all, Mr Ward?'

Kevin didn't stop, but mumbled his thanks as he strode by her and out the bank exit.

He yanked the Honda's door open. As he jumped into the car, Erica said, 'There you are. I was beginning to get worried.'

'Let's get out of here,' was the only thing he said.

As Erica drove, Kevin remained silent as he checked the meaning of 'adamas' on his cell phone's basic Web browser.

'Okay. I can't stand it anymore,' she said, interrupting him. 'What did you find? You were in there for a long time. I thought they had spotted the fake license.'

'I had a little problem, but I got into the box.' He showed her the notebook, and she glanced at the cover.

'What's Adamas?'

He looked at his phone. 'Adamas is Greek for an impenetrably hard stone.'

'What does that have to do with anything?'

'You may not believe it. I'm not sure I believe it myself yet.'

'What's in there? The formula for Coke?'

'No,' Kevin said, staring at the notebook. 'But it's

probably worth just as much. It's a chemical process. It has schematics, experimental data, methodology, everything I'd need to re-create it.'

'A chemical process? For what?'

Kevin looked up at her in amazement. 'According to Ward, he and I accidentally invented a method for making diamonds.'

Clayton Tarnwell burst through the door of the laboratory, almost knocking over a technician carrying samples in the other direction. The technician first cursed at him for using the wrong door and then, seeing who it was, apologized profusely. Tarnwell kept walking as if the man weren't even there.

Following him was his mousy, balding chief financial officer, Milton Senders, still garbed in a plaid shirt and hiking boots, dabbing the top of his perspiring head with a handkerchief. His flight had been late in arriving, and he had raced over to the office without changing when he'd gotten his messages at home.

'I . . . I'm sorry, Clay. There's no excuse. This should never have happened. ZurBank should have called—'

'It's too late for that, Senders. You're not going to weasel your way out of this. You gave me your word that Ward had no way of getting the money out.' Tarnwell crashed through another door.

'But he couldn't have if those assholes at ZurBank hadn't been so stupid. The bank had specific instructions to notify us before making any transactions over a thousand dollars involving the account. That would give us time to find out what he was up to. If he withdrew less than that, he'd have some spending money to play with, and he wouldn't get suspicious. It should have been foolproof.'

'Then what happened? Ten million dollars didn't just evaporate.' Tarnwell already had a headache, and this fool was just making it worse. Normally, four hours of sleep was enough for him, but he'd been up since Saturday following the operation to capture the Hamilton kid and getting ready to secure the loan to buy Forrestal Chemical. The loan talks had gone smoothly, and the buyout was practically a done deal. The Forrestal board had the contract in front of them, and Tarnwell expected them to sign it any minute. He had no doubt they would; they'd never get a better deal than twenty dollars a share for a company that was currently trading at twelve dollars a share.

'I talked to Hermann Schultz at ZurBank after I finished the work on the Forrestal contract,' Senders said. 'He faxed the detailed statements. The account isn't empty. There's a hundred thousand dollars left, probably so we wouldn't know he cleared out the account. Apparently on Friday he tried to make a withdrawal of ten thousand dollars. When the bank told him it would take several hours to complete the transaction, Ward changed his mind.'

Tarnwell stopped at a third door, simply marked 'Research.'

'What the hell are you getting at, Senders?'

'Beginning at six o'clock Friday morning Zurich time, Ward made eleven thousand withdrawals of nine hundred dollars each.'

'What! How?'

'He set up some kind of automated transaction.'

'Eleven thousand withdrawals in one day?'

'The computer registered one withdrawal every five seconds. It took about fifteen hours. He must have written a special program to do it.'

'Are you telling me that there was no cap on the amount that could be withdrawn?'

'We saw no need for it. You said you'd be willing to give up a few minor withdrawals to give Ward the illusion of a real account. And we had a hell of a time getting ZurBank to help us as much as they did. There was no way we were going to get them to limit the total amount Ward could withdraw—'

'I don't want to hear any more about how you screwed up, Senders. I want you to get the money back.'

The sweat on Senders's balding pate grew even more profuse. 'I can't. It was transferred to an account in the Bahamas and then out of that account. That's all we know. The money could be anywhere by now.'

'Fly to the Bahamas and talk to the bank—'

'It's no good. We may have had some influence in Zur-Bank because of our holdings, but we'll never get any help from the Bahamas. They'd laugh in our faces. Unless we can find some information from Ward's files, the money is gone.'

'You'd better damn well hope Mitch finds something in the files Lobec downloaded from Ward's computer. This Forrestal deal has eaten into my cash. You know the balance sheet.' Tarnwell had already signed the contract and given it to the lawyers to finalize the deal. He had more important matters to tend to. He'd wine and dine the Forrestal board later.

Senders risked a tentative smile. 'Now that we have the loan, the deal with Forrestal won't be a problem, even without the ten million. And once we announce the patent on the Adamas process, our stock will triple. We'll be able to pay off the loan the next day.'

Senders's phone rang.

'It's probably Harris. I told him to call when the Forrestal board signed the contract.' Senders answered it. 'Yeah?'

Select people within the company like Senders knew about Adamas, but besides Lobec and Bern, no one knew the true origin of the process. Senders and the lawyers thought the research staff had come up with it, and the research staff thought it had been bought from an individual inventor. That's why Tarnwell discouraged Senders from venturing into the research labs.

Tarnwell inserted an ID card into a wall reader. A light next to it turned from red to green.

As the door swung inward, Tarnwell said to Senders,

'Wait here for me,' and went through. Just before the door shut, it flew open again.

'I thought I told you to wait—' Tarnwell stopped when he saw it was Lobec. 'Oh, good, David, come in. Good news I hope.'

'No, the news is rather disturbing,' Lobec said without inflection, and then paused as a short, pudgy man wearing a white lab coat approached them. Dr Bruno Lefler was the chief scientist in charge of the Adamas project. Since they had obtained Michael Ward's notes the previous week, the staff had worked around the clock to set up the proper equipment and validate the process. They had to make sure it worked before the patent submission was complete. Tarnwell knew it was only a formality.

He was annoyed to see Dr Lefler frowning and carrying a three-ring binder.

'Mr Tarnwell,' Lefler said, pushing one of his sleeves up, 'I didn't know you were coming here. I was just about to call you. We have a problem.'

'Lefler, this is top priority. If you don't have some equipment you need, get it. Don't worry about the cost this time.'

'No, Mr Tarnwell, we have everything we need to validate the process. It works exactly as it is described in this notebook you gave me.'

'Then what's the problem?'

Lefler looked uneasily at Lobec, whom he'd never met. Tarnwell noticed his hesitation.

'Lefler, this is David Lobec, my chief of security. He knows all about Adamas. Now, go ahead.'

'As I was saying, the process works exactly as it is described. But what is described is a process for producing graphite, not diamond – industrial-grade or gem-quality.'

Tarnwell turned to Lobec. 'Is he joking? Did I hear him right? He has to be joking.'

'Dr Lefler appears to be serious, Mr Tarnwell,' Lobec said.

'Dammit!' Tarnwell glowered at Lefler. 'Explain.'

'I don't know if I can. I'm sure that key elements of the process have been left out. On the surface, I understand the general process for altering the structure of the carbon 60 to produce diamond, but after a certain point, these notes revert to a method of graphite synthesis that has been in the literature for several years now and already has a patent pending. It almost looks as if someone plagiarized a journal article's equations from that point on.'

'But I saw the process myself,' said Tarnwell. 'I didn't learn all of the details, but I remember enough from my chemistry degree to know that the overall idea was sound. I inspected the chamber before and after the experiment. It did produce diamond. The Adamas process worked.'

Ward had told Tarnwell the whole story of Adamas's genesis. On January 21 he and Kevin Hamilton were in the lab conducting an experiment when the laser overloaded and almost destroyed the lab. Once they got the situation under control, Kevin had to leave for class and therefore never realized what had truly happened.

While Ward was assessing the damage, he noticed something strange about the experimental chamber. A fine glaze had formed over the exterior surface of the test stand. At first he had no idea what it was. When he attempted to remove the target material from the test stand, it wouldn't budge. He unscrewed the entire test stand and examined it with an infrared spectrometer. Only then did the implications of the glaze become apparent.

A unique combination of events during the accident had resulted in a new and inexpensive method for producing diamond. For the next few months Ward spent every waking moment refining the process. Not only could he create a diamond film to coat any object, but he found that he could modify it to produce significant quantities of gem-quality stones. Ward had even shown Tarnwell the process in action and gave him the samples so that his own scientists could confirm that they were real diamonds.

Tarnwell had perused the copy of the notebook when Lobec recovered it to make sure it was the right one. The experimental setup Ward had shown him was described in the notebook, along with pages and pages of figures and data. There was no reason to think it wouldn't work.

'Perhaps it did work when you saw it. But this,' Lefler said, waving the binder, 'is not that process. You were duped.'

'That son of a bitch!' Tarnwell stared at Lobec. 'Ward planted a fake notebook. That means he was telling the truth about hiding it. Maybe about the videotape too.'

Lefler looked at Tarnwell with a puzzled expression.

'Is this notebook worthless?' Tarnwell asked Lefler.

'No, not at all. It provides great insight into the general nature of the research. Although the equipment itself can be set up in a matter of hours, the precise settings are quite complicated and time-consuming to configure. With a few years of experimentation, we might be able to replicate the process ourselves.'

'A few years!'

'Perhaps one year if we are very lucky and focus all of our resources—'

'Doctor,' Tarnwell said, 'we don't have even one month. We have a huge buyout that is dependent on Adamas being submitted for patent protection next week. If we don't get it, this company's credit won't be worth squat.'

'Then I suggest you don't make the buyout.'

Lefler was right. The entire pitch to the loan underwriters was based on Adamas. If he made the buyout and Adamas was a failure or delayed, he'd have no way to make the payments on the loan. He'd be insolvent almost immediately. Bankrupt. Which meant he had to stop the deal.

Senders! Maybe he could catch him before the contract was signed and tell him to withdraw it. Tarnwell raced back to the door and yanked it open.

Senders was replacing the phone in his pocket. Tarnwell's stomach sank when he saw Senders's huge smile.

'Good news, Clay.'

'**D**iamonds?' Erica said. She wanted to know exactly what Kevin was talking about before they decided what to do next. She pulled into a grocery store parking spot five blocks from the bank. 'As in "Diamonds are a girl's best friend" diamonds?'

'Yes, this notebook tells you how to make real, honest-to-God diamonds. It also tells you how to coat any object with a diamond film.'

Erica shook her head. 'How could you run an experiment for your professor without knowing you were making diamonds?'

'Because I wasn't,' Kevin said. 'The experiment we were working on the day I was fired was an investigation into high-temperature superconductors using carbon 60 nanoparticles. The diamonds were made by mistake.'

She must have looked as confused as she felt. 'Carbon 60? What's that?'

'Have you ever heard of buckyballs?'

'I've heard the word.'

'In 1985, some astrophysicists and chemists came across

them by accident while trying to simulate processes that produce interstellar dust. It's only the third known pure form of carbon, the other two being graphite and diamond. Since that accidental discovery, it's been in the newspapers a lot because whole new classes of chemicals can be made with it. The discoverers won the Nobel Prize.'

'"Buckyball" is a goofy name for a Nobel Prize–winning discovery.'

'The official name is buckminsterfullerene, but nobody liked saying it. The molecule looks just like a soccer ball, so "buckyball" stuck.'

'So you were using buckyballs in the experiment. What were they for?'

'We were trying to make high-temperature superconductors. Metal-doped fullerene crystals have been shown to be isotropically superconductive above thirty degrees Kelvin. That's a high temperature for a superconductor, even though it's actually about 240 degrees Celsius below zero.'

Erica just shook her head and gave Kevin a blank look.

'I'll back up,' he said. 'Superconductors are materials that have no electrical resistance and therefore no heat loss. The applications for them are endless. For example, we could make three-hundred-mile-per-hour trains that levitate above magnetic rails. Or we could send electricity from one end of the country to another because there'd be no resistance in the power lines. And superconductors would revolutionize microprocessors, making them a thousand times smaller than they are now because thermal failure is the main limiting factor in the size and speed of computers.'

'So what's the catch?'

'Right now, all superconductors have to be cooled down to a temperature near absolute zero using liquid helium. The cooling process requires a room about the size of a bus, and the whole setup costs over a million dollars. But if we could find a way to make a high-temperature superconductor, we could use liquid nitrogen as a coolant, which is cheap and requires only a small amount of equipment. Room-temperature superconductors are the holy grail. Ward and I were just doing basic research. We didn't really expect to find anything besides directions for future research.'

'But you did find something,' Erica said.

Kevin nodded. 'And I never knew it.'

'You were a part of it from the very beginning,' Erica said. 'You're a coinventor of Adamas.'

'Which would be very cool if people weren't trying to kill us.'

'Are you sure he was able to make diamond?' Erica said. 'Maybe this is all a hoax.'

'No, Ward may have been a jerk,' Kevin said, leafing through the notebook, 'but he was a damn good researcher. Ward talks about molecular fragmentation of C_{60} through a microwave discharge resulting in chemical vapor deposition of carbon. I thought about it only peripherally back in January, but I realize now that the method we were using to insert metallic ions into C_{60} molecules also forms the basis for chemical vapor deposition.'

Erica was completely lost. 'What the hell did you just say?'

'Sorry.' Kevin flipped to another section. 'I looked at this in the bank.' He pointed to a graph in the notebook. 'See? Here's what I mean. The infrared spectrometer data clearly shows a pure carbon matrix in the sample. Pure carbon. There are no significant quantities of any other type of element.'

'Which confirms it's real diamond?'

Kevin nodded. 'With all the properties that make diamonds special.'

'Like its hardness?'

Kevin looked off in the distance, as if he were an awestruck farmer who was seeing a city skyline for the first time. 'Right, but that's only the start. Diamond is also transparent, it's an almost perfect heat conductor, and it performs as a semiconductor at much higher temperatures than silicon. No other material in the world has that combination of properties.'

'So?'

He looked back at her, but the excitement was still there. 'People have been trying to find a cheap way to synthesize diamond for the past sixty years. In the fifties, General Electric found a way of making artificial diamonds, but it's still so expensive, it's only used for things like special industrial drills. And it's not pure enough for gems. The diamonds they make look like dirty glass. More recently some firms have created small diamonds that are being marketed to the gem industry. But imagine if you could put a diamond film on anything you wanted for tens of dollars per carat rather than thousands of dollars. You could even make large objects out of diamond. Computer chips, sunglasses, entire windows. Think of diamond stove tops and cookware. The patent for something like that is worth millions.'

'Or billions.' She paused to let the enormity of the discovery sink in. 'We have to take this to the police. Whoever's after us won't stop until they have that notebook. What about just posting it on the internet?'

'Where? My Facebook page?'

'I don't know. Send it to the *New York Times*. Or *USA Today*.'

'But why would they pay any attention to it? If I showed this to you, and you didn't know me from Adam, would you believe that this was a radical new discovery and not a hoax?'

He held up the notebook so she could see one of the pages with technical specifications on it. She noticed that the edge was jagged in between this page and the previous one.

'It looks like a page was ripped out,' she said.

'I saw that, but I don't know why he would do that,' Kevin said, turning the notebook for a closer look. 'It looks like his notes start on this page, so we have to assume they're complete.'

Erica traced her index finger across the top of the page. 'I think I can make out indentations of what he wrote.'

'We'll find out what it says later. Look at the specifications.'

Erica read starting from the first paragraph on the page. *To maintain a uniform face for vaporization, the metal-graphite composite target was supported over a water-cooled copper collector in a UHV chamber evacuated to 10 mTorr. The target was attached to a homemade liquid nitrogen cryostat and a magnetic suspended turbo molecular pump.*

The words were meaningless to Erica. She gave him the look again.

'See what I mean?' he said. 'Only a chemist would understand it.'

'So let's take it to a chemist.'

'Who? I can't go back to South Texas. You already found that out. And no professor's going to believe some student who walks in off the street with this wacko story. Even if he looked at the notebook, he'd have to study it to get an idea of whether it would work or not.'

'Will it?' Erica said.

'I'm not sure. I think so.'

'Then what chemist do we call?'

'We can't do that,' Kevin said. 'The first thing a chemist would do is call someone else, probably someone at South Texas. Then we're as good as caught. We need help from the FBI or somebody like that. In case you don't remember, people have been trying to kill us since Saturday morning.'

'What about making a copy of the notebook?' Erica said. 'It could be our insurance.'

'We'd have to give it to someone else. Look where that got Herbert Stein. He must have been Ward's attorney, and they killed him trying to get this notebook. I don't think I want that hanging over my head.'

'If they don't have the notebook yet, why are they trying to kill us? Wouldn't they kidnap us to tell them where it is?'

'You have a point.'

Erica shook her head, not knowing what to do next. 'Nothing else was in the safe-deposit box?'

'Dammit!' Kevin said, reaching into his pocket. 'I forgot about this.' He handed a digital videotape to her.

'This must be important if he put it in the box,' Erica said.

'I know. I guess I got so excited about the notebook, it slipped my mind.'

'Do you know what's on it?' she said, flipping it in her hands.

'I have no idea. The notebook doesn't say anything about it.'

She put the tape in her purse and started the Honda. 'Then let's find out.'

David Lobec closed the door behind him as he followed Tarnwell into the extravagant penthouse office. He knew Tarnwell wanted to impress everyone who entered with its marble floors, teak woodwork, and bear and elk hunting trophies lining the walls, but Lobec found it overbearing and tasteless. It was a total contrast to the spartan office Lobec maintained on the floor below.

Tarnwell clipped the end off a Cuban cigar and lit it. Instead of taking one of the chairs across from Tarnwell, Lobec sat on the sofa, away from the pungent smoke. 'So, how could these two kids be anywhere?' Tarnwell said, sitting at his desk. 'Last I heard, they were buying gas in Florida.'

Lobec suppressed a substantial urge to roll his eyes. He had little patience for Tarnwell's inadequacies. 'As I was explaining, Mr Tarnwell, they were only charging the cost of the gas to Erica Jensen's Visa card. It seems that they had worked out exactly how long it would take to drive from one city to another and then billed the credit card accordingly. They could have led us on for a good while longer, but they happened to choose an Exxon station in Georgia that was undergoing repairs and had no working gas pumps.'

Tarnwell rolled the cigar in his forefingers. 'We have got to find them, David. You heard what Lefler said.'

'As I said, the news is discouraging. We continue to survey all likely places they would turn up: the university, the medical school, known friends. We've also paid key people in each of those places to notify us if anything indicating the location of Mr Hamilton and Miss Jensen arises. But for all we know, they could still be in Houston.'

Tarnwell pounded with the cigar in hand, spraying ashes

across the desk. 'Dammit, David! Don't you have *any* leads?'

'Hamilton's father, Murray. He's our best bet because he's the closest living relative for either Hamilton or Jensen.'

'Do you think Hamilton would try to contact his father?'

'It's possible, but as far as we can tell, the two of them have had no contact in the past three years.'

'Where does the father live?'

'Dallas. We've had him under surveillance since Friday.'

'Go to Dallas and talk to him. Use the detective spiel. Find out if he knows where the kid is. But remember, now we need Kevin Hamilton alive. His girlfriend must have found the notebook in that library. We've got to get it before they do something that will ruin me, like give it to the police. I swear to you, if they bankrupt me because of this, you won't have to do the dirty work this time. I'll kill them myself.'

Kevin and Erica walked through the back-to-school signs toward the Radio Shack's camcorder section. The store had just opened and the lone salesman was helping a customer at the back.

Kevin could have kicked himself for not thinking of the most obvious place to watch it. He had been trying to come up with ways of getting the camcorder from the lab when Erica had suggested an electronics store. The nearest Best Buy hadn't had a working compatible camcorder to play their tape, so they were trying the stores at the Galleria next.

They quickly found the row of camcorders lined up for display, all tethered to the shelf by thin metal cables. This time they found a working model with a small LCD screen and speakers. Kevin unslung the brand-new backpack he'd bought to carry the notebook and videotape and fished out the tape. He loaded it and pressed 'PLAY.'

Nothing happened.

He tried pressing it a couple more times. Still nothing. Kevin checked the battery. It was inserted correctly and the battery indicator showed a full charge. This camcorder was much different from the old one they used in the lab, so he inspected it more carefully, holding it up to the light to better read all of the labels. *There must be thirty buttons on this damned thing*, he thought.

'May I help you?' a deep voice said behind them.

They turned to see a towering black man dressed in a Radio Shack shirt. 'Phil,' according to his name tag.

When Kevin hesitated, Erica spoke. 'Yes, we were trying to figure out how this one works. We brought our own tape so that we could compare the performance of this camcorder to others we're considering.'

Phil took the camcorder from Kevin. 'We don't sell many models anymore that use tapes. Everything is heading toward solid-state, but we keep a few tape models for legacy reasons. Now, you just press this button—'

Kevin put his hand on Phil's arm when he realized he was about to tape over what was on there. 'No, wait!'

Phil gave him a slightly startled look.

'What I mean is,' Kevin went on, 'the picture quality of the LCD panel is very important to us, so we brought a tape we previously made.'

'I see,' Phil said. 'In that case, you have to move this switch here to Playback and then press "PLAY." See?' He gave the camcorder back to Kevin.

'Perhaps you could tell me what price range and features you were looking for,' Phil continued. 'Some of the features of this camcorder include video editing, a remote control—'

'Thanks a lot,' said Erica. 'I think we just want to see the tape for now.'

Phil, sensing that they wanted to have some time alone, told them where he'd be and left.

Kevin pressed the PLAY button.

After a few seconds of static, an image of a room filled with an array of technical equipment appeared on the screen. In the middle of the room, a man was hunched over one of the instruments with his back toward the camera. In the corner of the screen, the time and the date 'January 21' glowed in red.

Kevin recognized the location immediately. 'That's Ward's lab! This must be a tape of the NV117 experiment.'

A second later he saw himself walk away from the camera. Through the speakers, he heard himself say, 'It's rolling.'

An older man in the video turned toward Kevin and said, 'Good. Then let's get going. We've got a lot to do today.' The man was Michael Ward.

Kevin turned to Erica. 'The following day I wanted to watch this to see if we could tell what happened, but Ward told me he taped over it. Asshole.'

Kevin knew that the next twenty minutes would be more setup, so he fast-forwarded through the tape. When it reached a point near the start of the experiment, he pressed 'PLAY' again.

Kevin and Erica watched hunched over the two-inch-wide screen.

Ward, standing at the computer control terminal, asked Kevin if they were ready. Kevin, who was standing near the test chamber, nodded affirmative as he walked back to the control terminal. Ward pushed a button on the keyboard.

At first, nothing seemed to happen. Kevin was peering at a monitor while Ward looked into the test chamber. Suddenly, Kevin was yelling 'Shut down! Shut down! Overload!' and a bright flash blanked out the screen. When it cleared, a piece of apparatus on the far side of the room was burning and smoke billowed to the ceiling. Ward frantically flipped switches on the emergency shutoff panel while Kevin raced across the room, yanked a fire extinguisher from the wall, and blasted the fire until it was out.

Kevin knew the next ten minutes were spent trying to ascertain what went wrong with the equipment. Kevin again fast-forwarded through it, then hit 'PLAY.'

'I think this is where I turned off the camera. I had a class to get to.'

Almost as he said it, the on-camera Kevin glanced at the camcorder and said, 'Oh, yeah.' He walked toward the camera and the screen returned to static. The two of them watched the static for a few moments, and then Kevin stopped the tape.

'This isn't going to help very much,' said Erica. 'Why would Ward hide it with the notebook?'

'He must have just wanted a record of the events leading up to the discovery. Maybe he wanted it as evidence. I don't know.'

Footsteps approached from behind. They turned to see Phil.

'Well, what do you think? Does it have everything you wanted?'

'No,' said Kevin. 'It's not what we were hoping for.'

As they dejectedly walked back to the car through the mall to avoid the heat outside, Kevin tentatively reached for Erica's hand.

'We'll get out of this somehow,' he said.

'I know.'

'You do?'

'Yes,' she said confidently.

'I'm glad one of us does, because I was just saying that. As far as I can tell, we're screwed.'

They passed the window display of a jewelry store and Erica stopped. A neat row of diamond rings and pendants rested on the velvet shelves. A picture of an enormous blue diamond hung above the display. In big letters at the top, it said, 'Why not get her the next best thing?' In smaller letters at the bottom, the caption read, 'The Hope Diamond. At 49.5 carats, it's the world's largest blue diamond.'

'It's hard to believe,' she said, 'that people would kill for something that makes rocks.'

'No, it's not. Look at how much some of these stones are going for.' He pointed at a one-carat diamond ring on sale for $2,499. 'Besides, they're more than rocks. Think of what the car companies alone would pay for windows not just coated with diamond but actually made of diamond. Windows that never break, never scratch. Not to mention tools that never wear out, unbreakable dishware, faster computers. Any one of those things would make somebody rich. But all together? That person would have more money than God.'

'Then why didn't Ward just keep it for himself?'

'I've been wondering about that, and I think I know why. There was no way he could use it and make any money.'

'What do you mean?'

'The way I see it, there are only two methods for making money off of this. One, you could make the diamonds yourself. But to make them in any substantial quantity, he'd have to have his own manufacturing plant, distribution sources, patent attorneys. In other words, he had to have money to begin with. I don't think there was any way he'd be able to convince the patent office that he'd come up with the process independent of the university. And if he had used university property to do the research, South Texas would own the patent. Ward would get his name on the patent, but the university would make the money.'

'And if he made diamonds on the sly with the university equipment,' Erica said, 'he couldn't make them too big or he wouldn't be able to sell them. And how do you sell a lot of small diamonds?'

'Right. After a while he'd probably get caught. The only way he was able to work on it as long as he did was to fire me and get me out of the lab. By the end of summer he would have had to hire new students. It would have been suspicious if he didn't. And there's no way he could take all of that specialized equipment out of the lab. It would have been missed. Which leads to the second way of making money: sell the process. That way he could make millions all at once, and the university would never know it came from him. That must have been what Ward meant about the deal with Clay.'

'But whoever this Clay is didn't want anyone else to know about it.'

'Including Ward,' Kevin said. 'They didn't want to take the chance he'd talk. Now we're the ones who these guys are hunting down, and the police won't believe us.' He threw his hands up in exasperation.

Erica pointed at the ad in the window. 'I bet if we strolled in with something as big as the Hope Diamond they'd believe us.'

'Yeah, they'd probably—' Kevin stopped abruptly. *That was it! Why not?*

He dug into his pocket and fished out the prepaid cell phone.

'Who are you calling?' she said.

'A friend.'

'Is he someone you can trust?'

'Absolutely,' Kevin said as he dialed Information.

'What can he do?'

'He's going to help us make our own diamond.'

Kevin was worried that his friend and former fellow student Ted Huang wouldn't be at home, but he answered immediately.

'Hello?' he said.

'Ted, it's Kevin.'

'Hey! Did you get a new number?'

'I lost the old phone.'

'How are you doing? Did you get the email I sent you Friday?'

'I did.'

'Where are you?'

'I'm in Houston. Listen, Ted, I wouldn't call you like this, but we are in a hell of a lot of trouble.'

'Who's "we"?'

'Erica Jensen. A friend. She's with me now. We're at the Galleria.'

Ted laughed. 'Kevin, if your car is broken down again, AAA is probably the place to call.'

'I'm serious, Ted. This is life-and-death. We need your help.'

Ted's voice sobered. 'What can I do?' There was nothing more Kevin needed to do to convince him. Their relationship had been like that for the last two years, each of them providing help whenever it was needed, no questions asked, but Kevin had never asked for any favor this big.

He held his breath before continuing, hoping Ted would have faith in him.

'Some men are trying to kill us.'

'What?'

'I know it sounds crazy, but it's true. We have something they want.'

'Have you gone to the police?'

'We've tried, but they aren't going to help us. Ted, believe me when I tell you that the less you know, the better. You might not believe it anyway. We need a favor.'

'Name it. Anything.'

'I want to use your lab for a few days.'

The other end of the line was silent. Kevin waited. Finally, he couldn't stand it.

'Ted? Are you still there?'

'Kevin, I don't know. I'm just an assistant professor, for God's sake. I've only been at Virginia Tech for two months—'

'I know it's a lot to ask, Ted, but this is our only shot. If you don't help us, we are going to die.'

There were another few seconds of hesitation. Erica gave Kevin a questioning look and he shrugged.

'When can you get here?'

Kevin sighed with relief. 'If we drive all night, we can get there by tomorrow evening.'

Ted gave Kevin his home address, and Kevin relayed it to Erica so she could map it on her phone.

'What kind of equipment do you need?' Ted said.

From memory, Kevin went down the list of items. 'An infrared spectrometer, a turbomolecular pump, a blue-light laser, a liquid nitrogen cryostat ...' He named a dozen other items.

'There's a problem. The lab has everything you just named except one. We had a catastrophic failure in our laser last month. It's totally shot.'

'What's wrong with it? Can it be fixed?'

'No way. We're getting a new one, but there's a buying freeze for the next two weeks.'

Kevin's heart sank. 'You couldn't bend the rules and get it any sooner, could you?'

'Kevin, I just started working here. I'm going out on a limb letting you use the lab in the first place. I'll try to get it sooner, but there are no guarantees.'

'That's all I ask.'

'Don't worry, man. You can hang low here until we get the laser. In the meantime, it'll be just like last year.'

'Yeah. Thanks, Ted. You're a lifesaver. Literally.'

'Just make sure you get here tomorrow. We leave at six o'clock Wednesday morning for Minneapolis.'

'Right, the conference. Don't worry. We'll be there.'

'Drive safely.'

Kevin hung up.

'It sounded like he was willing to help us,' Erica said. 'Who is he?'

They began walking toward the car.

'A chemistry Ph.D. who graduated from STU last year. He'll let me run the process in his lab.'

'You don't look too happy about it.'

'Their laser is broken, and they won't be able to replace it for at least two weeks. Without it, we can't make any diamond.'

'Two weeks! They might find us by then.'

'I know. But what other choice do we have? He's the only person I know who could do this for us.'

'What if you had this laser? How long would it take to make enough diamond?'

'Probably three days, depending on how much we want.'

'Do you know where we could get one?'

'I think so, but it doesn't matter. Those lasers cost about thirty thousand dollars.'

'Could we buy one ourselves?'

'Buy one ourselves?' Kevin asked. 'I just told you they are thirty *thousand* dollars.'

'I heard you. Just tell me if we could buy one ourselves today if we had the money.'

'Probably. There's a used scientific equipment dealer in Dallas that I ordered one from last year. The only problem was, it took a week to get what I ordered.'

'Then we'll have to go there in person,' Erica said. 'Can you find it or should we call first?'

'What are you talking about? I don't think they'll let us put a thirty-thousand-dollar laser on a credit card.'

Erica steered Kevin to a bench in a little-used side passage. She sat, and Kevin followed suit. She had an earnest look on her face, and Kevin had no idea what to expect. He waited while she searched for words.

'Remember when I told you at the party Friday that I'd had some money and family problems lately?' she finally said.

Kevin nodded, looking into her eyes. They seemed tortured.

She hesitated again.

'This is harder than I thought it would be. I haven't talked to anyone about this in' – she looked up, thinking – 'four years, I guess. Not even Luke.'

Kevin kept silent, not wanting to interrupt what was obviously difficult for her to say.

'About ten years ago, when I was a senior in high school, I was on the varsity diving team. I was pretty good, good enough that I was in contention for scholarships, and my parents were big fans. They would come to every meet, no matter how far away it was.

'The last meet of the year was in Fort Worth, a three-hour drive. I rode the bus with the other girls, but I saw my parents in the audience just before I went up for my first dive. They were sitting in the front row like they always were, clapping and yelling as my name was read off.

'We ended up winning that night. Naturally we were ecstatic, screaming and jumping around like lunatics. My parents wanted to take me out to celebrate, but I was so excited I wanted to ride the bus with the other girls and get pizza with them on the way home.'

Erica got a faraway look in her eyes. 'They understood, and I still remember watching them as the bus pulled away. My mom was waving a school banner, and my dad gave me a thumbs-up as we left. Everyone else was already talking about the state meet, but the only thing I was thinking at that moment was how proud I was that they had been there to see me. Of course, five seconds later I was laughing again with the other girls.'

Erica smiled as she said it, but her eyes began to glisten with tears.

'It was a Saturday, and of course we stayed out late partying. My friend Amy didn't drop me off at home until two in the morning, way past my curfew. I tiptoed straight to my room, hoping I wouldn't wake my parents.

'About an hour later, I heard a banging at the front door. It went on for a while, and I started to wonder why my father wasn't answering it. I got up and looked in my parents' room, but nobody was there. The bed hadn't even been slept in. Then I heard my name being called, and I ran downstairs thinking that my parents had locked themselves out somehow. I was so sleepy that it didn't occur to me to wonder why they were still out at that hour.

'When I opened the door, there was a sheriff's deputy

standing on the porch. He told me that my parents had been in an accident and that I should put some clothes on so that we could go to the hospital. I asked if they were all right. The deputy said he didn't know, but he was lying. He kept telling me to hurry, and when I stopped to call my grandparents, he said there wasn't enough time.

'A doctor at the hospital told me everything. As my parents were on their way home from the meet, a drunk in a pickup ran a stop sign and broadsided their car at sixty miles an hour. My mother and the drunk driver were killed instantly, but my dad revived enough at the hospital to tell them to come find me. He died fifteen minutes before I got there.

'The next three days were a blur. My dad's brother, Uncle Rick, took care of the funeral arrangements. Then I found out about the insurance. My mom and dad had policies totaling two million dollars, and I've been careful with the money since then. That's why we can buy a thirty-thousand-dollar laser. All I have to do is call my broker and transfer the money.'

When Erica had gotten to the part about the accident, Kevin's expression was a mixture of sadness and understanding. But when she mentioned the money, his jaw dropped in astonishment.

When he realized how he looked, he tried to explain.

'I'm sorry. I just ... I mean, I guess I know why you didn't tell me, but I had no idea you had that much money. Your clothes and town house are nicer than the other med students', but I just assumed your parents were paying for them.'

'In a way, they are.'

Something tugged at the back of Kevin's mind. 'But at the party you said you missed lunch because of money problems. I thought you forgot a car payment or something.'

'I did miss lunch because of money problems. I was speaking to my lawyer for about two hours. You know good old Uncle Rick? He was made executor of the trust that the insurance money was put into. I found out this year that he's been siphoning money from it ever since.'

'How much?'

'Close to three hundred thousand.'

Kevin's eyes bulged. 'Dollars?'

'Yeah. I was totally oblivious until I told my broker that I wanted to start getting the monthly statements myself. Up to that point, Uncle Rick was getting the statements and telling me how I was doing. Last summer, I attended a seminar for med students called Managing Your Money: A Doctor's Guide to Investment, and I decided I should start understanding how my finances worked. I didn't think to tell my uncle, since I was just going to monitor the statements. After I saw some weird withdrawals from the account – withdrawals that I didn't make – I asked for a total accounting of the finances for the last seven years. That's when it all came out. I've been involved in litigation with him ever since.'

'I don't know what to say. That's a lot to take in.'

'We've never really had a chance to talk about stuff like that before.'

Kevin patted her hand. 'I can't take your money. Thirty thousand dollars is too much—'

'Hey. This is for me as much as it is for you. We're in this together.' She smiled. 'Besides, we can always put it on eBay when this is all over.'

He hesitated, trying to decide whether to tell her about his father and the problem with his tuition. No, this wasn't the right time. It might seem like he was trying to take advantage of her wealth. Once they were safe, Kevin would tell her everything.

On her phone Erica found the Web site for SciSurplus in Dallas and relayed the 800 number to Kevin. He dialed, and she listened as Kevin explained to the sales representative what he needed. After five minutes of hearing Kevin try to convince the man that he was not joking, Erica was worried that they wouldn't be able to get one, but apparently Kevin finally succeeded. He haggled with the sales rep over the price and then hung up.

'Well?' she said.

'I talked him into selling me their last laser in stock if we came to pick it up today – with a fair markup for the sales rep's trouble, of course. I don't think I completely convinced him, though. He said it had already been promised to another customer, and if we don't buy it today, it'll be on the first UPS truck tomorrow morning. We have to be there by six o'clock to get it.'

'That should give us plenty of time.' Erica looked at her watch. 'It's only about ten thirty now. We can get to Dallas in about four hours or so.'

'Yeah, but the warehouse is on the other side of Dallas. That's another hour. If we get stuck in rush-hour traffic, it'll be tight.'

Erica was the next to use the phone. She called her broker to arrange the transfer, thankful for electronic transactions. Once she had the confirmation number written down, she was ready to pick up the cashier's check at any branch of her local bank.

They looked in the phone book and found a branch just outside the mall. In twenty minutes they had the cashier's check in hand and were headed toward I-45 north. Erica had still not caught up on her sleep from the week before, so she dozed while Kevin drove and listened to NPR.

A nudge from Kevin woke her. She saw a sign saying 'Dallas 15 Miles' and looked at her watch. It was a little past two thirty. They'd made good time.

For some reason Kevin was slowing down.

'We stopping?' Erica said, rubbing the sleep from her eyes.

Kevin jabbed his thumb toward the rear window. 'It's not my decision.'

She turned and felt her stomach somersault. Behind them were the flashing lights of a highway patrol car.

TWENTY-ONE

Kevin clenched the steering wheel tightly, feeling as if he were going to hyperventilate.

'Do you think it's them?' Erica said.

'I don't see how could they find us on the outskirts of Dallas. It's got to be the real police.'

'Thank God.'

A short siren sounded behind them.

'I didn't say that was necessarily a good thing. Remember, I don't have my license with me.' Kevin began to slow down.

'Were you speeding?'

'I don't know. I did speed up to pass a semi a few miles back.'

'They won't take us in just because you don't have your license with you.'

It sounded as if Erica was trying to reassure herself, but Kevin knew they were both thinking the same thing. If they were forced to go down to the station with the officer, it would be possible for their pursuers to learn their location.

The Honda rolled to a stop along the freeway shoulder.

They waited for the officer to approach the car, but no one got out. A minute later a second patrol car came to a stop behind the first. A female trooper wearing the standard wide-brimmed hat climbed out of the second patrol car and walked up to the first, leaning into the driver's window. Several times she looked in the direction of the Honda.

'What the hell is going on?' Kevin said, puzzled.

Erica shrugged and shook her head.

The door of the first patrol car opened, and a male officer got out and adjusted his gun belt. Kevin unrolled the window as the police officers walked toward him.

Both troopers wore dark aviator sunglasses, giving them a menacing appearance. The male officer's expression seemed to be practiced indifference, but Kevin noticed that his right hand wasn't far from his pistol. He leaned forward to look into the car. When he spoke, a monotone issued from between smoke-stained teeth.

'Sir, may I see your driver's license? And, ma'am, I'd like to see some identification from you as well.'

The female officer stood on the passenger side of the Honda.

'I'm sorry, Officer,' Kevin said as he handed Erica's license to the patrolman. 'I don't have my license with me.' There was no reason to tell him why he didn't have it. He sure as hell wasn't going to give the officer the license with Ward's name on it.

The officer took Erica's license. 'Then may I see some other form of identification?'

He shook his head, embarrassed. 'I don't have my wallet.'

The officer looked up at the other officer and then back at Kevin. His expression never wavered. 'What's your name, sir?'

'Kevin Hamilton.'

'Mr Hamilton, Miss Jensen, could you please step out of the vehicle?'

Kevin got out thinking that he and Erica would follow them back to one of the patrol cars, but what the officer said next shocked him.

'Now face the vehicle and put your hands on the hood.'

'Are you serious?' Erica's eyes widened.

'On the hood, sir. You, too, miss.' His voice continued in the polite monotone, but Kevin saw the serious look on his face. His hand was now hovering over the pistol.

Kevin did as he was told and faced Erica, who was leaning against the hood on the other side of the car. The officer patted his back and chest and then ran his hands up and down his legs. He tried not to squirm at the uncomfortable personal nature of the search, focusing on Erica's face. Her shocked expression mirrored his own.

The officer reached into Kevin's pocket and pulled out the driver's license with Ward's name on it.

'What's this?' the officer said. 'This identification says your name is Michael Ward.'

'I can explain that,' Kevin said.

'I'm sure you can.'

The officer grabbed his hands and Kevin heard a click from behind the cool metal of handcuffs shackling his wrists.

'What the hell is this all about?' Kevin said.

'Mr Ward, I stopped you for exceeding the speed limit—'

'I've been stopped for speeding before and I've never been handcuffed! And my name is Hamilton, not Ward.'

Erica made a face for him to be quiet.

'You are under arrest for grand theft auto,' the officer continued calmly. 'This vehicle has been reported stolen.'

'What?' Kevin said. 'That's impossible!'

'Officer,' Erica said, 'it can't be stolen. This is my car.'

'It was also reported that one of the occupants may be impersonating the owner of the car. The only identification Mr Hamilton' – the officer sarcastically drawled the name – 'has been able to produce is a license for someone named Michael Ward. I'd say that's sufficient evidence to make you suspects. You have the right to remain silent . . .'

Kevin listened to the litany of rights he had so often heard on hundreds of TV shows, almost unable to comprehend that they were now applying to him. He didn't respond when the officer seemed to be asking him a question.

'What?' he said.

'I said, do you understand these rights?'

They both answered yes.

'This is ridiculous,' Kevin said. 'How can we be under arrest for stealing her car? *It's her car!*'

'Sir, please calm down.'

'How can I be calm? I'm under arrest!'

'Officer,' Erica said, 'there's obviously some sort of mistake. All of my identification is in my purse. If you'll just check it, you'll see—'

'I'm sorry, ma'am. I'll take your purse with us, but this isn't something we'll be able to investigate here.'

Kevin remembered the backpack with the notebook and videotape.

'I need my backpack too,' he said. 'I can't leave it in the car.'

'What's in it?' the officer asked.

'Some very important papers of mine and a videotape. It'll be ruined if it stays out in this heat.'

The officer looked at Kevin for a few seconds. Kevin was about to say something else when the officer opened the Honda and retrieved the purse and the backpack.

'Where are we going?' Erica said.

'The local police headquarters.'

'What about my car?'

'I'll call for a tow truck and have the vehicle taken to the impound lot,' the female officer said. Kevin noticed that she didn't say 'your vehicle.'

Ten minutes later they entered a police station in Hutchins, Texas.

Because the station's internet connection was down, it took three hours of back-and-forth phone calls for the police to be convinced that Erica Jensen was, in fact, who she said she was. Relieved about the error being resolved, she gladly took back her belongings from Officer Brady, the patrolman who had stopped them. She looked at her watch. It was already five twenty. They had less than an hour before the warehouse closed.

'I'm sorry about the misunderstanding, Miss Jensen,' Brady said. 'You can be sure that we will be looking into this matter to make sure this kind of thing doesn't happen again.'

'Does this mean we're free to go?'

'You are, Miss Jensen. But I called about the identification with Michael Ward's name on it.' He jerked a thumb at Kevin, who was sitting at the desk of Officer Anson, the patrolwoman assisting Brady. 'There is someone with that name and Social Security number, but the license number is for someone named Maria Gonzalez. Therefore, it's a fake, not stolen. He claims he had it made as a joke. I'd be willing to let it go at that, but I still don't have any identification for him.'

Erica sighed with relief when she realized they hadn't made a connection to Ward's death. 'He was only speeding. That shouldn't be a big deal.'

'He was also driving without a license and in possession of a fake driver's license. Until I can confirm his true identity, he will have to remain here.' He continued quickly before she could object again: 'Under these odd circumstances, I have to be sure that there are no outstanding warrants for Mr Hamilton's arrest. He'll have to wait here until our internet link is back up.' He said Kevin's name with a slight but detectable air of skepticism.

'When will that be?'

'A couple of hours, maybe.'

Erica groaned. 'But if he shows you some ID, he can go?'

'A picture ID is necessary. If he can produce that, then yes, he will be free to go.'

'Okay. Where can I pick up my Honda?'

At the mention of her car, an embarrassed look crossed Brady's face and he seemed reluctant to continue.

'It was taken to the stolen vehicle impound lot,' he said after a pause.

'So?'

'There's a problem.'

'Of course there is,' Erica said, exasperated.

'I just talked to the lot. You can't retrieve the car until tomorrow morning.'

'What?'

'I'm sorry, but with the state budget cuts, the lot's only open until five o'clock. I tried to get them to make an exception, but they wouldn't.'

Erica stood up without saying a word and walked to Officer Anson's desk with Brady. Kevin looked as mad as she felt.

'What do I have to do to convince you that I'm not a criminal?' said Kevin, directing the question to both Anson and Brady.

'As I was telling Miss Jensen,' Brady said, 'all we need is a picture ID. Or you can wait here until we can verify your ID.'

Kevin looked at Erica, who knew what he was thinking. Every minute in the police station was dangerous. If the men after them could tap into police databases, they'd know where to find them. Not to mention that in half an hour they'd lose the chance at getting a laser for the next several weeks.

'Erica can go, can't she?'

'Of course,' Brady said. 'She's been cleared—'

Erica interrupted. 'No, I can't.' She told Kevin about the car.

Kevin fiddled with a paper clip from Officer Anson's desk, staring at it as he did so with a look of desperation. Erica wanted to pluck the paper clip from his hand and make him look at her, but she knew it was his way of occupying his hands while he thought.

Just as Brady seemed to get tired of waiting, Kevin said, 'All right.'

'What?' Erica said.

'There's only one thing I can think of.'

'What?'

'Something I'd really rather not do.'

'Will you stop that and say something meaningful?' Erica said, irritated.

'I have a passport. I got it six years ago, but I never used it.'

'At your apartment in Houston.'

'No, I left it at my home here in Dallas. I forgot to bring it with me to South Texas. I know exactly where it is. The top drawer in my old desk, unless my father threw it out.'

'You still have a house in Dallas?' Kevin had never talked about his parents to her except to tell her that his mother had passed away.

'Assuming he still lives there, it's about twenty minutes away.'

'"Assuming he still lives there"?' Erica asked.

'For all I know he moved a long time ago,' Kevin said. 'I haven't spoken to my father in three years.'

Lobec had the entire dossier Mitch Hornung had compiled on Murray Hamilton. He looked up from the file and buzzed the Gulfstream's cockpit.

'What is our ETA?' he asked above the jet engine's drone.

The intercom came to life. 'We're scheduled to touch down in thirty-three minutes, Mr Lobec, but we may be delayed by a thunderstorm moving through the area.'

'Get us down as soon as you can. Make sure the car is ready for us.'

'Yes, sir.'

Love Field was fifteen minutes closer to Murray Hamilton's home in eastern Dallas than DFW was. An inconspicuous Ford sedan would be waiting for them on the tarmac. The closer proximity, however, was no longer a factor. Hank Vincent, the local contractor Lobec had hired to track

Murray Hamilton, called twenty minutes ago to tell them that Hamilton had left his house and was heading toward southern Dallas. Lobec had instructed Vincent to follow at a discreet distance and to report back when Hamilton had reached his destination.

'Do you really think Hamilton's father is going to know where he is?' Richard Bern said. 'I mean, according to his phone records, the guy hasn't called his dad once since he got to Houston.' He sat across from Lobec, facing the other way. His feet were propped up on the leather upholstery, and he had the seat fully reclined. Besides them and the two crew members in the cockpit, the ten-passenger jet was empty.

'I don't know the reason for the Hamiltons' estrangement, but I've learned that the first place people in trouble turn is to their families. Hamilton may have no other choice.'

'He and his girlfriend could be in Guatemala for all we know. This is a shot in the dark.'

What Bern said was true. Lobec thought reporting the girl's car as stolen could prove useful because it might flush them out, but so far it hadn't yielded any results.

'If you have a better suggestion as to how we could use our time to search for them, I would appreciate enlightenment.'

Bern furrowed his brow, and Lobec could see him desperately trying to concoct a monumental plan. There would be none. Bern was a fairly capable assistant, but he would never command his own operations.

'In that case, Mr Bern, we will continue with our present

objective.' Lobec handed him the file. 'You will see that Murray Hamilton is a member of the NRA and a card-carrying Republican. He is licensed by the state to carry a concealed weapon and regularly hunts deer and quail. What does this suggest to you regarding our approach to the elder Mr Hamilton?'

Bern skimmed the ten-page file and then held a picture of the subject up to the light. It was a driver's license photo showing a man in his late fifties who hadn't aged well. Decades of smoking and drinking had left his cheeks and jowls sagging and wrinkled. Although he wasn't bald, the hair he did have was thinning, limp, and stringy. The photo belied the license's assertion that he carried 230 pounds on his six-foot two-inch frame, which indicated to Lobec that most of the weight was muscle developed during his years as a construction worker.

Bern dropped the photo back into the folder and said, 'I don't know. But I bet this guy ain't going to trust a couple of cops telling him his son's wanted by the law.'

'Exactly, Mr Bern. Very good. Therefore, we will need to take an entirely different approach. Your cover will be—'

The plane's intercom buzzed. Lobec picked up the handset.

'Yes.'

'I have a Mr Vincent on the line for you,' said the pilot.

'Put him through.'

After a click, the contractor tailing Murray Hamilton spoke from the other end.

'Mr Barnett?' Vincent said, drawling the syllables together.

'You have something to report, Mr Vincent?'

'Mr Barnett, I don't know why, but Murray Hamilton just came to a stop in the parking lot of the Hutchins Police Department.'

At one end of the squad room, Kevin and Erica sat on a wooden bench. Kevin stared at the clock. It said 5:41.

Erica clenched Kevin's right knee, stopping its bounce. Kevin hadn't realized until then that he'd been tapping his hand in rhythm with his bobbing leg. He gave her a half-hearted smile.

Because he had told the officers that his father was bringing the identification within the half hour, they'd let him wait with Erica in the squad room instead of in a holding cell. When Kevin had called his father, the conversation had been short. Although Kevin detected surprise in his father's voice when he'd told him where he and Erica were, his father hadn't asked any questions. Kevin just told him what he needed, and his father said it would take about twenty minutes to get to Hutchins and then hung up.

Knowing that they wouldn't get to the warehouse by six o'clock, Erica had called the sales representative at SciSurplus and sweet-talked him into staying late. He had some paperwork to do anyway, so if they got there by seven, they could still get the laser. It would be tight. The warehouse was forty-five minutes away in normal traffic; during the Dallas rush hour the travel time could easily double.

It had been fifteen minutes since Kevin had talked to his father. In that time he hadn't said much to Erica.

Still clenching Kevin's knee, she turned to him with a look of concern. 'Why didn't you tell me about your father?'

'That was a part of my life I wanted to forget about. I didn't think it was important to rehash it after that story about your parents. They obviously loved you. Why should I talk about how crappy my father was?'

'Kevin,' Erica said, the disappointment in her voice evident, 'after all we've been through the last few days, I thought you'd feel you could share something like that with me.'

'You're right. I'm sorry.' Kevin concentrated on the clock in front of them. 'Okay, here it is. My father was a drunk for the better part of my childhood. He had an accident on a construction site when I was fourteen and collected disability for the next ten years, drinking half of it because he didn't have anything better to do. He never wanted me to go to college and wouldn't pay for it, thought it was a waste of time. He wanted me to go into construction and be a real man. The only reason I went to college was because of my mother. She died of cancer three years ago. Her funeral was the last time I talked to my father until today.' He turned to face Erica. 'Not like your story, is it?'

'No, but he's coming. That should show you that he cares.' Erica nodded at the entrance and tapped Kevin's arm. 'That's got to be him,' she said.

Kevin looked up. At the other end of the squad room was Murray Hamilton, and Kevin realized why Erica had been so sure it was him. The figure striding toward them, clothed in a denim shirt, jeans, and work boots, was Kevin's height, but he'd lost thirty pounds of muscle since Kevin had last seen him, leaving a gaunt stick figure behind. Still, with the same square-jawed face, Roman nose, and wide hazel eyes, the older man's stubble-covered wrinkles and thinning hair made Kevin feel like he was looking at his future in a mirror.

He and Erica rose just as Murray reached them and came to an abrupt stop in front of them. He stood there without saying a word, just looking into Kevin's eyes.

Finally, Kevin broke the silence. 'Hello, Dad.'

'I might have known,' Murray said, 'that the only reason you would call me was because you were in trouble.'

Kevin expected his father to throw the passport at him, turn, and walk out as quickly as he'd come in.

'But I'm glad you did,' Murray said, and grasped Kevin in a tight hug.

Kevin was flabbergasted. His father had never been an affectionate man; in fact, Kevin could recall only a few times in his life when his father had hugged him, and even then it had been when he was much younger. Now it seemed as if his father would never let go. Still, Kevin couldn't bring himself to return the affection.

Murray released him and held him at arm's length.

'You look good,' said Murray. 'You've lost some weight, haven't you?'

'A little.'

'And put some muscle on those bones, I see,' Murray said, squeezing Kevin's shoulders.

'Did you find the passport?' Kevin asked without emotion.

'I got it right here.' Murray pulled the passport from his hip pocket. Kevin took it, opened it to check, and then called Officer Brady over to them.

Brady studied the passport carefully. After about thirty seconds he said, 'All right, Mr Hamilton. It looks like everything is in order.'

'Does that mean we can go?' Kevin said.

'Yes, but I'm confiscating the fake ID. Because of all the trouble we've caused you and Miss Jensen, I've decided to drop the charges against you. Just watch your speed from now on.' He nodded to Erica. 'Have a good day, Miss Jensen. Let me know if you have any trouble getting your car tomorrow.' Brady put on his hat and walked out the front entrance.

'Now, do you mind telling me what this is all about?' Murray said.

'It's no big deal. Thanks for the favor. See you later.' Kevin turned as if to walk away.

'Kevin!' Erica said. 'What's wrong with you?' She turned toward Murray, extending her hand. 'Hi, Mr Hamilton. My name's Erica Jensen. We really appreciate you going to all this trouble.'

Murray took her hand and smiled, showing teeth yellowed from years of smoking. 'No trouble at all. Pleased to meet you.'

'It shouldn't have been any trouble getting off the couch and coming over,' Kevin mumbled.

'Actually, you're lucky you caught me at home. I was just about to go back out to my job site when you called.'

'Grabbing a beer during your break?'

'No,' Murray said calmly. 'When I said my job site, I meant the one where I'm the foreman.'

Kevin looked at him in disbelief. This man he hadn't spoken to in three years, who'd been a drunk and lousy provider all his life, was now trying to tell Kevin that he had a steady job.

'You're kidding.'

'Had the job two years now. I tried to tell you, but you wouldn't return my calls.'

'Why should I have called you? You never cared about me or what I was interested in.'

Murray studied his shoes. 'Nick, I know I was an asshole when you were in high school. I was wrong about you going to college too. You seem to be doing pretty well for yourself. But before she died, your mother made me promise that I'd try to patch things up between us. I'm trying.'

Kevin said nothing. He wasn't sure why his dad was acting this way, but he wasn't going to let him redeem himself that easily, not after what he and his mother had gone through.

'Nick?' Erica said.

Murray turned to her and then, realizing she'd been talking to him, a look of understanding crossed his face.

'I forgot. He's going by "Kevin" now. Began using his middle name when he got to college. I don't think he ever liked being called Nick, though it still fits him in my mind.'

'My mother called me Nicholas.'

'I think you hated that just as much. Now, what's this about your car?'

Erica tucked her hair behind her ear. 'It seems that the impound lot where my car is won't be open until tomorrow morning. And we need to be somewhere by seven o'clock tonight.'

'Well, the least I could do is give you a ride.'

Erica started to speak, but Kevin interrupted her.

'Thanks, but we'll get there just fine.'

'Kevin,' Erica said, 'it's almost five forty-five. We'll be lucky to make it there as it is.'

'We can get there ourselves. We don't need any more help from him.'

Erica started to protest again, but Murray put his hand on her arm.

'Erica, it's a long story between us. If he doesn't want my help, that's the way it is. Like I said, I tried.' He turned back to Kevin. 'Good-bye, Nick ... I mean Kevin. Give me a call sometime.' With that, he walked out the front door into the dingy, gray afternoon.

Erica whirled toward Kevin with narrowed eyes. 'Kevin, I don't know what problems your family has had, but in thirty seconds we'll see our last chance to get the laser drive away.'

'We'll get a cab,' Kevin said, trying to ignore her logic.

'It will take the cab a half hour to get here, if it'll even come out this far.'

'Then we'll call the sales rep again. Get him to wait for us a little longer.' He saw the look on Erica's face and tried to preempt her. 'He is a drunken bum who didn't even tell me that my mother had cancer until a week before she died.'

'I'm sorry about that. That was a terrible thing to do. You can hate him all you want, but we need his help.'

Kevin looked at the acoustic tiling in the ceiling and let out a huge sigh. 'All right, but as soon as we can get your car, we're gone.'

Erica nodded and grabbed Kevin's hand as she started to run for the door. Kevin began to go with her, then stopped, feeling as if he were missing something. Suddenly he remembered and ran back to Officer Anson's desk to pick up his backpack.

When he turned around, Erica was already running toward the station's parking lot. He followed her outside, hoping that his father was already gone.

*

Minutes after getting the last call from Hank Vincent, Lobec received another one from the contractor. He'd given explicit instructions to Vincent that he was merely to follow Murray Hamilton. Under no circumstances was he to jeopardize his discreet observation by letting the subject know he was being tailed.

'What is it, Mr Vincent?'

'Mr Barnett, I do believe I may have some further information that you may be interested in.'

'Yes?'

'Well, I know my job is to just follow this Hamilton guy, but I did catch the drift that you were looking for someone.'

'We may be,' Lobec said cautiously. 'Why do you ask?'

'Would this someone actually be two someones comprised of a couple in their twenties, the guy about six two with short dark hair and his girlfriend a tan five-eight brunette?'

Lobec didn't want to let the man know any more than he needed to, but he seemed to be leading somewhere. 'As a matter of fact, we would be interested in determining the location of two people who fit that description.'

'I'd say you just determined it. Thirty seconds ago, they walked up to Murray Hamilton's truck.'

Murray had still been in the parking lot when Erica ran out, ready to chase down the road after him if she had to. He was sitting in the driver's seat of his pickup, talking on a cell phone.

The truck was a huge red Chevy dually, with its distinctive rear fenders flared to cover a pair of wheels on each side. As she walked toward the pickup, she could overhear a heated conversation through the open driver's-side window. She made out Murray's gruff voice more clearly as she got closer.

'No, dammit, you tell him that if he doesn't have the concrete on-site by eight o'clock tomorrow morning, I'm going with another supplier. This is Dorman's last chance. I've had it up to my ears with that guy.'

Just then he caught Erica in his peripheral vision and waved for her to approach the truck. Papers were strewn across the front seat, and a laptop was on the dashboard.

'You got that, Charlie? No excuses. Listen, I gotta go. I'll talk to you later.'

'Mr Hamilton?' Erica said.

'Please, call me Murray,' he said, stepping out of the cab.

'Murray,' she said, looking in Kevin's direction. He was about twenty feet behind her, studying the traffic going by, obviously trying to ignore her and his father. She lowered her voice slightly. 'We really need the ride. It's very important that we get to a place on the north side of Dallas called SciSurplus by seven o'clock. With the weather looking the way it is' – she looked up at the darkening sky – 'I'm not sure we can make it anyway.'

'We can make it,' Murray said confidently, even though Erica hadn't told him where SciSurplus was.

She stole another glance at Kevin. 'I've convinced Kevin to let you help us, but he probably isn't going to be very talkative.'

Murray considered it for a moment, then said, 'I guess there's not much I can do about that. He's probably not going to listen to me, either, so you'd better tell him to get in. I'll just clean the seat off for y'all.'

As he stowed the papers and laptop in the large cargo area behind the front seat, Erica walked back to Kevin.

'He said he'll take us there.'

'Fantastic,' Kevin said, with no trace of humor.

'It'll take an hour to get there. I think you can handle it.'

'All right, but he can leave as soon as we're there. We'll call a cab and find another motel until we can get your car.'

'Don't you think it might be better if we stay at his—'

'No.'

There didn't seem to be a point in arguing, so Erica walked around the Chevy and climbed in, knowing that

Kevin would want to sit as far away from Murray as possible. She had figured that the truck would reek of smoke, but the cab smelled surprisingly fresh, with just a hint of masculine sweat. Kevin climbed onto the bench seat next to Erica and closed the door.

Murray pulled a map from the door pocket. 'So let's see where we're going.'

'You don't need that,' Kevin said, holding up his phone. 'I've got the directions on here.'

'But,' Murray continued, 'do you know the best way to get there in rush-hour traffic? You haven't driven in Dallas for years.'

'Fine,' Kevin said. 'It's just off I-635 at Abrams Road. Taking I-45 to Highway 75 should be the quickest way, but you probably know better.'

'Until we get downtown it is, but the Dallas North Tollway will be faster from that point on. I think I can swing a few dollars for such a special occasion.'

As Murray drove toward the interstate, an awkward hush settled over the cab. It was a couple of minutes before the silence was broken.

'Are you a student, too, Erica?' Murray asked.

'Yes,' she said, 'but not in chemistry. I'm a medical student.'

'A doctor! Well, bless your heart.'

Another two-minute silence until Kevin sniffed and said, 'What'd you do? Quit smoking?'

'As a matter of fact,' Murray said, 'it'll be three years this

December.' He lowered his voice slightly and spoke to Erica. 'I was a two-pack-a-day smoker since I was a teenager. Except for losing Nick's mother, it was the hardest thing I ever went through.'

Erica waited for Kevin to correct his name, but he was quiet.

'So, Nick,' Murray said, 'you been hunting in the last couple of years?'

Erica glanced at Kevin.

'Not since high school,' Kevin said.

'Hunting?' Erica said.

'I used to take Nick hunting. He was a good shot. Bagged deer and ducks, mostly.'

'I heard you used to go to the pistol range together,' Erica said.

'It was about the only thing he was good at when he was a teenager, that and those damn video games. No way was he going to win awards for sports.'

Kevin let out an exasperated sigh but said nothing.

Erica kept quiet, not wanting to push it, but Murray didn't need encouragement.

'I mean, if he'd started lifting weights like I told him to, he'd have made one hell of a linebacker. But he was never interested, didn't mind being overweight. That's why I was so surprised when I saw him today. First time he's looked normal in his whole life.'

This line of conversation was going nowhere good, so Erica tried to change the subject.

'So, Murray, do you live on this side of town?'

Outbound traffic on the other side of the freeway was jammed, but the direction they were headed moved along smoothly.

'No, we live out on the east side actually. Or I should say I do. Nick's mother died about three years ago.'

'I'm sorry,' Erica said.

'Three years may seem like a long time to you, since you're so young. But to me I remember her like it was yesterday.'

At that, Kevin let out a dismissive cluck.

'What was that for?' said Murray.

'You could barely remember your name at the time.'

'You mean the drinking? I gave that up when I found out your mother had pancreatic cancer.' Erica winced, knowing Kevin's mother probably didn't live long after the diagnosis. 'I didn't have time after that to sit around drinking beer. AA helped get me through.'

'Yeah, I know how busy you were,' Kevin said. 'You didn't even have time to call me and tell me she was sick. You knew for two months, and you didn't have the decency to tell me. I wouldn't have known except for that fluke call from the hospital.'

'I know your mother explained to you why I didn't tell you.'

'What? That she didn't want to disrupt my studies? Bull-shit! She said that to cover your ass.'

'Nick, I tried to come clean at the funeral, but you

wouldn't listen. My God, why would I want to keep some-thing like that from you? I begged her to let me tell you, but she never would have forgiven me. She thought your edu-cation was too important to screw up.'

'You thought it wasn't serious, and you thought I'd over-react when I found out. She told me she didn't even get chemotherapy, for God's sake.'

'And I thought you knew your mother better than that. She read up on pancreatic cancer. She didn't want to go through all that chemotherapy crap just to live another month. It wasn't her way.'

'Whatever you want to believe,' Kevin said.

'Boy, you *must* be in big trouble to let me help you.'

'To tell the truth,' Erica said, 'we are. Someone should probably know in case ... something happens.'

'Well, it can't be trouble with the police, seeing as how they just let you go. Do you kids owe money to someone?'

Kevin looked out the side window, brooding. Erica knew that the issues between him and Murray weren't going to be worked out on this short trip, so she let Kevin sulk.

'No, it's not that simple. Some men are after us. We think we know why, but we still don't know who. They want something that we have. The place you're taking us has equipment that will help us get out of this.'

'Men are after you? Then let me help you—'

'You've done all you need to,' Kevin said. 'When we get the laser, we'll be fine on our own.'

'Thank you for offering,' Erica said.

'Just trying to help,' Murray grumbled.

'You have. We really do appreciate it.'

Up ahead, a sign showed the exit for the Dallas North Tollway.

'How long until we get there?' Erica asked. Her watch read 6:22. Rain was just starting to spatter against the windshield.

'About half an hour if we don't hit any traffic. I'd go faster, but the toll road always has plenty of cops during rush hour. We'd never make it if we got stopped.'

Erica smiled. 'I've had enough of the police for one afternoon.'

Thirty minutes later, they were still ten minutes from SciSurplus. A wreck on the toll road had slowed traffic, but it could have been worse. At six fifty-eight they pulled into the almost deserted SciSurplus parking lot, located in the middle of a long dead-end street off Abrams Road. Similar squat warehouse-type buildings lined the street. Like SciSurplus, most of the parking lots allowed open access to the street, but a ten-foot-high chain-link fence separated the rear delivery lot from the front, as well as the SciSurplus lot from the one next to it.

Only one car remained in the lot, and Erica prayed that it was the sales rep's. Activity at the other buildings along the street was nonexistent.

Murray stopped the pickup in front of the building. It was pouring now. Kevin hopped out, scurried through the rain to the front alcove, and knocked on the door. A man in his early fifties opened it. Erica cracked the truck's window to listen.

'You the guy who called about the laser?' the man said.

Erica was relieved. It was the same wavering voice she'd spoken with this afternoon.

'Yes, and she's got your check,' he said, pointing toward the truck.

'I was about to give up on you two,' the sales rep said. 'I was just locking up the place when you knocked. Come on in.'

Kevin ran back to the truck and picked up his back-pack.

'All right,' he said to Murray. 'We can take it from here. Have a good life.' Kevin began to turn and walk away.

'Will you call me sometime . . . Kevin?' Murray asked.

Kevin turned back and stared at him. 'I don't know,' Kevin said, surprising Erica because it wasn't a flat refusal. Then he walked into SciSurplus.

'What are you going to do now?' Murray said.

'We can call a cab. We'll be all right now. Thanks for getting us here in time.'

'I was glad to do it. And I'd like to ask you to do something to return the favor.'

'Sure, anything.'

'Can you work on him? You know, get him to call me sometime?'

'I can try.'

'I know it'll be hard, but I want to get some things cleared up before ...' His voice trailed off.

Erica had seen that look before. It was the expression of someone who didn't want to convey bad news. Now she understood why Murray was so gaunt.

'Is there something you should be telling Kevin?'

Murray sighed. 'I didn't want to tell him this to shame him into calling me, but you're going to be a doctor. You get it. I have lung cancer. I guess I didn't give up cigarettes soon enough.'

'What's the prognosis?'

'It's stage four metastatic. I'm going to tell him sometime. Learned my lesson with his mother. But now's not the right time. Just try and get him to call me. I have my friends and the job, but he's my only family.'

Erica saw sincerity in his eyes.

'I'll do my best,' she said.

'I knew you would. You seem like a fine match for Nick. Don't let him lose you.'

'We're just friends.'

'No, you aren't. I can tell. It's in the way you take care of him. If you're not together now, it's just a matter of time.' He winked.

Erica felt herself blush. 'Good-bye, Murray.' She shook his hand and climbed out of the truck, smiling and waving to him as he drove back toward the freeway. Then she went to look for Kevin.

*

Like most Texas buildings during the summer, the Sci-Surplus offices were chilly from the air-conditioning. A receptionist's desk stood in the first room. Through the doorway, Erica could see a hall with open offices on either side. She headed to the only one that still had its light on.

When she entered the office, the sales rep nodded and then returned his attention to Kevin, who was examining a piece of equipment. It looked like a telescope, about three feet long and six inches in diameter, cradled in a receptacle. It was connected to a three-foot-high metal cube by six cords. They'd have to call for a minivan taxi to cart it away.

'Is he gone?' Kevin said without looking up.

'Yes. Is this what we need?'

The sales rep chimed in. 'I believe so. The model XXP-2400 blue-light laser. The most reliable in the industry.'

'Yeah, it looks okay,' Kevin said. 'Do you have the check?'

Erica pulled the cashier's check out of her purse and handed it to the sales rep, who examined it as closely as Kevin had studied the laser.

'Before you came, I made sure that your bank's West Coast office was still open. I'll just need to make a call to them and verify this.'

After the sales rep left the room, Kevin began boxing up the laser.

'Why'd you have to be so hard on him?'

'What are you talking about?'

'He seemed like he was trying to make amends with you.'

'Oh, you mean my dad.'

'Who else would I mean?'

'I don't know. I guess I've been bottling up everything for so long, it had to come out somehow.'

'Then you don't hate him?'

'I never *hated* him,' Kevin said.

'You could've fooled me.'

'Well, maybe I did. Now I just try not to think about him. But seeing him brings up all these memories. It's more painful than anything else.'

'Then you'll call him?'

'I don't know. We'll see. Right now we've got to call a cab.'

While Kevin finished repacking the laser tightly in its box, Erica called for a taxi. She gave the address to the cab company and hung up.

'They said it'll be twenty to thirty minutes,' she said as the sales rep returned with a large smile on his face.

'The check cleared with no problem,' he said. 'Is everything to your satisfaction?'

'Yes, thanks.'

The sales rep put on his coat and escorted them to the front door, helping Kevin carry the laser. They placed it gently on the cement outside the building under the awning to protect the laser from the rain, which was now coming down in sheets. The sales rep locked the door.

'I'm sorry I can't let you wait inside,' he said.

'That's all right,' Erica said. 'You've done enough already. Our cab will be here soon.'

The sales rep looked curious and then shrugged. The circumstances *were* rather strange, Erica thought. But money was money, and he climbed into his car without asking questions.

A minute after the sales rep drove away, a Ford turned off Abrams Road. Erica didn't pay much attention to it; it was probably an employee returning from dinner for some late-night work at one of the other offices on the block. She was about to ask Kevin where they were going to go when the Ford suddenly veered into the SciSurplus parking lot.

'Oh, no,' Kevin said almost under his breath. The next word was shouted: 'Run!'

Erica's stomach churned when she realized the reason for Kevin's terror. He grabbed her hand and sprinted toward the far end of the parking lot, the downpour drenching them almost immediately. The sedan drove straight at them as if it were going to run them down. Kevin and Erica tried angling away from the chain-link fence separating them from the parking lot next door, but the car skidded to a stop ten feet in front of them, blocking the only way out of the enclosed lot.

A smiling man with perfectly trimmed black hair lowered the passenger window. In the driver's seat sat a beefy younger man with a crew cut. Erica's focus left the black-haired man's grinning face when he lifted a pistol into view.

'Good afternoon, Mr Hamilton,' he said. 'You can't know how happy I am to see you.'

Kevin couldn't believe he was seeing them again. But his eyes weren't deceiving him. In the car before him were Barnett and Kaplan, the fake policemen from Houston.

'I can tell you're surprised, Mr Hamilton,' Barnett said. 'We will have plenty of time to get caught up.' His gaze shifted to Erica. 'And I'm glad I finally get to meet Miss Jensen. You know, you both had us worried for a while. The trick with your credit cards was quite ingenious. I'll be interested to find out whose idea that was. Now, please open the back door slowly and climb in.'

Kevin looked at Erica with dismay. If he tried something stupid, like charging them, he'd only get shot. He was about to tell Erica to do what the man said when an engine roared from his left.

He turned in time to see his dad's truck hurtling toward the Ford from behind. In the next second, as he and Erica scrambled to get out of the way, the pickup smashed into the sedan, collapsing its trunk and catapulting it into the chain-link fence twenty feet ahead. The Ford hit the fence straight on and careened backward, coming to rest five feet from the fence, its engine stalled.

They wasted no time running to the truck. Even with such a heavy impact, the truck's front bumper suffered only minor damage. Murray was already opening the passenger door.

'Hurry!' he yelled.

Erica got in first, then Kevin.

'Nick, the glove compartment! My gun!'

Kevin opened it and found a Glock 17 in a leather holster. He hesitated and then saw woozy movement behind the Ford's limp air bags. Quickly, he unsnapped the holster and drew the pistol. His father was heading toward the parking lot exit.

'Wait! The laser! Dad, we need to go back!' They wouldn't get a second chance at it. Once Barnett and Kaplan figured out why they were at SciSurplus, they'd stake out every lab supply company in the country.

Murray threw him a surprised glance. 'What are you talking about?'

'The company entrance. We have to go back.' When he saw that his dad wasn't turning the wheel, he yelled. 'Go back!'

'I must be nuts,' Murray said. He yanked the wheel around and headed back to the SciSurplus front door, where the boxed laser was still sitting. As they screeched to a halt, Kevin glanced back at the Ford. He could hear the engine beginning to crank. The passenger door opened and Barnett climbed out. Blood streamed down his face.

'Dad! Put the truck between that package and the car.'

Murray pulled the truck's front up to the awning, its driver's side facing the sedan, and Kevin jumped out.

'Everybody use the passenger door.'

Erica and Murray followed him. Just as they did, Kevin heard the crack of a pistol. He pulled the slide to make sure a round was chambered.

'Get down!' He rose above the truck's bed and fired three quick shots in the direction of the Ford to give them some cover.

'Erica, help Dad put the laser in the back of the cab. I'll try and slow them down.'

He scooted to the rear of the pickup and peered around to see Barnett getting back in the car. Even with the trunk shortened by half, it was backing up. The rear suspension had come through the impact unscathed. Kevin had to put the car out of commission. A second car chase in as many days – this time hobbled by a lumbering truck – might not turn out as well.

He propped his right wrist in his left hand and sighted carefully through the notch on the Glock's barrel, letting the old habits come back. Despite the rain, the Ford's right rear tire was sharply in focus through the Glock's sight. He gently squeezed the trigger.

The tire blew out with a satisfying pop, sending the Ford spinning to the right. Kevin quickly repeated the motions, but the car was now moving much more wildly. This time it took three shots to take out the left rear tire.

Kevin turned to see his dad and Erica maneuvering the box through the rear access door into the cab's storage area. They'd be finished any second.

He'd kept the Glock pointed at the sedan and now saw its passengers scrambling out the other side. He realized that he'd unconsciously kept count of his bullets, just as he used to. He'd fired seven. If his dad had a full magazine in there, there should be ten rounds left.

Out of the corner of his eye, he saw first his dad and then Erica crawl into the truck cab. Kevin fired four more rounds and bolted for the open door. He dove in, pulling the door shut behind him.

'Go!'

He stayed on the floor as his dad backed up ten feet and then slammed the truck into drive. Bullets plinked into the driver's side of the truck and then the rear as they raced toward the parking lot exit farthest from the gunmen.

The truck veered crazily to the left as it sped onto the road, its rear end sliding to the right on the slick pavement. Kevin sat up in the seat. He could see his dad fighting to bring the pickup under control, steering into the skid.

The truck's nose shifted back to the right, pointing them straight at a shallow drainage ditch running along the opposite side of the road. But Murray was no longer attempting to turn the wheel. His hands rested almost lazily on the bottom arc.

Trying to avoid plunging into the ditch head-on, Kevin reached across and knocked the wheel counterclockwise. The truck again veered to the left, all six tires skidding. The Chevy tilted sideways, sending mud spraying to their right, and came to a rest with its right tires at the bottom of the ditch.

Kevin was about to yell at his father when he saw Erica's bloodstained hand.

'He's been shot,' Erica said. 'Left side, no visible exit wound.'

'Dammit!' Kevin said, looking back toward the Sci-Surplus parking lot through the rear window. Barnett and Kaplan were running toward the truck, pistols held in front of them. *Bastards!* Kevin crawled on top of the laser and yanked open the rear sliding glass. He shifted the pistol to his left hand and fired.

The gunmen dove behind the low retaining wall separating the drainage ditch on the other side from the parking lot.

'Kevin!' Erica yelled. 'He's hemorrhaging. We need to get him to a hospital now!'

Blood dripped from the door handle.

'You take care of him,' Kevin said. 'I'll drive.'

He kept aim on the retaining wall as Erica dragged Murray to the right. She was straining mightily, but gravity was on her side.

'Okay!' she said when she was in position.

Kevin fired the last of the bullets and crawled over the driver's seat. The truck had stalled, so he had to waste precious seconds shifting it into park, turning the engine over, and shifting it back into drive. In the rearview mirror, he saw a head poking around the end of the retaining wall only a hundred feet behind them.

He slammed the accelerator down, but the rear wheel spun in the muddy ditch. The rear was a live axle; if one wheel was spinning, the other wouldn't turn. Kevin swore and looked down, praying he would find what he was looking for. At first he panicked, not seeing it. *He's got to have it!* Kevin thought. *Where the hell is the knob?* Then he realized he was looking for the wrong thing. It wasn't a shifter. It was a rocker switch on the console.

'Thank God,' he said, and engaged the four-wheel-drive system.

He pushed on the gas again. This time all six tires bit into the ground. The truck wanted to stay pointed straight ahead, so he had to force the wheel to the left. The truck bounced as it came out of the ditch and onto the pavement. Looking in the side mirror, Kevin floored it.

Barnett and Kaplan were racing toward them, lifting their pistols to fire.

'Down!' he yelled, and heard the hail of bullets hitting the truck bed's tailgate.

They continued accelerating and Kevin raised his head. The gunmen were now a hundred yards behind them. Their pistols were now at their sides: they knew that they were too far away to take an accurate shot. Kevin came to the T-intersection and turned right without stopping.

'I think we're okay now. You can sit up.' His father was slumped against Erica. He wasn't unconscious, as Kevin had earlier thought, but he was on the verge. Erica unbuttoned Murray's shirt, which was soaked in blood.

'How is he?' Kevin said.

'It's hard to tell. He's losing a lot of blood.'

'Should we stop and try to do something for him?' He began to slow down.

'No, I've got some pressure on it now. I couldn't apply it as well when I was crouched down. The most important thing is to get to a hospital as soon as we can. Do you know where one is?'

'I think so. I saw one on the way here. It can't be more than five minutes away.'

Kevin wasn't paying as much attention to the road as he should have been, and the truck hit a deep pothole. The impact jarred Murray awake.

'What? Where are we?'

'It's all right, Dad. You just rest. You've been shot. We're taking you to the hospital.'

'I surprise you?' Murray slurred the words.

'Yeah, you did. Thanks. Now just be quiet. Erica's taking care of you.'

'After I dropped you off, I saw a car that was near my house this afternoon. Looked like the guy was watching you. I decided to hide and see what happened. Guy left, but another car showed up.'

'You did real well, Murray,' Erica said. 'Don't try to talk.'

'Saw their guns. Saw them chase you. Had to do something. I . . . ' Suddenly he began to wheeze, trying to take in huge breaths with great difficulty.

'Dammit!' Erica said.

'What? What is it?'

'It sounds like a hemothorax.'

'English!'

'I can't tell for sure, but I think he's got a collapsed lung. It's okay, Murray. Just try to breathe normally. We'll make you feel better in a few minutes.'

'What do we do?' Kevin asked.

'We can't do anything here. Just get to the hospital.'

Murray continued to gulp for air, clutching his chest. As the truck sailed through a green light doing seventy, Kevin spotted a blue sign with a large capital *H*. Below it, another blue sign said '2 Miles.'

Dr Jake Hammersmith studied the admissions board in Community North's ER. In his new position as chief resident, he had to make the tough decisions. Maybe he could get Neurology to take the head trauma in room three. It was really a toss-up; the man was babbling about miniature robots living in his brain, but Psych had already said they wouldn't take him without insurance. Maybe if—

The ER door burst open and a man ran in, skidding to a halt in front of Jake. The man was covered in blood.

'I need help!'

'It'll be okay,' Jake said as he scanned his body for wounds. 'What happened to you?'

'Not me! My dad! He's outside! Come on!' The man ran toward the door, waving for Jake to follow.

'Peter!' Jake yelled. 'Get a gurney outside, stat!'

He ran outside with the man. Peter was right behind him with the gurney.

A huge dually was parked with the driver's side next to the ER door. 'What happened?' Jake said as he climbed into the truck.

A woman in the passenger seat had her arms around a tall man who was unconscious. Both were soaked with blood.

'At least one gunshot wound to his chest,' the woman said. 'He's lost over five hundred cc's of blood. Possible hemothorax.'

'How about you two?' Jake said.

'It's his blood,' she said. 'We're fine.'

Jake removed the bundle of torn clothing the woman had been using as a compress. He tore away the man's shirt and inspected the wound. 'You a doctor?' he asked the woman.

'Not yet. Just started my fourth year at South Texas.'

'What's your name?'

'Erica.' She pointed at her male companion. 'This is the patient's son, Kevin.'

Jake didn't waste time with formalities. 'Kevin, is he on any medications?'

'I don't know.'

'It's possible,' said Erica. 'He has lung cancer.'

Kevin's eyes widened. 'What? How do you know that?'

Before she could answer, Jake said, 'Kevin, what's your father's name?'

'Murray.'

Jake gently rubbed Murray's sternum. 'Murray, can you hear me?'

Murray nodded groggily, still struggling for air. Then he passed out again.

They carried Murray from the truck and placed him on the gurney. Jake kept pressure on the wound while they moved him.

In seconds, they burst into the trauma room. Kevin started to follow them in. Jake was about to ask him to leave when Erica pulled him outside.

'They'll take care of him,' he heard her say. 'We'll just be in the way.'

An orderly moved the portable curtained partition so the trauma scene couldn't be viewed from the hall. Still, Jake knew that Kevin and Erica would be able to hear the commotion.

'On my count!' he said. 'One, two, three!' They lifted Murray onto the trauma table, and the five doctors and nurses in the room were on him immediately, starting IVs, hooking him up to instruments, and intubating him.

Jake put the stethoscope to Murray's chest, listening for breath sounds. The med student was right about the hemothorax. Blood filling the chest cavity on Murray's left side wasn't letting his lung inflate.

'I need a chest tube,' Jake said. He kept talking while he inserted it. 'Get a surgeon down here and call in a perfusionist.'

Once Jake had the tube in, blood came out in a torrent.

'No pulse!' a nurse yelled.

'Damn!' Jake said. 'Start CPR. Give him an amp of epi. What's the ETA on that surgeon?'

For the next ten minutes they continued to attempt resuscitation, but Murray's cardiac rhythm deteriorated to a flat line. By the time the surgeon arrived, it was too late. After confirming no cardiac activity, no breathing, and that Murray's pupils were fixed and dilated, Jake called it. Time of death was seven forty-one P.M.

Jake threw his scrubs away and went to break the news to Murray's son. He was surprised to see that Kevin and Erica weren't still standing on the other side of the partition. He went to the waiting area, but they weren't there, either.

Jake stopped one of the orderlies.

'Did you see where this guy's son and the med student went?'

'They went outside five minutes ago.' The orderly pointed at the ER loading doors.

Jake walked out onto the ambulance platform, thinking that he would see them smoking a cigarette or crying on the truck's tailgate. He looked around for a minute, but the dually was gone. They were nowhere to be seen.

It wasn't until half an hour later, when the police came to investigate the shooting, that Jake realized Kevin and Erica weren't coming back.

TWENTY-FIVE

A homeless man with a beard long enough to make him an honorary member of ZZ Top stared at Kevin from his booth on the other side of the Burger King. Kevin glumly stared back. He didn't know if the guy was trying to intimidate him or was so out of it that he thought Kevin was merely a hallucination, but either way Kevin didn't care. In fact he might have been happy for the homeless man to take a swing at him. It would be a fitting way to end the day.

The only reason Kevin had been able to make it this far from the hospital was because of Erica. Kevin had completely seized up, paralyzed by the sudden death of his father. Erica, who was more accustomed to extreme situations, had gently guided him back to the truck and driven off before the police arrived at the hospital.

She drove to the nearest Target and put on a jacket that had been stuffed in the cargo area of Murray's pickup. On her it was just long enough to cover the bloodstains on her shirt and pants. While Kevin waited in the truck, she bought new clothes for them and cleaning supplies to wipe down the truck's seats.

She'd planted Kevin in the booth at the fast-food joint while she washed out the pickup's vinyl seats and rubber floor. A burger and fries cooled on the table in front of him, but Kevin had no appetite.

After fifteen minutes Erica came in wearing her new T-shirt and jeans and sat next to Kevin.

'The truck's as clean as I could get it,' she said. 'I put the trash bag in the Dumpster behind the restaurant.'

Kevin just nodded.

Erica looked at his untouched food. 'Kevin, you need to eat.' She took a couple of fries as encouragement.

Kevin could feel the tears welling up and tried to choke them back. 'Why did I make him go back for that laser? That was so stupid.'

She put her hand on his and grasped it tightly.

'No, it wasn't. You were just doing what you thought we had to do. It's not your fault.'

'But we could have gotten another one.'

'It all happened so fast. You couldn't have known it would end that way.'

Kevin held her eyes. 'And what if you had been shot? How would you feel about it then?'

'But I wasn't. I'm okay.'

'And my father's dead. Because of me.'

Suddenly the tears gushed out and Erica drew his head to

her shoulder, patting his hair as he wept onto her brand-new shirt.

After a minute he collected himself and used a napkin to dry his face.

'Why am I doing this?' Kevin asked her. 'I haven't talked to the man in three years, and now I'm crying like a baby.'

'Because he's your father and you should be proud of him. He's a hero, you know. He died saving us. If it weren't for him, who knows what would have happened?'

Kevin realized she was right. Murray had been following them to make sure they'd be all right, and when he saw the car chasing them, he took action. Maybe he really had changed since Kevin saw him last.

Erica continued to caress the back of his head. The soothing motion took him back years.

'My mother was great,' he said after a long pause. 'She's the one who always encouraged me to keep up with school, even when I was depressed about not being part of the in-crowd. Being chunky and smart wasn't a recipe for popularity. She told me that intelligence was nothing to be ashamed of, that it was the other kids who should be ashamed for not trying their hardest to do well.'

Erica nodded. 'I know what you mean.'

Kevin fiddled with his fries as he talked. 'No, you don't. A beautiful diver like you couldn't possibly have been unpopular.'

'Are you kidding? With girls it's even worse. Jealousy can be a dangerous thing in high school.'

'At least you had a supportive father. My father didn't think being smart was such an asset. One time he said, "Nick, if you don't stand up for yourself like a real man, it doesn't matter how smart you are. You're still a wimp, and wimps don't get any respect." I guess in his own macho way he was just trying to make me stronger, but it made me feel like a loser at the time. The only time I really liked him was when we went hunting together by ourselves. Around my mom or his friends, he always had to act tough, but when we were alone, he was actually kind of a funny guy.' Kevin looked up and saw that the homeless guy was gone. 'How did you know he had lung cancer?'

Erica took her hand away and flushed. 'I'm sorry you had to find out that way. Your father had just broken the news to me when he dropped us off. He told me that he wanted to patch things up with you. He didn't have much time left.'

'And now there's no time left.' Kevin went silent again.

'So, what do you want to do now?' Erica asked.

'What do you mean?'

'The police will want to know what happened to your dad.'

'That doesn't change anything. We still don't have any evidence except the notebook and a bunch of dead bodies in our wake, and I don't trust the local police to help us. Do you?'

Erica thought about it for a long time and then shook her head. 'Then we keep to the plan?'

Kevin nodded. 'We'll go to Virginia Tech and make our evidence.'

'Do you want me to drive?'

'No, I need something to do. You need to eat and get some rest.'

They trashed the cold food on the table and ordered a fresh meal before getting in the truck and heading out of Dallas.

TWENTY-SIX

White-gloved waiters flitted around the softly lit dining room of the Houston Grill like bees tending the hive. The private supper club was unusually crowded for a Monday evening due to an oil convention in town for the week. Executives found it a convenient way to elegantly entertain guests while charging it to their companies' tabs. Many of the groups would later head to one of the numerous gentlemen's clubs on Houston's west side for further expense-account entertainment. No one blinked at the irony of using 'gentlemen' in reference to the high-class strip joints.

Clayton Tarnwell found them not only useful for convincing business associates to partner with Tarnwell Mining and Chemical but also as a frequent source of his overnight companionship. The food in the supper club was adequate, but Tarnwell was not a gourmet. All he needed was a good steak, which he had finished twenty minutes ago. Since then, all he had been thinking about was getting on with the evening's entertainment.

Milton Senders, the only one Tarnwell had invited from his company, knew about Tarnwell's eagerness to get to the gentlemen's club, so he hadn't ordered dessert. Unfortunately, the three executives from Forrestal Chemical ate with infuriating leisure, lingering over Bananas Foster and their third bottle of Cristal.

Eight days, Tarnwell thought, suppressing a shudder. Eight days from now, Clayton Tarnwell would be making his speech to the stockholders of both Tarnwell Mining and Chemical and Forrestal to praise the synergy the two companies brought to the merger. A speech in which he would announce a revolutionary new process that would take advantage of each of the companies' skills and make billions of dollars. Of course, he wouldn't mention that it would also make him one of the wealthiest men on earth. His skin began to tingle at the thought, but it grew cold when he remembered that the Adamas process still wasn't in his possession.

'Gentleman,' Tarnwell said, 'shall we continue the celebration of the merger at Ladies Inc.' Dierdre and Pauline were supposed to be working tonight, and he recalled how willing and adept they had been the last time he'd had them over to his River Oaks mansion.

As Tarnwell got up from the table, all thought of the girls vanished. David Lobec stood waiting for him in the lobby. As usual, Lobec's expression conveyed nothing about the success or failure of the operation.

'Gentlemen, I have to take care of some other business

for a few minutes. Milton will escort you in my limo to our next destination. I'll meet you there as soon as I can.'

Tarnwell walked Senders and the three staggering Forrestal executives to the elevator. When they were safely in, Tarnwell headed for the stairwell, followed closely by Lobec.

When they got to the third floor, Lobec said, 'This way,' and went through the door to the parking garage.

After entering the relative security of Lobec's new Chevy, Tarnwell got his first close-up view of him. A thin bandage stretched across Lobec's nose, which was swollen, and an ugly blue and green bruise circled his left eye.

'What the hell happened to you?' Tarnwell said.

'Which club?'

'Ladies.'

Lobec put the car in gear and drove toward the exit. 'Mr Hamilton is proving more troublesome than we had anticipated.'

'The Hamilton kid's father did this to you?'

'Yes, but I was referring to Kevin Hamilton. He was in Dallas today.'

Tarnwell tensed. 'Tell me you got him.'

'I can't.'

'At least tell me you got Adamas.'

Lobec shook his head.

'Dammit! Did you even see Kevin Hamilton?'

'En route to Dallas, I received a call—'

'Answer my question.'

Lobec sighed. 'Yes, I did.'

'All right,' Tarnwell said. 'See how easy that was? Now tell me how you found him.'

Lobec stepped through the events leading up to his confrontation with the Hamiltons and the Jensen girl. When he got to the part about Murray Hamilton ramming the sedan, Tarnwell exploded.

'You mean you let them get away because the father snuck up on you from behind?'

Lobec looked slightly embarrassed, an expression Tarnwell had never before seen on him. He definitely liked it.

'Although I was concentrating on the two students, I should never have let that happen. It was raining heavily, and neither Mr Bern nor I could hear his truck approach. I realized only later that Hamilton must have spotted our Dallas operative as he drove past. Mr Vincent wasn't careful while following Hamilton. He was parked much too close to the building where we found Kevin Hamilton. I suppose the elder Hamilton spotted Mr Vincent and became suspicious because he was watching the SciSurplus building and speaking on his cell phone. After Mr Vincent left, he must have seen us pursue Kevin Hamilton and Erica Jensen across the parking lot.'

'You've taken care of that idiot Vincent, I assume.'

'Yes, I have,' Lobec said. Tarnwell knew that meant Vincent was dead.

'So then what?'

After detailing the shootout, Lobec said, 'Kevin Hamilton must have fired pistols before. He was very efficient in disabling our car.'

'Did you hit any of them?'

'Murray Hamilton was driving the pickup and was the easiest shot. I suspected at the time that we had hit him because the truck was steered into a ditch.'

'You checked the hospitals?'

'Of course. Murray Hamilton was brought to Community Hospital North and died of a gunshot wound to the chest today. The younger Hamilton and Miss Jensen left before they could be questioned by the police.'

'And we have no idea where they are now.' It was a statement rather than a question, because Lobec was here instead of out searching for them.

'That's correct.'

Tarnwell threw his hands up in disgust. 'Well, you just screwed this up all the way around, haven't you?'

'Failure is not something I prize.'

'What now?'

'We continue our operation as planned. We're monitoring their email accounts in case either of them try to send any messages. Their known friends are under surveillance, and we are still searching for other people with whom they may seek refuge. Tomorrow I'll call SciSurplus and determine why they were there.'

'Have you questioned their friends?'

'We have discreetly attempted to find out if they have

knowledge of Hamilton and Jensen's whereabouts, but we didn't want to raise undue suspicion. I believe that the lower profile we maintain, the better.'

'There's no time for that. Question all of them. I want you to see to it personally. Tell them you're the police and that their friends are wanted for questioning. I really don't care. But we need to find them now. If I don't have the formula for that process by next week, I'm ruined.'

'In the long run, it's best that we try to be as discreet as possible. If for some reason I am connected to them, it may prove difficult to explain, particularly since I am an employee of yours.'

'I said I don't care. That's your problem. We have to find them.'

Lobec continued to protest. 'In addition, our resources could be applied better elsewhere—'

Tarnwell banged on the Chevy's dashboard. 'Maybe I've been sending the wrong message to you, David. This is not a partnership. You do what I say. As my chief of security, you can give your advice – once. I'll listen. But I am the boss. I make the decisions. Is that perfectly clear?'

'Of course, Mr Tarnwell.' Lobec pulled to a stop inside the Ladies Inc. carport, which glittered with light. Porsches and Mercedes lined the most visible valet parking spots.

A doorman opened Tarnwell's door and welcomed him by name. Tarnwell didn't acknowledge the man or get out.

'David, I bought you because you produce results.

Therefore, I expect results. You're too much of a professional for all of these excuses. In fact, you should feel a little ashamed.'

Another embarrassed look from Lobec, but quickly controlled. Tarnwell smiled inwardly.

'You can be assured,' Lobec said, 'that Mr Hamilton and Adamas won't elude me again.'

Tarnwell clapped him on the shoulder. 'You sure know how to sweet-talk me.' He unfolded his towering frame from the Chevy and saw the posters advertising this week's main attraction, a nightly performance by Dierdre and Pauline. Even though Adamas wasn't in the bag, at least he had something to look forward to.

TWENTY-SEVEN

Erica turned up the truck's fan in an attempt to keep her attention on the interstate. Kevin dozed next to her, snoring softly.

Since leaving the Burger King, they'd been on the road toward Blacksburg, Virginia, to meet Ted Huang, stopping only to gas up the thirsty Chevy. Their precarious situation meant they had to take some risks. They considered ditching the truck and getting another vehicle, but stealing a car or hiring a rental would only make things worse.

They were also putting Ted and his wife Janice in harm's way, and that prospect was even scarier now that Murray was dead. But they had no choice: they needed his lab to create their proof. Erica hoped Kevin was right in thinking that Ted's real name being Xiao-ping would make him harder to locate if they found Ted among his email contacts. Ted had made a reservation for Erica and Kevin at a local motel under his name and picked up the key before they arrived. Erica tried to imagine the look they would have gotten from the desk clerk if she and Kevin had showed up to claim the reservation.

Most of the trip to Virginia had been spent with one of them driving while the other slept. Meals consisted of fast food dispensed from drive-through windows. Erica grew tired of the greasy fare, but like Kevin, she wanted to put as much mileage between them and Texas as they could.

As they crossed the border from Tennessee into Virginia, a sign on I-81 indicated only 105 miles to Roanoke. Kevin had told her earlier that Blacksburg was about forty-five minutes southwest of that. About an hour to go.

Erica looked at the fuel gauge. The thirty-gallon tank was still half full; she'd be able to drive the rest of the way there easily. She didn't want to disturb Kevin, who had taken the first driving shift to let her sleep.

A semi came up fast behind them, moving into the passing lane. The minivan in front of it wouldn't yield, and the truck blasted its air horn. Kevin jerked. In one fluid motion, he opened the glove compartment with his left hand and plucked the pistol from its interior with his right. He looked around wild-eyed, ready to shoot.

'What the hell?' he said.

'It's okay! It's just a truck. Put that away before you shoot me by mistake.'

He calmed almost immediately, sitting back in his seat. 'I was dreaming about Barnett.'

She patted his knee.

'I know. I have been too.'

'I want you to learn how to use this,' Kevin said.

Erica was taken aback. 'I couldn't—'

'Yes, you can. It's easy. If it gets jammed, you rack the slide back like this.' He demonstrated the maneuver, popping a bullet out onto the seat next to him. 'There's no safety, so all you have to do is pull the trigger.'

'Will you be careful with that!' Erica yelled. 'Just put it away.'

Kevin pushed a button with his thumb and the magazine dropped into his lap. It was the full spare his father had kept in the glove compartment. After reloading the ejected round, he inserted the magazine into the pistol grip and put the Glock back in the glove compartment.

'We'll do it tomorrow,' he said.

'No. I don't care if I never hold a gun. I've seen what they do every day for the past two months in the ER. If you want to keep it for protection, fine. But I'm not touching it.'

'Okay.' He rubbed his eyes. 'Where are we?'

'We just crossed the Virginia border. How do you feel?'

'Like my neck has been in a vise. Have you got any aspirin?'

'I think so. In my purse.'

Kevin rummaged around until he found a small bottle of Tylenol. 'Close enough,' he said, and washed down two tablets with the melted ice from a McDonald's cup.

During the drive they had spent more time napping than formulating their next steps. Erica hoped that some sleep had given Kevin enough time to decompress.

'What are we going to do with the diamond when it's finished?' she asked.

'I've been thinking about that. We can either go to the

FBI or the *Washington Post*. What do you think? Get our story out there or get help from the Feds?'

'We haven't had much luck with the police. But the *Post* isn't going to be able to protect us.'

'Especially because we still don't even know who's after us. By the time the full story comes out, we'll be dead. They'll start checking their facts and the next thing you know, Barnett and his buddy will be all over us.'

'So it sounds like the FBI is the place to go. Might as well go to FBI headquarters, since it's in D.C.'

'But we're going to get only one chance at this. Once we go to the authorities, these people are going to know where to find us. Our luck has been crappy so far, and I don't think it'll be getting any better.'

She digested the idea of going to the FBI. After several miles she said, 'There's only one problem with your plan. When we go to the FBI, how do we convince them that we're not holding a big piece of glass? I know I wouldn't be able to tell a real diamond just by looking at it.'

A smile curled the corner of Kevin's lip. 'You know what else is in Washington?'

'What?'

'The Smithsonian.'

Two hours later Kevin and Ted were carrying the laser through the fifth floor of Derring Hall at Virginia Tech. 'I wish I'd thought about getting the cart,' Ted said. 'I'm sweating like a pig on a StairMaster.'

'It's your fault,' Kevin said. 'I've never heard of anybody wearing a jacket in September.'

'I didn't, either, when I was in Texas. I'd never been north of Oklahoma until I came here. But they say it's like this all summer.'

Actually, Kevin had been grateful when they'd stepped out of the truck into the cool mountain air. Blacksburg was nestled two thousand feet above sea level in the Appalachians of southwest Virginia and so was spared from the blistering summer heat by the altitude. When they'd arrived at the university at ten o'clock, Kevin and Erica hadn't been out of the truck since Knoxville, Tennessee, where the temperature had been ninety-five, so they were surprised by the sixty-degree evening.

Since Ted and Janice would be leaving early the next morning, Kevin had wanted to start getting the lab set up before they left. At the very least, he had to make sure he had the correct keys for everything and that he knew any idio-syncrasies with the rest of the equipment. Erica, who'd been exhausted from driving, decided to turn in for the night.

'Are you sure you didn't get the extra-heavy model?' Ted asked with exaggerated huffing, but Kevin knew it was all an act. Ted, who was in great shape, had been the person who'd introduced him to jogging.

'Oh, quit your whining,' Kevin said. 'You told me it wasn't far.'

'It's not.' Ted slowed, pulling a key chain from his pocket. 'Here we are.'

They put down the package with the laser, and Ted unlocked a heavy steel door, then opened it and flicked on a light switch. He propped it open with his leg while they picked up the package.

Once inside, Kevin could see why Ted had been so excited about the assistant professor position at Virginia Tech. A huge laboratory housed an impressive array of shiny new equipment. At one end, a row of three high-powered workstations lined a wall. Normally, the wall and desks would be covered with all sorts of personal artifacts by the grad students using the lab, but except for a few scattered papers and instruction manuals, the surfaces were empty.

'Nice, huh?' Ted said. 'I told you they had only the best stuff here.'

'No students yet?'

'The semester just started. All my students are new, and I didn't want them around the lab until I got back. My paper was accepted at the conference before I ever got the job, but I wish I weren't going.'

'Chomping at the bit to get the lab set up?'

'That and the fact that Miami is playing here this weekend. Janice wants to visit her parents while we're in Minneapolis, so we're staying there until Sunday. Hey, the faculty gets discount season tickets to the football games. Since we won't be using ours, do you want them? It's been sold out for months.'

'I'll be too busy. Besides, I'm not sure Erica likes football.'

'I don't envy you, then.'

'About Erica?'

'No, I like her. You two would make a great couple, if you ever took a chance.'

'What? We're just friends. Besides, she's not interested in me.'

'How do you know?'

'Because I'm not her type and I'm in the process of destroying her life,' Kevin barked. When he realized how testily he'd responded, he backed off. 'Sorry. So, why don't you envy me?'

Ted shrugged and started unpacking the laser. 'I just meant that they're repaving part of the stadium lot. Cars are going to pack the commuter lots, one of which is right outside this building. By ten o'clock Saturday morning, there are going to be seventy-five thousand rabid Miami and Tech fans in this town.'

'Great. Just what we need.'

'Stay in here and you'll be fine. Now, let's take a little tour of my new domain.'

After twenty minutes, Kevin felt more comfortable in the lab. All of the equipment was familiar to him, and he could have the Adamas process set up by the end of the following day.

Ted handed Kevin a set of keys hanging from a black Harley-Davidson key chain. 'The first one is to my office. I'll show you where that is in a minute. The next one is to the deadbolt on the lab door. This one is to the cabinets over on the far end. And this one is the key to the building. They lock the front doors around six. The other keys are to rooms you won't need to get into.'

'Are you sure no one's going to ask me what I'm doing here?'

'Almost all the professors will be at the conference. The people who are left will just think I've got a new student. Say that if anybody asks.'

'I really appreciate you doing this, Ted.'

'No problem. Just be careful with my equipment.'

'I will. And one more thing: Don't mention to anyone that we're here. I mean no one.'

Ted squinted at him. 'Well, I already told Janice, but I'll let her know. Someday I expect you to tell me what this is all about.'

'I promise.'

Ted locked up the lab and led Kevin down the linoleum-lined hall to a beat-up wooden door. He opened it to reveal a cramped office sparsely furnished with two bookshelves and the requisite metal desk. Books were still piled in boxes on the floor, and papers overflowed the desk space not occupied by the computer. Kevin bit his lip and nodded his head.

'I know. It's not exactly what I was hoping for,' said Ted. 'But it hasn't got that homey touch yet. One thing I do have, though, is a view.'

Ted raised the venetian blinds. From directly below the window to about a hundred yards out stretched the commuter lot he had talked about. Past the expansive lot, however, was a splendid mountain vista brightly lit by the full moon and dotted by lights from scattered houses.

'Bet you have fun running here,' said Kevin.

'You know it. Even after two months, my legs are still killing me from all these hills.' Ted paused. 'You sure you don't want to go to the police?'

Kevin hadn't told Ted about the run-in with the police yesterday or the death of his father. He worried that it might make Ted rethink letting Kevin use the lab.

'No. At least not yet. When we're done in the lab.'

'How long will you need it?'

'Five days at most. We'll definitely be out of here by Sunday night.'

'No problem. Stay as long as you need. Anything else?'

Kevin reached into his pocket and extracted four hundred dollars. Erica had gotten a three-thousand-dollar Visa cash advance in Dallas since their credit card scheme had been blown.

'For the motel,' Kevin said.

Ted hesitated for an instant before he took the money.

'I will let you reimburse me this time because the money will come in handy. I was going to tell you in a couple of weeks anyway, but since you're here, I might as well tell you now. Janice is pregnant.'

Kevin's jaw dropped. Then he grabbed Ted's hand and shook it furiously.

'Congratulations, you stud! I knew you had it in you, but I didn't know it would be so soon. When are you due?'

'March,' Ted said with a huge smile.

Kevin clapped him on the shoulder. 'You have to let me buy you a beer on the way home.' He was too tired to get any work done tonight anyway.

Ted looked at his watch. 'Eleven o'clock in a college town? I think we can find a bar that's still open.'

TWENTY-EIGHT

In a neighborhood near the Rice University campus, Bern drove as Lobec searched for a house on Albans. It was one P.M. on Thursday, and Lobec knew he was running out of time. The longer Kevin Hamilton and Erica Jensen remained at large, the greater the chance that he would never be able to recover the Adamas notebook, that they would turn it over to the police or to someone else who might understand the significance of it. Then the chase would be over. Every minute was valuable, and he and Bern were wasting it by following his arrogant boss's order to question their friends.

Lobec had assumed that not even Tarnwell would be foolish enough to bet everything on an untested technology. But Tarnwell had proclaimed to the shareholders that he would announce a revolutionary new process next Tuesday, five days from now. Lobec knew the stakes. If Tarnwell didn't have the invention in hand at the time of the press conference, the stock would plummet, leaving him with no way to service the debt on the new company. It was all or nothing.

Despite Tarnwell's orders, Lobec had taken time to find out why Murray Hamilton had left his son and Erica at SciSurplus. He had called the sales representative under his detective's guise. Since there had been nothing illegal about the sale, the man readily told Lobec that Erica Jensen had purchased a laser at well above list price.

The reason for the purchase was immediately obvious to Lobec. They had obtained the laser in order to repeat the Adamas experiment, to produce enough diamond for evidence. It was also possible that Kevin didn't even believe that the process worked or that he was planning to claim the process for himself. All of which led to the conclusion that they would acquire the rest of the equipment necessary and find somewhere to run the experiment. If Lobec found that place, he would find them.

But instead of looking for that location as they should, his men were staking out various locations throughout the city or maintaining phone taps, and the rest of the team – Lobec and Bern included – were interviewing anyone in Houston connected with Kevin or Erica. At least they'd made some good use of the time. The hospital confirmed that Erica Jensen had called the school on Tuesday to tell them she would not be in the rest of the week, again giving the excuse that she had a death in the family.

They'd also learned from the transaction for the laser that Erica had received a sizable insurance payout and used it to cut a check for the purchase. Lobec had instructed

Hornung to report Murray Hamilton's pickup truck stolen, but he didn't have much faith in the ruse working twice. His quarry could be anywhere in the contiguous United States by now.

'Here it is,' said Lobec, spotting the home's number through the branches of an ash tree.

Bern stopped the car in front of the house. They got out and prepared their identification as they walked toward the door. Lobec carefully touched his throbbing nose. During their interviews no one had mentioned his injuries, but he did observe several curious looks.

After two rings, the door opened to reveal a six-foot-tall black man.

'Are you Nigel Hudson?' asked Lobec.

'Yes,' the man said warily.

Lobec flipped open his wallet. 'My name is Detective Barnett, and this is my partner, Detective Kaplan. May we have a few words with you?'

'About what?'

'We need to discuss a friend of yours. His name is Kevin Hamilton.'

Hudson eyed Lobec and Bern suspiciously. 'All right,' he said after the hesitation. 'Come on in.'

Good. Perhaps this interview would be more productive. If Lobec worded his questions correctly, he would know if this man had communicated recently with Kevin. All he needed was one clue. Then he would have them.

*

At one P.M. on Thursday, Erica drove Murray's dually down Price's Fork Road away from Virginia Tech. Kevin was too busy in the lab to join her.

The day before, she and Kevin had made two phone calls. The first had been to the FBI to make an appointment with an agent for next week. The excuse they came up with was that they had some information they wanted to give about an ongoing case. When the agent, a man named Frederick Sutter, had asked what case, Kevin wouldn't say. He picked the earliest time Sutter would give him, which was nine o'clock Monday morning. That gave them plenty of time; Kevin thought he would be done even sooner than Sunday.

The second call had been to the Smithsonian. The request was unusual, so Kevin thought Erica should make it. He said she had a way with people. Although it took some convincing, the man she talked to, Quincy Downs, agreed to meet with them.

The rest of the day had been mundane, consisting primarily of moving equipment and adjusting settings per Kevin's direction. Bench research had never interested her, and the stuffy lab hadn't changed her mind. Eating greasy take-out pizza all day didn't help the situation. Once the setup was finished and Kevin didn't need her help anymore, she took the opportunity to find some food that was not made primarily of saturated fats. The obvious solution was the immense grocery store now in front of her. It was one of the megastores that had a pharmacy, a full-service bank, a deli, a Starbucks, and anything else they could cram in.

The lot was packed with students just returned for the fall semester, loading up on supplies. Erica had to park on the fringe, but it didn't bother her. She was looking forward to the walk, amazed that on a sunny September day the temperature hadn't been higher than seventy-five degrees. Maybe later she'd stroll around the campus.

When she saw the other students entering and leaving the store, she felt a pang of guilt for neglecting her own studies. But there was nothing she could do. At least this mess would all be over on Monday.

Erica followed two teenage girls into the store. She grabbed one of the shopping baskets piled at the front and dropped her purse into it. At the entrance to the produce section, a woman was holding a tray with bits of food. The teenagers each took a piece and popped them into their mouths.

The saleswoman held the tray up for Erica as she passed. 'Would you like to try a sample of NYC brand coffee cake?' Next to the woman was a stack of boxes to help her close the deal.

Though Erica was starving, she said, 'No, thanks,' and kept walking. Healthier foods were calling to her from the produce section.

A salad was her top priority, so she stopped at the salad bar and loaded up a couple of containers with fresh veggies. She selected a few apples and oranges, then went in search of the deli to peruse their selection of pastas.

As she rounded the corner into the grocery store's back

row, she saw the two teenagers again, this time standing by a dispenser containing cold drinks. They were facing away from Erica. Both were short and thin, one with dark, curly hair, the other with a blond crop. The dark-haired girl seemed to be comforting the blonde. As Erica got closer, she could hear what they were saying.

'Tory?' the dark-haired girl said in a voice that was tinged with fear. 'What's the matter?'

Tory's head was bowed and she seemed to be clutching her throat. At first Erica thought the girl was choking. But then Tory turned around, and Erica knew that the situation was much worse.

Tory's face was bright red, and her lips, cheeks, and neck were grossly swollen. Her eyes were beginning to shut because of the swelling. Tory responded with a mewling hiss as she gasped for breath through her constricting throat. It was a textbook case of anaphylaxis. If nothing was done in the next few minutes to halt the severe allergic reaction, Tory would go into shock and die.

When the dark-haired girl saw Tory's face, she screamed. A dozen eyes turned in the teenagers' direction, and without thinking, Erica ran over to them, as did a young man carrying a six-pack of Budweiser.

'What's wrong with her?' the man asked, holding the beer as if he wasn't sure if he should put it down.

'I don't know,' said the dark-haired teenager. 'She was fine just a minute ago.'

'She's having an allergic reaction,' Erica said, coming to

a stop in front of the girls and dropping her hand basket to the ground.

'You,' she said, pointing at the man, 'call 911 and tell them it's an emergency.' He nodded and walked off still cradling the cans in one hand and fishing a cell phone out of his pocket with the other.

She turned back to the teenagers. 'Is she allergic to something in that cake you just ate?' she said to the dark-haired girl.

'Tory asked about nuts, but the woman said there weren't any.'

Erica put one hand on Tory's shoulder and lifted her head. The swelling was spreading rapidly. Tory's face was now the color of one of the ripe tomatoes in Erica's basket.

Severe allergies to nuts were fairly common; a hundred people in the United States die from them every year. And sometimes the allergic person doesn't even have to eat the nuts themselves. The cake might have been baked with a nut oil, which would produce the same effect.

Tory lunged forward, panicking because she couldn't breathe. She stumbled over Erica's basket, scattering the fruit and the contents of her purse across the floor.

Erica clasped Tory's shoulders hard, knowing the only way to save her was to give her the dose of epinephrine that people with severe allergies like hers were supposed to carry.

'Tory, you're having an allergic reaction. I'm going to help you, but you need to calm down.' Tory shook her head but didn't resist.

'What's your name?' Erica said to the dark-haired girl as she held on to Tory.

'Maggie.'

'Maggie, I'm Erica. I need you to help me get Tory lying down. If she passes out and collapses, she might injure herself.'

'Are you a doctor?' Maggie said.

'Yes,' Erica said. She needed Maggie to have the automatic faith people put into a doctor's authority. 'Now grab her other side.'

Gently, they moved Tory to the floor. Her breath was now coming in shallow, ragged gasps.

'Where's her EpiPen?' Erica said, searching Tory's pockets.

Maggie looked at her, puzzled. 'Her what?'

'Her epinephrine. With her allergy, she should always be carrying it.'

'I don't—'

'Damn!' Erica said. All she found in Tory's pockets were her driver's license and seven dollars in cash. She wasn't surprised: both of the severe allergic reactions she'd seen in the ER resulted from the patients not carrying their epi kits.

'Did they call the paramedics?' Erica yelled.

'They're on their way,' someone said.

'How long?'

'They didn't say. Maybe five minutes?' The response was more question than answer.

The nearest EMS unit could be all the way across town for all she knew. She had to do something, otherwise Tory would asphyxiate in minutes. Even if she didn't, it wouldn't take long for the girl to sustain irreversible brain damage. In an emergency room, a tracheotomy might have been an option, but under these conditions and with her lack of experience, she could just as easily kill the girl. Erica's only choice was to stop the swelling before it got any worse.

By now more of the students had gathered around the scene. An obese man wearing a tie and name tag shouldered some of them aside.

'What's going on here?' he said in a gruff voice.

'Are you the manager?' Erica said.

'Yes. Is the kid all right?'

'No, she's about to go into shock.'

'Who are you?'

'I'm a doctor,' Erica said. 'Is the pharmacy open?'

'Sure,' the manager replied.

'Good. Go there and ask the pharmacist for an adult epi kit.'

'A what?' the manager said, obviously confused.

'A kit of epinephrine for ..' It was going to take too long to explain. The manager still had a bewildered look on his face, and if he brought back the wrong thing, it might be too late.

'Never mind,' Erica said. 'Where's the pharmacy?'

The manager pointed at the far end of the store.

'Maggie,' Erica said. 'Don't let Tory get up. Keep her still. I'll be back in a minute.'

'Where are you going?'

'I'm going to get some medicine.' She stood and faced the manager.

'Come with me,' she said, and sprinted down the aisle toward the pharmacy.

Ten seconds later she skidded to a stop at the pharmacy counter. A man in his early thirties was sorting pills near the back. When she hit the counter, he looked up, startled.

'I need ... an epi kit,' Erica said, gasping for breath, more from the stress than the exertion.

For a moment the man was taken aback. Then he said calmly, 'And your name?'

'No,' Erica said. 'This isn't a prescription.' As she said it, the manager caught up with her at the counter, huffing like he could have a heart attack any minute.

His eyes on the manager, the pharmacist said, 'Epinephrine is not an over-the-counter drug. I need a prescription—'

'Listen,' she said. 'A girl on the other side of the store had a severe allergic reaction to that coffee cake the woman was serving by the registers. If she doesn't get epinephrine in the next few minutes, she will die.' She glanced at the manager. 'Do you understand?'

The manager's eyes widened at the implications of a huge lawsuit. He looked at the pharmacist. 'I saw the kid. Her face was swollen like a balloon. This woman is a doctor. Get her whatever she needs right now.'

The pharmacist nodded. He hurried to the last shelf on the right and grabbed a box near the top. He gave it to Erica, who ripped open the package and withdrew a small syringe.

To the manager, she said, 'Go meet the paramedics outside so you can show them where we are.'

Without waiting for a response, she ran to Tory.

Erica approached the crowd and shoved two people aside. 'Everybody back up!' she yelled. The dozen people surrounding her complied.

Erica kneeled next to the supine teenager. By now Tory was no longer moving, and her breathing was reduced to shallow rasps. In seconds her throat would be completely constricted.

Maggie was now almost hysterical. 'Erica, do something, please! She's dying!'

'She's not going to die,' Erica said as calmly as possible. She jabbed the syringe's needle into Tory's left quadriceps and the medicine injected automatically. The epinephrine would quickly flow from the thigh muscle into the femoral vein and then straight to the heart. She withdrew the needle and pushed it against the floor to safely stow it in the injector.

After a few seconds of rubbing the injection site, the only thing Erica could do was tilt Tory's head back to clear the airway as much as possible. Cradling Tory's neck with her left hand, Erica gently pushed her forehead back. She leaned down and put her ear next to Tory's mouth. It was only the faintest of puffs, but she was still breathing. Erica hoped the epi had come soon enough.

Erica looked into Maggie's tearful eyes. 'She's going to be all right,' she said confidently, even though she wasn't sure. But the words had the desired effect. Maggie nodded and tried to smile.

Two minutes later she heard sirens blaring and then the honk of a piercing air horn. They were silenced as an EMS unit squealed to a stop in front of the store. The paramedics would be in here any second. Then another siren grew louder. The police, Erica thought with alarm. When they got here, they would certainly want a statement from Erica, including her name. She had to leave.

Her belongings were still scattered across the floor. She hurriedly scooped them up and stuffed them back in her purse. As she finished, the crowd parted and two paramedics holding emergency boxes pushed their way through.

Erica got up and spoke to one of them while he opened the box on the floor. 'Anaphylactic reaction. Severe throat constriction causing stridor. A dose of epi was administered via left quad.'

Before he could ask any questions, she ducked past the crowd. As she ran down the aisle, she could hear shouts behind her. 'Hey! Who was that? Come back!'

At the cash registers, she slowed to a walk when she saw a policeman. He was talking to the store manager, who had his back to Erica. She averted her face to avoid being recognized. As inconspicuously as possible, she turned away as the policeman followed the manager toward the rear of the store. She continued walking with her purse clenched tightly to her stomach and made it through the store's front door without being noticed. Outside, clusters of people were talking and pointing at the emergency vehicles. No one looked at her. Feeling as if she was about to hyperventilate, Erica ran.

TWENTY-NINE

Kevin gnawed on a piece of leftover pizza as he studied the figures on the computer screen in front of him. The graph of the spectroscopic analysis showed an impurity in the carbon of less than 0.001 percent, primarily in the form of methane and other organic molecules. He wasn't surprised that there was some impurity. Instead of requiring a pure vacuum, the process produced the greatest yield when performed in a vapor of hydrogen gas. Still, to the naked eye, or even under a high-powered loupe, no flaws in the material would be evident. Just as the notebook had promised, the Adamas process produced a clear, flawless diamond.

Kevin shook his head, still in a mild state of disbelief that it really worked. He walked over to the test chamber and stared through the door's porthole. The specimen sat in the middle of the chamber, imperceptibly acquiring new coatings of diamond every time the laser's light flashed. The coatings were fused to the previous layer so that the lattice retained its continuity and formed a single crystal, yielding the strength of the world's hardest known substance.

Kevin's contacts were bothering him, as they often did when he stayed up late. He rubbed his eyes and looked at his watch. Almost half past midnight.

'Ready for bed?'

Kevin whipped around, startled by the voice behind him. Erica's head peeked past the lab's open door.

'Hey, stranger. I didn't hear you. What are you doing here?'

Erica came in the rest of the way and closed the door behind her.

'What kind of greeting is that when I came all the way over here to find out how you were doing?'

'Sorry. Been a long day.'

'I know what you mean.' Erica walked over to peer into the chamber. When she saw the specimen, she gasped and then chuckled. 'So that's how we're going to prove it's an artificial diamond.'

'It was the only thing I could come up with.'

'I like it,' Erica said. 'How much do we have?' She pulled up a stool and sat next to him.

'Not as much as I'd hoped. It looks like we might get forty grams by Sunday.'

'How many carats is that?'

'I was wondering that myself, so I looked it up on the Web. One carat equals two hundred milligrams.'

After the slightest pause for a calculation, Erica exclaimed, 'That's two hundred carats!'

'Yeah. I figured it would be enough to prove our point.'

'Jennifer Lopez might not be impressed.'

'She wasn't. I've already got her order for a three-hundred-carat diamond.'

Erica nodded. 'I might have known. She likes her bling.'

Kevin smiled, then couldn't stifle a yawn.

'You need to get some rest,' Erica said. 'You've barely slept the last two nights.'

'I'm all right. What did you do all afternoon?'

'The reason I'm here is that I couldn't sleep. Something happened today. I wasn't going to tell you because I knew it would upset you, but I thought you should know.'

'What?' Kevin's mind raced through a number of possibilities, all bad.

'Today, when I went to the store, there was an emergency. A girl, a teenager, had a reaction to something she ate.'

'And?'

'She was severely allergic and went into anaphylactic shock.'

'Wow! Did she live? Is she going to be okay?'

'I'm not sure, but I think so.'

'That's good ... Wait a minute. What does this have to do with you?'

Erica took a deep breath. 'I was right there when it happened. By the time anyone noticed, she couldn't breathe. I guess my instincts took over, otherwise she would have died right in front of me. I had to help. She was suffocating.'

'What did you do?'

She pulled up a Web site on the lab's computer. The

banner said *Roanoke Times*. She scrolled down to a story on the bottom of the page.

Kevin read the story twice before he looked up.

'Don't tell me the unidentified woman was you.'

Erica nodded.

'Are you insane? What were you trying to prove?'

'If I had waited until the paramedics arrived, she could have become brain-damaged or even died.'

'But the police. They were there—'

Erica shook her head. 'I got away before they could talk to me.'

'Do you realize the risk you took?' Kevin said, his voice rising.

'Like I said, it didn't seem like I had a choice. It all happened pretty fast.'

'Erica, we have been just one step ahead of these ... psychos, whoever they are. What if the police had taken you in?' Kevin was off the stool now, pacing.

'What would you have wanted me to do? Let that girl die?'

'Don't be ridiculous. Of course not.'

'Oh, so I'm the one being ridiculous?'

'You could have waited.'

'No, I couldn't.'

'Are you sure? How do you know? You're not a doctor yet.'

'I've spent the last two months in the ER. It was a judgment call. I made it. That's my profession. Deal with it.'

'Your heroics have lousy timing.'

'I'm sorry emergencies aren't more convenient for you.' Erica jumped to her feet and picked up her purse.

Kevin grabbed her shoulders and shouted at her, 'Don't you get it? If Barnett finds you, he'll kill you. I'm not going to let you die because of me.'

'Why not?' Erica yelled back.

'Because I'm in love with you!'

Erica stared at him, and Kevin suddenly realized what he'd said. Before he could backtrack, Erica pulled Kevin toward her in a rush and kissed him deeply. Kevin pressed himself to her and inhaled the light scent of fresh soap from her skin, cradling her head in one palm and holding her to him with the other.

After what seemed like an hour but had to have been only a few seconds, Kevin released her and held her hands.

'Why didn't you tell me that before?' Erica asked.

'Recent events haven't exactly lent themselves to a romantic moment.'

'I meant, why didn't you tell me before last week? I thought you just wanted to be friends.'

'I don't know. Because I didn't think I was your type. I can't compete with a guy like Luke.'

'Why not? I've always thought you were cute.'

'Exactly. And he's a doctor who looks like he could be on the cover of GQ. He's every woman's dream. Whenever I stand next to him, I feel like the "before" image for a plastic surgery ad.'

'Luke was also a jerk. Charming, yes, but in the same way an unneutered Labrador retriever is charming. He's every woman's dream for about a month. I've always been stupid enough to go for men like him. You, on the other hand, are a solid guy. To tell you the truth, I used to think that meant you were predictable.'

'And I'm not?'

Erica let out a throaty laugh.

'Nicholas Kevin Hamilton,' she said, 'after the past week, I can absolutely confirm that you are about as unpredictable as it gets.'

She suddenly planted another long kiss on him.

When she pulled away, Kevin grinned. 'So are you.'

Erica looked at the equipment. 'Can this stuff stay un-attended for an hour or so?' Then she looked back at him with a mischievous smile.

Kevin punched a large red EMERGENCY STOP button. The whine of the machinery ground to a halt, and just to be even more unpredictable, this time *he* was the one to kiss *her*.

THIRTY

'STU Financial Aid and Student Affairs, this is Teri, may I help you?' Teri Linley recited the line with the boredom of innumerable repetitions.

The answering voice spoke in a dreadful southern drawl. She sounded young, maybe a teenager. 'Hi, my name's Maggie Burleson. I was told you were the right person to talk to.'

'What can I help you with?' Teri glanced at the wall clock. Only two hours until the weekend. Friday afternoons were always the slowest. She hoped it wouldn't take as long to get out of here as last Friday did.

'Yesterday, a friend of mine had an emergency. She ate some cake with peanut oil in it and had an allergic reaction.'

'So, why are you calling this office?'

'Because this is who they told me to call to find a student. One of the people at the emergency was a South Texas student. Her name is Erica Jensen.'

Teri perked up at the name. It was one of the two she'd been told to be on the alert for. That priggish black-haired guy had told her she'd get a two-hundred-dollar reward if she could tell him where Erica Jensen was.

'Go on, Ms. Burleson.' Two hundred dollars would make the weekend a lot more fun. 'You said you saw Erica Jensen?'

'Yeah. I was wondering if you could tell me her number.'

'We're not allowed to give out that information for confidentiality reasons. Where did you say you were?'

'It . . . the emergency happened in Blacksburg.'

Blacksburg? Where the hell is that? 'Blacksburg, Texas?'

'No, Blacksburg, Virginia. Uh, I really need to talk to her.'

Teri decided to take another approach. 'Maggie, I shouldn't be doing this, but Erica is a friend of mine. If you tell me the message, I'll make sure she gets it and calls you back.'

The line was silent for a few seconds. 'She's a friend of yours?'

'We're in med school together. I just work here for extra money.' When Maggie hesitated, Teri said, 'In fact, I'm going to see Erica when she gets back to Houston. I forgot that she was visiting her relatives in Virginia.'

'All right,' Maggie said, the apprehension apparent in her voice. 'You should be proud of Erica. She saved my friend's life yesterday. The doctors at the hospital said Tory, my friend, might have died if Erica hadn't given her epinephrine.' She said the word slowly, trying to pronounce it properly.

'Oh, my God! Is Erica with you now?' Teri impressed herself at how well she was doing. She was definitely earning that two hundred dollars.

'No, and that's why I was calling. Erica ran off just as the paramedics and police got there. Just after she left, I found her medical student badge. It must have fallen out when Tory knocked her purse over. I put it in my pocket without telling anyone. I've been wondering all day whether I should tell them or not, but I'm worried she might get in trouble for saying she was a doctor but she's only a med student. That's why I'm trying to call her, to see if I can tell the police.'

'No!' Teri said, too forcefully. She lowered her voice. 'No, you did the right thing. I'll give Erica the message. She probably just wanted her privacy.'

'That's what I thought.'

'All student IDs have an address printed on the back. Just mail it there. She'll get it back. Thank you very much for your help, Maggie.'

'I was pretty scared yesterday, but Erica helped me a lot. I'm glad I'm able to help her.'

On Fridays at six fifteen, the parking garage Lobec had chosen for the meet was about as empty as it ever got. He motioned for Bern to wait in the car while he got out to meet with Teri Linley. As he expected, she wasn't going to give the information over the phone when two hundred dollars was on the line.

None of the friends, including Nigel Hudson, had provided any useful info. This was Lobec's best chance to track down Kevin and Erica. Through rush-hour traffic, it had taken almost an hour to get across Houston after her phone call. Teri's Toyota was parked in front of them at the deserted end of the garage's fourth level.

A big-haired girl in her twenties got out of the hatchback and approached him. On the other side, a young man opened the door and stood. He wore a bodybuilder's tank top and had the physique to match it. Obviously he was the boyfriend along for protection. He puffed up to his full six-foot height and casually leaned on the open door.

'Do you have the money?' she said.

Lobec pulled two hundreds out of his pocket and handed the bills over to her. 'Where was she sighted?'

'It'll cost you another two hundred.'

Lobec didn't blink. 'The offered price was two hundred. I suggest you take it.'

'It sounded on the phone like you really want this information, and by the looks of you, you can afford it. Four hundred or you don't get it.' She held out her hand for the money.

Without moving his eyes from hers, Lobec grabbed her hand like a viper snatching its prey and pulled her toward him, twisting her arm back with his right hand. She gasped but was too surprised to scream.

'You'll tell me now for two hundred or you'll tell me for nothing after I've broken your arm. Which shall it be?'

Out of his peripheral vision, Lobec saw the bodybuilder move in and throw a punch at his head. He ducked under it and slammed his left fist into the man's crotch in the same movement. Teri screamed. As the man doubled over, Lobec threw his elbow into the amateur's face. Teeth cracked with the impact. The man groaned and vomited, spitting up blood.

Bern was still sitting in the car, smiling. According to procedure, Bern was to assist only if Lobec's attacker drew a weapon.

Lobec grabbed the woman's face. 'Now, stop screaming.'

The woman, wide-eyed at her groaning boyfriend lying on the ground, exhaled in jittery sobs.

'Good. Unfortunately, I will now have to repeat myself. Where was she sighted?'

'B-B-Blacksburg, Virginia. Please, God, don't hurt me.'

'You can help matters by answering my questions. Why was she there?'

Teri's words came out in a rush. 'A girl said Erica Jensen saved her friend's life and ran off before she gave her name to the police or anyone else. The girl found her South Texas ID. It had Erica's name on it. That's all I know, I swear!'

'When?'

'Yesterday. She didn't say what time.'

'And you're very sure it was Blacksburg, Virginia?'

'Yes, yes!'

'Thank you,' Lobec said, releasing her arm, satisfied that she was telling the truth. 'I hope you've learned a valuable lesson in negotiation. Never bargain when you don't have the advantage.'

As Bern drove out of the garage, Lobec opened his cell phone and dialed.

'We going to Blacksburg?' Bern asked.

'No, I am calling Mitch Hornung.'

'What for? The girl just said she was in Blacksburg.'

'Exactly. She *was* in Blacksburg. Yesterday. For any number of possible reasons. She and Hamilton could easily have been passing through on their way to another location. Before we go on another wild-goose chase, I want to find out if there is any reason they would be there.'

After five rings, the line clicked over to Hornung's voice mail. Lobec left him a message with what he needed.

During the next three hours, Bern and Lobec tried calling the people they had already met with for information about anyone Kevin might know in Blacksburg. Relatives, friends, schoolmates from grade school on up, anyone Erica and Kevin had ever been in contact with. The few people who were home on a Friday night were useless. Finally, Hornung called back. Lobec was livid. Though he was the best hacker money could buy, Hornung's lack of dependability had always been a problem.

'Mr Hornung, I gave specific instructions that you were to be on call at all times until this matter was resolved.'

'Sorry, man. I was with Monica.' He said it as if it were supposed to mean something to Lobec.

'Mr Bern and I will be at your computer in fifteen minutes. Meet us there.'

'But Monica—'

'Do as I say, Mr Hornung. I am not always this pleasant.'

When Hornung arrived at his office exactly fifteen minutes later, Lobec explained the problem.

'Man, I don't know. This could take a while.' Hornung looked at the screen in front of him. 'Says here that Blacksburg has a population of 22,921, but including all the students at Virginia Tech and the people in the surrounding area, we're talking over 100,000.'

'I didn't say it would be easy,' said Lobec. 'But I could go to this town and never find them if I don't know where to look.'

'So you're saying you want me to compare every name in that town and the university's database to the name of every person either of these two have ever met and see if I get a match?'

'That is the gist of it.'

'These guys must have screwed Tarnwell out of some serious cash.'

'More than even *you* have,' Lobec whispered into Hornung's ear. Hornung smiled at Lobec, but when he saw Lobec was serious, his smile faltered. He quickly turned to the computer and began tapping on the keyboard.

*

Given the task, Lobec wasn't expecting an answer until well into the next day. But Hornung was good, which was why Tarnwell let him get away with skimming a few measly thousand each month. At three in the morning, he said, 'Bingo.'

Lobec got up from the couch where he was lightly dozing and went over to Hornung's computer. Bern followed from the chair he was sleeping on. 'You have something?' Lobec said.

'I got lucky. The only reason I found it so quickly was because the name was a little odd. Xiao-ping Huang. Both Hamilton and Jensen are getting graduate degrees, so I thought maybe one of them knew a student at Virginia Tech. Then I broadened the search to include professors. Guess where Xiao-ping Huang, the new assistant professor in chemistry, got his Ph.D.'

'South Texas?' Bern said.

'Very good, Dick,' Hornung said. 'That only took you a few seconds.'

Bern grabbed Hornung's arm. 'Why, you little—'

Lobec held up his hand. 'That's enough.' Bern let go, and Lobec turned to Hornung. 'When did he graduate?'

'This past summer. Huang's nickname on Facebook is Ted, and Hamilton has a Ted listed in his cell phone directory and email contact list. Looks like he and Hamilton went to school together for a couple of years. Huang's got a vita about a mile long posted on the Web. He and Hamilton are even coauthors on one of the papers.'

That was enough for Lobec. He took out his cell and dialed the charter company that operated Tarnwell's jet, which would be returning from Washington at eight A.M.

'Mr Hornung,' Lobec said as he waited for the call to be picked up, 'text Dr Huang's address to me and find the airport nearest to Blacksburg, Virginia.'

It was Saturday afternoon, and the sun shone brightly through a cloudless sky. The commuter parking lot was full of cars, many with Virginia Tech banners flying from their antennas. Erica was surprised how many of the cars had University of Miami flags. But she knew from growing up in Texas how big football games could be, drawing fans who would have to travel a thousand miles to attend. Few spots were left in the commuter lot. It was three o'clock. The game had started at noon and would probably be over soon.

The door to Ted Huang's office opened. Erica turned away from the window to see Kevin enter and close the door behind him.

'How's it look?' he asked. 'Crazy?'

'These people know how to tailgate.'

'I'm starving, and the last of the pizza is gone.'

'We could get another one delivered,' she said.

'No, I'm sick of pizza, if you can believe it. I'm going to Wendy's. You want anything?'

Erica was feeling slightly claustrophobic and wanted to go with him, but they had already agreed that she should show her face in public as little as possible to avoid running into someone who might recognize her from the grocery store incident.

'A grilled chicken salad if Wendy's has that. Vinaigrette on the side, please.'

'Okay, but first I have something to show you.' The look on his face was noncommittal as to whether it was a good something or a bad something.

'What?'

'Come with me.'

He led her to the lab. It was totally quiet for the first time in days. None of the equipment was running.

'What's wrong?' Erica said. 'Is something broken?'

'Nope. I ran out of raw material to make more bucky-balls, but I think what we have is enough. Take a look in the chamber.'

Erica went over to the chamber window. She gasped when she saw the specimen. She hadn't seen it since Thursday night, and it was now ten times the size it was then.

'By my calculations,' Kevin said, 'it should weigh about forty grams.' He tapped the Adamas notebook, which was lying on the workbench. 'Looks like old Mike and I had ourselves a winner.'

Erica smiled and shook her head. 'This is incredible. You're going to be famous.'

'Maybe. I know I won't be rich. The university will own the patent. I guess I can see why Ward tried to sell it instead. I have to say, it's hard not to be tempted.'

Kevin saw how she was looking at him.

'I'm not saying I *agree* with him,' he said, 'just that I can understand why he did it.'

'So, what do we do now?' she said.

'The only thing left is to remove the specimen from the chamber and take it to Washington. The chamber is still hot. It'll be an hour or so before we can take it out.'

'How?'

'I soldered the target to the top of a quarter-inch-diameter nut. Then I just screwed it onto a bolt that was out of the laser's path. Not pretty, but it worked. All you do is unscrew it. If you'd like, I'll let you do the honors when the chamber's cooled.'

Erica did a slight curtsy. 'It would be my privilege.'

'Now, before my stomach implodes,' Kevin said, 'I am going to get some food.' He handed her Ted's key chain. 'Keep both rooms locked, even if you're just going to the bathroom.'

'I think I'll hang out in the office. At least I can get some sun there.' They were both starting to relax at the thought that this ordeal would soon be over.

'Oh, and one more thing before I leave.' He pulled her to him and kissed her, then drew his lips down her neck. The feeling was delicious. 'While I'm away, you can think about how we'll pass the time until we leave tomorrow.'

With a wink, Kevin was gone.

*

According to Lobec's phone, the rental car he and Bern were in was halfway to Blacksburg from the Roanoke airport. The Montgomery County executive airport would have been closer, but getting a car would have been more difficult. With the interstate traffic as light as it was, they'd be at the university in under thirty minutes.

'Ted Huang's house or the lab first?' Bern asked.

'The lab. Fifth floor, Derring Hall. If he's not there, we'll try Dr Huang's home.'

'I'll be glad to get my hands on him.'

'We are not going to harm either him or Miss Jensen until we have the notebook in our possession. Understood?'

'Yeah, but you must be ready to take a crack at him, too, after what he did to us in Dallas.'

'Mr Bern, if you ever want to be a true professional, you'll have to learn how to suppress your need for vengeance. This is our job. Nothing more.'

'Whatever you say. So what turnoff am I looking for?'

Lobec checked his phone. 'Highway 460.'

He had the route all mapped out. It would be easy to find the lab.

It had been nearly half an hour since Kevin left, and Erica was beginning to wonder where he was. Because the lot was still devoid of fans, she guessed that the game had gone into overtime.

A boom like thunder rattled the windows in defiance of

the sunny sky, the sixth time it had happened today. Erica had read in the school paper during her long stretches of boredom in the last few days that a cannon was fired by the corps of cadets every time Virginia Tech scored. The Hokies were celebrating another touchdown.

Erica found herself absently tapping on the desk and stopped. She chuckled, amused that she was starting to pick up Kevin's bad habits. It was the first time in years she didn't have to study, and now she didn't know what to do with herself except stare out of the window, imagining everything that could go wrong in the next two days. What if their appointment got canceled? What if the FBI didn't believe them? Could the *Washington Post* help them? And most of all, what if they were found by Barnett and Kaplan?

As the thunder faded, Erica heard a new sound. It was faint at first, but grew steadily louder. The heavy footfall of shoes in the hallway outside the door, two pairs. Both had the slow rhythm of men marching in lockstep rather than the quick staccato of women's heels. They were probably fifty feet away by now.

They suddenly stopped to her left, just about where the lab would be. Erica pressed her ear against the door. She heard low mumbles. Definitely two men. One of them knocked on a door.

What if it's them? But that was absurd. Nobody knew where they were except Ted and Janice, and they were in Minneapolis. No, she was just being paranoid.

So, why don't you open the door and take a look?

She put her hand on the doorknob. More footsteps. Another knock, this time closer. More mumbling.

She hesitated. *You're just being silly. Just a couple of students trying to find one of their friends.*

Even if it was them, what was she going to do about it? Her purse was in the lab along with her Mace. The gun was in the truck's glove compartment, and if she did have it, she didn't know if she'd be able to use it. No, might as well open the door now while she had a chance to run.

Erica turned the knob as quietly as she could, waiting to pull the door toward her until the latch was totally disengaged. She'd have to stick her head out to see who it was. She eased the door inward and peered down the hall to the right. No one was in the field of view. As the door opened wide enough for her body, she yanked the door open, slid to the right, and turned in one motion, tensing her muscles for flight.

When she saw the two men, she almost ran, but then she realized they were wearing dark blue maintenance uniforms and both had on tool belts. They turned at the sound of the door hitting her back. One was about Kevin's height, blond, and had a gap where a tooth should have been. The other was about five inches shorter, with dark hair and a pug nose. Neither of them was the one who had ambushed them in Dallas, the man with the black hair and steely gray eyes. Both smiled when they saw her. The taller one spoke with a heavy Virginia accent.

'Excuse me, miss. We're looking for Dr Haber. He said he was going to be in one of these labs, but we can't find him.'

Erica let out the breath she didn't know she'd been holding.

'Miss?' the man repeated.

'I'm sorry,' she said. 'I'm not really familiar with this building.'

'I thought he said 519, but—'

A door opened beyond the two maintenance men, and a pudgy, bald man stepped out.

'Thank God you're here,' he said in a thick German accent. 'I was in the back of the lab, but I thought I heard knocking. The air-conditioning is completely broken now. Come. The equipment will be ruined soon.'

'I think we found him,' said the gap-toothed one, and the two men followed Dr Haber into the lab.

Erica retreated into the office and closed the door, chiding herself for being so foolish. Then her phone rang, and she nearly jumped onto the desk.

She opened the phone and saw that it was Kevin.

'Hello?'

'Hey, I had a hell of a time getting some food.'

'What happened?'

'I'll tell you when I get up there.'

'Where are you?'

'I'm in the truck. I've been looking for a parking spot for the last ten minutes. Can you see one from up there?'

Erica smiled and went to the window, scanning the

parking lot for a second. There he was. The huge dually slowly turned a corner and headed up the fourth row from the building.

'Yeah, I see one. You'll have to go up the next row and come over to the other side of the lot. It's almost at the back. I think you'll be able to fit.'

'Okay, I'm on my way.'

After a few more instructions, Kevin found the spot.

'Thanks,' he said as he opened the truck door. He waved and began walking toward the building.

'Can you see me?' she said, waving back.

'Sure. The fourth window from the right.'

'I'm glad you're back.'

'Hungry?'

'That's not the only reason.'

'Oh, really?'

'That's not what I meant. Where were you?'

He held up a white bag and pointed at it. 'You're the reason I'm late.'

'Me?'

'I checked the order after I came out of the drive-through. They messed yours up and I had to go back in and wait until they got it right.' He was about halfway to the building. Another car pulled into the parking lot.

'That was awfully thoughtful of . . . ' Erica froze. The car, a brown Ford, stopped about seventy-five feet from Kevin and its occupants got out. Both were dressed in suits, the driver a beefy guy with a crew cut, the passenger with jet-black hair and sunglasses. They were far away, but she thought of the moment in Dallas when another Ford had stopped in front of them in that rainy SciSurplus parking lot. Even though it seemed impossible, she had no doubt. It was them.

'Oh, my God!' she yelled. 'Kevin, get down!'

His bewildered voice replied. 'What? What are you talking about?'

'It's them! Barnett and Kaplan! Get down before they see you.'

'Shit!' Kevin dropped to his knees behind a blue sports car, but it was too late. They'd spotted him. Barnett and Kaplan crouched down, drew guns from their jackets, and began creeping toward him.

THIRTY-TWO

The commuter parking lot had ten rows parallel to the building, with multiple cross lanes connecting each row with the next. In the fourth row, about three hundred feet away from Erica, Kevin crouched behind the sports car, the bag of food spilled at his feet. Kaplan, the burly one, edged one row toward the building and continued moving in Kevin's direction. Barnett circled around the other way with the fluid motions of a practiced hunter.

'Are they still there?'

'Yes,' Erica said. 'Stay down.'

She searched the lot for other people. There had to be someone left. There! To her far right were a couple of stragglers walking toward the stadium. Then she realized they would be of no use. Even if she could get their attention, what could they possibly do?

'Kevin. I'm going to hang up and call the police.'

'No,' he whispered. 'There isn't time. They'll find me before the police get here. You have to tell me where they are so I can get back to the truck.'

He was right. If she hung up, Kevin would have no way

of knowing where they were. As long as they didn't know she was up in the office spying on them, she and Kevin had an advantage.

'Where are they?' he said. 'Why didn't they just run over and get me?'

'Five days ago you shot at them. Would you take a chance on running at someone who may have a gun?'

'Good point. Only one problem. The gun's in the truck.'

'I know,' Erica said. 'Okay, start moving toward the back of the blue car, and when I tell you, go to the next row.'

'All right.'

He scooted to the back of the car, which was flush with the open space of the next row, and began to peer around the corner.

'Don't do that!' Erica said. 'Keep your head down. Let me be your eyes. I'll tell you when it's okay.'

The parking spaces in each row were staggered. It looked to Erica like it would be difficult for them to see between cars beyond more than one row. As long as Kevin kept ahead of them, he had a chance.

Barnett nodded to Kaplan and they raced to the next row, only one away from Kevin's.

'Now!' Erica said.

With a gait that would have been comical in any other situation, Kevin scuttled like a crab. Kaplan ducked behind a sedan and Barnett stood behind a minivan. Then Barnett flattened himself on the ground.

'Kevin! Barnett's trying to look under the cars for your

feet.' Kevin was almost to the next row. 'Get behind the tire of that green car you're coming to.'

Kevin ran the last few feet and huddled against the green car beside its front tire.

'What's he doing—'

'Shh! He's only about fifty feet from you now. He's still down.' Barnett's head rose into view. 'Now he's getting up. I don't think he saw you. No, he's pointing to the left of you and peeking around the minivan toward his partner.' Suddenly, Kaplan began running toward the back of the lot. Erica heard Kevin curse under his breath. 'Move back!' she yelled.

Kevin edged toward the open part of the row.

'No! I mean in between the two cars in your row.'

Kevin turned and reached the point between the two cars just as Kaplan entered the open drive five cars to the left. If Kevin had still been at the front of the car, Kaplan surely would have seen him. Instead, Kaplan kept his head down, running toward the far end of the lot.

'What's he doing?' Erica said.

Kevin whispered a reply. 'I heard Barnett yell something about the truck. He must have spotted it. They're trying to cut me off.'

The phone was slick in Kevin's hand. He wiped his sweaty palms on his jeans.

'Erica, if anything happens to me, call 911, and then get out of there.'

'Nothing's going to happen. Just be quiet. Kaplan's to the

row just before the truck now. That's about three rows past you. Barnett's still two rows back toward me. He's moving now. He's looking between each pair of cars. Kaplan's doing the same thing.'

'How far down the row are they?'

'I think Kaplan's too far from you to see you if you stay down. But Barnett's six cars to your left, moving faster now. He'll see you in a few seconds unless you go behind the red car.'

The red car was a Chevy sedan behind the green Mazda he was next to. He scurried behind it so that the Chevy and Mazda were between him and Barnett. His heart pounded as he listened to Erica give the play-by-play.

'Five cars now. Four cars. Three cars. Two cars. One. He's right behind you. Okay, he's past.' She waited a few seconds. 'You can talk now.'

'This isn't working,' Kevin said. 'A few more times looking under cars and they're going to see where I am. The window on this Mazda is open. It has a fold-down back seat. If I can get in, I can crawl into the trunk through the backseat and hide there until they leave. Keep me posted if they get near me.'

'Okay,' said Erica.

With his back to the Chevy, he slid around to the opposite side until he was at the driver's door of the Mazda. The Mazda's window was only half open. He tried the door handle, but it was locked. Looking through the window, he could see the passenger door's lock release on the inside of the door, next to the handle. It would be the same for the driver's door.

'Erica,' he said, 'I'm going to have to stand up to get to the lock release. Are they looking this way?'

'No. A crowd is streaming into the lot on the other side from you. The game must be over. They're both looking in that direction.'

Good, Kevin thought. It was a perfect distraction. They were both looking away from him. He stood, trying to keep his head behind the car's door pillar. He snaked his arm through the window opening and felt the velour cloth of the door's interior. He reached forward. His fingers ran over the nubby plastic of the area surrounding the lock and then rested on the smooth contour of the lock mechanism. He pushed it forward and heard the whine of the locks. A red indicator on the passenger lock appeared.

Kevin pulled his arm out and bent down again.

'It's unlocked. I'm going to open the door now. Am I clear?'

'They're both about fifty feet from you and facing the other way, but they may turn around any minute. You'd better do it now.'

As he lifted the handle and popped the door open, the shriek of a car alarm ripped the air.

Even from the enclosed office, Erica could hear the alarm. Through the phone, it was piercing. She yanked the phone away from her ear.

Kevin fell backward in surprise, and his phone flipped closed as his hand hit the ground. Barnett and Kaplan were already running in his direction. In his attempt to get away from the green car, Kevin scrambled around the corner directly into Barnett's vision.

Erica felt helpless as she saw Kevin stand and look around desperately before running away from Barnett.

'The crowd!' she screamed at the window. 'Get help from the people in the crowd!'

As if he could still hear her, Kevin veered toward the mass of people. Barnett followed, but Kaplan ran toward the brown sedan they had arrived in.

Not knowing what else to do, Erica hung up the phone and dialed 911.

Kevin had never run faster in his life, glad he had lost those thirty extra pounds from high school. His long legs were giving him a slight lead over Barnett and Kaplan.

A sidewalk split the parking lot in half. He leapt over some bushes into the other side of the lot, where the hooting masses were still celebrating the obvious victory. The crowd was getting denser by the minute. Kevin might be able to meld with the throngs and lose them.

'Stop that man!' Barnett shouted from behind him. 'Police! Stop him!'

Four bare-chested college students with their shirts dangling from their shorts were directly in front of Kevin. Their whoops of joy ceased when they heard Barnett. Kevin tried to maneuver around them, but two of the students tackled him. Kevin kicked at them to get away, but the other two held down his legs.

'Let go!' he yelled. 'You don't know what you're doing!'

Barnett skidded to a stop and pointed his gun at Kevin.

With his left hand, Barnett withdrew a wallet from his jacket and flashed a badge at the students. 'Police. This man's wanted for murder.'

'He's lying!' Kevin said. 'He's not a policeman!'

'Nice try,' one of the students said. They weren't about to question a policeman apprehending a crazed criminal, especially when the cop was holding a gun. In fact, they were high-fiving each other for catching him.

'That car alarm you hear,' Barnett said, 'was the result of this suspect breaking into a vehicle. He was attempting to get away.'

By this time a crowd had gathered around them, but it parted when Kaplan stopped the Ford near them and got out. He walked around, pulling handcuffs from his pocket.

Kevin knew it was no use trying to get help from these people. He didn't resist as Kaplan pushed him against the car, patted him down, handcuffed him, and shoved him into the back seat. In the distance, Kevin heard sirens.

'You're not going to wait for the Blacksburg police, Barnett?' Kevin said, sneering the name.

The man who had called himself Barnett six days ago slammed the door and looked back at Kevin from the front seat, his hollow gray eyes smiling. 'Allow me to introduce myself, Mr Hamilton. My name is David Lobec.'

Erica bounded down the staircase two steps at a time. To get the police's attention quickly, she'd told them that somebody had been shot in the commuter parking lot during a fight. When she was convinced that the police were coming, she hung up and ran for the stairs, stopping only to retrieve her Mace from the lab, ready to do what she could to free Kevin.

She got to the first floor and burst into the hallway, her lungs burning. She ran through the outer door, squinting as she stepped into the sun, and stopped.

To her right, the crowd continued to flood the parking lot. To her left, the flashing lights of a police car were visible cresting the hill. She quickly scanned the rest of the lot, but there was no sign of the brown Ford.

They were gone.

THIRTY-THREE

Kevin was driven to an isolated spot far from campus where they waited for thirty minutes, enough time for any cops to have left the commuter lot. Then the three of them returned to the university.

Bern and Lobec led Kevin to Derring Hall's fifth floor. With every step, he prayed that Erica had taken the diamond specimen and left.

'Here it is,' Bern said as they approached the lab. He looked at the number on the door. 'This is Huang's lab.'

'The key, Mr Hamilton,' Lobec said, holding out his hand.

'I don't have it.'

Lobec nodded at Bern, who patted him down more thoroughly than when they had first caught him. Kevin was almost getting used to the process.

After a minute Bern shrugged. 'He's clean.'

'Miss Jensen must have it. No matter.' Lobec withdrew a small kit from his pocket and took out two slivers of metal.

He inserted both into the lab's deadbolt, and within twenty seconds he twisted the handle opening the lab.

Kevin was impressed. He was scared, too, but he didn't want them to know it. 'That was fast. You must get locked out of your house a lot.'

'I'm glad you can still see the humor in this, Mr Hamilton. Mr Bern, wait outside while we look around the laboratory.'

Followed by Lobec, who had his gun drawn, Kevin entered the lab and breathed a sigh of relief when he saw that it was deserted. Erica's purse was gone, and some papers were strewn on the floor near where it had been.

Lobec walked directly to the experimental equipment, first inspecting the laser, then peering inside the chamber. 'It appears that your purchase from SciSurplus was not wasted. The laser is still warm to the touch.'

Kevin's stomach sank. Lobec realized what they had done.

'It appears Miss Jensen took the diamond with her.' Lobec turned away from the chamber and looked at Kevin. 'You warned her. How?'

A grin spread across Kevin's face. He shrugged.

'It doesn't matter,' Lobec said. 'I don't think there's any point in searching the laboratory. Even in her hurry, Miss Jensen wouldn't have left the notebook. And we don't want to dawdle in case she has called the police again. We should, however, check Dr Huang's office to be sure she isn't still here.'

A search of Ted's office revealed nothing more than that

Erica had left in a hurry. She'd had the presence of mind to lock both doors, though the gesture had been futile.

Inside the office, Lobec looked out at the parking lot below. 'I see. She observed our chase from here.'

Once they were back in the car, Lobec said, 'I think it's safe to assume Miss Jensen is no longer in Blacksburg.'

'What do we do now?' asked Bern from his seat beside Kevin. 'She's got the notebook.'

'Yes,' Lobec said, training his eyes on Kevin, 'but we have something equally valuable.'

At the Roanoke Regional Airport, Kevin and his captors got on the most luxurious jet he had ever seen. His hands were cuffed in front of him the entire time, but he was otherwise unrestrained. The plane trip lasted less than an hour. The window shade next to him was closed, but the angle of the sun through the other windows of the plane indicated a northeasterly direction. At a hangar in an airport he couldn't identify, he was put into another car. As they exited the airport, he saw a sign confirming his suspicions: 'Dulles Airport.' Washington.

Thirty minutes from Dulles, after a drive through lush horse farms and rolling pastures, the car turned into a long driveway shielded from the afternoon sun by elms and oaks. It wound for what seemed like a mile, then the arbor opened to reveal a stunning white plantation-style mansion. The paint gleamed on the huge columns and stately frontispiece, indicating a recent restoration. Kevin noted with discomfort that his entourage had made no attempt to disguise their route or even provide him with a blindfold. He knew exactly where they were and how to get back. Which meant they intended to kill him.

Lobec took him out of the car, released his handcuffs, and led him up the front steps into a marble-floored foyer. Large doors on each side flanked a spiral staircase straight out of *Gone with the Wind*. Lobec pointed to the door on the right, directing Kevin into a library with delicate Persian carpeting and handsome leather furniture. Few books lined the cherry shelving, which were instead filled with mementos and awards.

'Ah!' said a man sipping an iced tea in one of the library's wing-backed chairs. 'You're right on time as usual, David.' The man stood up, stretching to a height four inches taller than Kevin. He walked over with his hand outstretched. 'Kevin Hamilton, I'm Clayton Tarnwell,' he said with a clipped Texas twang.

Kevin ignored the hand. 'So you're Clay. What do you want?'

With a bemused look, Tarnwell dropped his hand and returned to his chair. 'Sit down while we talk, Kevin. Do you want an iced tea?'

Kevin didn't move. 'I said, what do you want, Tarnwell? If that's your real name.'

Tarnwell looked at Lobec. 'A little like me, don't you think, David?' To Kevin he said, 'Good. No bullshit. I think you know what I want.'

'I don't know what you're talking about. Last Sunday, your goon here tried to kill me and my girlfriend, and we've been on the run ever since.'

'By the way, Clayton Tarnwell *is* my name. Ever heard of Tarnwell Mining and Chemical?' Kevin shrugged. 'No? That's understandable. Our annual revenue is less than a billion dollars, chump change in the mining and chemicals industry. But in three days, my company's value will quadruple. Everyone in America will know its name because of something I bought from your professor.'

Kevin remained impassive. Tarnwell arched an eyebrow and continued.

'I know that Erica Jensen paid over thirty thousand dollars for a new laser, which is very interesting, because an instrument like that could be pretty useful in the process I bought. You see, like you I'm a chemist, so I know what the hell I'm talking about.'

'Oh, you're like me, huh? I don't seem to recall ever killing someone because I didn't get what I wanted.'

'If you mean Michael Ward, that son of a bitch was trying to swindle me. I saw the possibilities for his process, and I was willing to invest in it, to make it work, to put my company and reputation on the line. As thanks for my willingness to take these risks, what does he do? That bastard double-crosses me. Steals ten million dollars from me – which, by the way, I don't think I'll ever see again. Not only that, but the money wasn't enough for Michael. He wanted the money and the Adamas process too. A terrible tragedy, his wife and him dying in a fire like that.'

'That fire was no accident.'

'The news reports said it was.'

'Give me a break. What about Herbert Stein? What about my father?'

'Yes, Michael did think I had Herbert Stein killed, but murders are common in Houston. As for your father, too bad about that, but as I understand it, David and Richard were only defending themselves after he plowed into their car. That's why they had to take you in Blacksburg the way they did.'

Kevin ground his teeth. 'You're a murderer. You can't explain it all away that easily.'

'I just did,' Tarnwell said with a wicked smile. 'It's exactly what I'll tell anyone who asks if your girlfriend goes to the authorities with that notebook. What do I want? I want what I paid for. Nothing more, nothing less.'

Lobec spoke up. 'And the videotape.'

Kevin tried to hide his surprised reaction, but it was too late. Lobec saw it and smiled.

Damn, Kevin thought. *How did he know about that?*

'Ah,' Tarnwell said. 'I can see by the look on your face that Michael wasn't bluffing. Yes, then. The videotape too.'

'And I suppose you'll let us both go free if she gives them to you.'

'Of course.'

'Bullshit.'

'Why shouldn't I? Once I have Adamas, who do you think anyone will believe? A wealthy businessman who's a pillar of the community, who's donated over a million dollars to charities and political causes around the state? Or a struggling student and his girlfriend who've recently had trouble with the police?'

Kevin walked over to the window and looked out at the lush green lawn. 'And you expect me to believe that once you get the Adamas notebook, you'll be satisfied?'

'It's all I've wanted from the first day Michael contacted me. In a way, Michael was trying to cheat both of us. If I'd known you were one of the inventors, I wouldn't have left you out of the deal. In fact, I'm willing to pay you the balance of what I was going to pay Michael. How does ten million sound to you?'

After Erica topped off the gas tank, she took a bathroom break and stretched her legs at the Phillips 66 truck stop just outside of Front Royal, Virginia, about an hour and a half west of Washington's Beltway. At eight o'clock on a Saturday night, the air of the packed parking lot was rank with the smell of diesel fuel and truck exhaust.

When she saw that Kevin had been abducted, Erica immediately ran back to the lab and gathered her belongings, including the notebook, videotape, and the diamond specimen, all the while terrified that Barnett and Kaplan would burst into the lab at any moment. The specimen had been difficult for her to dislodge without Kevin's help, but after ten minutes she worked it free. Then she ran to the truck, only to realize that Kevin still had the key.

She had no idea how to hot-wire a vehicle, so the pickup was useless to her. At first she panicked, frozen at having her only method of escape cut off.

She remembered Murray's Glock was still in the glove box. Erica climbed into the bed and through the rear sliding window to retrieve it. She put the gun in her purse, although she didn't know if she would actually be able to use it if they came after her. The only thought she could focus on as she got out of the truck was that she had to get to Washington and ask for help from the FBI.

That was enough to get her feet moving. As she'd wandered back toward the campus in a haze, taking in the swarm of football fans streaming to their cars. Vehicles were already jammed up trying to leave the parking lot, and it dawned on her that some of them had D.C. plates. When she found a group that seemed nonthreatening – two girls and a guy who didn't look much older than she was – she waved down their Lexus and made up a sob story about getting stranded by a no-good boyfriend.

The girls had sympathy for her and offered to give her a ride back to Washington, where the three Virginia Tech alums – Marcy, Paul, and Rita – were new associates at a lobbying firm. Now they were taking turns in the truck stop bathroom and buying coffee and snacks to tide them over until they got supper in Washington. As a thanks for the ride, Erica had offered to gas up the car.

Alone with her thoughts for the first time in three hours, Erica obsessed about Kevin's fate. She didn't know when or even if the kidnappers would try to contact her. She had called Kevin's phone several times, but it always went to voice mail. If she didn't hear from them by Sunday night, she'd have to conclude they weren't going to call. She had no idea where to find him or the identities of the men who'd taken him, leaving her with only one option. Given the situation, there was no alternative but to meet FBI agent Sutter on her own.

While she paced, her phone rang. No one had this new phone's number except Kevin. She opened it with trepidation.

'Hello?' she said, her heart in her mouth.

'Erica Jensen,' said a man with a Texas drawl, 'I'm so glad we were able to contact you.'

'Who is this?'

'As you might guess, I'm reluctant to give my name out over the phone. I believe we each have something the other wants.'

'What have you done with Kevin?'

'I haven't done anything. He's right here. Do you want to speak to him?'

'Put him on.'

After a slight pause, she heard Kevin's voice. 'Erica? Are you okay?'

'I'm fine,' she said, choking back tears. 'I got out before they came back.'

'I know. Don't worry about me, and don't deal with them. Stick to our plan—'

She heard a scuffle on the other end of the line. Then the Texan was back on the phone.

'That's too bad. I thought we had convinced Kevin to cooperate. I even offered him ten million dollars for Adamas. You know what he did? He tried to spit in my face.'

'Good.'

'You two are a pair, aren't you? Well, it doesn't matter. Erica, do you want Kevin to live?'

Erica's breath caught in her throat.

'I said, do you want Kevin to live?'

'Yes.'

'Then we'll have to do some horse trading. Find your way to Washington, which will be much more convenient for us. I'll have the two men you met earlier take Kevin and meet you at a warehouse on the Potomac. The address is—'

'No. I may not have done this before, but I'm not stupid. It has to be someplace public.'

A second's pause. 'All right. Where?'

Erica had lived in Washington during a summer job after her sophomore year in college. She worked downtown, but hadn't had a car at the time. Instead, she avoided the crush of the Metro by biking in each day from her apartment in Arlington through the Mall. On her route from Virginia she had crossed one of the busiest bridges in the Washington area, the Arlington Memorial Bridge, directly across from the Lincoln Memorial. It was almost always crowded, especially during rush hour, and the moment she thought of the bridge, she got the inkling of a idea.

'The middle of the Arlington Memorial Bridge, north side. The only ones I want to see with Kevin are the two I've already met. If I see an army of guys out there, I'll leave and send a copy of Adamas to every internet site I can think of.'

Another pause, probably to discuss the risks of the location. 'All right, Erica. The Arlington Memorial Bridge tomorrow at noon.'

'It has to be Monday morning,' she said, trying to stall for time.

'Why Monday? Time's important to me, Erica.' She was nauseated every time the Texan said her name.

'Too bad. If you want the notebook, you'll have to wait.' She looked at her backpack. 'I can't get to where it's hidden until tomorrow night.'

A sigh. 'Seven A.M. Monday morning. Oh, and there's something else I want you to bring. A particular videotape that you found. You have that too?'

'Yes,' Erica said, reluctantly. Although it didn't show much, it *was* a link between Kevin and the Adamas process.

'Good. I can't afford for you to miss this appointment, Erica. If you're not there, they'll never find Kevin's body, and we'll eventually deal with you too. Same thing if you don't have the notebook and the videotape or if you bring the police. Get it?'

'I get it.'

'I'm glad we got to talk finally. I'm sure you're just as smart as you are pretty. Don't make a dumbass mistake like Michael Ward did.' Then the phone went dead.

She put it back in her pocket, then suddenly realizing how alone she was, she leaned against the car door and cried. She wept until she felt a tap on her shoulder.

Marcy was holding out a tissue to her.

'Men,' she said, shaking her head as Erica took the offering. 'If you ask me, you're too good for him. Now, I've got a nice cup of coffee and some donuts for you. That should help.'

Erica smiled at Marcy's kindness and wiped her face before getting back in the car with her band of Good Samaritans.

THIRTY-FOUR

'**H**ey! Hey, out there! Franco!' Kevin continued to pound on the bedroom door. 'I have a problem in here.'

Kevin stepped back as the door swung inward. Franco, as Bern had called him, stepped through wearing an Italian-style gray suit.

'I told you dinner wasn't for another hour.'

'I know,' Kevin said, 'but there's a problem with the bathroom. I think the toilet's broken.'

Franco came farther into the mansion's bedroom while a second man waited behind him. The room was sparsely furnished with a bed, a nightstand and lamp, a delicate writing desk, and a cane-backed chair. All decorations had been removed from the room just before Kevin's arrival. Holes in the wall were visible where picture hangers had been removed. The window above the desk was nailed shut. If he broke it and attempted to jump the twenty feet to the ground, the guard posted outside his door would be alerted and capture him before he could climb through. Besides, he had no doubt it was hooked up to the alarm system. A bathroom with a glass-enclosed shower, a sink, and a toilet was separated from the bedroom by a louvered door. All of its contents had been removed except for a hand towel.

'Did you take a dump in it?' Franco asked, walking toward the bathroom but never taking his eyes off Kevin.

'No, I just took a piss, and then it started to overflow after I flushed it.'

'Sit down in that chair while I take a look. And I don't want to see you get up.' Kevin did as he was told. Franco went into the bathroom.

Kevin surprised himself with his acting ability. True, the toilet was stopped up, but Kevin knew exactly why. He had torn a piece of the sheet from the foot of his bed and stuffed the wad into the toilet so that only a plumber's tool would be able to get at it. Kevin was sure they wouldn't risk bringing a stranger into the house while he was held hostage. He just hoped they'd let him use another bathroom.

Franco came out after a minute.

'What's the problem?' Kevin said.

'Do I look like a plumber? How the hell should I know?'

'What am I supposed to do? I can't use that toilet. It's filled to the top with water. If I try to flush it, it's going to flood the whole room.'

'I thought you college guys were smart. You said you just went. If you have to go, don't flush. Now, don't bother me again.'

The door slammed shut. Kevin could only wait in the barren room, helpless.

Two hours later, dinner still hadn't come. Kevin was famished; his lunch was still lying in the Virginia Tech commuter lot. He lay in the bed on top of the covers, staring at the ceiling in the lingering twilight coming through the window. The events of the past week weighed heavily on him. He'd never experienced so much death and destruction. In fact, up to this point he'd never lost anyone close except his mother.

Now he was just like Erica. No parents. No family.

But he did have her. He hadn't realized how strong his feelings for her had grown during their ordeal until he'd blurted out his profession of love so ham-handedly. She was the only reason he'd been able to get through all of it. He missed her with a ferocity that edged aside his hunger pangs.

A key rattled in the lock. Kevin sat up as the door swung open.

A tray came through, held by Franco. Following him was David Lobec.

'I understand from Mr Francowiak that you have had some plumbing problems.'

Franco placed the tray on the desk. The only things on it were a paper plate holding a sandwich, potato chips, and a paper cup turned upside down.

'Boy, you guys are really going all out,' Kevin said,

pointing at the meager meal. 'You're just trying to butter me up, right? I mean, before you offer me twenty million instead of ten million.'

'You're an amusing young man, Mr Hamilton,' Lobec said. 'I am sorry that we haven't been able to provide more luxurious accommodations, but I am sure you understand our position. It wouldn't do to have you escape before we have the Adamas notebook in our possession. This is obviously the most secure room in the house. Nevertheless, someone will be outside the room at all times.'

'You could at least have given me a working toilet.'

'Yes, of course you're correct. I have decided to let Mr Francowiak and his replacements take you to another bathroom down the hall. I have instructed him to let you use it only if you behave. If you attempt to escape or cause any mischief, he will tie you to the bed for the rest of your stay. Is that clear?'

'If I'm good, do I get a lollipop?'

Lobec came to within a foot of Kevin. 'Do you realize, Mr Hamilton, that if Miss Jensen does not meet us at the Arlington Bridge on Monday, you will die?'

'You're going to kill me anyway. In fact, the only way I'll live is if she doesn't show up, because then you'll need me.'

'You can believe what you want, Mr Hamilton, but I can assure you that no one wants this situation resolved peacefully more than I. Monday morning I will escort you to the rendezvous.'

'I'm looking forward to it.'

'Enjoy your meal. Mr Francowiak will escort you to the bathroom when you're finished.'

As he flashed a last corrupt smile at Kevin, Lobec followed Franco out the door. Kevin stood staring into space, wondering if he had a chance in hell of getting out of this.

At first apprehensive that the sandwich contained poison, Kevin dismissed the idea as ludicrous. If they wanted to kill him, it would have happened hours ago, probably under torture. Tarnwell had grilled him about Adamas, but the precise settings were too complicated to reconstruct completely from memory – not that Kevin had tried very hard.

He wolfed the sandwich and potato chips, followed by several cupfuls of water from the sink. Then, invigorated by the food, he did what he would have thought disgusting in any other circumstance. With the water running to mask the sound, he urinated into the sink.

After he was finished, he knocked on the door.

'Hey, Franco, I'm through with dinner.'

The door opened. 'Stand over there,' said Franco, pointing to the chair that was now by the window. Kevin did as he was told, and Franco took the tray into the hall.

He came back in and said, 'You need to hit the can before you go to sleep?'

'Yeah.'

Franco drew a Beretta automatic and waved it toward the hallway. 'Come on.'

Kevin, with Franco and the gun at his back, walked

down the hall he had come through earlier. A Persian runner stretched down the middle of the hallway and polished oak flanked it on either side. Antique tables lined the hall at regular intervals, and fine tapestries hung from the walls. Intricate wainscoting ran the length of the hall. In all, Kevin supposed the effect was to be one of lavish opulence, but he found it overdone, as if someone had given an unlimited budget to a fledgling interior decorator.

The mansion was large enough so that the hall formed a complete circuit joining the large staircase at the back of the house. A balcony overlooked the foyer but ended about halfway around the circuit, giving way to several rooms. From his first walk to his room at the front of the house, Kevin had seen only one other room with its door open, and that had been a bedroom.

'Here,' Franco said when they had walked about fifty feet down the hallway. Kevin turned and saw him pointing to an interior room, obviously chosen because it had no windows.

Kevin opened its door to find a bathroom that equaled the unbridled opulence of the hallway. Marble floors, brass fixtures, beveled mirrors, all shined and polished to perfection. He flicked the light switch and track lighting came on, accompanied by the hum of a fan.

Franco shoved him into the spacious bathroom. 'Go ahead.'

The door was still wide open, and Kevin began to shut it. Franco pushed it back, almost slamming it into the wall.

'Uh-uh.'

Kevin was worried that he wouldn't get the privacy he needed, so he tried to appear angry. 'Can't I take a crap in peace? What are you afraid of? Where the hell am I going to go?'

Franco thought about it for a second, appraised the room's dimensions, and then relented, releasing the door. 'Okay, but I don't want to hear that lock click. We got the key downstairs anyway, so don't bother.'

'Thank you,' Kevin said, and closed the door.

After loudly propping up the toilet seat lid, Kevin set about quickly but quietly searching the cupboards for anything that might be of use to him, hoping that they hadn't cleaned out this bathroom like the one in his room. The cabinet under the sink was bare, as were the six drawers to either side. It was a minute before he got to the cabinet behind the mirror. Still nothing. Kevin looked around the large bathroom, about to give up on finding anything, when he saw a linen closet that doubled as a stand-up mirror.

The closet had no handle, and the edge cut out to open it had been so ingeniously integrated into the mirror's design that he almost hadn't noticed the door. He tiptoed over and held his breath as he opened it.

Six evenly spaced shelves went from top to bottom. The first five shelves were empty, and it appeared that the top one, which lay about two inches above his eye level, was as well. But standing on his toes, Kevin caught a glimpse of color toward the back of the shelf.

He strained as high as he could and saw a number of bottles and cans shoved together at the back. He couldn't be sure from this angle, but one appeared to be ammonia and another, a blue and white bottle of Clorox bleach.

Whoever had emptied out the bathroom must have been shorter than Kevin. From a lower angle, the person would never have been able to see the cleaning fluids bunched on the top shelf. It was exactly what Kevin had been hoping for.

He reached his hand to the back and the tips of his fingers brushed against one of the cans. He felt it nudge and gasped involuntarily when he realized it was about to fall. The noise would surely raise suspicions outside. He strained even harder, feeling as if his arm would come out of its socket, until he was able to steady the can.

He looked at his watch. He'd been in the bathroom three minutes now. Any longer and Franco might barge in on him without knocking. He didn't have time to inventory what was up there. It would have to wait for the next visit.

Kevin silently closed the closet door, then flushed the toilet. After washing his hands and toweling off, he opened the door. Franco stood on the other side of the hallway with his gun drawn.

'I guess this one worked,' he said.

Kevin nodded, stepping into the hall. 'I like this bathroom a lot better.'

The next morning a new guard took Kevin to the same lavish bathroom. This time he tested the bottom shelf and found that it was sufficiently strong to bear his weight. While the fan covered what little noise Kevin made, he inventoried the items in the cabinet.

A gallon jug half full of generic ammonia; a full bottle of the Clorox bleach he'd seen last night; a spray bottle of Windex; a can of air freshener, which was what he'd probably almost tipped over; two small bottles of nonabrasive tile cleaner; a tin of shoe polish; a tube of superglue; a brown vial of iodine; a pack of Q-tips; three sponges; and a rag.

Whatever he was going to do, it would have to be with these items. MacGyver he was not, but one thing he did know was how to mix chemicals to produce an effect.

Kevin immediately saw several possibilities. He stuffed the tube of superglue into one sock and the vial of iodine into the other, knowing that they might be seen in his jeans pockets. The Q-tips might come in handy, so he took twenty out of the box and put them in his underwear. He needed the ammonia, too, but it would have to wait. He put away the rest of the items, flushed the toilet, and exited the bathroom.

After lunch, Kevin was able to make another trip to the bathroom. He ran the water in the sink and emptied one of the bottles of tile cleaner, which would be small enough to fit in his waistband and go unnoticed. As far from the door as he could get so that the guard wouldn't smell the fumes, Kevin poured some of the ammonia into the bottle until it was full. After capping the ammonia and putting it away, he waved his arms to dissipate the odor. Finally, he took one of the sponges and the rag. The sponge he put down his pants, along with the bottle in his waistband. He wrapped the rag around his ankle and pulled his sock tight over it.

As usual, he flushed the toilet and began the walk toward his room. As he did so, he felt his sock inch down under his pant leg. The rag began to fall loose. It flopped against the inside of his pants, but he didn't dare alter his walk to compensate. He felt it slipping lower and lower until, only five feet from the door, he was sure it was peeking out from the bottom of his cuff. If the guard saw it, he would certainly check Kevin to see if he was carrying anything else and that would lead to a search of his room. Any hope of escape would be gone.

Kevin walked into the room and turned, sighing with relief as the bedroom door closed behind him. The corner of the rag was brushing the floor, about half of it exposed.

If the guard had looked down for any reason, he would have seen it.

Kevin picked up the rag and took the sponge and bottle of ammonia out of his pants. Then he went to the bathroom and removed the other items from under the sink. He thought about creating a more elaborate hiding place but decided there was no point because if they made a deliberate search of the room, no niche would be overlooked.

He examined the array of items before him. The guard opened the door only to bring in food, and Kevin hoped he would keep to that regimen because the desk was now covered with illicit objects. He had to work quickly.

He spread the rag flat on the desk to protect the surface from staining, which would reveal what he was doing. On top of the rag he placed a thin paper plate, an extra from lunch that had stuck to the bottom of his sandwich plate.

He uncapped the bottle of iodine and poured some of it onto the plate. Then he poured a little water from his paper cup and mixed them together using one of the Q-tips. To this mixture he added some ammonia and stirred.

After several minutes Kevin was pleased to see the mixture became a sticky paste. While he stirred, he silently thanked Daryl Grotman and the injury that had taken him to Erica in the ER. The computer whiz had been hurt after mixing a homemade contact explosive, ammonium triiodide. Kevin had made it himself years ago at Texas A&M, just for fun. He and his friends would flick quarter-inch drops of the purple concoction onto the sidewalk, then stand back and let it dry. People would step on the dried droplets, setting off a pop about half as powerful as a firecracker. The unsuspecting pedestrian would jump and Kevin and his friends would laugh hysterically. But Daryl Grotman found out how dangerous it could be in larger amounts.

From the state of the mixture in front of him, Kevin was confident that he'd remembered how to prepare it correctly. After he was sure it was ready, he hurriedly emptied out the rest of the iodine bottle into the sink. The mixture would dry quickly in the open air, and he had to get it safely stored before he put a hole in the desk. Kevin scooped the paste carefully into the empty iodine bottle, where it would remain inert. He capped it and wiped it clean with the corner of the rag, which was now soaked with iodine. Then he ran water over the paper plate to remove the remaining residue and rinsed the rag out, the paste diluted by the water. All of the objects went back under the sink.

The whole process had taken about two hours, which left him with plenty of time to go over his plan. He stood at the window, staring at the woods flanking the front drive. They were thick with foliage from a warm, wet summer – perfect for a nighttime escape.

Kevin's dinner consisted of another sandwich and chips. Apparently the chef had the weekend off. Twenty minutes later, as Franco cleaned up the remnants of the meal, he asked if Kevin needed to go to the bathroom, but Kevin declined. There were still about two hours of daylight left. He had to wait for nightfall.

Kevin wondered if his plan would actually work. Despite his careful preparations, he was still relying on a lot of luck, even before he got to the woods. But for now he had to make his own luck, even if that meant running into fate head-on.

Finally it was dark. Kevin quietly leaned the cane-backed chair against the door and pushed the top of it up to the knob. He removed the bottle of ammonium triiodide from its hiding place and spread six-inch-diameter circles on the floor, a few inches from where the chair legs were wedged against the floor.

He closed the bottle and put the remaining triiodide in his waistband. Then he moved the chair back to its normal position at the desk and turned off the lights. Standing close to the door, Kevin knocked and told Franco he was ready for the bathroom. The door swung open, and Kevin noted with relief that the door's arc did not overlap the painted circles. Franco didn't see them, or if he did, he didn't remark on them.

Once in the bathroom, Kevin opened the triiodide to pour a larger circle on the bottom of the under-sink cabinet, using up the rest of the bottle. From the tall cabinet, he retrieved the bottles of Clorox and ammonia. Then he poured most of the Clorox down the sink and waited. When he thought the triiodide had dried, he poured some ammonia into the bottle of Clorox, screwed on the lid tightly, and placed the mixture and the bottle of ammonia next to the circle. He closed the cabinet and knocked on the door, knowing he didn't have much time.

When the door opened, Franco said, 'Did you take a leak?'

'Of course I did,' Kevin said, too defensively.

'Then flush the toilet, for God's sake.'

With horror, Kevin realized he had completely forgotten to act his part. He couldn't afford any more mistakes like that.

'Happy?' he said.

'Come on,' Franco said, pushing Kevin into the hall.

He tried to walk casually down the hall, but the urge to run was strong. He had only a minute at most. At last, he opened the door to the bedroom – slowly, to avoid a sudden change in air pressure that might set off the explosive. Kevin cast his eyes downward, peering to see the dark spots on the floor. If he stepped on one of the circles, he might lose a foot. He turned without moving farther into the room and closed the door behind him. Franco gave him a funny look, probably wondering why he was doing it instead of letting Franco, but Kevin didn't have time to worry about it. When the door was closed and locked behind him, Kevin took the superglue from beneath the sink and squirted it into the lock mechanism.

He lifted the chair and carried it to the door, always keeping an eye on the two purple dots on the floor. With the top of the chair again wedged under the doorknob, he placed it gently on the floor and shoved until it was held tightly in position. He glanced at the watch they'd let him keep. He had only seconds left. He needed to get to the window.

Hand towel and rag in hand, he moved the desk so that the top was even with the window. The desk was light enough so that he could lift it without making noise. He sat up on the desk with his feet toward the window. Kevin waited.

He didn't have to wait long. A loud bang echoed through the hallway, followed almost instantly by another, larger explosion. The concoction had worked exactly as planned. The mixture of ammonia and bleach had blown the bottle apart as it formed deadly chlorine gas, setting off the ammonium triiodide contact explosive poured onto the shelf next to it, bursting the bottle of ammonia. If he was lucky, smoke and fumes were now billowing from the bathroom.

His answer came a second later as an earsplitting alarm sounded throughout the house, no doubt set off by the smoke detector. He heard the guard outside yell 'Fire!' and then race down the hall. Now was his chance. He hoped they were too distracted by the blaze to worry about him.

Kevin held on to the desk and kicked at the window with both his feet. The glass shattered. Normally it would have set off the alarm, but the explosion had already done that. As he had hoped, the fire alarm and the burglar alarm were one and the same.

Clearing the smashed window of glass shards, Kevin

raised the screen and looked over the edge. No guards in sight. Twenty feet below the window was a hedge about four feet high. To his left was the top of the portico covering the front porch.

Another shout down the hall. This time Kevin heard his name. Footsteps pounded toward the room. He began to climb out feet first.

The lock rattled.

'Hurry up!' someone said.

'I'm trying!' yelled Franco.

'Open it!'

'It won't work!' said Franco. 'That asshole did something to the lock.'

Kevin's legs dangled over the side. He slid his waist across the edge and supported himself with his elbows.

'Forget about the damn lock!'

The door shuddered as someone kicked it. It held, but several more blows would splinter the wood.

He had to jump now. As Kevin pushed off, another kick caused part of the frame to crack. Kevin saw the chair slide three inches toward the purple spots. Then he was free-falling.

If he hit a sturdy branch in the hedge, his ankle could be easily twisted or he could even break his leg. His butt came in contact with the hedge first, but the myriad tiny branches brought him to a gentle stop. The hedge's sharp needles scraped him in dozens of places, but otherwise he was fine.

Above him, he heard the pop of twin explosions as the chair legs hit the ammonium triiodide.

'He's got a gun!' Franco yelled.

Shots blasted into the room.

'What the hell are you doing?' screamed the other voice. 'We can't kill him!'

Their voices lowered, becoming inaudible to Kevin. He didn't care. In a few seconds they'd realize he was no longer in the room. He had to get to the forest before that happened.

He rolled off the top of the hedge and crouched on the ground with his back to the front porch, ready to sprint.

Two shots rang out behind him and the rounds pinged off the ground next to him. He spun to see David Lobec and Clayton Tarnwell standing on the porch twenty feet from him.

'Mr Hamilton,' Lobec said, 'I can assure you that I could have hit you from this range, and I can tell you from experience that getting shot in the leg is not pleasant.' He threw a sideways glance at Tarnwell, who stared at Kevin in fury and disbelief. 'Didn't I tell you he was resourceful?'

Franco, still huffing from his mad dash down the stairs, led Kevin up the front steps until he was facing Lobec and Tarnwell.

Franco patted him down and said, 'He's clean.'

Bern came to a stop in the doorway. 'There wasn't any fire. But the smoke was some kind of poison gas. Two of our men have to get to a hospital. We'll need to air out the upstairs.'

Tarnwell got nose to nose with Kevin. 'You wrecked my house, you little prick.' He turned on Lobec. 'You were supposed to clean out that bathroom.'

'I'm sorry, Mr Tarnwell,' Lobec said, glaring at Franco with bald contempt. 'I trusted Mr Francowiak to do the job. I'll make sure he is disciplined severely.'

Franco's eyes bugged out when he realized he was the one responsible.

'I could have sworn I cleaned out—'

'But you didn't,' Lobec said. 'Wait for me in the kitchen.'

'But I—'

Lobec shot Franco another look and he shut up, seeming to shrink two sizes.

Tarnwell sneered at Franco and just nodded as Franco went inside.

Kevin had blown his only shot at escape, but at least he had the satisfaction of causing serious damage to the expensive mansion. 'Is that going to cost a lot to fix?'

'You think you're funny?' Tarnwell said.

'Mr Hamilton,' Lobec said, 'as I warned you, any attempt on your part to cause trouble would force me to have you restrained. Mr Bern, get some rope.'

Three hours later, with Kevin safely locked in another bedroom and all traces of the gas vented, Tarnwell motioned to Lobec to close the library door. He poured a snifter of Courvoisier and took a hand-rolled Cuban cigar from the mahogany humidor. Tarnwell noticed that Lobec stayed far on the other side of the room as he lit the cigar.

'Care for one, David?' he asked, knowing full well what the answer would be.

'No, thank you.'

Tarnwell blew a smoke ring in Lobec's direction, then closed his eyes as he sipped the cognac. After a long pause to savor the taste, he swallowed and opened his eyes. 'David, you were damned careless tonight. Your plan for tomorrow better be an improvement. Tell me about it.'

Still standing at the other side of the library, Lobec's eyes followed the smoke ring until it dissipated. 'It's very simple, really. I will have two men in separate cars posted at each end of the bridge. They can't get there too early or police may stop to ask why they are holding up traffic. We will let Miss Jensen approach, if she is not already there. Once I verify that she has the notebook, we make the exchange and let them leave.'

Tarnwell raised an eyebrow. 'You'll let them leave?'

'At least give them that impression. Since Mr Bern and I must be on foot, it would be risky to terminate them in the middle of the bridge. Too much attention would be drawn to us, with no way to escape easily.'

'Then where do you get them?'

'My men have instructions to take them at the end of the bridge. I have an unmarked panel van ready. We can then dispose of them so that there will be no connection to us.'

'Don't you think they might have thought of that?' said Tarnwell.

'Of course, but they will have no defense. As a last resort, we may have to kill them there, but we will avoid that if we can.'

'What about the water?'

'Unlikely. They would have to swim a quarter of a mile to get to shore.'

'Are you worried about Erica bringing the police?'

'She has no proof. The police won't believe her. Besides, if they try to stake out the bridge, we'll see them.'

Lobec's reasoning seemed valid. 'It sounds like you've got things under control, David. Just make sure you get the right notebook. We don't have time for any more delays. In case Erica doesn't show up, I'll be handling our contingency. Call me when you've succeeded.'

With a wave of his hand, Tarnwell dismissed him. After the door was closed, Tarnwell pressed an intercom button next to his chair.

'Come in, Richard,' he said.

Through the library's other door came Richard Bern. He stood uncomfortably in front of Tarnwell.

'You wanted to see me, Mr Tarnwell?'

'Yes, Richard, I did. You have a real strong future in this company. You've become one of my go-to guys, and you know that I treat my trusted employees well.'

'You sure do, Mr Tarnwell. I'm lucky to be working for you.'

'The reason I asked you in here is because I need someone I trust on my side. David's foul-up tonight makes me worried, like his head's not in the game. I need you to keep an eye on him.'

'Sure, Mr Tarnwell, anything.'

'What do you think of his plan tomorrow?'

'Seems solid to me.'

'Good. I don't need any more mistakes. Just make sure that notebook gets back to me in one piece. It contains something that will make us all rich, you included. This will be the most important job you've ever had. Don't let David mess this up. Do whatever it takes to get that notebook, I mean anything. Are you up for that?'

'You pay the bills.'

'All right,' Tarnwell said. 'See you tomorrow.'

Bern took the cue and exited.

Tarnwell turned the cigar over in his fingers, treating himself to one more minute of relaxation. In less than twenty-four hours, such moments would be rare. Even with the Adamas process, it would be hard work becoming the richest man in the world.

After a sleepless night tied to a four-poster bed, Kevin ached all over, and his eyes were gummed from sleeping two straight nights without removing his contacts. At six in the morning, Bern, who was uncharacteristically dressed in gray sweatpants and a blue hooded sweatshirt, came in to untie the ropes. He led Kevin to a different bathroom, but this time the door remained open.

Kevin was given water but no breakfast. He thought he could hear Bern chuckling at his growling stomach as they walked downstairs to the library.

Lobec stood as Kevin and Bern entered the room. He, like Bern, was casually dressed, in jogging shorts, a long-sleeved cotton pullover, and an Orioles baseball cap.

'I hope you slept well despite the conditions,' Lobec said.

Kevin had caught a glance at himself in the upstairs mirror and knew he looked like hell.

'Where's Tarnwell? Doesn't he want to join in on the fun too?'

'Mr Tarnwell has business in Washington this morning.'

Lobec looked at his watch. 'Are you ready to meet Miss Jensen?'

'I don't have much choice, do I?'

'Of course not.'

Lobec nodded at Bern, who cuffed Kevin's hands in front of him. The three of them went outside to a sedan waiting for them at the mansion entrance. A new guy was in the driver's seat. Franco was nowhere to be seen.

'Just the four of us?' said Kevin as they pulled away from the house. 'I would have thought you'd bring the whole goon squad.'

'Mr Wilson will be dropping us off. There is no reason to upset Miss Jensen unnecessarily with a large contingent.' Even though Kevin couldn't tell from the smooth voice, he knew Lobec was lying. Lobec probably already had men stationed around the bridge, waiting to tell him when Erica arrived.

Forty minutes later, Wilson stopped at the eastern side of Arlington National Cemetery. It was a ten-minute walk to the bridge.

As Bern dragged him from the car, Kevin said, 'So, what's the plan?'

'We will escort you to the middle of the bridge, where Miss Jensen should be waiting for us,' Lobec said. 'She'll leave the notebook and videotape on the sidewalk and you'll be free to go.'

Kevin tossed out a contemptuous chuckle and held up his cuffed hands. 'Can I at least get these off?'

'No. You've already shown a penchant for causing trouble. I'll release your hands before we make the exchange.' Lobec draped a sweatshirt over Kevin's cuffed wrists.

Bern pulled his hood up, and they began walking toward the Arlington Memorial Bridge. The western face of the Lincoln Memorial was still in shadow, and in the distance Kevin could see the Washington Monument and the Capitol. They climbed down the incline, crossed a busy interchange, and walked onto the north side of the bridge.

The bridge was essentially a six-lane road with ten-foot-wide sidewalks on both sides. Cement railings lined the edge, with lamps embedded in square pillars every twenty feet. The half-mile span arched over the Potomac seventy-five feet below. A fine mist rose from the river's placid surface, and the rising sun cast long shadows across the water.

As Kevin expected, several early-morning exercisers jogged or biked across the bridge. Traffic was brisk, but not heavy. That would change nearer to eight o'clock, especially on the other side, where traffic was flowing from the Virginia suburbs into the District. No cars were allowed to park on the bridge at any time, which was probably why Lobec had agreed to the location. There was nowhere for the police to observe the transaction without him seeing them.

Erica would come by one of two ways to meet them for the exchange. She would either pull up in a car and leave it for a few seconds while they made the trade, or she would walk. He didn't like either scenario. Lobec and Bern could easily force him and Erica into a car. And if she walked, they had to trust that Lobec would let them get to the end of the bridge to whatever mode of transportation she had waiting.

They reached the center of the bridge and stopped next to a cement pillar. All three stood facing traffic, scanning both directions. Kevin looked at his watch. It was six fifty-seven.

From a distance, it was difficult to tell one walker from another, and Lobec and Bern had several false starts each time they saw lone women coming toward them.

The traffic heading toward Virginia suddenly stopped, blocked by a cab that had come to a halt a hundred yards away. A single woman got out, looked both directions, and walked toward them while the cab drove on.

Kevin had trouble seeing her face through his dirty contacts. The tall, slender form matched Erica's height, but her hair didn't cascade over her shoulders as Erica's usually did. This woman wore a T-shirt and shorts and carried a bag at her side. But despite his blurred vision, Kevin had no doubt. The long legs and distinctive, purposeful stride were Erica's.

On her cab ride from the L'Enfant Plaza Metro station, Erica had been careful to look out for any sign that she was being followed. In fact, for the last day and a half, she'd had a continuous, almost paranoid awareness of her surroundings. If Kevin's abductors even guessed at what she was about to try, she'd never get away with it.

Up ahead she saw Kevin, but he made no sign that he recognized her. She couldn't see the two men behind him clearly. One wore sunglasses and a baseball cap and the other's head was covered by a hood. She guessed that they were the same two who had kidnapped Kevin from the parking lot at Virginia Tech.

Erica didn't see anyone else, but that only made her more nervous. She knew they had to be around somewhere and searched for all the clichés: a parked car with a man reading a newspaper, a sidewalk vendor, a jogger taking a slow walk to cool down. There were joggers and walkers of all types, but cars couldn't park on the bridge and vendors were nowhere to be seen. As far as she could tell, there was no one out of the ordinary. She didn't like it.

She walked slowly toward them, trying to detect any unusual movement in her periphery. Footsteps pounded behind her. She clutched the bag close to her chest and whirled around to see a sixty-year-old woman focusing on the ground as she plodded past Erica. Erica tried to calm herself and continued toward the middle of the bridge.

When she was fifty feet from Kevin and his escorts, she moved toward the side of the bridge and held the bag over the railing as she walked. The concrete railing was about a foot wide and at shoulder level, so Erica had to stay close to the edge with her arm outstretched. Inside the bag was a kayaking pack she'd bought yesterday at an outdoors store. She'd wrapped the pack in a canvas bag to hide the fact that it was waterproof.

Thirty feet away from Kevin, she stopped. She could tell from this distance that she was right about the men's identities. Barnett was in jogging shorts and a cap, and Kaplan's bulky frame looked at home in the sweatpants and sweatshirt he wore. She could also see that Kevin's hands were cuffed in front of him. Kaplan shoved him, and they began to walk toward her.

'Don't come any closer, Barnett, or whatever the hell your name is,' Erica said, shaking the bag. 'I'll throw the notebook in the river.'

'Their real names are Lobec and Bern,' Kevin said, nodding to each of them.

'Be quiet,' Lobec said, He held a pistol to Kevin's right side, out of sight of the passing traffic. 'How do I know that what I want is in the bag?'

'First, I want to know if Kevin's all right.'

Lobec nodded for Kevin to speak.

'Except for a couple of bruises,' he said, 'I'm fine. Are you okay?'

'Considering the circumstances, I'd rather be doing what I was doing the night my parents died.' She looked at the river, hoping to give an impression of sadness to Lobec and Bern. Then she looked back at Kevin.

His eyes flicked twice to the river. 'I know what you mean.'

Good, he got the message. Now they had to find the right time. Maybe they could make it a few yards down the bridge before they attempted her plan.

'Miss Jensen. The contents of the bag?'

Erica climbed onto the railing and sat, keeping the bag over the river. She unwrapped the kayaking pack inside the bag, out of Lobec's view. She withdrew the Adamas notebook and flipped a few of the pages to show him the writing.

'And the videotape? You have that as well?' said Lobec.

She replaced the notebook and took out the videotape. He seemed satisfied. She stuffed it back in the kayaking pack and Velcroed it shut. Her arm was again outstretched over the water.

'I suppose you expect me to trust that those are the originals and that no copies have been made,' Lobec said.

'Just like I have to trust you to let us go once you have them. Now, let Kevin go or I'll drop the bag in the water and no one will ever see the Adamas notebook again.'

'I don't care,' Lobec said.

She was taken aback by the statement. Kevin furrowed his brow. Even Bern seemed puzzled.

'I'm serious,' Erica said. 'I'm going to drop it.'

'I certainly hope you're serious,' Lobec said. 'Go ahead. Drop it.' Then he turned and shot Bern.

THIRTY-SEVEN

Kevin had been ready to act ever since he realized what Erica was planning. When Lobec said, 'Drop it,' Kevin knew it was time. He twisted and swung his arms at Lobec's head. At the same time, he heard Lobec's gun fire, but he didn't let that slow him down. The full force of Kevin's blow snapped Lobec's neck sideways and he staggered away.

Kevin ran to the side of the bridge while Lobec was still stunned. Erica was already standing on the concrete railing. He shouted, 'Go!' and Erica jumped.

Kevin didn't bother climbing onto the railing. He vaulted over it, praying that the river was deep enough for him to make the running dive.

As he fell, Kevin could imagine Erica entering the water in a perfect pike position. In contrast he had no control and spun end over end. He tried to stabilize his trajectory in the two seconds of free fall he had, aiming his feet at the water. Then the soles of his feet slammed into the murky Potomac.

He sank for what seemed like forever despite his attempts to stop. Finally, his direction reversed. The impact had knocked the wind out of him, and his lungs were already crying for fresh air. He kicked furiously.

Just when he thought he was never going to breathe again, he caught a glimmer of light and kicked harder. He broke the surface and gasped, the crisp morning air filling his lungs.

Kevin looked around for signs of Erica, panicking when he didn't see her. He took a deep breath, about to dive back under and begin a search, when he heard, 'Kevin, over here.'

He spun around. The impact of water must have jarred his contacts loose, because all he saw was an indistinct blur bobbing in the water. She had already swum twenty yards to the next bridge pylon. She waved for him to swim in her direction and disappeared behind it. He tried to swim freestyle, but the shackles on his hands made that impossible. The best he could manage was a lame dog paddle.

Kevin propelled himself as quickly as he could to get past the next pylon and under the bridge. As he came around the pylon, he looked for Erica's face, but instead he saw a large object come into view, bobbing on the surface of the water next to the concrete wall of the pylon. As he got closer, he saw letters painted on its side. He squinted. *Lady Luck*.

'There's a ladder on the left,' Erica called from the boat's deck. 'Hurry. They could be here any second.'

Kevin sputtered through the water. 'I'm swimming as fast as I can. The handcuffs aren't helping.'

He gripped the top rung of the ladder with both hands

and pulled himself up to get his feet to the bottom rung. Erica grabbed his arms and pulled, heaving him up so that he lay on the deck with his feet dangling over the back. From this position Kevin was able to sit up. The boat looked to be a sixteen-footer.

'What can I do?' he said, trying to catch his breath. He rubbed his eyes, and one of his contacts came back into focus. The other one was lost in the jump.

'Here. Untie this mooring while I start her up.'

He awkwardly worked on the tie-down while she started the noisy outboard motor. After wrestling with it for a few seconds, he finally released the knot, and *Lady Luck* floated away from the pylon.

'Clear!' Kevin yelled.

Erica gunned the throttle, and the boat shot forward, its bow rising high above the water's surface. Within seconds, they were cruising south on the Potomac at thirty-five knots.

'Where are we going?' Kevin said.

'Bayshore Marina. That's where I rented this. I brought you some dry clothes in the bag. Your gun's there too.'

'You're a smart woman.' He wanted to celebrate their reunion properly with a big hug and kiss, but now wasn't the time. 'How far?'

'The marina's about fifteen minutes from here. We should have plenty of time before our meeting with Sutter.'

Kevin looked at his watch. It was seven fifteen. The meeting with the FBI agent wasn't until nine o'clock.

'Jumping off the bridge,' he said, shaking his head. 'I'm impressed.'

'I'm just glad you got the reference to my diving meet. I didn't want Lobec to get even a hint that we'd try that.'

'When did you get the idea?'

'During that phone call. When I lived here six years ago, I biked to work every day. I came from the Virginia side, over the Arlington Bridge, and around the Mall. I always saw boats on the river. I didn't know if it was deep enough to jump until yesterday when I checked the navigation charts at the marina. They said it's up to ninety feet deep in the middle. It was a chance.'

'I'll take jumping into a river over getting shot any day.'

To the left, a white rounded shape rose above some trees. He'd never been to D.C. before, but Kevin recognized the Jefferson Memorial's domed top from photographs. An engine roared above them, and Kevin looked up to see a jet. He wasn't sure, but it looked like it had just taken off. It banked to the left and headed up the Potomac.

'Reagan National Airport,' Erica said, pointing to her right. 'About a half mile ahead is the end of the runway. Looks like the bleachers are still there.' Three planes were lined up to take off.

'Bleachers?'

'Yeah. The jogging path goes right by the airport. Someone set up bleachers just on the other side of the fence surrounding the airport. A lot of people take breaks to watch the planes taking off.' Erica paused. 'Why did Lobec do it?'

Kevin looked at her. 'You mean shoot Bern?' She nodded. 'He probably wanted Adamas for himself. Once he got all of us out of the way, he could disappear and sell it to the highest bidder. But, of course, not until after he applied for the patent. It would be no good without the patent protection.'

'Who was the guy in charge? The Texan.'

'Clayton Tarnwell. He owns a mining and chemical company. Tarnwell would probably have gone after him, but this guy Lobec is smart. He would have gotten away.'

His hands still cuffed, Kevin looked around at the boat for something to use to pick them. The bow was open and lined on either side with bench seats. An aisle split the main console, which had a bucket seat behind it on either side. More bench seats lined the aft section. A one-hundred-horsepower Mercury outboard thrashed a spray of water into the air.

When his eyes reached the top of the ladder fastened to the back of the boat, he stopped and gasped. They both had been so focused on their destination that neither of them had bothered to look behind them.

One hand curled over the stern. Then a grimacing face rose above the hand. Kevin stared in disbelief as David Lobec smiled and continued to pull himself up.

THIRTY-EIGHT

After Kevin had hit him in the head back on the bridge, Lobec was dazed for only a second, but it was enough for Kevin and Erica to jump over the side of the bridge without Lobec firing a shot. The undeniable pleasure he'd taken in shooting the insufferable Bern provided the rest of the distraction.

Lobec recovered quickly from the blow and ran over to see Kevin splash to the surface, his girlfriend already taking cover under the bridge at the next pylon west. Unfortunately, some of the passing cars stopped to investigate, leaving no chance for Lobec to take them out from above. Erica and Kevin disappeared under the bridge.

For the benefit of the bystanders, Lobec pointed at Bern and yelled, 'My God! Someone shot him and jumped off the bridge!' Then Lobec ran. If Tarnwell's men had been stationed at the ends of the bridge, they could have intercepted Erica and Kevin as they swam to shore. But he had lied to Tarnwell about the reinforcements: extra men didn't fit into his plans.

Lobec sprinted toward the Virginia end of the bridge,

pausing at the next pylon to see if he could find them in the water. That's when he heard the boat's motor fire up and realized they would get away unless he did something drastic. There were only a few small docks north of the bridge, so he took a chance that they were headed south.

Lobec tucked his SIG Sauer into the waistband of his shorts and sprinted through the slow-moving traffic, crossing the six lanes in seconds. Without stopping, he leapt off the opposite side of the bridge. When he surfaced, he swam around the support and saw a boat puttering out from under the bridge ten feet in front of him. He lunged forward and thrust his arm toward the aft ladder just as the boat went to full throttle. He caught his hand in between the rungs of the boat's ladder and gritted his teeth as the force of the jolt dislocated his left shoulder, nearly ripping his arm from its socket.

It took all of his concentration to keep his legs from being tossed by the waves into the exposed propeller. After a minute, though, he was able to grab hold of the ladder's side with his other hand, extricate his injured arm, and raise himself enough to get a foothold. Then he inched his way up. As his head rose above the boat's edge, he smiled at seeing Kevin's shocked face, although the surprise had come earlier than he hoped.

Kevin's inaction lasted only a fraction of a second. Cursing, he began fumbling with a bag lying next to him. The girl turned around and screamed when she saw Lobec.

'Shake him loose!' Kevin yelled.

Lobec was still climbing into the boat and had to hold on tightly to keep from being thrown into the water as Erica swerved the boat from side to side.

Kevin found what he was looking for, withdrawing a Glock pistol from the bag. He yelled in the girl's direction.

'Okay. Stop the boat.' Kevin held the Glock with both hands still cuffed.

Erica pushed the throttle to STOP and turned to face Lobec.

'Keep your hands where I can see them,' Kevin said.

Lobec couldn't draw his own weapon because his right hand was holding onto the ladder and his left was useless. He couldn't raise the injured arm enough to grab the pistol, let alone fire it accurately. Given Kevin's marksmanship, Lobec slowly eased his legs over the side of the boat without trying to draw.

'That's far enough,' Kevin said. 'Now, with the thumb and forefinger of your right hand, grab only the butt of the pistol in your shorts and toss it over the side.'

At a range of three meters, Kevin would not miss if Lobec tried to draw the awkward pistol-and-silencer combination. But he had no intention of doing as he was told. He dropped it to the deck.

Kevin's eyes narrowed. 'I said into the water.'

Knowing that he now had the opportunity to grab the pistol and take his shot, Lobec bent over to retrieve it.

'Stop!' Kevin shouted. 'Stand up!'

Lobec complied. He was impressed that Kevin hadn't fallen for his ruse.

'Slide it over here with your right foot,' Kevin said.

'Or what,' Lobec said. 'Or you'll shoot me?'

'You killed my father. Give me one good reason why I shouldn't blow your head off.' Kevin had to raise his voice to be heard over the sound of an airplane throttling up at the end of the runway.

'Kevin, don't,' Erica said.

'He won't, Miss Jensen. And I have a very good reason for you not to kill me. Because I can tell you what this is all about. Besides, I am an unarmed man. I doubt that you've ever shot anyone in your life. And you won't shoot me.' He moved his left leg forward. Even with his dislocated shoulder, Lobec merely had to get close enough to disarm Kevin. Two arm's lengths would do it.

With feline quickness, Kevin shifted the gun and shot Lobec in the left calf. Lobec stumbled, for the first time surprised, but he caught himself on the other leg. He didn't look down. The pain was no worse than other gunshot injuries he'd endured, probably little more than a flesh wound.

'Are you convinced now?' Kevin pointed the pistol at Lobec's head.

'Quite.' With his right foot, Lobec tapped the SIG Sauer, which slid along the deck to Kevin's feet.

'All right, then,' Kevin said as he slowly dipped to the deck to pick up the SIG, never taking his eyes off Lobec. He put the pistol in his waistband. 'I decided I want to hear what you have to say. Sit on that cushion.' Kevin pointed at the back of the boat with his head. 'And remember to keep your hands in the air.'

An interesting predicament, Lobec thought as he sat with a squish on the cushioned ledge. To be at the mercy of his captors, most likely to be turned in to the authorities, was a situation he'd never before faced. But despite his injuries, his hand-to-hand skills were still formidable if he could find an opportunity to use them. He had to get Erica and Kevin off guard. And presently, he had only one way to do that. Tell them the truth.

'I can't believe you shot him,' Erica said.

'It's only a minor wound,' Kevin said, seeing that Lobec's expression hadn't wavered. 'He wouldn't have stopped if I hadn't. He'll be all right.'

Which was true, but for the moment Lobec was a mess. Blood was streaming down his leg and pooling on the deck. His left arm dangled awkwardly at his side.

'You are probably wondering why I shot Mr Bern.'

'We know why,' Kevin said. 'Because you're a greedy son of a bitch like Tarnwell. You wanted Adamas, and you weren't willing to share.'

'Then why did he tell me to throw the bag into the river?' Erica said.

'What?'

'When I told him to let you go or I'd throw the bag in the

river, he said that he didn't care. He told me to drop it into the Potomac.'

'He was bluffing.'

'On the contrary, Mr Hamilton. She's right. My hope was that she would drop the bag in the river.'

'Oh, really?' Kevin said sarcastically. 'And why did you shoot Bern? So you could let us go?'

'Mr Bern's death was tragically unavoidable in the protection of my employers' interests.'

'Tarnwell's interests involve you killing one of his men and destroying the Adamas process?'

Lobec smiled. 'No. But then again, Mr Tarnwell is not my real employer.'

'What are you talking about?' Kevin said. 'Who are you?'

'I thought that would be obvious by now. I'm a spy. The corporate type.'

Out of the corner of his eye, Kevin could see Erica turn to him in surprise, but he didn't take his eyes off Lobec. The pistol was still pointed straight at his head. The pool of blood was slowly expanding at Lobec's feet.

Kevin was dubious. 'Who are you?' he demanded again. 'Who *do* you work for?'

'My real name is unimportant. As for my company, I represent a coalition of mining firms that are in competition with Tarnwell Mining and Chemical. His acquisitions have been accumulating quickly, and my backers were wary of his growing power in the industry. Originally, I was just to observe his dealings and report back. Of course, he thinks I'm a mercenary for hire, bowing to his every wish because he believed that he arranged my release from a Mexican prison.'

'But then Adamas came along and changed everything.'

Lobec nodded. 'The companies I represent have substantial holdings in diamond mines around the world. A process that would make those investments worthless would be an unacceptable risk.'

'So you were just going to have me destroy Adamas?' Erica asked.

'The firms didn't like the idea of sharing. Messy. There is *one* item of value in your bag. If Michael Ward wasn't lying, that videotape would have given me something to use against Tarnwell.'

'What do you mean?'

'You haven't watched it?'

'We watched it,' Erica said. 'It was the whole experiment where Kevin's equipment melted down. So what?'

'Then Ward *was* lying,' Lobec said with surprise. 'It doesn't matter. Tarnwell's easy enough to manipulate without it.'

'So you never were helping Tarnwell?'

'Oh, my missions occasionally helped him just to maintain the illusion, but losing Adamas would almost surely ruin him. Tarnwell has all of his money riding on a merger with Forrestal Chemical. If he doesn't have Adamas by tomorrow, his company won't be worth enough to pay off the interest on his loans.'

Kevin chuckled. 'You expect us to believe this load of crap?'

'It's the truth.'

'The truth! You've already given me two names. Lord knows how many others you have. You killed my father, Ward, Stein, Bern. Pardon me for thinking this is a bunch of bullshit. Erica, start the boat. We're taking this guy to the police. Let them figure out whether he's telling the truth.'

'I must point out that I'm merely trying to protect you. Tarnwell has thirty men still looking for you. They'll find you, just as I ... found ... ' Lobec's voice trailed off and he stumbled, catching himself on the gunwale.

'We need to stop the bleeding,' she said. 'He's going into shock.' She started toward him.

Kevin put his left hand out to stop her. 'Wait until we get to the marina. It'll only be a few minutes.'

'If you nicked an artery, he may not have that much time.' She struggled against his arm, and Kevin turned his head to face her.

'Erica, I'm telling you, this guy is dangerous. If he—'

Kevin's left arm suddenly exploded in pain. The impact of Lobec's foot knocked the gun from his hand. The Glock ricocheted off the port side of the boat. Before he could react, Lobec slammed him backward against the console.

In the next instant, Kevin could feel a hand pawing at his midsection. He realized what was happening and wrapped both hands around Lobec's wrist just as the SIG Sauer was being drawn from his waistband.

Erica, who had nearly fallen overboard when Kevin glanced off her, regained her balance and came up behind Lobec, grabbing his injured shoulder. Lobec yelled in pain and released his grip. The SIG clattered to the deck. In a single twisting motion, he swung in a 180-degree arc and threw his fist at Erica. She ducked to avoid a direct blow, but Lobec managed to catch the top of her head. It was enough to send her reeling toward the bow.

Kevin stooped to pick up the fallen SIG. As his fingers brushed the grip, Lobec threw his knee into Kevin's chest, knocking the wind out of him. Then Kevin felt himself being tossed to the back of the boat.

While he struggled to breathe, Kevin saw the Glock lying underneath a life vest in front of him. He scrambled over to it. In a prone position, Kevin raised the pistol and turned to point it at Lobec.

At the same time, Lobec rose next to the console, holding the SIG Sauer. But it wasn't pointed at Kevin. It was pointed at Erica, now standing at the bow of the boat.

'Hold it!' Kevin yelled.

Lobec remained facing Erica. 'I saw you retrieve the Glock, Mr Hamilton. Drop it or I'll kill her.'

'What if I kill you first?'

'You're in handcuffs and in an awkward position. I am not. My chances are much better.'

'If you kill her, you'll die and I'll still have the Adamas notebook. Now, put down the damn gun!'

Erica looked at Kevin. Oddly, she didn't seem as terrified as Kevin was. Instead, she was concentrating on him. Her eyes almost imperceptibly moved toward the water and then back to him. Her legs were bent, ready for action. Kevin understood what she was thinking. But Lobec was standing no more than eight feet from her. She'd never be able to dive into the river before he shot her. Kevin shook his head.

'Kevin, we both know how this is going to end—'

The roar of a jet taking off drowned out Lobec's words. His eyes flicked toward the noise, and Erica dove over the side. Kevin, who was ready for her to use the distraction, pulled the Glock's trigger and shot Lobec in the chest. It wasn't enough to put Lobec down. He fired the SIG as Erica flew backward, getting three shots off within the second it took her to hit the water.

'No!' Kevin shouted. Lobec turned to face him. There was no expression on the man's face. No sadness, no remorse, no anger, no pleasure. Just the determined look of a professional carrying out his duty.

He swung the SIG in Kevin's direction. Without thinking, Kevin fired three more times, all three bullets slamming into Lobec's chest, blood spraying with each impact. The gun dropped from Lobec's hand. For a moment he just stood there as if nothing had happened. The only change was his expression.

He looked puzzled.

The expression quickly faded. His eyes closed sleepily and he pitched forward, his lifeless body smacking the deck.

Kevin pushed himself to his feet and ran to the bow, expecting to see Erica's body floating facedown in the water. But all he could see in the placid surface of the Potomac was his horrified reflection.

THIRTY-NINE

Afraid that Erica had gotten stuck under the boat, Kevin dropped the Glock and prepared to dive in. A bubble broke the surface on the starboard side. Then another and another. Erica's head burst out of the water. She gasped for air and looked up to see Kevin.

'You're alive!' Kevin said, amazed.

'So are you!'

'Are you injured?' he asked, holding out his still-cuffed hands.

'No, I'm all right.' Erica pulled herself up and over the railing. When she was aboard, he pulled her to him and she hugged him fiercely.

'I was afraid you were gone.' Kevin's hands began to shake and his teeth chattered.

'Are *you* okay?' Erica said.

'Yeah. It's just beginning to sink in. I had to . . .' He hesitated.

'Lobec?'

Kevin nodded toward the back of the boat. 'Dead.' The shivering got worse.

'Are you sure?'

He didn't answer. She went behind the console and sucked in her breath when she saw the body.

'He's dead all right.'

'I thought you were too,' he said. 'He shot you. You fell backward—'

'No, I *dove* backward. I thought he might assume I'd dive forward. Apparently, he did. I heard one of the bullets zing past my ear.'

'Oh, that makes me feel a lot better.'

'Let's not dwell on it. It happened. Now let's get you out of those handcuffs.'

They retrieved the keys from Lobec's pocket, then moved the body away from the console and laid it against the port side. Kevin draped the boat's rain tarp over the corpse while Erica used the boat's handheld bilge pump to wash down the bloody deck.

After a long discussion about reporting the shooting to the police before their meeting with the FBI, Kevin and Erica decided they didn't want to take the chance of being taken in by the local police for a homicide before they could prove why they were on the run.

When they got back to the marina, Erica told the rental agency they would need the boat for another day. After she paid in advance with cash, the clerk promised that it wouldn't be disturbed.

The Metro station nearest the marina was a five-minute walk, and they had one stop to make before nine o'clock.

*

The white concrete of the J. Edgar Hoover Building gleamed in the morning sun, forcing Kevin to squint until he and Erica were inside. He glanced at his watch. 8:56. Right on time. The walk from the National Museum of Natural History had been only two blocks. Kevin breathed a sigh of relief. The worst was over. Now it was just a matter of getting someone in authority to believe them.

Normally, the FBI directs people reporting a crime to the Washington field office six blocks to the north, but Kevin had insisted on the headquarters because of its close proximity to the Mall. Carrying a loaded weapon into the Hoover Building would have been idiotic, so he had left the Glock on the boat. After showing their IDs and passing through a metal detector, Kevin and Erica were met by a frumpy woman in her fifties.

'I'm Marian James, Mr Hamilton. I'm an office assistant for Special Agent Sutter.'

'Hello. This is a friend of mine, Erica Jensen. Where's Agent Sutter?'

'He's waiting for us. He asked me to bring you up to the conference room.' She led them to an elevator and she pressed the button for the fifth floor. 'You know, until a few minutes ago, I thought you wouldn't be coming.'

What is this woman talking about? Kevin looked at Erica. She seemed just as puzzled as he was.

The elevator opened and they got on. 'I'm sorry,' said Erica to Marian. 'I don't understand. Kevin made this appointment last week.'

The elevator door opened again, and Marian walked down the hall as she spoke. 'Yes, but yesterday Mr Tarnwell left word that you wouldn't be coming, so I canceled—'

'Tarnwell?'

'Clayton Tarnwell. You know him, right?'

'Yes, I do. What did he say?'

'Just that we shouldn't expect you to keep the appointment. I'll have to let Special Agent Sutter explain the rest.'

Of course. Kevin's cell phone. He had called the FBI on it. Tarnwell would have gone through the call log, discovered that they were planning to meet with Sutter, and canceled the meeting.

They stopped at the door of a small conference room. Two men were talking. One had his back to them. The other, a slender black man in his forties with a receding hairline and dressed in a dark suit, stood up when he saw them.

The second man turned and stood as well, and Kevin stopped short when he saw who it was. The expression on Clayton Tarnwell's face matched the shock that Kevin felt.

'Kevin. I ... I didn't expect to see you here.' Tarnwell quickly recovered. 'I'm glad you've decided to turn yourself in.'

The black man walked over to Kevin. 'Mr Hamilton, Miss Jensen, I'm Special Agent Sutter. Perhaps we should all sit down and discuss what Mr Tarnwell has been explaining to me.'

Kevin didn't take his eyes off Tarnwell. 'Agent Sutter,

whatever this bastard has told you is a lie,' Kevin said, barely restraining himself from yelling.

Tarnwell smiled at Kevin. 'No need to lose your cool now that I've exposed your plot.' He turned to Sutter. 'Don't let him fool you too. I've never met this girl before, but Kevin here is the slickest con artist I've ever seen.'

Kevin took a step toward Tarnwell with clenched fists. 'I should—' Before he could get any farther, Erica grabbed him, holding him back.

Erica spoke to Sutter. 'I don't know what Mr Tarnwell has told you, Agent Sutter, but Kevin has discovered a revolutionary new process that could change almost every industry overnight.'

'He's got her in on this thing with him too,' Tarnwell said. 'Clever kid, Kevin. Two voices are always better than one. But as I was just telling the special agent here, your plan's a failure. When I found out about your meeting with Agent Sutter, I thought I'd better come down and clear up any misunderstandings you might have caused. He needs to know how you and Dr Ward tried to swindle me out of an experimental process that is rightfully mine.'

'He's lying,' Kevin said.

Sutter put up his hands. 'I need to hear both sides of this story before we go any further—'

'I have evidence.' Kevin reached into his pocket for the specimen he'd completed two days ago.

'Ah, yes,' Tarnwell said. 'Let's see this evidence.'

Kevin walked over to Sutter and handed him a diamond the size and shape of an egg. It was perfectly clear, a flawless specimen, except for one thing: the safe-deposit box key fused in its middle.

Kevin had known he'd need some way of proving that it was actually fabricated and not mined. The key was the most appropriate thing he could think of.

While Sutter inspected the specimen, Kevin took the notebook out of the backpack and tossed it onto the conference table.

'It's all in there, sir. How we discovered it, how it works, everything. You are holding in your hand an artificially manufactured two-hundred-carat diamond.'

'All this proves is that he stole the process from me,' Tarnwell said.

Sutter held up the diamond. 'I don't know if I believe either of you. How do I know this is real?'

'If you'll just be patient, sir,' Kevin said, 'I'm sure we can show you in another minute that this is a real diamond.' Kevin repeatedly looked at the door to the outer office. *Where is he?*

'If you want to leave this with me, I can have it tested in a few days.' Sutter picked up the phone.

'No, you're our last hope. Tarnwell will have us killed before the night is over.'

'Will you listen to this?' Tarnwell said. 'The lies just go on and on. I promise you, Agent Sutter, that I am going to ask you to prosecute them to the fullest extent of the law.'

'Sir, you have to help us,' Erica said. 'Kevin's telling the truth. You have to arrest Tarnwell.'

Sutter bristled. 'I don't have to do anything.'

'They're afraid I'll have them killed?' Tarnwell said in affected bewilderment. 'Come on, Erica. Don't make this any worse for yourself.'

'Everyone sit down,' Sutter said, and they all took seats, with Tarnwell across from Kevin and Erica.

Sutter continued. 'Now I don't know what's going on, but—' The ringing of his phone cut him off. Sutter answered. 'Sutter ... Who? ...' He turned to Kevin but kept speaking into the phone. 'He did? ... You verified his credentials? ... Okay. Send him up.' He put the phone back in his pocket. 'I said sit down.'

'What's going on?' Tarnwell asked him.

Sutter looked down at the egg-size diamond. 'I guess we're going to find out.'

Marian came to the conference room with a man in a short-sleeved dress shirt, solid blue tie, and black poly-blend slacks that were a little too tight and a little too short. A battered leather briefcase was in his left hand.

Sutter stood and went over to him. 'Mr Downs?'

'Dr Downs. Quincy Downs. Are you Agent Sutter?'

'That's right. And this is Clayton Tarnwell. I believe you already know Kevin Hamilton and Erica Jensen.'

Downs nodded at Kevin and Erica. 'I do.'

Tarnwell stood and jabbed a finger at Downs. 'Who is this?'

'I'd like to introduce Dr Quincy Downs,' Kevin said, 'a geologist from the Smithsonian.'

'I actually work at the National Museum of Natural History. Mineralogy department.'

Tarnwell's eyes narrowed. For the first time this morning, Kevin smiled.

'I understand Mr Hamilton invited you here today,' Sutter said.

'Yes. And I was happy to come. This is very exciting.'

Sutter held up the diamond specimen and pointed at Kevin. 'Mr Hamilton claims that this clear material is a diamond. Is that true?'

Downs took the specimen with a gleam in his eye. 'When Kevin and Erica first came to my office this morning, I thought that this couldn't possibly be diamond.'

'Why not?'

'Well, for one, it has a key in the middle, which means it would have to be artificial. I've seen a few artificial diamonds, but this one's ten times as big as the largest I've ever heard of.'

Downs opened his briefcase, withdrew a jeweler's loupe, and examined the diamond.

'I couldn't see any flaws, but that doesn't mean anything. Fakes are getting better and better. It's especially difficult to tell without facets.' He removed a small scale from the bag and then took out a piece of electronic equipment. He placed the specimen on the scale.

'Two hundred and thirty-two carats. Minus, of course, whatever the key weighs.' The electronic equipment was a four-by-six-inch box with a display. Two wire leads came out of the box's top and ended in metal-tipped probes.

'What's that?' asked Sutter.

'This measures the electrical resistance of any material. Diamond has a unique resistive signature.' Downs pressed a button to turn the unit on and placed the two probes against the diamond's surface. 'I calibrated this instrument an hour ago, before I tested the sample with Kevin and Erica earlier this morning. It conclusively demonstrates that this material is diamond.'

Sutter picked the specimen up again and looked at Kevin. 'Where did you get this?'

'I made it.'

'It's incredible,' Downs said. 'This is as pure a diamond as I've ever seen.'

'But it's huge,' Sutter said. 'It must be worth a fortune.'

'With this clarity and color ... if it were cut and polished into gemstones, it would be worth nearly twenty thousand dollars per carat.'

'That's over four million dollars,' Erica said.

'Without the key in it, it would be worth far more. A stone that size hasn't come on the market in thirty years. It would create a sensation.'

'How do you explain this, Mr Tarnwell?' Sutter asked.

For a minute Tarnwell said nothing. 'I was hoping I wouldn't have to do this, Agent Sutter. I wanted to keep the process a secret until we had the patent issued, and I wanted to get this mess resolved without Kevin going to prison. But he's forced my hand. My scientists developed this process over six months ago. Kevin stole it.'

Kevin couldn't stop himself. 'This is insane!' he yelled. 'He's lying!'

'I was trying to settle this some other way,' Tarnwell continued, 'but I guess that just isn't possible now. Dr Michael Ward, a professor at South Texas, was working as a consultant for me. In particular, he was providing me with some important information on how to refine the diamond-making process. Although Michael was careful, Kevin got wind of it somehow and wanted it for himself. I think you'll discover that he's been having some financial troubles. I know how people can get desperate when they have no money, but I think we can all see how this has gone too far.'

Sutter appraised Tarnwell. Kevin hoped that he wasn't buying the story.

'Dr Ward and I discovered this process on South Texas University property with STU equipment,' he said.

'Kevin's telling the truth,' Erica said.

'Unfortunately,' Tarnwell said, 'Kevin's brought Erica into his scheme as well. Now she's going to be responsible for this along with him.'

The situation wasn't going the way Kevin had planned. He was beginning to worry that Tarnwell might actually talk his way out of this.

Erica whispered to Kevin. 'What about the tape?'

He whispered back. 'That won't prove anything. Sutter

won't know one experiment from another.' Then he
remembered Lobec specifically asking about the tape. He'd
said Ward had told him something about it, something he
might have used against Tarnwell. Maybe there was a
chance.

'Do you have a camcorder here?' Kevin said to Sutter.

'Why?'

'There may be something on a tape I have that will convince you that I really did invent this.'

At mention of a videotape, beads of sweat formed on
Tarnwell's forehead.

'All right,' Sutter said. 'What kind of camcorder do you
need?'

'It's a digital videotape.'

He dialed his phone. 'Marian. Please bring a digital
videotape camcorder to the conference room.'

'Agent Sutter,' Tarnwell said, 'I'd like to call my company's attorneys so that they can come in and consult on
this matter before we go any further.'

Sutter shook his head. 'You can leave if you like, but it's
not every day I see a two-hundred-carat artificial diamond.
I think we'll look at the tape.'

'Thank you,' said Kevin. He turned to Tarnwell. 'Lobec
didn't tell you what was on the tape, did he? Just like he
didn't tell you he was a corporate spy working for a con-
sortium of companies.'

'You're babbling to get yourself out of this mess you've
created. David Lobec is my head of company security.'

'That's what he led you to believe after he got out of that Mexican prison. I bet he was in there on purpose, just to make your releasing him seen convincing. His real name wasn't even Lobec.'

Tarnwell's face was a mask of pure shock. 'How did you know—'

'After he got Bern out of the way, he told us.'

Tarnwell recovered quickly from Kevin's revelations. 'As for your tape, Dr Ward was trying to blackmail me, cooking up some kind of evidence to do so. That must be what the recording is.'

Sutter had been listening to their conversation. 'After we watch this tape, you both are going to tell me who Lobec and Bern are.'

Marian walked in with a camcorder in hand. She took it over to the conference room's TV and began hooking it up.

'I'll tell you what's on the video,' Kevin said. 'It's the lab experiment where Ward and I first accidentally discovered the Adamas process. But Lobec seemed to think there was something more on it.'

Kevin took the tape over to the camcorder and inserted it. As it ran, he narrated the experiment in detail, referring to the notebook when it was appropriate. As he watched, he looked for anything he and Erica might have missed the first time they'd seen it.

As before when they had watched it in the store, the tape went to static after the Kevin on the screen switched off the camcorder. Kevin couldn't understand. He stared at it, hoping for a revelation about what he'd just seen, but nothing seemed especially significant.

Tarnwell didn't think so, either.

'Is this all you have to show us?' he said. 'Because I can tell you that I don't see what the big deal is. For all I know, that experiment could have been anything.'

'If we look closely at the equipment in the tape,' said Kevin, 'I think it's clear that we had the setup described in the notebook.'

'Even if it was the Adamas process,' Tarnwell continued, 'how do we know when you made the tape? You could just as easily have stolen the process from me, run the experiment with Ward later, and changed the time stamp on the camcorder. That kind of thing is faked all the time.'

'There's got to be something.' Kevin went over to the camcorder to rewind it to the beginning and play it back again.

'Agent Sutter,' said Tarnwell, 'I think one viewing is enough to see that there wasn't anything there.'

Just as Kevin reached for the camcorder, a new picture flickered into focus on the screen. He stopped and stepped aside to let the others see. It was the lab again, freshly cleaned and the damaged equipment replaced, but this time it was from a different point of view. The tripod was visible across the room. The camera was on the other side of the lab, probably on one of the lab shelves. The picture moved around as adjustments in the camera view were made. Then a voice said, 'Dammit!' Kevin recognized it immediately.

The camcorder stopped moving. Michael Ward walked past the camera into the field of view, tinkered with a piece of equipment, and left the room.

'Do we need to see this again?' Tarnwell said.

Kevin looked at Sutter. 'This is something different. I haven't seen it before.'

'Keep going,' Sutter said.

Nothing was happening on screen, so Kevin hit the FAST FORWARD button. After about a minute the lab door opened. Kevin released the button and watched the screen intently.

Michael Ward walked in and opened the lab's door wider.

'Come on in,' he said.

Another voice could be heard outside the door.

'David, wait for us out here.' Even muffled, the Texas drawl was unmistakable.

Ward's guest followed him into the lab. Although Ward was six feet tall, he looked puny next to the massive frame of Clayton Tarnwell.

FORTY

'**W**e've got about half an hour until my class starts,' Ward said on-screen as he closed the door. The lens of the camcorder captured almost the entire lab.

'That's all right,' the on-screen Tarnwell said. 'I don't have much time anyway.' He looked into the test chamber. 'Good. Nothing here but the test stand. All right, you can go ahead.'

As Ward began the experiment, Tarnwell wandered around the room, casually observing the equipment. When he looked directly at the camcorder, Kevin held his breath, afraid that Tarnwell had seen that it was recording. But after a second Tarnwell continued. The recording light on the lab's camcorder had been broken for months before the NV117 accident, so Tarnwell would have no way to know he was being recorded.

With a nod, Ward indicated he was ready.

'Let's see it,' Tarnwell said.

A hum emanated from the TV for a minute or so, then it was quiet. Ward walked over to the test chamber and opened the door. After a few seconds' inspection, he turned to Tarnwell.

'Take a look for yourself,' he said.

Tarnwell peered into the chamber. He began to reach in, but Ward grabbed his hand.

'Be careful. It's hot. Here.' Ward handed him a pair of tongs. A minute later Tarnwell held a metal pin in his hand. A target on top shined.

'The coating is only a couple of microns thick,' Ward said, 'but it's real diamond. You can take this back to your lab for testing.' Ward scratched the glass of the lab's door, leaving a five-inch streak, then handed it to Tarnwell.

Tarnwell looked in awe at the diamond-coated sample in his hand.

'Holy hell, Michael,' Tarnwell said. 'I wouldn't have believed it if I hadn't seen it with my own eyes.'

'Incredible, isn't it?' said Ward. 'I've been perfecting it for three months. I could produce fifty carats a day if I ran it around the clock.'

'Which makes me wonder why I'm here,' Tarnwell said. 'Why not just make them yourself?'

'Two reasons. The first is that I have other people around here all the time. The only time I get work done in the lab is late at night when no one else is around. That's why it's taken me three months to get as far as I have.'

'And the second?'

Ward closed the test chamber. 'I can cut sections off the

target, but it's difficult to do. I tried selling some of the diamond samples, but unpolished stones raised eyebrows. They wanted to know where I got them. After a couple of times and a lot of questions, I stopped. I figured it was better to sell the whole process at once rather than keep making diamonds myself. The only catch was to find someone who I trusted that had enough money to make it worthwhile.' Ward smiled. 'Of course, the first person I thought of was my old college buddy.'

'I appreciate that,' Tarnwell said. 'Of course, you realize that this is highly illegal.'

'Of course. I knew you'd see past any potential legal issues.' Ward smiled, and Tarnwell returned it.

'Good. Now that I've seen ... what did you call this process?'

'Adamas.'

'Now that I have seen Adamas, how about we talk business?'

They walked toward the lab door together.

'I think you can comprehend the value of something like this,' said Ward. 'You'll easily net over a billion dollars in the first year of production.' He stopped at the door.

'So, what are you thinking of?' said Tarnwell.

'Let's start with a nice round number. Fifty million.'

Tarnwell didn't blink. 'Why don't we talk about it over dinner?' He opened the door, and the two of them left. After a few seconds of fast-forwarding, it was obvious that the tape would run out recording the empty lab. Kevin pressed the STOP button, and the conference room went silent. He looked at Sutter and then Tarnwell.

'What do you have to say for yourself, Mr Tarnwell?' Sutter said.

Tarnwell didn't move. He stared at Kevin, his eyes closed to slits, his lips curled in a sneer.

'Lobec told us about the merger,' Kevin said. 'You bet it all, didn't you? Without Adamas, your company is nonexistent. Murdering Ward was the dumbest move you ever made.'

'Murder?' Sutter said with alarm. 'Ward was murdered?'

'Along with Herbert Stein, Richard Bern, and my father, Murray Hamilton.' Kevin leaned forward and looked Tarnwell in the eye. 'You're going to prison, you son of a bitch.'

Without warning, Tarnwell launched himself from the chair over the table. 'You little prick!' Kevin pushed Erica out of the way, and before he could do anything to protect himself, Tarnwell knocked him to the floor, straddled him, and gripped his throat, his meaty thumbs digging into Kevin's larynx. He had an insane look in his eyes, as if he didn't give a damn anymore. He probably didn't, which terrified Kevin. He was a man with nothing to lose.

Sutter grabbed Tarnwell from behind.

'Let him go!' Sutter yelled. Tarnwell released one hand and threw a massive elbow at Sutter, the lucky hit breaking a facial bone with an audible crack. Sutter reeled backward against the wall, screaming in pain.

As voices yelled in the background, Tarnwell whispered to Kevin, 'You're gonna die this time. And guess what? I'm going to plead insanity. You'll be dead and I'll be out of the asylum by next year.'

Kevin gasped for breath as he tried to pry Tarnwell's hands off his throat. He reached for Tarnwell's eyes, but his arms were five inches shorter than Tarnwell's.

Erica jumped onto Tarnwell's back. He let go of Kevin's throat and threw her off, which gave Kevin enough of an opening. He pushed Tarnwell away and launched his foot with all his strength, kicking Tarnwell squarely in the crotch.

Tarnwell grabbed himself and collapsed to the carpet in agony. At that moment two agents rushed into the room.

With his hand pressed to his eye, Sutter pointed at Tarnwell. 'Take this guy away. And make sure you cuff him.'

Kevin crawled over to Erica and she clasped him to her. 'I'm all right,' she reassured him. Then she let go and went over to examine Sutter's face. 'We'll have to get you to a hospital.'

'I'll be fine,' Sutter growled as he watched the two agents struggle to lift Tarnwell.

Kevin pulled himself to his feet and looked at Sutter, who peered back with his one good eye. His voice a raspy croak, Kevin said, 'Now do you believe us?'

A light breeze played through the lush foliage of the South Texas University campus, enhancing the unusually cool September evening. The sun was just setting over the chemistry building, and Kevin turned to admire it as he walked toward the meeting place. He stopped and removed his sunglasses to see the dazzling pink and orange sky, the result of a volcano that had erupted in the Philippines three months earlier. After a moment he continued walking, reminding himself to savor every sunset from now on.

He reached the bench in the middle of the quad but decided to stand. He'd been sitting at the computer all day. Maybe he'd go for a run after dinner to work the kinks out. To his left, Campbell Library was undergoing renovations. It was almost exactly a year ago that Erica had found Michael Ward's safe-deposit box key. Kevin wondered where he'd be right now if she hadn't. Probably dead.

'Hey, stranger!' a voice said from behind.

Kevin turned to see a weary-looking Erica. She'd been in another tough ER rotation. Kevin hadn't seen her for three days. Despite the circles under her eyes, she was still beautiful.

After a long hug and kiss, they sat on the bench.

'That feels good,' said Erica. 'I've been standing for the last twelve hours.'

'How are you handling it?' She'd been an emergency medicine resident for two months. Because she'd graduated at the top her med school class, she'd gotten her pick of residencies. She chose the trauma center at Memorial Hermann, one of the best in the country, which also let her stay in Houston with Kevin.

'I've never worked this hard in my life. Right before I came over, I was stitching up a guy who walked through a plate-glass window. Nothing serious, but he had about forty places where he needed stitches. Then there was the burn victim—'

Kevin put up his hand. 'Okay, thanks for the update. But if I'm going to eat dinner, I'll need to talk about something else. Check these out.' He handed her his sunglasses.

She inspected them. 'Are these the first ones?'

He didn't answer her. Instead, he took his keys out. He picked the ignition key to his new Mustang convertible and ran the point of it along the lens. The surface was unmarred.

'Try it,' he said, handing her the keys.

She rubbed the key on the lens. Any other sunglasses would have been severely scratched by now, but these still looked brand-new.

'You could drive a tank over them,' he said, 'and the lenses wouldn't have a mark.'

'How thick is the coating?' Erica asked.

'That's the great thing. There *is* no coating.'

'You mean the whole lens is diamond?'

'Yes. And that's just the tip of the iceberg. The university got two more licensing contracts today: one from a stove manufacturer who wants to make clear stove tops out of diamond, the other from a chain-saw company to make diamond-coated teeth for their saws. Now, if we can just deal with De Beers, we can run with it in the gem market.'

When the university learned of the magnitude of the discovery and the role Kevin played in retrieving it, they decided to give him a percentage of the licensing grosses. It was only a fraction of a percent, but it still would be worth millions over the next few years. So far, all he'd done with the money was replace his beloved but destroyed Mustang and rent a larger apartment for Erica and himself. He was so busy finishing his degree and overseeing further research with the Adamas process that he didn't have time to spend the rest of it.

'Did you hear the latest on the trial?' Kevin said.

'No. I tried to catch a little of it on CNN yesterday, but I was so tired, I fell asleep before the story came on.'

Tarnwell's trial for conspiracy to commit murder, among other charges, was the hottest news topic in Houston. Kevin and Erica had testified the week before, after months of procedural wrangling by Tarnwell's lawyers during which

Tarnwell had been held without bail as a possible menace and a flight risk. Leave it to the lawyers. Tarnwell was spending what was left of his money on his defense. None was available for his private security force, meaning Kevin and Erica had little to fear.

'It should be over soon. Tarnwell brought in some character witnesses, but I don't think they did much good. Not after Bern's testimony.'

Although at the time of his shooting Bern's wound seemed mortal, Tarnwell's meaty employee had proved to have a strong constitution. Kevin's blow had apparently spoiled Lobec's aim, and the bullet just missed Bern's heart.

When Bern recovered, he believed Tarnwell had set him up. The bullet recovered from Herbert Stein's body matched Bern's gun perfectly, so it was a slam-dunk case against him. To reduce his sentence, Bern had turned state's evidence against Tarnwell. Together with Kevin and Erica's testimony and the videotape, the prosecution's case was practically open-and-shut, and ballistics analysis confirmed that Lobec's gun was the one used to kill Murray Hamilton. By revealing his orders to kill Kevin and Erica, Bern had even helped provide evidence that Lobec's death had been a case of self-defense.

'Do you think Tarnwell will get the death penalty?' Erica asked.

'I don't see why he wouldn't.' He saw her disturbed expression. 'I know what you think, but if anyone deserves it, he does. Besides, it'll be years before it happens.'

He looked at the library. 'You want to go see the renovations we paid for?'

'We didn't exactly pay for them.'

'You want to put Tarnwell's name on the donation?'

'No, "Anonymous" was the right name to use.'

As they got up and strolled toward the library, Kevin could see the sign at the front with the list of donors. At the top was the word 'Anonymous,' and next to it, '$2,500,000.' Similar signs were on buildings being renovated or built at the STU med school, Texas A&M, and Erica's undergraduate college, the University of Kansas.

When Kevin found out how much Ward had taken from Tarnwell, he realized that the money had to be stashed somewhere. Then he'd remembered the page ripped out of the Adamas notebook and the impression of a number and some letters on the next page. While he had been deciphering the notebook, he had written down what the impression had left and then covered over all traces of it in case it would provide him additional leverage later. It was only afterward that he realized the two numerical sequences and the words 'Trust One, G.T.' represented a numbered bank account and pass code that would let the bearer access the funds.

Kevin and Erica had toyed with the idea of keeping the ten million, but only for a few minutes. Financially, they were set for life. Besides, it would be fairly difficult to explain to the IRS how they had suddenly obtained ten million dollars. They'd also considered turning the information over to the Feds, but the money might have made its way back to Tarnwell, and he'd just spend it on more lawyers. Though the anonymous donation had been risky, it was the best compromise they could think of. Kevin and Erica had both wanted to give the money in their parents' names, but that would only have raised more questions.

Kevin and Erica took a short walk through the construction. The renovations seemed to be coming along nicely. Most of the linoleum was being replaced with carpeting to deaden the sound of footsteps, and new, comfortable cubicles took the place of the torn and battered ones. The rest of the money was spent on restoring or replacing worn-out books.

As they left the building, Erica said, 'It's amazing that all this was made possible because of a process that makes shiny little stones.' She looked down at the one-carat diamond on her finger. Kevin had tried to tell her that diamonds weren't going to be valued as jewelry much longer, but she had insisted on a traditional engagement ring. A simple gold wedding band nestled beside it.

'I like to think that we had something to do with it too.' He took her hand and smiled. 'Now, Mrs Hamilton, where would you like to eat dinner? The sky's the limit: Wendy's, Taco Bell, you name it.'

'I was thinking about a nice quiet dinner at Sambuca and then back to the apartment for a bit of R & R.'

'Rest and relaxation?'

She winked at him and flashed a sultry smile. 'Rum and

romance. You didn't have more interesting plans, did you?'

The idea of going for a run after dinner no longer held any appeal.

'Didn't you know?' Kevin said, leading her by the hand toward his car. 'Nothing interesting ever happens to me.'

AFTERWORD

When I originally wrote this novel in 1995, the technology at the heart of the story did not yet exist. Diamonds had been made in a laboratory, but the process was difficult, expensive, and didn't produce gem-quality stones in large quantities. Then in September 2003, *Wired* magazine unveiled a cover story about the invention of revolutionary new chemical processes for making diamonds, processes very similar to the Adamas method that I envisioned when I first wrote the novel.

Since that article was published, I've updated the story to make the Adamas process even more revolutionary. I'm sure scientists will eventually make breakthroughs that will make the new Adamas a reality, too.

Chemically perfect gem-quality diamonds can now be produced artificially at reasonable prices and great quantities. It is such a huge threat to De Beers that they have spent millions of dollars convincing consumers that mined diamonds are better than laboratory diamonds, even though the two are identical in structure. A diamond is a diamond, no matter whether it's natural or artificial.

The industry will really change, though, when everyone can buy those cool sunglasses with the diamond lenses.

Enjoyed **The Catalyst?**

Turn the page to read an extract
from Boyd Morrison's

The Midas Code

Eighteen Months Ago

Jordan Orr's thumb hovered over the detonator. Two dead guards lay at his feet. He threw one final glance at his accomplices, who both nodded ready. Orr tapped the button, and a Mercedes in a car park near Piccadilly Circus exploded three miles away.

Orr didn't know and didn't care if there were casualties, but at three in the morning he didn't expect any. The important thing was that the authorities would suspect a terrorist attack. The response time from the London police for any other call would more than double, leaving Orr and his men plenty of time to empty the auction house's largest storage vault.

Orr pulled the balaclava over his face. Russo and Manzini did the same. Disabling the cameras inside the vault would take time they didn't have. The alarm would go off the moment the door was opened.

The vault door was guarded by the double lock of a card key and a pass code. The card key was now in his hand, courtesy of one of the dead guards. He inserted the card, which prompted the system to ask for the code. Orr examined the touchpad. The clever design scrambled the arrangement of the numbers on the keypad every time it was used, making it impossible to guess the code simply by watching someone's finger movements. But the manager had been careless the day before, when Orr cased the facility as a prospective client. He made no effort to shield the screen from Orr, who recorded the code with a pen-shaped video camera in his jacket pocket.

Typical complacency, Orr had thought. Security system planners always forgot about the human element.

Orr typed the code, and the door buzzed, signaling that it was unlocked. He yanked it open and heard no Klaxon, but he knew that the broken magnetic seal had set off the silent alarm at the security firm's headquarters. At this time of the morning, no one should be accessing the vault.

Unable to reach the guards, the security company would call the police, but their problem would be a low priority. A terrorist event took precedence over everything else. Orr loved it.

He led the way in. He'd seen the interior in person, but Russo and Manzini had seen only the video.

The fifteen-foot-by-fifteen-foot vault was designed to showcase the objects that were to be formally appraised the next day. Jewelry, rare books, sculptures, gold coins, and antiques – valuables hidden away in an English manor's attic for a hundred years – were illuminated for optimum effect. Together, the items were expected to fetch in excess of thirty million pounds at auction.

One item was the prize of the collection. In the center display case was a delicate hand made of pure gold. Orr marveled at the lustrous beauty of the metal.

Manzini, a short balding man with powerful arms, removed a sledgehammer from his belt.

'Let's get rich,' he said, and swung the hammer toward the case. The thick glass shattered, and Manzini reached in, removed the golden hand, and wrapped it with bubble wrap before stuffing it into his bag. He moved on to the jewelry case.

Russo, so skinny that his pants could have been held up by a rubber band, used two hands to swing his own hammer. He smashed the back of the case holding a Picasso drawing and withdrew it carefully to keep it from getting cut by the shards.

While Manzini and Russo gathered the rest of the jewels and rolled up the artwork, Orr raced to the back of the vault. With a single blow, he liberated three ancient manuscripts and carefully placed them in his duffel. The collection of rare gold coins was next.

In three minutes, they had emptied the vault's entire contents into their bags.

'That's it,' Orr said. He opened his cell and dialed. The call was answered on the first ring.

'Yeah?'

'We're on our way,' Orr said, and hung up.

They stepped over the bullet-riddled guards and ran to the building's entrance. Outside, Orr could make out sirens in the distance, but they were going in the other direction. A stolen cab was waiting for them. The driver, Felder, wore a flat cap, glasses, and a fake mustache.

They tossed the bags into the car and got in.

'Success?' Felder asked.

'Just like the video,' Russo said. 'Thirty million pounds' worth.'

'A third of that on the black market,' Manzini said. 'Orr's buyer is only paying ten million.'

'Either way, it's more money than you've ever seen,' Felder said.

'Drive,' Orr said, impatient with their giddiness. They still weren't done.

The cab took off. Because London has the highest concentration of surveillance cameras in the world, they kept their masks on. After a theft like this, Scotland Yard would pore over every single video for the one clue that would lead back to the thieves.

Orr was confident that would never happen.

As they had practiced, the cab reached the boat slip at the Thames river dock only five minutes later. They left the cab sitting at the dock car park and made their way to the cabin cruiser Felder had hired. Orr knew the boat might be traced back to Felder, but by the time it was, it wouldn't matter.

As soon as they were on board, Felder, a native Brit who

had plied these waters for ten years as tug crewman, threw the throttle forward. They wouldn't stop until they reached the Strait of Dover, where the plan was to go ashore in Kent and use a rental car to make their final escape on a SeaFrance ferry to Calais.

While Felder navigated, the rest of them emptied the contents of the bags in the blacked-out forward cabin to take stock of their haul. Russo and Manzini cackled in Italian. The only word Orr, an American, could understand was when they mentioned their hometown, 'Napoli.' Naples. He ignored them and carefully inspected the three manuscripts. He found the one he wanted and set it aside. The other two were worthless to him, so he put them back in the duffel.

By the time they finished sorting the goods, the boat had entered the English Channel. It was time.

Orr turned his back to Russo and Manzini and drew the silenced SIG Sauer he'd used to kill the guards.

'Hey, Orr,' Russo said, 'when do we meet your contact? I want my money soon, *capisce*?'

'No problem,' Orr said, and whipped around. He shot Russo first, then Manzini. Manzini toppled onto Russo, the necklace he'd been fondling still in his hand.

The wind and the engine noise were so loud that Felder couldn't have heard the shots. Orr made his way up to the wheel deck.

Felder turned and smiled at him.

'Mind taking a few minutes at the wheel?' Felder said. 'I'm dying to check out my share.'

'Sure,' Orr said. He took the wheel with one hand, and when Felder's back was turned, he shot him twice. Felder tumbled to the deck below.

Orr checked the GPS and twisted the wheel until he was heading toward Leysdown-on-Sea, a small town on the coast, where he'd parked a second car. The car Felder had hired would stay where it was until it was towed away. Orr didn't care. There would be nothing to link him with it.

When the boat was three miles from town, Orr brought it to a stop. The water here would be deep enough.

Down in the cabin, he lashed all three of the bodies to the interior, planted two small explosive charges below the waterline, and readied an inflatable raft and oars. Once he triggered the bombs, which were just big enough to tear openings in the hull, the boat would sink within minutes.

He sealed the golden hand, jewelry, coins, and the lone manuscript in a waterproof bag and put everything else into lockers that he battened down. There would be no trace of the boat once it was on the bottom of the Channel. The items like the Picasso were valuable, but they were also too recognizable to sell. He couldn't take the chance that they would lead back to him. The jewelry and the gold could be broken apart and sold for the gems and metal with little risk. He expected to net two million pounds from them, enough to pay off his debts and fund his ultimate plan.

But the golden hand and the manuscript he would keep.

Although Orr's accomplices hadn't known it, the document was the most valuable item they had taken from the vault. In fact, it was arguably the single most valuable object on the face of the earth. The owner must not have realized what it contained, or he would never have tried to auction it.

Orr *did* know what it contained. He had checked it himself while Russo and Manzini had been fawning over the gold and the jewels. To the layman, the most important line, heading a section at the end of the document, looked like a string of random Greek letters, but it confirmed the document's importance.

ΟΣΤΙΣΚΡΑΤΕΙΤΟΥΤΟΥΤΟΥΤΟΥΓΡΑΜΜΑΤΟΣΚΡΑΤΕΙΤ ΟΥΠΛΟΥΤΟΥΤΟΥΜΙΔΑ.

The manuscript was a medieval codex transcribed from a scroll written two hundred years before the birth of Christ. It contained an ancient treatise by antiquity's greatest scientist and engineer, the man who kept the Romans at bay for two years through his ingenuity alone, a Greek native of Syracuse named Archimedes.

The codex was written without spaces or lowercase letters, making it tedious to translate, so the manuscript's complete contents were unknown. But that one line convinced Orr that the manuscript at his feet held the secret to the location of a treasure worth untold billions.

Orr climbed into the raft and, for the second time that night, pressed the button of a detonator. The explosive charges blasted open two breaches in the boat's hull. He rowed away but kept close to confirm that the boat was gone before he made his way to land. As Orr watched the boat sink beneath the placid sea, the translation of Archimedes' text flashed in front of his eyes as clearly as if it were written on the water's surface.

He who controls this map controls the riches of Midas.

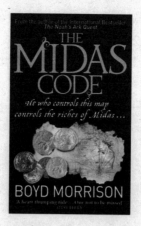

From the author of the international Bestseller
The Noah's Ark Quest

THE
MIDAS
CODE

*He who controls this map
controls the riches of Midas...*

BOYD MORRISON

'A heart-thumping ride... One not to be missed'
STEVE BERRY

Top army engineer Tyler Locke is given a mysterious ancient manuscript. Written in Greek, it initially seems indecipherable.

But with the help of classics scholar Stacy Benedict, Locke comes to understand that this manuscript could provide the clues to the greatest riches known to mankind – the legendary treasure of King Midas.

However, there are others who are also hot on the trail – and it rapidly becomes a race against time to crack a code that is both fiendishly difficult and potentially deadly . . .

'Boyd Morrison hits his stride and delivers another smart, sassy tale fraught with action. The coiling plot crackles with tension and imagination from the first to the last page. It's a heart-thumping ride, firing on all cylinders. One not to be missed'
Steve Berry

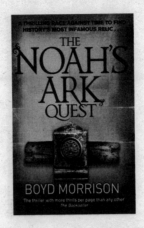

Do the remains of Noah's Ark really exist?

Before he dies, the father of ambitious young architect Dilara Kenner leaves her tantalising clues about the location of the legendary historical artefact – Noah's Ark.

The most fabled relic of all time, the search for Noah's Ark has obsessed many over the years. And when Dilara starts her quest – aided by former army engineer Tyler Locke – she rapidly becomes transfixed by the thought of discovering it.

But there are sinister forces gathering who have deadly reasons for wanting to be the first ones to get to the relic.

From a helicopter crash in the Atlantic, to a sinister sect in Arizona's Mojave desert, to the remote slopes of Mount Ararat, this thrilling page-turner blends nonstop action with fascinating historical fact.

'Lightning-paced, chillingly real, here is a novel that will have you holding your breath until the last page is turned' James Rollins

One man. One hour.
One million people to save . . .

THE TSUNAMI COUNTDOWN

BOYD MORRISON

Bestselling author of *The Noah's Ark Quest*

One man. One hour. One million people to save . . .

Over the remote central Pacific, an airliner is rocked by a massive explosion and plummets into the ocean, leaving no survivors.

Twelve hundred miles away in Hawaii, Kai Tanaka, the acting director of the Pacific Tsunami Warning Centre in Honolulu, notes a minor seismic disturbance but doesn't make the connection with the lost airplane. He has no reason to worry about his wife, manager of a luxury hotel, or his daughter, who is enjoying the sunshine at Waikiki beach.

But when all contact with neighbouring Christmas Island is lost, Kai is the first to realize that Hawaii faces an epic catastrophe: in one hour, a series of massive waves will wipe out Honolulu. He has just sixty minutes to save the lives of a million people, including his wife and daughter . . .

'Opens with a bang-literally-and then takes the reader on a watery thrill ride of terror. This is top-notch suspense, with crisp plotting, believable characters, and well-researched science. A classic disaster novel, up there with the very best' Douglas Preston